Whisky From Small Glasses

D. A. Meyrick

Ringwood Publishing
Glasgow

First published in Great Britain in 2012 by
Ringwood Publishing
7 Kirklee Quadrant, Glasgow G12 0TS
www.ringwoodpublishing.com
e-mail mail@ringwoodpublishing.com

ISBN 978-1-901514-08-7

British Library Cataloguing-in Publication Data
A catalogue record for this book is available from
the British Library

Typeset, printed and bound in Great Britain by;

www.direct-pod.com

Dedication

For my family: my lovely wife, Fiona; Rachel and Sian.
Also, the memory of my late parents,
Alan and Elspeth Meyrick.
God Bless you all.

Acknowledgements

Writing a novel is not the solo pursuit many would have you believe; rather, the finished work is down to the hard work and dedication of many.

Firstly, I would like to thank my dear wife, Fiona, for endless revision of the text before anybody else read it. My family, especially Rachel, Jason and Sian for their encouragement and support.
Sandy Jamieson and all at Ringwood Publishing for having faith in me and my writing. My long-suffering editor, Joanne Durning, for her patience and sound advice, as well as the others who have checked and re-checked the manuscript prior to publication.
Special thanks are due to Karen Appleyard who designed the front cover. (*http://www.karenappleyard.com/*)

Finally I would like to thank, albeit posthumously, revered Kintyre author, Angus MacVicar, who told an eager schoolboy, many years ago, that he should be a writer.

PART ONE

<u>Prologue.</u>

Lights sparked and flashed before her eyes. The movement of her limbs slowed as though of their own accord. The pain she had felt was dull now; the panic subsiding. She was aware that her bowels had opened; she no longer cared. Her last, her remaining emotions, were a fading mixture of anger, injustice, and overwhelming sadness, the cause of which she could barely recall.

All she was, all she had ever been, was seeping slowly away: her loves, desires, likes and dislikes, the things that made her angry, the things that made her sad, made her laugh, made her cry; now all curiously diminished. Her final moments were descending into a fading abyss - the surreal detachment of the brain soothing its own way to oblivion.

Suddenly, as the lights began to dim, the face of a small, blonde, blue-eyed child filled her thoughts. Only for an instant did the terrible choking pain, the struggle for breath, the fight to stay alive, return.

1

The body ebbed and flowed rhythmically in concert with the seaweed and flotsam and jetsam trapped in the bay of the low, rocky cove. A styrofoam cup, a fisherman's glove with three fingers missing, a drinks bottle, label so bleached by sun and sea that only a hint of its former contents were now discernible, and bright orange plastic netting which had ensnared a small crab, reluctant to quit the purpose for which it was intended: all of these floated and bobbed in unison with the corpse.

The naked body of a woman lay face down in the water, limbs spread in a lazy 'X' shape. Her skin looked waxy - a horrible cross between yellow and grey, turning black at her feet, hands, and the back of her neck. The remains were bloated, consistent with time spent in water. Small areas of her lower back and thighs were gnawed, most likely by prawns, indicating the cadaver had spent at least some time further out to sea.

Surprisingly though, most repellent, were the two bright red ribbons that held her hair in bunches, a hairstyle redolent of childhood and happiness, horribly incongruous with the rotting corpse now souring the sea tang of the mild spring day.

With almost six years' service in uniform, Detective Constable Archie Fraser was new to the CID. That new in fact, he hoped that he was surveying the scene on the beach with what could be considered the appropriate degree of professional detachment. A young WPC, and the pale looking dog-walker - who had alerted the police - looked on with the mixture of abject horror and fascination, so common in humanity faced with death; especially of the gruesome variety. A large, black labrador snuffled and pawed at the sand, unaware and undisturbed by the corpse.

"Could you put your dog back on the lead please, Mrs MacPherson?" Fraser bellowed with a confidence he did not feel. It would not be beyond possibility for the dog to catch an unusual scent on the air and proceed to wade into the water to investigate its source.

His short time in Kinloch had already been difficult. Only last month his ultimate superior - one Inspector MacLeod, Sub-Divisional Commander - had cause to reprimand him on discovering a young female shoplifter handcuffed to a very hot radiator while her captor answered an urgent call of nature.

"Focus boy, focus!" MacLeod shouted in his high pitched, sing-song, Highland accent. "The last thing I need is the Discipline Branch descending on me because you have seen fit to roast some daft bint. You're bloody lucky she was too stupid to make the complaint."

Fraser noticed how his boss always referred to *the* something, in the way a foreigner would; tourists regularly took him for a German or Scandinavian and not from the Isle of Harris that was his home. A long period of admonishment ensued, after which Fraser resolved to improve in every way and pay many less visits to the *Taste of India* restaurant.

"Karen, could you come over please?" Fraser summoned the WPC. She walked slowly towards him, never taking her eyes from the body, in the way a child would having been asked to pat a snake. "What's up?" he enquired. "Surely this isn't your first stiff?" Her doe-eyed nod was barely perceptible.

Having worked his probationary period in Glasgow, Fraser was no stranger to dead bodies: murders, drowning, suicides, accidents - occasionally even some natural deaths; all were part of the daily diet of Glasgow's finest. The difference now was - for the time being at least - the crime scene was his responsibility. No van full of colleagues likely to appear; the Serious Crime Squad over a hundred miles away; even his DS off sick, laid low with a persistent 'early retirement' back. Right here, right now, he was the senior CID officer on duty in the Sub-Division: he was the only CID officer on duty in the Sub-Division.

"It's no' jeest that, Archie," the WPC had a thick local accent. "I mean this is Kinloch - I probably know her."

How could he forget? The crime locus was three miles away from one of the most unique places he had ever been to, let alone lived and worked in. Kinloch. The town was situated on a peninsula a hundred and fifty miles away from Glasgow, on Scotland's rugged West Coast; alternatively, miles away from anywhere, as Fraser had come to think of it. Around ten thousand people lived in what could best be described as a modern alternative to the Nineteen-Fifties. Everyone knew everyone else, down to the merest detail of family, even personal life. Sometimes, when working on a case, the young policeman had the distinct impression that everybody knew what he was trying to find out, but of course, were never going to tell.

Another symptom of such a close-knit community was an inherent distrust of strangers - including policemen. Fraser's uncle - himself a retired police officer - had advised him to always have friends outside *The Job*, as the force was habitually known to initiates. He believed that many cops both worked and socialised together, leaving them isolated, introverted, and out of touch.

"You keep your ear to the ground, son - especially in a wee place like Kinloch," Uncle Davie had declared sagely. "I mean you're never goin' tae find anything oot about these people unless you get out an' talk tae them. Get yourself out, socialise - spend a few bob, buy a couple o' drinks; you'll see they'll soon open up."

Archie had mixed feelings about this strategic advice: for a start, Uncle Davie had had his ear to the ground, and bought so many drinks, and so regularly, that he was now awaiting a liver transplant. Also, this was Kinloch, a place most definitely apart. However, he thought that some of what Davie had said could be useful. As the town was his first posting as a DC, he resolved to immerse himself in the community. He tried to join the local golf club, though sadly they were full. Unabashed, he tried the local tennis and cricket clubs, both with same result. He was briefly elated when the town's Gaelic choir had contacted him in the hope he could sing and swell their dwindling numbers; sadly Fraser was about as tone deaf as it was possible to be.

He had tried visiting the local pubs when off duty. Kinloch had a goodly number of such establishments - far too many according to some of the town's more temperate residents. They conformed to small communities within the community; for instance, regulars at the *Shore Bar* wouldn't normally consider crossing the threshold of the *Royal Borough* across the road.

Subtly, each establishment catered for a slightly different clientele: rowdy youth attended *Pulse,* a noisy disco-bar in the Main Street, whilst their more cerebral peers became habituates of *The Old Bothy,* in the square. Roman Catholics preferred the *Douglas Arms*, while so called *blue noses* headed for the *Royal*. There was a pub that catered for lawyers, doctors and businessmen, another inhabited by tradesmen and factory workers; indeed one hostelry was dedicated solely to horse racing, the 'sport of Kings' playing all day and all night on large screens. It was situated conveniently next to the bookmakers on the High Street. *Jenny's,* lurking on a small back street, was the end of the line. Those who behaved badly enough to be banned from all of the other premises - and many had - gravitated there. The 'tick book' was legendary, as were the fights. Locals referred to it as the *Star Wars Bar,* for reasons that were obvious.

Fraser had visited them all. Typically, as he walked into the room the conversation would stop, resuming in a more modulated fashion moments later. People would gradually drift away, leaving the young detective with one of Kinloch's small army of drunks who barely knew nor cared where they drank, as well as a glaring publican, counting the cost of lost customers. A polite welcome inevitably led to an unspoken invitation to make his stay short.

"Can I say something?" Mrs MacPherson spoke timidly. "The tide's on the turn... well could it - she - not drift back out?"
The young Officer had not considered this, "Right, Karen, time to get your feet wet; we'll need to get her above the water line, even

if we corrupt forensics, it's better than her ending up on Islay."

"Can ye' no' dae it yersel', Archie? This gi'es me the boak."

He gently reminded the WPC why she was being paid, and after removing shoes, tights and socks where appropriate, the pair waded into the few inches of water.

"OK, grab her other arm, Karen - and mind pull gently - we want to disturb this as little as possible." The policewoman looked doubtfully at the cadaver, but did as requested, looking away as she grabbed the left wrist, lips pursed in distaste.

"One, two, three…" they started to pull.

To the collective horror of all three on the beach, the corpse, with a great issue of dark fluid and some more solid matter, broke neatly apart, with the deep sucking noise of a plunger working on a well blocked sink. Both police officers, having put more effort into their task than required, fell backwards onto the shingle, the top half of the deceased now some two feet away from the rest of the remains.

In what seemed like a split second, the fetid stench emanating from the newly cleft body induced the dog to stand tall on all fours and emit a mournful howl, as the WPC retched copiously over her uniform, still sitting on the shingle where her assistance to the CID had left her. Body fluids seeped darkly into the sand; even the local seagull population had registered the events and were now swirling in a squawking frenzy over the bay.

"Fuck," Fraser swore vehemently, forgetting the presence of Mrs MacPherson, who was herself looking on in disbelief, as though she was waiting for someone to come bounding from behind a rock to confirm the whole ghastly episode was all one elaborate joke, of the type played out in down-market TV.

Just then, movement to his right caught Fraser's eye. Three figures were walking purposefully down the beach towards him. The slight, taut figure of Inspector Macleod was unmistakable at their head.

It took the Inspector a few moments to grasp exactly what was in front of him.

One of his DC's was getting up from the sand, leaving the torso of a dead woman, and a WPC spewing copiously at his feet. A woman he did not know was issuing convulsive sobs, while a large black dog happily wagged its tail at the new arrivals. Only feet away, the rest of the body could barely be made out in the badly discoloured water. A sickening stench was all pervasive.

"What the fuck are you doing, boy?" MacLeod's temples displayed throbbing veins. "In all my years in the police I have never seen the like."

"I was merely trying to…" Fraser's excuse was cut off.

"You were merely trying to fuck things up, as usual," the Inspector was incandescent. "Aye, and all of our careers along with it. I dread to think what they taught you at the training college. In my day you were shown how to preserve the crime scene, not tear it in half!"

As though suddenly remembering others were there, MacLeod visibly took hold of himself, turning to address the uniformed Sergeant next to him. "Sergeant Shaw, please do your best to ensure that the remains are contained at this locus," turning to a man in a well-worn sports jacket with patched sleeves, he said, "Sandy, are you able to make any kind of examination under these circumstances?" At that he looked towards Fraser with a thunderous glare.

The stocky man, whom Fraser recognised as one of the local doctors, ran his hand through greying locks as he surveyed the scene. "Well, Charles, I can only concur with your very accurate assessment," his accent was straight out of the Scottish public school system. "I too, have never attended such an incident in thirty years of medicine." He looked at the young DC with a flat lipped grimace that spoke of nothing but pity, then lent over the landed portion of body, rubbing his chin.

MacLeod walked away from the others, gesturing to Fraser to come with him. Once out of earshot, he grabbed the younger man's arm and on tip-toe addressed the DC's right ear with spitting vitriol.

"You listen to me, constable; since you arrived at my station you have lurched from one crisis to the next." Fraser could feel his face redden. "As soon as this sorry mess is over I will be recommending to HQ that you are not only unsuited to the CID, but to police work in general. Be absolutely sure that the *cach* will land on your head, not mine. We'll be the laughing stock of the force by tea time."

Fraser wanted to grab his superior and fling him bodily down the shout from the doctor turned both of their heads.

"One for the big boys I'm afraid, Charles." The doctor was brushing sand from his trousers as the policemen walked back over. "Murder - nasty business."

"How can you be so sure, Sandy?" The Inspector looked doubtfully at the medic.

"Oh, quite easily, Inspector MacLeod; she has a ligature around her neck."

2

Detective Inspector Jim Daley reflected on the dispiriting nature of trouser shopping, as he handed his credit card over to the assistant in the fashionable clothes store.

In his twenties - even in his thirties - he had been able to maintain a respectable waistline without the deployment of starvation diets or drastic fitness regimens. Now in his early forties - as he liked to think of forty three - and especially since giving up cigarettes, he felt his stomach now capable of gaining inches overnight. It was not without a little trepidation that he eyed a suit or a pair of jeans he had not worn for a few weeks. Often, on trying to get them on, there would follow the desperate tugging at a straining zip, a grunting wrestle with a recalcitrant waistband, holding in both breath and stomach, as he fought to get the garment into a position whereby he could move, sit, or stand without a trouser button shooting into the air like a misdirected bullet; worse still, without hearing the sickening rip of sewing tearing apart over a more than ample backside.

He had resolved therefore to make a new start as far as trousers were concerned: go out and buy a pair that more suited his thickening frame, regardless of how unpalatable the thought of having his age and waist size matching was. After all, he would get older, diet and join a gym, ensuring these numbers would diverge in an acceptable manner in the near future.

He caught a glimpse of himself in a fitting mirror as he left the shop. Was that fattening, middle aged man really him? He consoled himself with the fact he was six feet three, still had his hair and his own teeth. Sure, women found him attractive, just not the woman he wanted to, or so it seemed. Tall, dark, getting fatter, older and handsome - that summed up Jim Daley.

The theme tune from the *Sopranos,* jolted him from thoughts of sartorial insecurity to an equally perplexing subject: his wife Liz. She called infrequently when he was at work and he had become used to these calls containing at least a modicum of bad or unwelcome news.

"Hi, Liz, everything OK?" He always heard himself sounding lame when he had to speak to her unexpectedly. He felt an involuntary frisson of excitement at the sound of those familiar, well-spoken, smoky tones.

"Oh hi, darling; that was quick. Are you OK to talk?"

"Yeah, no bother, I'm actually…" habitually, she gave him no time to finish his answer.

"Great, just to let you know, Jill wants me to go up to the caravan at Granton for a few days. Anyway I thought, the weather's nice and it's not as though we'll be doing anything, so I'm leaving in a couple of hours."

Daley was used to a fait accompli. He marvelled at the easy way Liz, again, managed to impart her intention to do as she pleased, while at the same time make him feel as though he was in some way responsible.

He attempted a rear-guard action: "I'll be home about five; we could go to the wee pub for a couple of drinks, or get a curry or something - make a night of it. You could go up to Jill's in the morning."

Without a pause, Liz's reply was as predictable as it was swift, "Oh, what a pity you didn't mention it before. She's invited me to dinner tonight as well; Mark has some boring guest to entertain. I've already said I would go - sorry, darling."

"Oh - OK," was all he could muster. He guessed it was true what people said, once a partner had been unfaithful, it was really difficult to regain the trust that was so important in any relationship. Liz had been spectacularly unfaithful.

The first incident - he knew of - was with her gym instructor.

Sent home early by the force Medical Officer after taking a baseball bat across the head during a drug raid, he thought he heard noises as he gained the stairs of their new detached home in the village of Howwood. The vision of Liz on hands and knees on their bed while her paramour worked energetically behind her was burnt onto his memory. Suffering from a hair trigger temper as well as an acute headache, Daley proceeded to render the third party insensible with a swift upper-cut, dragged him by the hair onto the small bedroom balcony, and dispatched him neatly over the railing and onto the garden below.

The sight of a naked man struggling to get up, with what looked like a broken leg, from a neighbour's garden, accompanied by the shrieks of an obviously frantic woman, constituted more than enough reason for the good people of Howwood to call the police. Eventually, after much pulling of strings and dire warnings regarding the diminishment of his prospects, a deal was done behind the scenes and Daley - forced to attend anger management classes - was left to resurrect, as best he could, the remnants of his career. Having reached Detective Inspector in his mid-thirties, Jim Daley could have reasonably hoped for Superintendent or beyond, before retirement. This was now most unlikely.

As for Liz, she had vowed undying love for him, citing boredom and loneliness as an excuse for her behaviour. Daley realised he was wrong, however, his almost cloying love for her saw him take the only action that seemed palatable: forgiveness.

Since then, even when close friends and colleagues had alerted him to likely dalliances, he chose to ignore them, having neither the strength nor will to do the sensible thing and leave her. Though he would never let her know, he was head over heels in love with her, and, even though he barely believed it himself, was prepared to accede to almost anything in order to keep their relationship afloat.

She said and did all the right things: she showed great interest in him, they made passionate love, declared satisfied happiness, promised unerring loyalty; all to no avail. Now trust was absent, only the slavery of obsession remained.

Daley was forced to endure the nods and winks of colleagues; the police of course being a small community where gossip was rife.

Had Liz been less attractive her indiscretions would have probably gone unnoticed, however, such were the rumours of her wanton nature, every male colleague now reckoned that they had a chance with her.

"Anyway, you know what the traffic's like in the morning." Liz pronounced *morning* with that annoying intonation that had crept into everyday usage from the popularity of Australian soap operas, as though the knowledge or concept of the morning was something entirely alien to the listener. The habit annoyed Daley, who hardened his reply.

"Yeah, whatever you think, Liz. When will you be back?"

"Oh, you know, darling - go with the flow - you know me." He did. "Anyway, better dash. I've left one of those *boil in the microwave* curries out for you. Bell you later, bye. Love you." That was an afterthought.

Daley stood with the handset to his ear for a few moments. So little said; so much left unsaid: it summed up their marriage. He walked back to the car park, made a mental note to get his car washed, then drove to the station.

Jim returned to his office by way of the coffee machine. On gaining the second floor he could clearly hear the dulcet tones of his DS as he swore volubly at his computer.

"You know, I'm buggered how they think that getting us tae dae all this typing ourselves is cost effective." DS Brian Scott was more agitated than normal, which was indeed saying something. "When I joined up you just had tae scribble something doon and wait for some daft wee lassie in the typing pool tae dae the business. Noo, well I'll tell ye, Paisley's goin' like a fair, while I'm up here learnin' tae be a fuckin' secretary."

"Ah, DS Scott," Daley aped the clipped Kelvinside tones of their boss, "it's incumbent upon us all to integrate with new policing methods." He smiled at Scott's exasperation.

"Aye, fuck him tae. It's getting tae be you need a degree in this shit jist tae dae yer ain job." Scott was smiling in spite of himself. An IT specialist he most certainly was not; he most certainly was however, a highly effective, sometimes inspired police officer. His brusque manner, and tendency to ignore the rule book, had hampered his progress through the ranks; he would no doubt, end his career as a DS. Daley felt that it was a role that had been tailor made for his gritty determination, and valued his assistance more than he would ever admit. Simply, they made a good team.

Daley walked to the large paper strewn desk in the office he shared with Scott. A yellow *Post-it* note placed on top of a mountain of files announced: *Numpty wants to see you!* - in Scott's bold, untidy hand.

"When did his magnificence call?" Daley enquired, looking up just in time to see Scott's computer screen turn a brilliant blue. "Oh, just efter you left; he's in a right stooshie aboot somthin'. He didna' even pull me up aboot whit a coup this place is." He swung his chair around to face Daley, left hand outstretched in gesture of disbelief at his computer screen. "I mean, whit the fuck's this a' aboot?"

Draining his coffee, Daley got up and walked to Scott's desk, where he deftly pressed a few keys on the computer, turning it back to the report on which the DS was working.

"Just how many computer courses have you been on? It seems like dozens."

Scott's face took on a look of rueful resignation, "Aye, a few, but you've got tae remember, Jim, every time I get a chance tae go up tae the college its mair like a break from my dear lady wife. That's a great wee bar they've got there; an' well, by the time yiv sobered up in the morning, yiv well an' truly lost the thread aboot whit the fuck they're on aboot."

Daley chuckled to himself as he took the lift to the top floor of the building. As the elevator doors swished open he yet again marvelled at the steep upward curve in the standard of opulence in this portion of the station. Gone the bare functionality of the other three floors, to be replaced by dark wood panelling, tasteful paintings, picked out by soft up-lighting, thick carpeting punctuated by tall, verdant pot plants. Even the civilian staff were of a seemingly more aesthetically pleasing variety; an attractive woman in a tight fitting skirt wiggled past him in a cloud of expensive perfume that reminded him of Liz.

Behind the closed door the sound of a giggling female was plain. The nameplate read simply: 'Superintendent John Donald. Commander Div. CID.' Daley knocked loudly three times.

After a few moments of mumbled voices, the familiar *come,* served as an invitation for Daley to enter. He opened the door, stepping inside straight backed and confident.

Donald was sitting behind an impossibly large desk that made even this large office seem reduced. Yet another attractive female stood over him clutching a file, looking intently on as the Superintendent busily appended his signature to a document.

"Ah, Jim," Donald's eyes flitted towards him then back to his papers. He gestured airily with his left hand, "make yourself comfortable while I satisfy the rapacious appetite for my time this young lady seems to harbour."

Same old, same old. Jim was used to his boss's eccentricities; indeed, it felt much as though he had worked for this man for most of his career. As a young probationary cop Donald had been his shift sergeant, on his first posting to Paisley CID, as a raw DC, Donald was his DS. Not long after his promotion to detective sergeant in 'A' Division in Glasgow, Donald arrived as the all-powerful DCI. They were once described as star-crossed. He wished they weren't.

The man that sat in front of him now though, bore hardly any resemblance to the foul-mouthed, over-weight philistine figure of, what seemed like, so long ago.

Steadily, he had ironed out all of his imperfections. He stopped drinking, took up running, golf, and squash; consequently losing piles of weight. He spent a great deal of time abroad or under a sun-bed ensuring that his permanent tan was indeed, ever present. Even his hair had undergone a similar transformation: gone, the thick black curls paired close to the scalp; now thinning, his gelled back coiffure made him look like a hackneyed version of an East-end gangster.

His manner had changed accordingly too, the harsh accent of Glasgow's East end, modulated to the clipped tones of middle-class Bearsden, taking him much further socially than it had done in geographic reality. His notorious temper was kept in check by smarmy sycophancy to superiors, or aloof arrogance to those of a lesser rank. Daley though, had never been in any doubt as to how thin this veil was; indeed, Donald was as notorious for his self-seeking ruthlessness, as he was for being a mediocre police officer transformed into a truly talented administrator and political bon vivant. The letters BA, LLB after his name bore testament to the determined hard work it had taken to climb from the mire of a piss poor childhood, to his current middle-class magnificence.

Donald flourished his signature at the bottom of the document then flamboyantly waved the paper in the air to dry the fountain pen ink he had used.

"Now, Di, don't be frightened to bring in as many papers for me to sign as you want; my door is always open, you know." He leered a smile at the young woman who nodded dutifully, then left the room, Donald appraising her departure with the fixed gaze of a satyr.

"Now, Jim, sorry about that, breaking in a new girl, so to speak; one long round of paperwork in here. Now where did I put that… ah, here it is." He lifted a black file from the desk and removed what looked like a number of printed e-mails. "Bit of bother in our new dominions; Kinloch to be exact. There's no point me blustering on, scan these and we'll get on wi' it."

Daley noticed how the polished edge of his accent had tarnished slightly since the secretary had gone. For many, this would have appeared to be an acknowledgement of their shared past, to Daley however, it was more of an indication of how far down he was in the pecking order. Donald obviously felt there to be little point in turning on the charm for his senior DI. He opened the file and began to browse its contents.

After a few minutes he looked up from the papers and cleared his throat to divert Donald's attention from the copy of *Perfect Home* magazine his superior was avidly consuming.

"Oh right, Jim. So, there you have it. Bit of a crisis down there in terms of manpower and experience too. The Sub-Division is run by a teuchter called Charles MacLeod - a right little shit - the very worst kind of social climber. They have a DS who is no more use than ornament, and a few eager young DCs. Do you remember Davie Fraser from 'A' Division? - his nephew's there."

"If he's anything like his uncle, the pubs will be doing a fine trade." Daley had a sinking feeling in his stomach.

Strathclyde Police had undergone yet another phase of reorganisation in an attempt to save money. His Division had been amalgamated with what had been the old Argyll Constabulary, meaning that headquarters in Paisley was now responsible for parts of the West Coast of Scotland that few could pronounce, never mind find on a map.

"Quite so, quite so, Jim; poor man. I think his liver is on the way out; never met a man who loved a drink more," Donald looked rueful. "Anyway, I'm reliably informed his nephew is cut from entirely different cloth."

Daley hoped so; his experience of Davie Fraser was one of having to follow him from bar to bar when he was a young cop, watching the man supposed to be showing him the ropes steadily becoming more inebriated and objectionable by turns.

"Do you mind me asking what this has to do with me?" He knew what the answer was going to be, however being direct would mean Donald would be unable to dollop his usual helping of sugar onto an unpalatable request.

"Straight to the point, Inspector Daley; that's what I like to hear." Daley had the impression that Donald was a bit disappointed, and would rather still have the chance to dish out his usual speeches on duty and chances for advancement, that were the normal precursors of a shit job. "I need someone there with a bit of experience - get this solved quickly - prove to these yokels that our way is the best way. Fuck knows, we'll have to get them to toe the line somehow; this affords us the perfect opportunity."

"So you want me down there, sir?" Daley moved the conversation away from a lecture on the difference in policing methods between city and county divisions.

"Yes, Jim, in fact I would like you down there first thing tomorrow morning. The body is on the way to the mortuary in Glasgow. Under the circumstances, that prick Crichton will do the necessary this evening at about seven. I would like you to be there."

Daley paused momentarily to take this in. He was being sent to a far outpost of the empire to investigate a murder that could take forever, while the wayward Liz was at the other end of the country doing - well he dreaded to think.

"I see, sir. What about personnel?" was all he could think of to say.

"I have you booked on the first flight in the morning. You will of course be much better informed after the PM. Take a look on the ground yourself; then we'll decide who we can spare to send down there with you - take that file. I'll send anything else we've got downstairs. No doubt we can spare Tweedle Dum and a few other bodies, should the situation require it." Donald had what could best be described as a *strained* relationship with DS Scott.

Daley's mind returned to the images he had seen on the e-mails: a young woman, ligature, body dumped at sea, and a locus distant from usual amenities; he mentally surmised that this was not going to be an easy enquiry.

"Have the Support Unit been informed yet, sir?" He was referring to the group of elite Strathclyde Officers who specialised in various disciplines now required of a modern police force: firearms, dog branch, crowd control, underwater unit etc. Daley reckoned the latter would be handy bearing in mind the apparent circumstances surrounding the death.

"Not as yet, Jim. I think it wise to wait until we have some kind of results from the PM, no matter how preliminary. Of course you realise, in terms of expenditure this is going to be a killer; we've already had a full SOCO team down there. The burden of expense falls to us, the investigating department. I hope you will bear that in mind when you're on the ground?"

"As you know, sir, cost is always to the forefront of my mind during every enquiry." Daley smiled openly, knowing his boss was more than well aware about his attitude to the bean counters many senior officers had been forced to become.

"Luckily," Donald chose to ignore the irony of the last statement, "because this is new territory so to speak, we are able to introduce a degree of flexibility into our spend. However, Jim, the pot is by no means bottomless; please take that on board."

Daley was about to make some sarcastic reply, when Donald began to speak again on an entirely different subject without the need for an intake of breath; he, it seemed, had developed all the skills of the politician.

"How is Liz? Everything back to normal in that department?" Daley bridled as the leer returned to Donald's face. Only a few weeks had passed since Liz had flirted outrageously with the superintendent at a retirement party. The couple had rowed late into the night when they returned home, Liz claiming that she was only trying to advance his career with a little networking; yet another modern term he couldn't stand. Anyway, Donald's body language had pointed to the fact that networking was the last thing on his mind. Loyally, DS Scott had administered a left hook to a colleague who had insinuated that something illicit was afoot.

"Mrs Donald and I really must have you for dinner."

Mrs Daley's more likely to have you for breakfast, he thought, somewhat uncharitably.

"Anyway, better get on, we both have plenty to do. Oh, by the way, pick your tickets up from Kirsty next door - she's had them googled or something - and don't forget to keep me informed; googles will do. Don't take any shit off that little bastard MacLeod. Any trouble there and I've got a few tricks up my sleeve."

"Good hunting, Jim." The Superintendent stood, hand

outstretched. Daley shook it in acceptance of the tacit dismissal.

3

"What's this with googles?" Daley and Scott were driving into Glasgow in Scott's car. The DS had opted for a post mortem instead of an evening with his in-laws.

"Aye, he's one stupid bastard wi' that," Scott laughed heartily. "He telt me the other day he wiz away tae poke Sheila Robertson - you know, that wee cracker in the child protection unit. Fuckin' Facebook he was on aboot. Though ye canna be sure." The laughter became raucous.

"I'd love to read his Facebook page," tears were streaming down Daley's face.

"Better on Twatter," they laughed the car around a corner in Argyle Street, towards the city mortuary.

It didn't matter how long it had been since Daley's last visit to Glasgow's Mortuary: it hadn't been long enough.

Part of the training of young police constables in years gone by included at least one trip to this place to witness a post mortem. Around a dozen pale, putative police officers would huddle around a bluff pathologist, as he hacked, cut, tore, drained, and generally showcased his talents in a way only the most strong-stomached could withstand.

He had managed not to faint or be sick; however he was in the minority. These incidents of revulsion were so common in fact, that each Muppet, (as trainee cops were then affectionately known), would be given a paper bag and told to be ready to grab whomever was next to them, in the likely event they passed out.

The young WPC who had stood next to Daley was so traumatised that she left Police College that day, never to return.

Things had changed: brushed aluminium sheets replaced the badly grouted Victorian tiles that had served as ubiquitous wall covering; heavy footed industrial carpet silenced the ominous tread of the cracked linoleum flooring; soft, mood lighting illuminated, where once the harsh glow of humming strip lights had served to augment a visceral scene of blood, shit and gore.

One thing had not changed - not in the slightest - the smell. The olfactory sense being as it is, instantly transported Daley back to his first visit every time he came here. A cloying, sickening mix of death, decay, disinfectant and refrigeration. A smell in fact, that no matter how you tried, would be your unwelcome companion, uninvited house guest for days on end after departing this Faustian repository of hell on earth.

Not everyone was affected in the same way, of course. Scott, slouched along the corridors untroubled by odour or clammy taint that the building seemed to impart.

"Aye an' see if he disna' get another centre half - he can forget it," the DS was expostulating on his favourite subject: Rangers Football Club. "That fuckin' 'keeper's fuck a' use un a'." From different sides of the West of Scotland sectarian divide, Inspector and Sergeant usually kept up a healthy banter on the subject of football. At the moment though, Scott found his interlocutor uncharacteristically silent. "Are ye followin' me, Jim?" The clatter of a large mortuary fire-door being slammed shut startled both men and negated the need for an answer.

"Well, well, if it's not the dream team." The sarcasm was palpable, even at a distance of ten yards. Another thing was unchanged from the first time Jim Daley had been to the mortuary, and he was now trying to secure a fire door with one hand as he pocketed a black pipe into a short, white coat with the other: Chief Forensic Pathologist Andrew Crichton.

"Still at the pipe, Andy? - I dread to think what shape your lungs are in." Daley walked towards Crichton and slapped him on the back. "How are you keeping? Surely you must be past retirement age." He smiled at the older man affectionately.

"One of the advantages of a professional career, Inspector Daley, is that one doesn't have to retire in one's forties and get a job delivering newspapers or doing odd jobs in order to make ends meet." Crichton was referring to the fact that most junior uniformed police officers retired after thirty years of service. Many would indeed find themselves in rather menial employment, either from boredom, or the real need to supplement an inadequate pension. In the CID, and from the rank of Inspector and above, the situation was different; the higher grades regularly stayed well beyond thirty years in *The Job*. However, forces were slowly encouraging ordinary cops to stay on as well, realising that there was indeed, no substitute for experience.

"Aye, listen tae it," Scott held an expression of mock outrage. "It'll be nae bother fir you tae get a wee part time job; that butcher in Kilmacolm's a'ways needin' help - an' think, no reports tae write or fuck a'."

"I'm so glad those elocution lessons you took have paid off, Brian; your ready turn of phrase never ceases to amaze me." Crichton surveyed the DS with a critical eye, "All that drink is having a devastating effect on your looks, too; good grief man, you look like you've aged ten years in the last two."

"Cheeky bastard," Scott chuckled. "Anyhow me an' the boss havn'a time for a' this, he's getting sent tae the wilds tomorrow. Whit have you got for us, Andy?"

"Well, gents, as you can no doubt discern with the use of your legendary detection skills and the pall of expensive pipe tobacco, I have been having a smoke; really nothing is sacred these days. My old professor never had a cigar out of his mouth when he performed a post mortem; now, if you light up within ten feet of the building, you're liable to go down for ten years."

"Aye, an' you've ay'ways been a stickler for the rule book, Andy." Ironic laughter filled the corridor as they headed for the pathology theatre.

Two technicians were working on a body lying on a metal operating table. The room itself was dimly lit, however a large bank of lights suspended in a metal frame above the operation emitted an ethereal glow, illuminating the scene with an ice-white precision.

"Be so good as to put these on." An assistant had arrived bearing green aprons, masks, and rubber overshoes. Crichton removed his white coat, then headed over to a large metal sink, where he rolled up his shirt sleeves and soaped his hands and forearms copiously, operating the taps with his elbows when he was finished. This done, he shrugged on his green rubber overall with a great deal more ease than the two police officers had displayed, having required the help of an assistant.

Now fully kitted out, the three proceeded to the operating table where Daley recognised the blackened, slightly bloated features of the deceased he had first seen on the e-mails in Donald's office. The body cavity had been exposed, both sides of her ribcage and flesh pinned back with large stainless steel clamps. As usual, Daley had to suppress his gagging reflex, Scott, however took the scene in intently, eyes visible over his mask, which was moving in a less than flattering manner as he continued to chew an ever-present piece of gum.

"Aye, you've had a good start, Andy." Scott's eyes flicked from the eviscerated corpse to the pathologist.

"When I heard who was in charge of this investigation, I thought I would get any sawing over with before you got here, Jim." Daley could only imagine the broad grin hidden by the older man's mask. "Right, progress so far…"

"As you can see we have managed a pretty comprehensive examination of the subject," Crichton was talking in a more business-like manner now, almost matter of fact, like a dentist announcing to his nurse which teeth were to be filled. What appeared to be a large microphone hung down above the scene, ensuring no utterances from anyone around the operating table were missed.

"At first glance - despite one or two anomalies, which I will come to - a straightforward strangulation. However, if I may, can I draw your attention to this?"

Surprisingly, Crichton moved down the corpse to an exposed leg. "This mark around the ankle indicates restraint." He pointed to a band about two inches thick encompassing the right ankle. The skin here was a lighter hue than the rest of the body, which was turning regulation black as the process of putrefaction began. "However, this mark was left on the body post mortem, so someone felt the need to tie her up even though she was dead."

Without giving the officers time to take this in, or ask any questions, he pulled the green sheet which had been covering the waist of the dead woman asunder, revealing a deep black gash, bisecting the remains. Daley could taste bile in the back of his throat.

"Again, after death, the body suffered a major trauma, completed I am told by your colleagues in Kinloch, who saw fit to pull the subject apart like a Christmas cracker." Crichton looked towards Daley, laughter lines visible above his mask. "If you need a chair, please just ask, Jim."

"Very good, Andy," the Inspector changed the subject quickly. "How - when - could that have happened?"

"If you're asking me to make a wild guess, I would say she was nearly cleft in two by a large, sharp metallic object - a ship's propeller for example. The wound is precise and clean, which suggests to me a swift slice, rather than the kind of sawing or cutting that would be required if manpower, or even a tool had been used. I'll have to do more tests on the flesh surrounding the wound. That will take a couple of days though."

"Fucking hell, this is some mess, Jim. Fuck, yer better taking Sherlock Holmes doon with ye, rather than me." As normal, Scott had displayed his uncanny knack of distilling the most complex of situations down to the lowest common denominator.

"I must admit, in my many years as a forensic pathologist, I have never encountered such circumstances. However, as I say, we have a number of lab based tests yet to perform: stomach contents, other bodily fluids etc. She definitely had sex within the last forty-eight hours. I will be in a position to tell you more on that point after yet more lab work."

"What do you mean, Andy?" Daley was curious; he had known Crichton for so many years that he had become used to the nuances of his voice and presentation. He suspected the pathologist had discovered something significant.

"Oh, merely a theory - nothing more. By the time you've had lunch down in Kinloch tomorrow, I should be able to give you some answers."

Suddenly Crichton raised his head from the body and looked at the police officers. "Wonderful place, Kinloch. I have a friend down there: great fishing, golf; fantastic scenery," he had a far-away look. "People are as mad as fuck, though."

"What are you? - A shite tourist board?" DS Scott, straight to the point. "Once you're done wi' the rough guide, mebe you'll tell us how long she's been deid for."

"Again, immersion in water has made that more difficult - no more than sixty, no less than twenty-eight hours, I would say. Sorry to be repetitive, I'll be able to be more precise within the next day or so."

"What about her age, Andy; any distinguishing marks?" Daley was intrigued; despite the gruesome surroundings, attending the post mortem had whetted his appetite for the investigation.

"I was just coming to that. I would say she was between twenty-five and thirty. She has given birth within the last three years or so; oh and look at this." He moved the corpse's right leg. On her inner thigh, the letters 'IS', had been tattooed, roughly. "As you can see, not professional - ink and knife job if you ask me - most unusual for a woman to let herself be disfigured in that way - don't you think gents?"

For once, DS Scott had nothing to say.

4

Daley hated waiting. He was sure that on his death bed he would bitterly regret the hours, days and weeks he had spent in the limbo of being unable to do anything whilst waiting. In this particular instance, Scott was fifteen minutes late and although he would still easily make his flight, he fretted that the time he had added in lieu of any possible delay was fast disappearing.

He looked around his lounge absently, subconsciously noting that all of the décor, ornaments, choice of furniture - even photographs and paintings - were really all the work of his wife. Not for the first time he felt like a stranger in his own home; an alien environment, pandering to the tastes and comfort of another.

He remembered being a teenager: the posters on his wall, the black paint that had so infuriated his mother when she had discovered it adorning his bedroom, from floor to ceiling. He had even painted his bedroom furniture white: black and white which matched his taste in SKA music. The music centre, that he had coveted for so long, sat on top of an old chest of drawers that his father had '*acquired*'. A *Roberts* transistor radio dominated his bedside table, the rest of the small space occupied by an ancient angle-poise lamp and whatever book he happened to be reading at the time.

He had managed to cobble together a low cabinet, which contained his records and tapes, the former stored end-on, in alphabetical order. Now he had this equipment, he was able to make up compilation tapes that he gave his father to play on the car stereo whenever they embarked upon some of the gargantuan journeys that were the habitual precursor to visiting some ancient relative.

All this had been his pride and joy; the indication to anyone who cared to wonder, that he was now an adult who had his own likes and dislikes - his personality encapsulated by a few sticks of rough furniture, poorly applied paint and low-end hi-fi equipment. Nothing special - but his. Even his eventual choice of career had reflected the black and white check.

Standing now in his expensive home, in one of the well-appointed, *reception* rooms, graced with the cream of soft furnishings and de jour art - stark realisation that he had allowed his personality to be subsumed by the whims and itinerant fancies of Liz, slowly dawned. This room - in fact the whole house - was someone else's stage; a stage on which he was merely an ensemble member, an insignificant and unaccredited player. He shied away from acceptance of the fact that this relationship was consuming his soul; his reason for being was evermore entwined and predicated on his dynamic with a person he felt he grew further from every day.

Unnecessarily, Scott was loudly sounding his horn as he drove up the short, gravel drive. "C'mon you; you'll miss that bloody flight if we don't get a fuckin' shift on." Daley pushed the front door twice, ensuring it was properly closed, walked down three steps and opened the door to Scott's car, the acrid smell of cigarette smoke hitting him like a wave of unwelcome nausea.

"You know, Brian, this car is a complete health hazard," Daley eased himself into the front passenger seat.

"Fuck me, am good enough tae take ye o'er tae the airport, an' a' ye can dae is gie me a hard time. You've been a right pain in the arse since ye stopped smoking. Do you know that?" Scott stubbed his cigarette out in the overflowing ashtray with exaggerated vigour; involuntarily, he coughed the deep, unhealthy rasp of the confirmed smoker.

"See, when you're in the oxygen tent you'll wish you'd done the same as me and given up. How do you think I managed to afford that big plasma TV you like so much?" Scott coughed an expletive filled answer as they drove towards the main road.

Daley realised that he had become difficult since quitting fags. He definitely did not miss the hacking cough, the bad breath and the huge amount of money they relieved you of in the course of a year; he hadn't even suffered any noticeable sign of withdrawal. No, his post smoking self, had developed a visceral hatred of cigarettes, something he supposed the body prompted in order to protect this new, nicotine free, existence.

Scott broke the spell, "Mind you met my brother, Willie, at the fitba'?" Daley grunted in the affirmative. "Aye, well I'd forgotten he wiz doon there workin' aboot three years ago - he's a sparky, mind?"

"I remember, he swears more than you. I didn't think that was possible. Anyway, how did he like Kinloch?"

"Fuck me, we had tae wring his liver oot wi' a mangle when he came back, he says they're a' near daft doon there. The wife reminded me last night, you know, when I says I might be goin' doon for a while. A' mad wi drink; fight wi' their ain shadows - aye, an' close knit tae. I'm thinking yer in fir a fuckin' hard time wi' that mob, for certain sure."

Daley looked out at the leaden sky as he pondered Scott's theories on Kinloch society. Small communities were always difficult places in which to carry out an investigation. However, in a way, all investigations took place within one community or another, whether it be a housing estate, tower block, company or ethnic enclave. Glasgow's Asian and Chinese communities were notoriously difficult to infiltrate - and as for some of the schemes - well, he didn't expect Kinloch could be any worse.

As they neared the airport, large signs announced a change to parking procedures around the terminal buildings. In fact, it was more appropriate to say you couldn't drive anywhere near them. An attack on the airport by terrorists with a car full of gas canisters had made sure of that.

As a young cop, he had worked for nearly six months at Glasgow Airport. In those carefree days, all the police worried about was where they could get a free coffee, or where best to view nubile young holiday makers as they navigated their scantily dressed way through the terminal. Now; well now, things were different. Even here, on Paisley's doorstep he was aware of a change in attitude. People viewed anyone remotely Asian or Arabic in appearance as a potential threat. The landlord of his local in Howwood had implored him to look carefully at the soles of the shoes of any suspicious looking passengers.

"Think aboot it," he said, "when wiz the last time anybody looked at your shoes when you checked onto a flight? – it's obvious, Jim." Since then Daley had to make a real effort not to stare at fellow passengers' footwear. Maybe people were right to be suspicious, perhaps danger was ever present; definitely, the world had changed.

Scott dropped him as near to the terminal building as was humanly possible and Daley made his way along pavements and walkways crammed with bright faced, pale travellers, chatting excitedly as they made their way into the airport; or their tanned, yet quieter counterparts, returning to the greyness of reality from holiday idylls. The scent of cool rain on warm tarmac mixed with the heady odour of aviation fuel and car fumes permeated the air.

He hated any kind of terminal building: whether it be train, bus, or airport. It was not that they were large, often busy, usually impersonal places; no, it was the air of melancholy that inhabited them. To him, they spoke loudly of parting, of sorrow: people saying goodbye. Not for him thoughts of a mother greeting a long lost child, or lovers re-united; these buildings were filled with a resonance of something coming to an end. Without meaning to, he thought of Liz.

He made his way to the check-in, where an attractive young woman issued his boarding pass and processed his luggage. She reminded him of the fragrant secretaries that populated Donald's floor of the station. He pondered how many women were passed over for work just because they were not in possession of the requisite looks; life was indeed as unfair as it was ridiculous.

He strolled to the departure gate via a newsagent, where he bought a paper. A quick scan of the front page revealed that, inevitably, the press had got a hold of the murder story. No doubt he would have to appear at a press conference at some point; something he hated. He wished he had chosen to wear a different tie and resolved to change it at the earliest opportunity.

Daley couldn't help smiling on discovering that the same woman who had checked him in, was now collecting his boarding pass. She noticed the smirk, "We're a small operation, sir; everyone has to pitch in." She nodded her head once to underline what she had said. He detected an unusual lilt to her voice; not the sing-song of a Highland accent, nor the questioning intonation of the central belt - something different, longer vowels - a more laconic pace.

A low floored bus drove them towards a small aircraft. At first, he thought they would drive past this mini plane, until the bus pulled up and another uniformed flight attendant entered and ushered them from the vehicle towards the aircraft. Daley was normally a confident flier, however, he was unprepared for the cramped cabin he now entered, hunched over, walking sideways like a crab. The flight attendant showed him to a window seat on the right hand side of the aisle. As he adjusted his belt he heard a stream of expletives issuing from two youths, as they were seated in front of him. The young men were not being intentionally offensive; in the West of Scotland, punctuation was gradually being replaced by curses. He and Liz had recently spent a weekend in York. He remembered being surprised by the absence of swearing. Even the small pub in the Marygate, close to their hotel, offered a warm welcome in an oath free zone. Along with good beer, it made a pleasant change from the raucous, febrile ambiance prevalent in the boozers he frequented.

Momentarily, the young men fell silent as a slight, middle aged Asian man was shown to a seat at the front of the aircraft. A snort of suppressed laughter indicated that they had registered his presence.

"Fuck me Bobby, start saying your prayers. That cunt's lakely got a bomb up his arse."

Daley contemplated intervening on the behalf of decency;

however, he was beaten to it by the prompt intervention of the attendant. "Right you, Camel Johnstone, any mair o' that an' the only arse you'll need tae worry about is yer ain as it bounces off the tarmac when I throw you off the plane. Unnerstan?"

Daley smiled, this was certainly not the type of approach he was used to from airline staff, however, it proved most effective as both young men were now quiet and had adopted blank, slightly embarrassed expressions. He had noticed the long vowels again, both from the boys and the stewardess; this was, no doubt, the Kinloch accent. The flight attendant stared pointedly at them both, her expression hard to gauge under the requisite thick layer of gaudy make up.

He mentally repressed feelings of claustrophobia as the engines burst into life and they began to taxi slowly along the runway.

Without warning the plane rose sharply from the ground, engines straining to get them airborne. Daley's heart missed a beat as the engine noise dropped suddenly as they attained the required height. A grey curtain at the front of the aircraft was flung open revealing the cockpit: one pilot was seated, clearly flying the plane, while the other stood hunched with a radio mike in his hand, ready to address the passengers.

"Good morning, Ladies and Gents, aye an' you Camel Johnstone," - Camel was clearly a well-known figure. "We'll be flying at a height of fifteen hundred feet for most of the journey, which will last around twenty-five minutes. The weather in Kinloch is much the same as in Glasgow, so we will be taking the scenic route over Arran, then down the Kintyre peninsula. If you have any questions, please address them to our lovely flight attendant, Morag," she managed to turn the corners of her mouth into a smile under the cake of make-up. The rest of her features didn't appear to move. "I'm Lieutenant Moran, your pilot today is Captain Witherspoon. Thank you for flying Scotia Airways. Morag will now take you through the safety procedures."

As she stood up, the flight attendant obscured the young pilot as he retreated into the cockpit. After jumping involuntarily, she announced, perfunctorily, the usual list of safety instructions. Daley guessed that Lieutenant Moran had nipped her arse through the curtain, though her plastered expression gave nothing away.

He looked lazily out of the window: cotton wool whisps of cloud floated above a patchwork of tiny fields and the grey snake of roads beneath, familiar landmarks took on a miniature appearance from the air. Bright sunlight issued from the blue sky now, reflecting from the silver wing of the plane, making Daley wish he had brought the designer sunglasses Liz had so proudly presented him with at Christmas. Her attitude was that if it did not possess a fancy designer name and an outrageous price tag, then it wasn't worth buying.

Beneath, the fields were replaced by an iron grey sea, flecked with the white tips of waves. Daley thought the sea looked out of place; too cold for what was a warm, spring day. He shuddered at the thought of the corpse of the young woman floating in this forbidding expanse of water. He had always been wary of the sea; though he swam well, he restricted his aquatic pursuits to swimming pools. The sea seemed too big, too unfathomable; filled with the unexpected and unknown. He had read that we knew more about the surface of Mars than the hidden depths of the ocean - he wasn't surprised.

His thoughts drifted to Liz. He had managed to get her on the mobile late the previous evening. Despite ringing since six and leaving copious messages, she seemed surprised by his call. The noise of a pub: clinking glasses, singing, loud music, over exaggerated laughter, was the backdrop to their conversation. She greeted his news about the Kinloch investigation with the platitudes he supposed she felt were her dutiful responsibility - *I'll miss you... hope you won't be away long...oh, the house will be so empty* - all the time he could hear muffled voices, suppressed laughter; the way a teenager talked to a worried parent from a uni bar whilst being taunted by friends. Amongst the conspiratorial mumbles, a familiar voice: Mark.

Mark Henderson was married to Liz's sister Jill, and as such, was Jim Daley's brother-in-law. The pair hated each other from the word go. In fact, mutual friends would often comment how mismatched both couples were. Mark was more like Liz: haughty, dismissive, arrogant, immodest, sly, vengeful, petty, shallow, good-looking, and extremely clever. It appeared to many that the sisters had married the wrong men. Jill, though almost identical to Liz in a long limbed, languid, stunning way, was of a much more reticent nature. The younger sibling by two years, she lacked Liz's supreme confidence, which, accidentally perhaps, had imbued her with greater empathy, sensitivity and understanding. She could almost mirror the role Daley played in his marriage. Mark was a notorious philanderer, having been a more than willing party to a number of affairs. He worked as a corporate lawyer to an international firm of accountants; two of the slippiest professions under the one roof. Who was less trustworthy? - the accountant constantly seeking the loophole or the uncrossed T, or the lawyer who habitually watched his back?

Daley liked Jill. He was able to gauge by the way she looked at Mark how devoted she was, and the pain and devastation caused by his infidelity. They had spoken about it on a Portuguese beach, as they sat in a secluded bay watching Mark and Liz's horseplay in the sea.

"Do you think they've slept together?" Her question was sudden and perplexing. However, on examination, Daley knew that he had often wondered the same thing, doing what he always did with unpalatable thoughts about his wife: banishing them.

"No, they're too alike to be attracted to each other," he had lied. He remembered the wan smile that had crossed her face by way of a reply. It was a *he knew, she knew, he knew,* situation. After that, they had kept their own council on the matter, each aware of the bitter, unspoken truth, just unwilling to grant it the life of acknowledgement.

Jill and Mark did share something that it seemed he and Liz would never have: a child.

Beth was their pride and joy. She shared her mother's long limbs and easy grace, had her father's round intelligent face, which framed deep, watchful blue eyes, slightly turned down at the corners. A nest of curly hair crowned her busy three year old head, hanging in ringlets when her mother let it grow long. She had, as Daley's mother used to say, *Been here before.* Talking fluently before she was two, she combined tireless mischief with quick thought and flawless parody. When Daley visited, she grabbed her favourite Noddy book, climbed on his knee, and demanded to be read to. She chuckled her way through a story with him, mimicking the voices he used for various characters. He didn't envy Mark Henderson his money, his board level career, big house, fancy car; even the fact he had probably had his wife: no, he coveted his daughter, dearly wishing that the beautiful little girl was his own.

Liz it seemed had no intention of ever having a child. The five *S's,* she called it: screams, shits, sick, sleeplessness and stretch-marks. "Bugger that, who in their right mind would want a baby?" Her attitude to children encapsulated in a few words.

"Ladies and Gentlemen, we have just emerged from some cloud cover. Below, you can see the east coast of the Kintyre peninsula."

Daley looked out of the window at the prompting of the intercom. The uninviting grey sea had been replaced by a low, rocky coastline, dotted at intervals with white, sandy beaches. To his untrained eye, the landscape looked more verdant than it had twenty minutes before, as though the fecundity of the season was somehow at a more advanced stage here.

"Everything OK?" Morag the air stewardess was making her way up the aisle, tending to her temporary charges, holding a small basket filled with brightly wrapped sweets. He had developed a sweet tooth since stopping smoking, something he blamed for his recent weight gain. So, inevitably, as the confectionery was waved under his nose he chose two sweets, being careful to avoid the golden wrapped toffees that had been responsible for him losing a filling last Christmas.

Out of the window the chimneys and rooftops of a small town could be distantly discerned; he guessed that this was the fabled Kinloch.

As though to confirm this, the intercom burst into crackling life once more: "Ladies and Gents, as you can perhaps see we are approaching our destination: Kinloch. We will be landing in around five minutes or so. Please ensure that you remain seated, and that your seatbelts remain secured."

Daley continued to look absently out of the window, his head resting on the headrest. The buildings below were more distinct now; unexpectedly grey he thought. Strangely, the street pattern of what looked like tenement buildings reminded him of Paisley. Unlike most seaside towns, built around the sea front, it looked as though Kinloch's streets were at right angles to the loch around which the town sprawled.

The pitch of the engines changed again as the plane began its descent over an airfield, which looked to be only a few fields away from the town. The hangers and other airfield buildings bore a distinctly military feel, though Daley could not see any matching aircraft. From some distance along the runway, a red fire appliance could just be made out speeding towards their likely landing point.

"Ladies and gents, as you will be aware we are beginning our descent into Kinloch airport. Please remain seated, with your seat belts fastened. May I take this opportunity to thank you again for travelling Scotia Airways and hope that you enjoy your time amongst the colourful residents of the area." That had been said with tongue firmly placed in cheek. Daley wondered just how different this place, and these people could be? - in any event he was about to find out.

The plane bumped down noisily onto the runway with the usual screech of skidding tyres and creaks and groans of the undercarriage. The fire engine looked much larger now as it pulled up beside the aircraft. They taxied a short distance to a small terminal building. A green light flashed in time to a dinging alarm from the intercom, indicating that it was safe for the passengers to remove their seatbelts and begin the stooped crab walk down the aisle.

Morag stood slightly hunched at the exit, handing passengers carefully onto the plane's steps, as an identically dressed colleague stood at the bottom of the stairs repeating this function. The two were carrying on a shouted dialogue in the long vowels he was now sure belonged to the natives of Kinloch. He ducked through the exit door and down the few steps onto the tarmac. The tang of the sea was strong as he walked towards the terminal building. The temperature seemed higher than that he had left in Paisley and there was such a freshness to the air here, that he drew deeply through his nostrils, already relishing being away from the fetid air of the city.

A cadaverous man stood in the doorway of the terminal building, examining the identity documents that were now a routine, even on internal flights. As Daley got to the front of the small queue, and before he could produce his warrant card, the man, who was probably nearer sixty than fifty, held up his hand indicating the policeman need not worry about ID.

"You'll be fine, Inspector Daley," he had the musical lilt of the Hebrides. "There's a boy out the front to pick you up." Junior officers were often described by cops of old as boys. This, coupled with bearing and demeanour, led Daley to his next comment.

"How's retirement treating you?" He smiled knowingly at the man.

"Aye good, very good, Inspector. Lachie Bain, thirty years before the mast, aye and heartily glad not to be before it any more," he held out a large hand for Daley to shake.

"Jim Daley - but you know that already."

Now it was time for the older man to smile. He had a broad, infectious grin, though Daley suspected that it was not something he did very often. " Aye well, as you'll find out yourself, old habits die hard - I saw your name on the passenger list - and anyhow this is Kinloch, the whole town will likely know that you're on your way, aye and why you're here."

"Like that is it? Looks like a reasonably sized place, I didn't expect gossip to be so rife."

Bain laughed again, this time tossing his head back in mirth, "It's the biggest gossip hole this side of Benbecula, aye and vicious with it. If you ever need a friendly ear, I'm in the bar of the County Hotel about half five most days - after the last flight - only for an hour or so, you understand," he added, with a serious look.

"Thanks, I'll certainly remember that, but I think I'll have my hands pretty full - I needn't tell you…"

Bain held his hand up again, "Och, no doubt you'll not have troubles to seek - but you'll be billeted there anyway - mind all work and no play…"

Daley grinned as he headed into the terminal. It was already clear that there were few secrets in Kinloch. He picked up his luggage and walked through the automatic doors of the small building.

5

A large, red-headed young man was sitting on the bonnet of what - with Daley's experience – he recognized immediately as a CID car.

"Inspector Daley, I'm DC Fraser," he held out his hand to greet the senior officer. "Hope your trip was OK; it can get a bit hairy on that wee plane when the wind's up. Not so bad today."

Daley noted the similarities between Fraser and his infamous uncle: while both men were tall, heavily built, with red hair, the young officer in front of him bore none of the signs of debauchery that had marked out his uncle as a more than heavy drinker. Indeed, he looked like the kind of cop that you would be glad to have at your side going into sort out a pub brawl in Paisley, not the short, slight, graduates that now seemed to be favoured by force recruitment.

"Hello, DC Fraser. I used to work with your Uncle Davie - how's he doing by the way? I heard he hadn't been well."

"Eh - don't hold that against me, sir - he's on the waiting list for a liver transplant; don't suppose I need to tell you why." Fraser looked ruefully at the Inspector.

"Ach, don't worry son, there's a lot worse than Davie cloaking about," Daley lied. "You're getting a bit of a reputation yourself, ripping murder victims in half." He smiled at the DC benevolently, he was quite sure that the young man had heard plenty of that particular incident.

Fraser's face was now a deep red, as he stooped to pick up the Inspector's bags, putting them into the open boot of the car.

"Would you like to drive, sir? Our boss always insists on driving if he's in the motor."

"No, no - take the wheel, DC Fraser. This'll be Inspector MacLeod you're talking about?"

"Yes, sir," Daley noted his colleague's raised eyebrow, "he has his eh... routines, so to speak." They both got into the car, and leaving the small airport car park, headed along a single track road.

"How far's the town?" Daley said absently, remembering to switch his mobile back on after the flight, and noticing, not without some dismay, that he had a missed call from Liz.

"Oh, only about four miles, sir - we'll soon be on the main drag; have you been here before?"

Daley only had hazy memories of coming to Kinloch on one of the old steamers with his granny, in what seemed like a lifetime ago.

"Aye, once when I was a wee boy - so you'll forgive me if I don't remember much about it." He put the phone back into his pocket, resolving to call Liz as soon as he got a bit of space. "How are we doing with this enquiry - anything turned up?"

Fraser gave a resigned sigh. "We've done the rounds, sir - y'know, local fishermen, missing persons - the usual. Nobody seems to know anything. She was a bit hard to recognise with the bloating an' all. What did the PM show?"

Daley smiled, "If you're worried about your little mishap, well don't be. The corpse was nearly severed, anyone trying to move it would have had the same problem. Oh, by the way, she had *IS* tattooed on her thigh - ring any bells?"

Fraser shook his head, Daley could tell he was thinking about saying something, but wasn't sure what kind of reception he would get.

"Spit it out, Archie; I believe that everyone on an investigation should be allowed an opinion, so don't ever be afraid to speak your mind if you think it's relevant. In this job, the smallest push can topple the most robust wall of silence. Oh, and, I get this fireside philosophy from my - our - boss, so take heed." He winked at the younger man.

"Well, sir, it's just that... well when you get used to Kinloch, you realise that nothing really happens that the whole community doesn't know about, within minutes usually. I don't understand why we haven't got a lead yet. If somebody was missing, well, it would stand out a mile to friends, family. Do you know what I mean, sir?"

Daley had of course considered this, however, there were a number of problems: the Post Mortem had shown that the body had not been exposed to water for very long, even though the corpse had likely spent time out to sea. Also, by all accounts, the prevailing weather conditions seemed to negate the likelihood of the body being washed up where it had been at all. Then there was the strange mark on the ankle, possibly left by a restraint. Maybe he should send for Sherlock Holmes.

They were now pulling into the outskirts of Kinloch. He was surprised to note that it did bear a resemblance to Paisley on the ground as well as the air; only a Paisley from twenty years ago. Four storey tenements in red sandstone, bordered both sides of the road; under each a small shop of the type that had all but disappeared back home. In those days, butchers, bakers, cobblers, pubs, tailors, grocers, hairdressers, funeral parlours, newsagents - all could be located on the High Streets of every town in Scotland. Now, huge supermarket chains and massive *out of town* shopping malls had all but put paid to the local emporium. Not though, in Kinloch.

The town appeared to be cosseted on three sides by hills that stood out starkly against the flawless blue sky. Now they were getting nearer to the centre, he noticed that his colleague was being waved at repeatedly, a number of cars were even flashing their lights and sounding their horns - most unusual. Fraser was acknowledging all this in an understated manner, most likely not wanting to make the wrong move in front of the Inspector.

"Straight to the office, sir?" They were now at a *T* junction, where the good people of Kinloch took the opportunity to stare into the vehicle with unrestrained interest.

41

"Aye, fine. I'll get settled in and have a word with your Inspector MacLeod, then I want to meet the team here. Have you set up an incident room yet?"

Fraser looked anxiously at the Inspector, "Well, sir, it's been a bit difficult. My gaffer is on the panel - with his back, y'know?" Daley nodded, indicating he wanted him to get on with it. "Well, Inspector MacLeod said that was your job, sir." Fraser's embarrassment was plain, his face was almost a beacon-like red.

"OK," Daley tried to work things out in his mind, "how many do we have in CID here?"

"Four, sir, me included."

"Oh," was all Daley had to say in reply. They turned right into what Daley assumed to be the main street of the town, up a hill, and towards a structure that looked like a cross between a medieval castle and a Victorian prison. Fraser turned the car through an opened gateway and into a car park at the rear of the building.

"Here we are, sir." Fraser was already getting out of the car.

Daley was in the middle of insisting that he was perfectly capable of carrying his own bags from the car, when a dapper figure, dressed in the perfectly creased uniform of an Inspector, appeared from a steel security door which led out onto the car park. A full head shorter than Daley, the well-polished peak of his hat was adorned with silver braid. He stopped suddenly, obviously not expecting to see the other two officers.

Daley was the first to speak. "Good morning, Inspector, Jim Daley. You have an unusual office here."

Macleod was eyeing him the way some would, having been presented with a less than desirable meal.

"Daley, yes of course we've been expecting you, though why we need assistance from the city, I will never know." He had a similar accent to that of Lachie Bain at the airport, though more highly pitched and faster paced. The sneering aspect to his face riled Daley immediately, though he tried hard not to let it show. He was also unhappy that while he had given MacLeod his designation, his opposite number had seen fit only to grace him with his surname.

MacLeod turned on his heel, and held the steel door open with eyes downcast, a reluctant invitation to enter the hallowed portals of his domain. Fraser and Daley, now in the corridor, waited while MacLeod entered, letting the door swing shut slowly on its transom.

"Fraser, take those bags to the CID room. Daley, you can follow me."

Fraser took the luggage from Daley with a doubtful look. MacLeod was doing his best to stamp his authority over the interloper. Daley refused to descend to his level, so much more meekly than he felt, followed MacLeod to his office, the door of which reminded him of Superintendent Donald's: Insp. C. MacLeod. Sub. Div. Commander. - was picked out in bold, larger than normal, letters.

"Sit." MacLeod's instruction was terse, though Daley did as he was bid, as he desperately tried to remember the mantra he had learned in anger management, about the man who could keep his temper always winning the argument. MacLeod had removed his hat, exposing a bald head fringed by neatly cropped, silver-grey hair.

"Now, let me make myself clear, I..." Daley held up his hand to indicate that he was not listening.

"No, Inspector MacLeod, please let me make myself clear," maybe some of those classes in temper control had worked. "In the future when you address me, you will be good enough to use my designation - which is incidentally - the same as yours." MacLeod opened his mouth to speak, but Daley raised his voice, making it clear that he was not finished. "You may be the Sub Divisional Commander here, however, I am running a murder investigation, with which I require your every assistance. I will keep you informed of my requirements as, and when they arise. I will also keep you abreast with the progress of the investigation as I see fit - is that understood?"

MacLeod's face was red, verging on purple. "Inspector Daley, I really must protest, here in Argyll we have a different way of proceeding than in the city. I am…"

Again his words were cut short.

"You are subject to the Force Standing Orders of Strathclyde Police - the force of which you are part. I don't give a shit what passed for organisation here in the old county days. If you have any problems with that, I suggest you contact Superintendent Donald, who is ultimately in charge of this operation, and to whom I will be reporting regularly. I've got him on speed dial - here."

He handed his mobile to MacLeod, who looked as though he was close to tears, he did though straighten himself up in his chair, eschewing the offer of the mobile phone.

"Very well, *Inspector* Daley," the rank was said in a long, exaggerated way. "I will accede to your requests - I have however, my own hotline to a superior." He smiled a wan, yet arrogant smile, looked down at his desk, and opened a file.

Daley stood up, then lent forward, resting his large frame on outstretched arms, his hands now fists, knuckles white against the dark wood of MacLeod's desk.

"Fuck me about at your peril, you little prick." He stood, turned and walked to the door which he opened as if to leave; he stopped though, in the open doorway, turning to face the seated figure. "Oh, I'll be wanting to meet with the local CID Officers and two of your best uniformed constables - I'll leave the choice to you - in half an hour. Please see to it. Now, where the fuck's my office?"

Daley sat in the glass box that served as the inner sanctum for the senior officers within the larger CID room. He hated open plan offices: no privacy, too much faux camaraderie - a feeling of enforced togetherness; which, in his opinion, only served to heighten resentment and ill-feeling amongst ambitious officers, promote a steep upward curve in the sedentary behaviour of their more 'easy going' colleagues and prompt an absolute requirement for a good set of blinds. He noted that such had been thoughtfully provided in his box as he pulled the various cords in turn, ensuring he had at least, some modicum, of privacy.

He was unhappy that MacLeod had breached his temper so

44

readily, however he felt that their unfortunate first meeting had clarified how he wished to proceed. To that end, he had been shocked to see just how little effort had gone into the operation so far from the Kinloch CID's point of view.

The large 'clear boards' on which SOCO images of the victim, locus, and eventually suspects were in place, but unused. A computer database (all important in modern murder inquiries), had been started, but had pitifully little input for a case that was already twenty-four hours old. The four young DC's - three men and one woman - had conducted some door-to-door work, spoken to fishermen and other seafarers who may be of help, stopped cars at, or near the locus where the body was recovered, etc. In short, done the basics. The local investigation lacked any organisation or impetus: that was what he was here to provide.

Through the narrowed slats of his blinds he could see them now: four DC's and two uniformed officers; he couldn't help noticing how young they seemed. This was he supposed, the curse of the older, experienced officer. He recalled, vividly, that his initial experience of CID work was one of ignored drudgery: ploughing through endless files, records, bank statements, phone bills, CCTV footage - anything that could provide that crucial piece of evidence to crack an investigation. His opinions or theories had been, most definitely, not required.

He opened his glass door, the conversation between the local officers stopped.

"As I am sure you all know I'm Inspector Jim Daley, and before anyone says it, I most certainly go to the gym daily." That got a laugh. "I'll get to know you as we go along. I'm afraid for reasons of logistics and man-power, we're chasing our tail slightly with this one, however, we're already some way along the road so to speak."

He walked over to a desk from which he picked up a large manila folder. "Constable Fraser, if you would be good enough to append these PM images to the second of our boards there in number order. Could you... sorry what's your name?" He was gesturing towards the WDC, who stood in a formal way.

"Dunn, sir Mary Dunn - this lota bastards call me '*Yoor getting*'- you know, by way of puerile male entertainment." She looked wearily at her sniggering colleagues.

He forgave her the regulation rise in intonation, and then gave her the pictures of the victim that had been taken by SOCO on the beach. She affixed them to the first clear board, and then stood waiting for further instructions.

"OK, DC Dunn," he threw a white marker pen at the young Detective, which she caught adroitly, "please write up all relevant information that we know for sure, such as time, date, method of discovery etc. Which of you is the computer buff?"

A slight, pale-faced DC, whose pock marked face gave him the look of a teenager he couldn't be, stuck his hand in the air.

"Me, sir, Neil Cluckie."

"OK, Neil, I want you to be responsible for updating the database; at least until we can see where we're going with this. I'm sure I don't have to tell you what's required, but I know different investigators have different standards, so in this case, I want everything put in there: who we interview, when and why, the statement itself, the opinions of the interviewing officers - feelings. I hope you all know how important feelings and instinct are in this job." Heads were nodding vigorously. He walked over to the window, which looked from their elevated position straight down the sunny main street of the town. The road was busy with cars, the pavements an unexpected throng of people, which surprised him.

"Is it always this busy here? - fuck me, there's over two-hundred shopping days till Christmas."

"It's Thursday, sir," the familiar voice of DC Fraser. "The local paper comes out about ten every Thursday morning - everyone rushes out to buy it; it's like a local community event."

"From my brief experience of your lovely town, I would have thought a newspaper was the last thing they needed - everyone seems so well informed." Daley got a laugh again, but he was only half joking. Tight-knit they may be, but in small communities like this, information changed hands so much that some of it must eventually come the way of the police. He turned back to face his new team.

"Right, let's get this show on the road."

It took him a couple of hours or so to get them on track. Cluckie remained in the office updating the database, while WDCs Dunn and Keith, another large, agricultural type, were sent to every shop, pub, office and café, in fact, anywhere that someone may have heard, seen, or been told something of relevance. He called the force Public Relations Unit, and arranged for a press conference to be held in Kinloch the following day.

It turned out that the two uniformed cops had to spell another who was guarding the locus; and in the very likely event of the investigation continuing over the weekend, all three would be required to bolster what seemed like a considerable show of strength in the face of the unruly revellers of the town. In short, he was woefully undermanned, and sent an e-mail detailing this, and a short summary of his run-in with MacLeod to Superintendent Donald. Pass the buck - he had enough to do without coping with bruised egos, or preening selfishness. He was pretty sure that Donald would appreciate all of this.

His next visit was to the Harbour Master. Now they knew that the body had spent at least twelve hours in the sea, he wanted some idea as to where their victim may have entered the water.

"The Harbour Master's office is on the pier, right?" this question was to Fraser who he had chosen as a local guide and advisor.

"Yes, sir, do you want to check into the hotel en route? It's on the way."

"Not just now, Archie. Get one of the uniforms to take my bags down, tell them I'll want some food later. I fancy a stroll down to the pier; it's a nice day after all, and I want to try and get a feel of the place."

They left the station by the front door, passed the local court, and some lawyers' offices, and then headed down Main Street,

Kinloch.

"Well, at least the office is central for the court; not much of an excuse if you're late though." Daley spoke easily to Fraser, he sensed that he already had gained the younger man's trust, indeed he felt sympathy with the DC; having to deal with the peccadilloes of Macleod was unlikely to be easy.

"Aye, sir, the town centre is pretty compact, it's mostly over this side of the Loch, mainly residential over the other side; a few shops, a hotel, nothing much."

"Hello, Inspector," two elderly women were shuffling towards them, arm-in-arm, "we're all glad you've come down to sort this out. What a dreadful, dreadful crime." The thick set woman, who was short with round glasses, was doing the talking; her slight, white-haired companion was merely nodding, as she drew in her breath sharply by way of agreement with her friend.

"Thank you, ladies." Good PR was essential in isolated areas; however it was clear that he would have no need to announce his arrival to anybody. "I hope that if you hear anything you'll tell my officers - no matter how trivial, mind." He smiled at the pair indulgently.

"Oh, don't you worry, Inspector, we're well acquainted with your handsome constable; you could say he is a drinking companion of ours. Is that not right, Archie?" The plump old woman smiled broadly at the DC, displaying an assortment of teeth in various stages of brown decay, whilst her companion continued to nod sagely, drawing her breath in as occasion demanded.

Daley wondered just how many shades of red his colleague's face was capable of displaying, as they made their excuses and continued down the street, leaving the two old women in their wake.

"Nothing to be embarrassed about, son. When I was your age, I liked them a wee bit older too."

Fraser turned suddenly, about to assure his new boss that he only saw the old ladies in the pub now and then, when, by the look on Daley's face, he realised he was being wound up.

"Very good, sir - aye very good."

The day was warmer still, as it was now mid-afternoon. They made their way through what was now the town's centre, passing the County Hotel where Daley was to be accommodated. The building was - like many others in Kinloch - built from red sandstone; however a faux *Juliet* balcony and equally contrived crenulations had been included in the architecture, in an attempt to give the hotel a *Scottish Baronial* feel. If failing in that regard, it did ensure that the façade was difficult to miss, even by the most geographically challenged guest.

As they progressed, they were greeted with nods and hellos. A group of smokers outside one of the many bars regaled them with shouts of 'here's the cavalry', and 'fuck me, a proper polis in the toon at last'. Unperturbed, the pair crossed onto a well-tended roundabout, then across another road on to one of Kinloch's two piers.

The air was a heady mix of ozone, fish and the diesel fumes emitted by a small number of wooden fishing boats, which were accompanied by the raucous shouts of crew members, radios playing music - all bass and drums - and seagulls wheeling, diving, and squawking. Daley surmised that their arrival coincided with the fishing boats landing their catch of the day.

Again, he was instantly transported back to his childhood, standing on this very pier with his grandparents: his granny, short, bustling and stout; his grandfather a thin, almost skeletal figure, tall for his time, but dressed in keeping with the period, in an old grey suit, the trousers of which were held up by thick, maroon braces. Papa George laughed wheezily as he drew on a Capstan full-strength. To the young Daley he had seemed like an old man; in fact he was destined not see past his fifty-seventh birthday, his lungs wrecked by years of heavy smoking, and a lifetime spent down the coal pits of North Lanarkshire.

He walked slowly over to the side of the pier, placing his foot on an iron stanchion built into the side of the construction, allowing boats to affix extra moorings in case of bad weather. Dark, oily water lapped at the supports of the jetty. The afternoon was warm, scent laden - almost idyllic. He looked out over the water to the head of the loch, which was about a mile away. His thoughts returned to the investigation; he shivered involuntarily as he turned to Fraser.

"The people here might be a bit dodgy, but the scenery is beautiful."

They made their way along the pier towards the green building, in which the harbour master had his office. A top-of-the-range Jaguar motor car sat impressively outside the office complex, which was shared with the RNLI and the Fishery Protection as well as other private companies. Fraser led him through a white door, and on into a corridor. At the very end, a varnished wooden sign - another intimation of importance - was attached somewhat incongruously to a to a plain white UVPC door, announcing in gold letters: 'Capt. A Flynn - Harbour Master.' Fraser knocked, and a disembodied voice bade them enter.

Flynn, was a small, neat man, dressed in what could be taken for the uniform of a Royal Naval Officer. His shirt was perfectly creased, as were his trousers, shoes *bulled* to perfection. His cap was a pristine white over a shiny black peak, which reflected a cap badge embroidered with a golden anchor. He was dark-haired, with a neatly clipped *goatee* beard. Putting the man in his fifties, Daley pondered idly whether or not both hair and beard were dyed.

The office, which smelled strongly of pipe tobacco, looked as if it had been furnished sometime before the war. A large wooden bureau sat solidly at the end of the room, adorned by a muddle of papers, pens, books, and a laptop computer, looking out of time. At right angles to the bureau, facing the window, sat an even older looking desk which bore further detritus. Next to it, sitting in a basket chair at the desk, an old man with a parchment coloured face, directed his startlingly blue-eyed gaze at the new-comers. His steady, unblinking appraisal gave the impression of great sagacity; he didn't attempt a welcome, and was motionless in his seat.

"Hello, Inspector," the man in the uniform held out a meaty, calloused hand. "Alan Flynn - pleased to meet you." He gestured the policemen to two rickety-looking chairs. "Sorry about the mess. I do try to tidy up from time to time, but bugger me, when I dae, I can never find a bloody thing. So much paper-work in this job, you wouldna believe."

"I'm sad to say I would believe," Daley shook Flynn's hand. "I think the police force could break all records as to the use of unnecessary paper." He sat down heavily, suddenly feeling tired.

"Just so, Inspector, preaching to the converted. Now how can I be of assistance to you?"

Daley pondered the contrast between the neat man, and the chaos he appeared to work in; however, more pressing matters ensued.

"I have an idea how long our victim spent in the water and I know you've already talked with DC Fraser here," Flynn was nodding, but looking as though he had something important to say. Daley though, carried on, "however, I'd be most grateful if you could go over things with me." He lifted his hand palm up, indicating to Flynn that he acknowledged that he was desperate to talk.

"You see, that's just it, Inspector," he was standing over the laptop at the untidy desk, "in my opinion…"

"I'm sorry, Mr Flynn," Daley realised just how tired he was, "as you know we are conducting what is a murder inquiry. I would be obliged if you addressed your thoughts to us, alone." The old man didn't take the hint.

"Of course, Inspector, of course - how stupid of me. Hamish I told you the Inspector would want to talk to me by myself. Why don't you get up to the fish shed and make sure that none of these rogues are up tae no good? Watch out for that *Lady Kate* mob - they're ay' at it."

The old man sat still, and just as Flynn was about to speak again, he cleared his throat noisily and looking directly at Daley, began talking in a low, rasping voice that was barely more than a slow whisper.

"Noo, Officer, surely a man of your conseederable experience

51

can answer me wan question?" He had the long vowels of the area, pronouncing 'considerable' as though it contained two *U's*, and more than two *E's*.

Daley, now getting used to the local drawl smiled.

"Sure, what would you like to know? Within reason of course." Hamish continued with his unblinking stare, "Ye wid never be able tae guess whoot age I am?" His face suddenly cracked with a broad grin, he threw his head back and laughed manically.

Daley paused. He knew age to be a very touchy subject with the very old; it was as though they were constantly expecting confirmation of how kind the years had been. He was about to say eighty, though he suspected the man to be at least ninety, when Hamish stopped laughing abruptly.

"Seeventy-three, Inspector. Aye, seeventy-three; noo ye wirna' expecting that?" The broad beam returned to his face, narrowing his eyes, giving him an almost oriental expression.

Daley honestly agreed, as Fraser looked on, bemused by the whole exchange. They sat in silence for a few seconds, until Flynn walked over to his elderly companion and took him by the arm.

"Noo, come on, Hamish, these men have a lot on - let's be having you - don't roll over, roll out and a' that."

Hamish got up, slowly but straight-backed. He picked his pipe from the table and began to walk towards the door. When he reached Daley's chair he stopped; any trace of a smile was gone and he looked as though he had bad news to impart.

"Fair's fair, Inspector, you gied me a courtesy, noo it's my turn tae dae lakewise." The blue of his eyes were at their most piercing at this close proximity. Daley smiled; though he wanted to get on with proceedings, he indulged the old man.

"Yir wiman, the wan that's flying doon at the weekend," he had everyone's attention now, not least Daley's. "Weel, you'll need tae make up your mind up wance an' fir a' aboot things. Aye, an' forby, the man's she's wae, he's no good - no good at a'. Mabes yer passed caring though, eh? But heed this: ne'er let herm come tae the things that ur precious tae you."

With that, he smiled briefly, put his pipe to his mouth, and left the room.

Flynn looked embarrassed, "Jeest ignore him Inspector, he's forever making prophecies of doom."

"It depends how accurate they are, Mr Flynn." Daley was strangely relieved that Hamish had gone, he had found something about the man unsettling.

"That's the thing, Inspector, he's got a name for it - you know, predicting the future an' a that - his family's a' the same. His grandfether predicted the Second World War."

Fraser spoke up in defence of his new boss. "Och, lots of people predicted that, you just had to have a look at what was happening in Germany at the time; Churchill predicted it too."

"Aye, no' in nineteen-twenty-two he didna', time date an' everything. They still talk aboot it in the toon tae this day. You must remember constable, superstition's still strong in wee places like this, especially amongst the fishin' community. Now gents, take a look at this." He walked back over to the laptop.

Daley coughed, anxious to move on. "Yes, Mr Flynn, back down to business."

The laptop screen was a live satellite image of the Kintyre peninsula, superimposed on which were a complex swirl of what Daley recognised as isobar lines, and numbers which he did not understand. The map refreshed itself about every thirty seconds. Flynn started typing on the keypad of the computer, with what Daley thought was impressive speed.

"You see, Inspector, I'm now going back over the last forty-eight hours or so. These numbers are indications of tide and direction of the wind - it's quite complex, takes a wee bit of getting used to, but I wish I had something like this when I was at the fishing myself." He tapped a few keys and suddenly the image enlarged, showing the area around where the body had been found.

"I recognise this, Mr Flynn, the body was found about here," Daley pointed his finger at the swirling image, without touching the screen. He was glad he had spent time the previous evening pouring over Google maps of the crime scene and the area in general. "What does this indicate to you?"

Flynn rubbed his well-trimmed beard. "If you're asking me for an opinion, Inspector, I'll give it freely - it's an opinion mind - but based on what I know of these waters, and the help I get fae this kit; you canna ever be certain with what happens at sea..." his voice tailed off.

Daley was anxious to push on, "I understand that this is only an indication, Mr Flynn. No-one is going to question your judgement if it's proved wrong. I really need some kind of idea of how, when, and from which direction the body came from to end up where it did, at the time it did." Daley nodded at the harbour master, who straightened up from leaning over the screen, crossed his arms and pursed his lips. Whatever he was about to say, Daley realised that he didn't really want to say it.

"Well, in my opinion, if the time-scale you have given me for this poor lassie entering the water is correct, there is no way possible she could have been washed into that bay by the force of wind or tide: in fact, the opposite. If she drowned in the sound here," he pointed again at the screen, "she wid likely be somewhere out in the Atlantic by now, or maybe washed up on the North Antrim coast, aye or even Donegal. But Machrie Bay - na, no chance."

"The Post Mortem indicated that the body had been gnawed by shellfish, probably prawns - surely they are only present in deeper water."

"Aye, you're right there, Inspector. There's no such things as prawns in Machrie Bay - into the sound aye: crab, lobster, prawns, and langoustines - but definitely not in the bay. Anyway, we're not talking about a big stretch of water, are we, Mr Daley? If there had been a body floating aboot in it, someone wid have spotted it before they did. Wid ye not think?"

Daley looked at the computer image. The bay was indeed small, it seemed unlikely that a cadaver would have remained undetected for what was a reasonably long period, and then there were the bite marks on the body.

"So, taking this into account, our victim would have had to

have been put where she was found?" Daley's face was a study of concentration.

"So you're saying, sir, that she was dumped in, or spent time out to sea, then was moved into Machrie Bay?" Fraser had not thought of this possibility.

"Either that, or could she have been dragged into the bay inadvertently by some vessel, Mr Flynn?"

"Aye, it's possible; but mind you, the bay itself is quite shallow. The only craft you get in there are small boats - lobster boats, pleasure craft - and the like. I canna see a vessel like that hauling a body intae the bay without noticing." He shrugged his shoulders to reinforce the fact that he felt this option unlikely.

"Are there many lobster boats there?"

"Ach, nooadays only six or so. Used tae be a lot mair, aye an' scallop boats too - that trade's dead now after the ban - the scallops got infected by sewage. Well they said they were. If you ask me there were nathin' wrong wi' them - that was my trade Inspector - scallop fisherman."

Fraser was frowning, "I know the fishermen out there, sir, and they don't miss much,"

Daley ran his hand through his close-cropped dark hair. It looked very much as though the body had been dumped in the bay, rather than being washed up there; then there was the restraint mark around the ankle of the victim.

"I take it you have a record of which vessels moor here, Mr Flynn?"

"Of course, Inspector," Flynn appeared suddenly on the defensive, "I make sure that my books are meticulous." Flynn looked at Daley and Fraser in turn; the latter had his eyebrow raised at this sudden rush of self-justification.

"Sorry, chaps," he laughed, eyes downcast, "a bit of a touchy subject actually. That's what did for my predecessor y'see. The place was a shambles when I arrived here."

Daley looked around, unintentionally making his thoughts public.

"I know its untidy, Mr Daley, but I know where everything is."

He reached under a pile of papers on the bureau and pulled out a heavy, leather bound ledger, that looked as antiquated as the furniture. "Everything is here. I've no' had time tae put it on the machine yet, but all the information is up to date. I even log the fishing boats in and out these days. No need to really since they're moored here permanently, but well, there's so few of them now."

"So it's only visiting boats you would normally register?" Daley hoped he was wrong.

"Na, na Inspector, that used tae be the case; but, you know, we're no' all that busy just noo, so I like to keep myself goin', in case somebody takes it intae their mind that I'm no' required, if ye get my drift," he laughed nervously.

"What about the yachts over there?" Daley pointed out of the window at some pleasure vessels moored at a wooden pontoon. There were three small sail-boats and a couple of expensive-looking cabin cruisers.

"No, Inspector, they're no' my responsibility; well unless somebody breaks the harbour rules, or in some kind of emergency. It's owned and run by a private company - Newell Enterprises - James Newell's the main man."

"Where can I find him?" Daley took out his notebook, prompting Fraser to do the same.

"Aye, as well as running the pontoon, he has wan o' these big RIBs."

"RIBs? What's that?" Daley's lack of nautical knowledge was beginning to show.

"Rigid Inflatable Boat, sir," Fraser's time in Kinloch had not been wasted, "Big powerful boats - they go like f -" He managed to stop himself.

"He takes passengers on trips, Mr Daley," Flynn filled the gap. "He's away a trip tae Ballycastle with a party o' tourists. He always lets me know his plans - for safety you understand. He's a nice big bloke. Used tae be a Captain in the Royal Navy; a wee bit haughty sometimes, but sure, we all have our faults."

Daley was looking back out of the window. "When is he due back? I'd like to have a word with him."

"No' until tomorrow, they're staying overnight," not to be out-done, Flynn brought his own notebook out of a breast pocket in his shirt. "Let me see. Aye, due back about two tomorrow, I've got his mobile number here if that's of any help?"

"Yes please. Take a note will you, constable."

Fraser jotted the number down in his notebook, and stood pen poised, just in case he had to write anything else pertinent.

"Well, thanks, Mr Flynn, you've given us a lot to think about." Daley again held out his hand. "I trust you will keep our discussions to yourself for the time being - not add to the rumours - eh?" He smiled at Flynn, who was now shaking his hand enthusiastically.

"Just so, just so, Inspector. And mind, if you need anything else, jeest give me a shout. I'm here all day, and half the night sometimes as well," he said, somewhat ruefully.

The harbour master led them out of the office and down the corridor to the exterior door. As he again shook Daley's hand, he looked around to see who could be watching.

Noting Flynn's apparent unease, Daley nodded towards the Jaguar. "Who belongs to this wonderful beast?"

Flynn looked embarrassed. "Well, me actually, just a little in-dulgence. I'm sure you treat yourself now and again, Inspector?"

"A treat for me is a good malt, though I'm afraid I couldn't stretch to anything like this. It must be, what," he looked along the lines of the car, "best part of sixty k?"

Flynn laughed awkwardly. "Oh no, Inspector, that is to say I got a good deal on it. I sold my scallop boat when I got this job; a treat, as I said."

The thought crossed Daley's mind that this was indeed a guilty pleasure, judging by Flynn's discomfort. His thoughts were dragged away from the car when his phone rang, and he made his excuses, and walked to the side of the pier to take the call.

"Hi, darling," it was Liz. "You're a hard man to get a hold of."

"Sorry, I've been a bit..." as usual she cut him short.

"Listen, I've got some hot news," she was clearly in a bar or restaurant, he could hear the chink of glasses and the animated conversation of people consuming alcohol. He had learned to beware of his wife's idea of 'hot news', so he listened in with no little trepidation.

"Mark has had a brainwave," *Oh no.* "His company has just bought a helicopter, and he has the use of it if they're not ferrying clients about, or anyone else senior is using it. Apparently there's a gorgeous golf course down there. So to cut a long story short - I'm coming to visit you in Mark's chopper, while he plays boring old golf."

Mark's Chopper had elicited a raucous response in the background, much hee-hawing and guffawing.

"Well, it'll be nice to see you; I've got a lot on, so…"

"Never mind that, darling, I'm sure we'll find some time…" at this an exaggerated *'oo'* from those listening in. "Anyhow, got to dash. We'll be down at about lunch-time tomorrow. Bye, my love." With that the sound of nothing from his mobile, which he was well used to.

He felt as though he was being watched, and turned to look down the pier. Standing apart from a group of fishermen, Hamish was staring straight at him. The old man nodded his head and gave Daley a stage wink.

6

Daley was silent as they walked back up the Main Street. That this investigation was puzzling, there was no doubt. He was also well outside his comfort zone in terms of the location of the case, which surprised him; he had not considered just how different an investigation could be this far away from Glasgow.

Then inevitably, his mind turned to his wayward wife. Why was she coming all the way from Granton to Kinloch? He felt sure that all this had been Mark's suggestion. What better than spending a weekend winding up the man he saw as a worthless civil servant, a poorly paid lackey - hardly worth consideration.

He was grim faced as he caught sight of his paunch reflected in a shop window and involuntarily pulled his stomach in.

"Any ideas, sir?" Fraser was looking as bemused as Daley felt.

"No. Well, yes and no really," he had the DC's attention now. "My theory is that our victim was murdered elsewhere, then, for whatever reason, her body was taken to the bay and dumped. Either that, or we are dealing with a spectacular suicide." He smiled wanly at Fraser to indicate that he was indeed joking.

Inspector MacLeod was getting into a car as they walked to the rear door of the office through the car park. On seeing Daley and Fraser, he ducked back out of the car and stood at the open door, his hand resting on the frame.

"Your man has been on from the Glasgow Mortuary, you have to phone him as soon as possible." With that, he reseated himself in the car, started the engine and pulled off, taking care not to look at the two CID Officers as he passed.

"I take it that's your boss being civil? Well, he can stick it up his arse." Daley waited as Fraser punched the security code into the door entry system. He was tired and hungry. He sincerely hoped that Crichton had not uncovered yet more mystifying post mortem data.

He sat in his glass box, picked up his phone and pressed 2# to enter his voicemail - at least this method was standard all over the force. He heard Crichton's familiar tones, hung up, then dialed the pathologist's direct number. It was six-thirty, but Daley knew that when Crichton was working on a case, he might as well throw his watch away; he was dedicated above and beyond the call of duty.

He was just about to put the phone down, when a breathless Crichton answered.

"Dear God, I swear they're making that corridor longer. Give me a couple of seconds, Jim." Daley heard the clunk of the phone being put down on Crichton's desk, then the rustling of papers mixed with the sighs and breathless oaths of the pathologist.

"Now, Jim, here we are," there was a short pause for effect. "Your victim from lovely Kinloch, she had sex with two different men prior to her death."

"Aye, you said as much last night Andrew. I thought you had some piece of hot news; probably just as well you haven't, this investigation's going to be a bastard as it is. Do you have a DNA profile of the two semen samples?"

"Three semen samples Jim."

"You said two Andy; my memory's not that bad."

"I said she had sex with two men just prior to death; she also contrived to have sex with another man - post mortem."

There was a brief silence as Daley mentally processed this new information, even then his response was halting.

"Necrophilia - are you sure, Andrew?"

"Afraid so, Jim. We have well defined tests for that sort of thing now. Fascinating, yet macabre at the same time. None of the samples match in terms of DNA, to answer your question."

"So we're talking about three men right?"

"Yes, three men. The first two had their wicked way with our victim within a relatively short space of time - maybe even at the same time. Our third man, so to speak, some eight or nine hours later - most unusual."

Again, both men were silent.

After a few moments of mutual consideration, Crichton spoke again.

"I'll send the DNA profiles to the database of course. You should get a match, if there is one, early tomorrow."

"This is a strange one, Andy: a victim, no missing persons, no suspects - now necrophilia. Anything more on that mark on her ankle?"

"Only that is was made by some rough type of plastic - like that interminable binding they wrap parcels in these days - much thicker of course."

Daley finished his call with the pathologist; he knew that the possibility of getting a DNA match from the semen samples found in the post mortem with someone already on the database was remote. Right now though, it was his only hard lead. The grinding process of checks would continue through the night. A young WPC was settling down to check the footage from all of the CCTV cameras operational in the town in the forty-eight hour period prior to the victim's estimated time of death. He had contacted all of the neighbouring police forces, including the Police Service of Northern Ireland, the coastline of County Antrim being less than twenty miles from where the body had been found. So far, no response.

He took his mobile from the inside pocket of his jacket. Within seconds the familiar sound of DS Scott coughing volubly could be heard on the other end of the phone.

"What a way to greet your superior; you sound as though you're on your way out, Brian."

"Aye, happy Christmas tae you too. Should you no' be stripping the willow, or whitever they get uptae in Choochterland?"

Daley smiled. He was tired, hungry and baffled, but he was

realising what a tight team he and Scott had become. He had forgotten all of the things that his DS would have attended to as a matter of course, until today when he had had to make sure all the bases were covered himself.

"I thought you'd be pleased, a trip to the country at this time of year. Just the thing."

"No' when you've tae listen tae all the pish I've had tae pit up wi' today. First His Majesty gein' me the pep talk aboot representin' the division. Noo my dear lady bendin' my nut wi' how much she'll miss me, an, how will she manage tae get the shoppin?' etc., etc."

Scott told him to hang on; muffled oaths were more than audible as Scott imparted some more wisdom to his long-suffering wife.

"Sorry aboot that - she's burst intae tears noo - y'id think I wiz headin' off tae Afghanistan. Will you shut up wiman, I'm talking tac Jim," Daley heard Mrs Scott shouting hello as though there was nothing amiss.

"Have you managed to read the PM report, Brian?"

"Aye, in between a' the shit. Some right goings-on doon there. Lucky I'm comin' doon tae watch yer back."

"Wait until you see Inspector MacLeod - he's a cracker."

"Oh, I've got something for you from on high. I'll give you it tomorrow when I get there. Who dae ye want me tae bring? They're all on standby, as ye can imagine."

Daley thought for a moment. Thinking was getting difficult, so he left the choice of personnel to his sergeant.

"How long dae you think it'll take me tae get there in a minibus, Jim?"

"Well, wait a minute," Daley swivelled around in his chair to consult a large map on the wall behind him. "Seems as though you're going a long way for a short cut, you've got to go north before you head back south, towards us. One of the lads here said it takes about three hours by car; so I would guess it'll take you more like four."

"Aye, very good. Whit's this hotel like?"

Daley looked at his watch, time seemed to fly here, all he had eaten were a few sandwiches, and a mug of truly dreadful mug-a-soup from the vending machine in the office.

"I'll tell you when I get there. What time are you leaving tomorrow?"

Scott coughed loudly again, regained his composure, then answered, "No' before six, so I'll see you aboot ten. Fuck me, it's like the voyage o' the damned."

After more deeply held opinions about rural Scotland from the DS, and a brief description of the large, A4 envelope that Scott had been given by Superintendent Donald, to pass on to Daley, they ended the call.

Daley went for a pee. He looked at himself in the mirror as he dried his hands under yet another inefficient dryer. He was getting grey at the temples, and the flesh under his chin was getting loose: he was turning into his father. How was that happening?

He unbuttoned his trousers, able to exhale properly for the first time in hours. After smoothing creases from the tail of his shirt, he pulled the trousers back up and then buttoned them again with a sigh. He wasn't getting any thinner, despite the paucity of his lunch. Looking at himself side-on in the large mirror, he let his stomach relax again. A large paunch showed over the waist of his trousers, he yawned absently, as the hunger and the tiredness of the day began to tell.

Who was this woman? What had happened to her - and why?

Daley and Fraser walked back down the Main Street, this time heading for the hotel.

The entrance was broad; they walked along a short vestibule, then through a heavy, glass-panelled door into a reception area. On their right, a wide centre-carpeted staircase swung up to floors above; the banister painted in what looked like faded gold leaf, giving it the appearance of an installation more suited to an old cinema. Dark wooden panelling covered the walls to well above head height, then gave way to red and gold striped, textured wallpaper, of a type popular over thirty years ago in such premises.

To their left a foyer area was populated with chairs and tables, the former upholstered in red velvet, worn thin by numerous posteriors. The latter, covered in an indented brass, was again, redolent of days gone by.

A large glass-fronted box was the obvious reception desk. Sliding windows lay open over a varnished shelf, on which the open register sat beside a large brass bell. Fraser, obviously no stranger to these surroundings, picked up the bell and sounded it enthusiastically, leaning his head into the reception office.

"Aye, aye - gie'us a meenute," a woman's voice sounded through a door at the other side of the reception box. "I'll be with yooz directly." The rear door opened, allowing the distinctive murmur that only a bar-full of contented drinkers could produce, quiet chat punctuated by short bursts of raucous laughter. Whatever was happening in Kinloch, its citizens seemed to be a cheery bunch.

Daley took in his surroundings. This hotel was strangely familiar; he had felt this first when they had walked past the unusual frontage earlier in the day. The sweet, inviting smell of alcohol, mingled with the aroma of freshly cooked food and a strong chemical odour which reminded Daley of his primary school.

Through the door, a small, dark haired woman in her middle years appeared, closing it behind her.

"Good evening, officers. How'ye daein', Erchie? You'll be wantin' tae check in, Inspector." Yet again, there was clearly no need for introductions. "The kitchen will be closing in a wee while, so dae ye want tae order noo? - or I'll get a hell o' a time fae big Wullie, and you'll get nathin' tae eat." She handed Daley a large brown menu, bound in a leatherette cover, slightly stained by previous diners. "There nae beef left, and I widna touch the lasagna since he made it the day before yesterday. The fush is ay'ways quite good. Noo, could you fill this in?" She turned the open ledger around to face the Detectives.

Daley busied himself with the usual details, filling in his

address as c/o Paisley Police Office, and using the number of the Kinloch office as his contact. He slid the ledger back across the desk, along with the menu.

"I'll take your recommendation on the fish. I hope my luggage arrived earlier - my name's Jim by the way."

The receptionist reorganised the register, then reached behind her chair to a wooden board peppered with keys on hooks, attached to large wooden key-rings, all bearing the legend: 'Property of The County Hotel.'

"Please tae meet you I'm sure, my name's Annie. Aye, all your kit's up in room six, third door on yer left on the first flair."

Daley and Fraser made their way from reception further down the corridor to where the noise of drunken banter was emanating. He had persuaded the DC to have a meal with him; he hated eating alone, and in any case, the younger man had had no more chance than his superior of getting a decent meal all day. Fraser had opted for a chicken curry; a choice that saw Annie raise her eyebrows, though she fell short of making any comment. That they had decided to eat in the bar made her brows arch even further.

Fraser made his way through the frosted glass door that read *Public Bar,* in an old-fashioned, swirling script. The warm smell of alcohol enveloped the officers like a wave, though the conversation stopped instantly.

There were about twenty customers in all, some standing at a varnished wooden bar, while the rest were spread amongst a number of randomly placed chairs and tables. They appeared a cross-section of ages, however regardless of vintage, all of the women were seated. Clearly, standing at the bar was a purely male preserve.

"Aye an' whoots wrong wi' a' yooz?" the formidable Annie was back behind the bar. "It reminds me o' that werewolf fulm; jeest get back tae yer conversations, an' lea' the officers get their tea."

A young man at the bar looked confused, "Whoot werewolf fulm dae ye mean Annie –'Dawn o' the Deed'?"

"Na, you eediot - American Werewolf in London. You know; the

65

bit where they go intae the bar, an' everyone jeest shuts up. Noo get on wae yer pint, Danny Finlay."

An elderly woman sitting at a table expressed her opinion that Lon Chaney had been her favourite werewolf to no-one in particular, and then drained her glass, resuming her blank gaze. Two older men eyed Daley up and down. One of them was wearing yellow oilskin trousers over green Wellington boots, and smelled strongly of fish.

"Yer wasting yer time, Inspector, that poor lassie could be fae anywhere - there no reason as tae how the sea gi'es up her dead, no reason at a'." The man was smirking the grin of a smart-arse.

Daley reached into his pocket, fetching out his notebook. "And your name is, sir? I'll take a quick note and get you up to the office for an interview tomorrow." The smirk left his interlocutor's face.

"Noo, wait a meenut - I mean, I wiz jeest gee'in an opinion - I'm no'saying…" He didn't get a chance to finish his sentence, Daley had winked at his companions and they greeted the winding up of their mate with great hilarity.

"Aye, very good, you should see your face, Jackie. Lake a skelpit kipper. Fuckin' eediot."

"Good for you, Inspector," this was Annie. "Noo, whoot can I get yiz?"

"I'll get these," Fraser reached into his jacket pocket. "What do you want, sir?"

Daley looked along the gantry; the County Hotel had no mean stock of single malts. He asked for a large Springbank, much to the dismay of his colleague, who took another ten pound note from his wallet.

"There a seat at the back there," Annie served the drinks with a smile. "That'll be eighteen pound, sixty pence Erchie - since it's you we'll call it eighteen." He handed the money over grim-faced, and the policemen made their way through the chairs and tables to their seats at the rear of the bar-room.

Daley had forgotten how expensive Springbank was and offered Fraser some money in compensation, which he refused.

"Well, if you're sure, Archie. I suppose it goes some way to squaring me up after all the drinks I had to buy your Uncle Davie over the years." The pair laughed, each with their own memories of Fraser's uncle.

The meal arrived without undue haste. Fraser's curry was an unusual shade of green, but it didn't seem to bother him as he took his fork to it with great enthusiasm.

Daley's fish on the other hand, looked delicious: a large haddock, covered in golden, crispy batter, accompanied by marble-sized marrow fat peas, thick, home-made chips - which also looked perfectly cooked - and a small ramekin of tartar sauce. A huge chunk of badly cut lemon rather spoiled the look of the dish; however, the Inspector was as hungry as his subordinate, so he tucked in with equal relish.

"Well, they certainly know how to cook fish in this neck of the woods," Daley pushed his empty plate across the table. "What was yours like, Archie?"

The younger man had managed to spill some curry down his tie, which he was desperately trying to remove with a red, paper napkin.

"Bloody thing," Fraser cursed as he examined the stained tie. "I've only got another one, and it doesna' match my other suits. Bugger it."

Daley suppressed a smile; sartorial elegance was very important to some CID Officers. He had known colleagues buy some ridiculously priced suits and shoes, only to have had them torn, burnt, stained with blood, soaked in the rain, or a multiplicity of other hazards that faced police officers on a daily basis. Personally, he had always chosen the cheapest suits on offer; having his own private celebration when one of the big super-markets began selling the garments for twenty quid.

"I've got a couple of spare ties in my bag. I'm sure I can spare one."

Fraser looked relieved. "Thanks, sir. You don't want to have to buy any clothes here. You'd need to take out a mortgage first, the shops are extortionate."

"What have you done with your clothing allowance?" Daley was referring to an annual allowance CID personnel were given to buy their clothes, which was habitually used to buy golf clubs, a weekend away, a new computer, or a range of other expenditure that had nothing to do with clothes.

"Too little to go round, sir," Fraser was grinning. "Anyway, I've put on a stone since I've been off the beat; keep having to buy a whole new set of clothes."

"Tell me about it," said Daley wryly. "A few less pints, and a few more hours in the gym, my boy. Take a leaf out of my book," he said with a smile. If there was one thing that he could empathise with, it was sudden weight gain; even now his belly was protruding over his waist band in a painful, and constricted manner - and these were his new trousers.

He resolved to follow his own advice and signalled to Annie behind the bar that they were ready for another couple of drinks - the same again.

Annie arrived with the drinks on a tray, depositing them on a table, then removing the dishes onto the tray in their stead.

"Yooz were hungry right enough," she pronounced *hungry* with a soft *g*. "I'd keep an eye on the young fellow here, he'll lakely be in intensive care by the'morrow. Big Wullie's great at plain food, but he canna cook fancy stuff tae save himself." She smiled at the policemen. "Whoot time wull ye be wantin' yer breakfast the'morrow? I'm daein the cooking, so if ye choose continental or jeest a cereal, I'll be o'er the moon."

Daley ordered a full Scottish breakfast for six-forty five. Annie took a note, raised her eyebrows, and returned to the bar, shouting at one of the younger male customers, who had just spilled his pint and was swearing copiously.

The police officers finished their drinks. Daley was aware that almost all of the other customers were either trying to hear what they were saying, or throwing cursory glances in their direction on a regular basis.

"Time to hit the sack, Archie," Daley was rubbing the bridge of his nose with his forefinger and thumb. "Keep your mobile on

- you never know how an investigation like this will turn out. Or when we'll have to do likewise, come to that."

They made their way through the tables, shouted goodnight to Annie, and then walked out into the Hotel foyer. A ragged chorus of 'Cheerio,cheerio,cheerio', issued from some of the more rowdy element they had just left behind, closely followed by Annie's now familiar voice leaving them in absolutely no doubt she wanted them to shut up.

Daley said goodnight to Fraser, fished his room key with the impossibly large, wooden fob from the inside of his jacket, and made his way up the faded grandeur of the hotel staircase to the first floor.

Gaining the landing, he faced a glass-paned fire door, of the type common in schools when he had been a boy. A bright green *Exit* sign shone vividly above it; the transom shuddered to a creaking close as he made his way to room six.

He turned the key in the Yale lock, and pushed his room door open. Running his hand up and down the inside wall beside the door, he located a light-switch, which prompted a strip light in the ceiling into blinking illumination.

The heavy door swung shut at his back. Facing him was a double bed, which would have been a tight squeeze for two adults, however was perfectly adequate for one. The bed was covered in an old-fashioned candlewick bedspread. The diamond patterned top-sheet had faded from what he suspected had once been a light red colour, to a candy pink. He had one exactly the same in his room when he had been a boy.

At the side of the bed, a cheap cabinet served as the base for an ancient angle-poise lamp, which looked as though it would snap in two if any attempt was made to change its position. His luggage was on the floor beside the bed, which he sat on as he unbuckled and unzipped his suit-bag. In front of him now, and to the side of the door, sat a small pine wardrobe. On investigation, Daley discovered that it contained five metal coat-hangers, and smelled strongly of mothballs. He hung three suits, a sports jacket, a pair of trousers, and six shirts up, and then closed the doors.

From another bag, he removed a pair of chinos, a pair of denims, various socks, pants and t-shirts, and arranged them in one of the four drawers of the chest, that sat to the right side of his bed, directly across from a sash window. Antiquated, the window was adorned with faded, red velvet curtains and full-length net curtains the colour of old parchment. An assortment of dead flies and moths populated the dusty window sill. The single-glazed window resisted all of his strained attempts to get it open. He gave up and stared at the street below, illuminated orange in the acetylene street lights.

To his surprise, one of the old women that he and Fraser had met on their way down the street was standing at the bus stop across the road. She looked up at his window and gave a hearty wave, smiling broadly. Daley, automatically waved back, and on having done so, felt faintly ridiculous. It didn't seem to take long to make friends in Kinloch.

Closing the curtains, he switched on the bedside light. Which, to his surprise, worked perfectly, allowing him to extinguish the ceiling strip-light, silencing the loud humming noise that it had started to make.

His en-suite bathroom was a much grander affair: all Victorian tiling, and large brass bath taps. Liz would probably have paid thousands to some trendy design company to achieve the same effect. This though, was the real McCoy. He placed his toiletries on a shelf near the large sink and on another shelf at the side of the bath.

Addicted to radio since he was a child, the penultimate item that he removed from his luggage was his portable radio-alarm clock. Again to his surprise, he found a spare socket, plugged it in, set the time, and turned on Radio Four.

Finally, he took his copy of Patrick O'Brian's '*The Wine Dark Sea*', from his case, lay back on the bed, and placed it next to him. It was only then he noticed where the television was located, set well back, on top of the wardrobe. Using the deductive powers for which he was famous, he opened the flimsy drawer of the bedside cabinet and there - sure enough - was a battered TV remote, the batteries held in by black electrical tape, which was shrunken and peeling with age.

Daley had a bath. There seemed to be plenty of hot water, and unlike the modern variety, this old bath was deep and wide. He luxuriated in the relaxing warmth for a few minutes. He got out, then towelled himself down, donning a pair of shorts, that were his habitual sleeping garment.

He lay in the bed. It was a warm night, and the room was stuffy as the window was stuck. He had toyed with the idea of calling reception, but decided against this course of action. Firstly, he thought it unlikely anyone would be about the hotel at that time of night who would actually be prepared, or able to fix it. Secondly, such was the racket of cars going up and down the Main Street, plus the shouts and guffaws of local revellers; he reasoned that the window best remain shut.

He tried to concentrate on the discussion programme which was currently being broadcast, but decided that was impossible. He picked up the novel, and admired the cover. Unfortunately, by the time he had found the right page, his eyes refused to obey his mental commands, and danced over the words. His eyelids began to droop. Leaning over, he flicked the lamp off, and turned onto his side. Within moments, he was asleep.

7

He was in a bar - but not like one he had ever been in before. He sat on a tall bar stool, hunched over a glass of whisky. Behind the bar tender, on a raised stage, naked women cavorted, suggestively, using long metal poles as a prop of phallic seduction. Beside him, a large, balding man was gesticulating at him with a clenched fist, save for his forefinger and pinky, which were pointing aggressively in his direction, gold rings visible on the remaining fingers, folded into the palm. All was loud music, shouting and whooping males...

Reality.

He realised that the ringtone of his phone had prompted the dream, and for a few seconds he had been in the *'Bada Bing'*.

"...*Got a Blue Moon in Your Eye...*" Daley picked up the mobile, his eyes were blurred with sleep, and being in strange surroundings, he was slightly disorientated. He answered the phone automatically.

"Daley." There was a short pause on the other end, then a woman's voice.

"Sir, sorry to call you at this time. It's WDC Dunn, there's been a development - I think you better come up to the station."

"OK, what kind of development?" Understanding was flooding into his brain replacing the confusing numbness of sleep, but he was still playing for time.

"We've had a report of a missing woman who closely matches the description of our victim, sir. Her husband is here."

Daley rubbed his eyes with the thumb and forefinger of his

right hand.

"Have you told him anything; shown him any pictures of the deceased? Does he know we have a body?"

"He knows that a woman has been found dead, sir. He's a fisherman, he lives in Kinloch, but he works out of Dublin on a deep sea trawler - away for three weeks at a time. It's quite complicated. But no, to answer your first question, we haven't said anything to him; thought we better wait until you were informed. How should we proceed, sir?"

Daley was fully awake now. He looked at his radio-alarm clock; it was three thirty-five; whatever sleep he'd had would have to suffice.

"OK, DC Dunn, I'm on my way - give me ten minutes or so - leave the guy in an interview room until I get there; get him a cup of coffee or something, but don't tell him anything. I'll talk to him myself - you've done well." He heard a slight sigh on the other end of the line.

"I hope that wasn't a pun, sir." The line went dead.

The Main Street was deathly quiet. Daley left the hotel, taking the short walk to the station. There was an unexpected chill in the air, and he wished he had brought his overcoat. The sky was a carpet of stars, visible through the orange glow of the street lighting. Light pollution was nowhere nearly as bad as in the Greater Glasgow area. Again, unexpectedly, he heard a bird squawk overhead with a distinctive whistle, a repetitive shrill note. He resolved to test Fraser's ornithological knowledge. The all-pervading smell of the sea provided the olfactory backdrop.

He went around the back of the station, keying the security code into the pad on the door that led from the car park. The office was bathed in a subdued blue light. He passed the control room, hearing the intermittent crackle of sub-divisional radio traffic echoing through the corridors, reminding him of his own time on nightshift as a uniform cop.

WDC Dunn met him outside the CID offices. She looked tired and slightly harassed.

"Sir, so glad you're here. It's been a bit of a strain trying not to tell this poor guy that his wife's probably dead."

"You sound very sure - what's he been saying?" They entered an interview room and closed the door. Daley leaned on the table, while the young WDC stood, formally, as though she was about to deliver a speech.

"The guy is Michael Watson. He's a fisherman - deep sea - he used to fish out of Kinloch, but he's based in Dublin now. He works off one of the big trawlers that fish mainly far out into the Atlantic; three weeks on, two weeks off. He still lives here."

The detective spread her hands over her dark-blue skirt, smoothing out non-existent creases. "His wife and son live here too, well...."

"OK, so what do we know about her?" Daley took out his notebook; he was about to interview this man, and he wanted to have his facts straight before he did.

"She's about the right height, build and age for our victim, sir. He has a photo of her; but what with the bloating on the corpse, and the fact she has dyed blonde hair in the picture - well it's difficult to tell."

Daley scratched under his chin while he thought, a habit that infuriated Liz.

"It's a strange time to report her missing - the reason?"

"Yes, his mother has been looking after the wee boy for the last three days. She and her husband have been up the city shopping. They came back early yesterday, couldn't find Mrs Watson, heard about the body being found, and put two and two together. They wanted to wait until Watson arrived before they contacted the police. He arrived on a RIB from Dublin about two hours ago. His fishing boat had just returned to port. His bosses hired the RIB to get him here quickly."

"What's his wife's first name?"

"Isobel, sir, Isobel Watson."

Daley stood back up just as a knock at the door announced the arrival of DC Fraser, who leaned his head round the corner. Daley noticed that his hair was sticking up, and he wasn't wearing a tie, the offending article having been stained by curry earlier.

"Right, DC Dunn, give me five minutes to get our casually dressed colleague DC Fraser up to speed, then show Mr Watson in." Fraser's face reddened as the WDC left the interview room.

After imparting the facts, Daley had a surprise for the young DC.

"I want you to conduct this interview, Archie. I want to observe our Mr Watson. We'll get a bit of background, then, depending on how it pans out, we'll have to arrange some kind of ID. That won't be easy considering the body's a hundred and fifty miles away."

"Under these circumstances we normally use CCTV from the mortuary, sir; distances taken into account and all that. We only take people up to Glasgow if things get complicated."

The door sounded again. WDC Dunn opened it, standing to the side, to reveal a thick-set man, short, with a broad pale face and a shaven head. He was wearing jeans and a t-shirt, his right forearm adorned with a large, blue, thistle tattoo, the legend *Scotland Forever* showing proudly in red.

Daley cleared his throat, prompting Fraser into action.

"Mr Watson, please take a seat." The young DC was on his feet as he slid a chair back inviting the fisherman to sit with a silent gesture of his hand.

As he was getting back into his own chair he introduced himself and the Inspector. Both officers had opened their notebooks. Fraser asked Mr Watson if he would mind if they recorded their discussion. He acceded to the request, though he looked uncomfortable.

"Come on, guys," the accent was pure Kinloch, even at this brief exposure, "I'm worried sick here. I want to know whoot's goin' on. Gie'us a break, eh?" His eyes were pleading, arms held straight out in front of him, both fists clenched.

"I need a few details first, sir," Fraser's colour was on the rise again. "You must understand we have to be really careful in situations like this - so please." He pointed at his notebook, an action which saw Watson deflate slightly, as some of the tension left his shoulders.

"Aye OK - ask away."

Watson answered the usual round of questions: firstly giving his name and address, details of his work, recent movements, and how he had heard about the discovery of the dead woman. He then went on to give his wife's details, including a general description, and summary of her personality, habits, etc.

Tiring of this line of enquiry, he looked directly at Daley. "Now, Inspector, jeest be straight wi' us - can I see the body?"

Ignoring his question, Daley had one of his own.

"What was your wife's maiden name, Mr Watson?"

"Sneddon - Isobel Sneddon."

"Did she have any tattoos? I'm thinking of one in particular…"

"Aye on her leg, she had…" his expression changed to one of grim realisation, "aw - for fuck's sake." He held his head in his hands and started to sob.

"Whoot the fuck am I goin' tae tell the wee man?"

Daley got up and walked to the other side of the desk, placing his hand on Watson's shoulder. The fisherman's body was racked with convulsive sobs. Fraser looked on hopelessly; this was an aspect of police work that he not did like.

"We're going to have to ask you to identify the body formally, Mr Watson." Daley was calm and authoritative. He knew the value of maintaining a front on these occasions, though he realised that his reaction would have been the same, had anything like this happened to Liz. He felt compassion for Watson, but his job was to find her killer; and now he was sure that they had an ID, time was of the essence.

Daley left Fraser with Watson, finding WDC Dunn at her desk in the large CID office.

"I want you to go and comfort Mr Watson. I think his wife is our victim, but I need to get him to make an official identification." The young detective was nodding solemnly. "Once we have that, I want you and a couple of uniforms to go to their house. We'll need to go through everything. I'm leaving you in charge of that. OK?"

"Yes, sir." She looked suddenly preoccupied, as though already working out some kind of plan of attack suited to trawling through someone's personal possessions.

"What about Mr. Watson? Will he have to be present?"

"Not at the moment, I'll get his permission of course. Now tell me, how quickly can we organise one of these CCTV identifications?"

As it turned out, things took longer to organize than Daley anticipated. For a start, they had to wait for the Glasgow Mortuary day shift to turn up, which wasn't until seven-thirty at the earliest. The nightshift was there, but they were not able to use the video equipment.

And all the problems were not at the other end. Permission from the Sub-Divisional Commander was required before their audio-visual equipment at the station could be used, and MacLeod could not be raised. Daley sent a reluctant Fraser to his home to rouse him.

He had texted DS Scott with the latest developments, and had received a terse acknowledgement of same in return - *Aye great - c u soon - on my way* - which he supposed was at least functional.

He had also spoken at greater length to Watson. It appeared that all was not well in their marriage; though Daley had already guessed that. Isobel Watson, had apparently taken to going out regularly, and according to her husband, was associating with the underbelly of Kinloch's society, where lots of alcohol, drugs and sex were the order of the day. Watson had illustrated how difficult it was to maintain their relationship when he was away so much; a sentiment with which Daley could empathise, especially since he found his relationship hard to maintain, even at close quarters.

On the whole, he found Watson an uncomplicated, even pleasant individual; in extremis, he conducted himself with a kind of rough and ready dignity that the Inspector found to his credit.

He had looked carefully for signs of feigned surprise when Watson had discovered that his wife may well be the likely murder victim. He had found none. Nonetheless, he had contacted the Garda in Dublin to make sure that his story of being *deep-sea* for the last three weeks, checked out.

The Inspector, WDC Dunn, and two uniformed officers were in attendance in the station's audio-visual room, with Watson, who was sitting forward in his chair, looking exceptionally stressed. A large plasma screen was currently displaying the force *Semper Vigilo* logo.

The door burst open, and a sleepy-looking MacLeod breezed into the room; not wearing a uniform, but a tracksuit with a hooded top, which he seemed to wear uneasily. This leitmotif of youth clashed with his balding head, fringed with grey hair, and his stiff, abrasive manner.

"I can't for the life of me understand what all this rush is about. You're lucky to catch me, I was about to go for my five miler along Westbay sands." He looked around, as though this revelation should illicit some kind of praise.

"A courtesy only, I can assure you," Daley didn't look in MacLeod's direction. "If DC Fraser had been unable to find you, I'd have authorised this myself."

MacLeod's face took on a look of extreme distaste. He walked over to the unit, and picked up what looked like a large mobile phone. After dialling a number, and waiting for a few moments he started to speak.

"Yes, Kinloch Sub-Division, authorisation Delta Mike 281165." A further pause, and then the screen began to flicker into life; the force logo was replaced by a view of the PR room in Glasgow Mortuary. A table with small microphones sat in front of three chairs, backed by a brown screen which bore the name of the institution, plus the Glasgow City Crest.

Daley saw Watson tense; he was clenching then unclenching his fists which were resting on his knees, as he sat even further forward in his seat. He was pale and tired-looking. Daley made a mental note to make sure that he sent the fisherman to his parents, to try to get some sleep once this, the first of many ordeals, was over.

A woman appeared on screen wearing a white coat with three pens arrayed along the top of the breast pocket. Daley recognised her, but did not know her name. She was a Junior Pathologist, and the Inspector recalled Crichton referring to her in what could best be described in less than politically correct terms: in short, even at this hour, her good looks were evident. He saw Fraser's expression register this too.

"Good Morning." She stood in front of the table, speaking in a low voiced, business-like manner. "Mr Watson, could you acknowledge that you are present, and can see the screen at close quarters without any hindrance?"

The fisherman grunted a reply and then coughed nervously. They were communicating through omni-directional microphones that hung from the ceiling of the Kinloch video suite.

"Could all serving officers present please state their names and designations for the record - starting with the Senior Investigating Officer, then in descending order of rank.

Daley and MacLeod both started to talk at the same time. MacLeod stopped, his face pinched with rancour.

"James Daley, Detective Inspector, Senior Investigating Officer."

MacLeod now took his chance. "I would like to make a point of order please. You, whatever your name is -" he didn't give the pathologist a chance to reply. "I'm Sub-Divisional Commander here, and by rights my name should be submitted first."

Everyone present looked in disbelief at the short man in the hooded top. MacLeod stood in the middle of the room in an impromptu aisle, formed by the small rank of chairs. The pathologist however remained focused and unfazed.

"Sorry, sir, the procedure in this matter is clear. The Senior Investigating Officer takes precedence, even to those of a higher rank.

"Which you are not," Daley spoke, clearly furious with MacLeod. "Please sit down, Inspector MacLeod. I'm sure Mr Watson is finding this hard enough as it is."

MacLeod muttered something under his breath, but retreated

to the back of the room and took a seat. The remaining police officers gave their details, and the pathologist continued.

"My name is Judy Kelly. I'm Assistant Pathologist in Greater Glasgow." She walked behind the desk and took a seat behind the microphones. "Mr Watson, when you are ready, I will begin to show a number of images of the deceased. Please feel free to ask me to stop at any time, if either you can make a positive identification, or you want a break. I must warn you that the deceased has been exposed to salt water for a period of time, which may make her features appear swollen or bloated - so please take this into account. Please say yes when you are ready to proceed." She looked directly into the camera, waiting for Watson's reply.

"Aye, go ahead." Watson's voice was clear, but ready to break with emotion.

Instantly, an overhead view of a body shrouded in white sheets was visible on the widescreen; only the face and hair were exposed. Daley noted that the sheet was placed high up on the neck, obscuring the ligature marks.

"Can I see?" Watson was peering at the screen. The image zoomed onto the face alone.

"Dear God," Watson looked heavenward, his hands clenched, like a child in prayer; he quickly crossed himself, then bowed his head.

"Aye, that's Isobel." His voice was almost a whisper. "She...she looks different, but that's her." Again, he hunched over and sobbed.

The Pathologist thanked Watson, and expressed her condolences. After a pause she asked Daley to acknowledge the positive identification. The gruesome job was over.

The screen flickered back to the force logo.

Daley, sitting beside Watson, had his arm around his shoulder.

"Thank you for that, Mr Watson, I know how hard it must have been. C'mon, let's get you a coffee, eh - or perhaps something a bit stronger?" Despite the early hour, he was sure that Watson would appreciate a dram.

The pair stood, and headed for the door - as Daley opened it Watson stopped. A shaft of bright morning sunshine pierced the gloom. The fisherman turned to where MacLeod was sitting.

"You're a real fuckin' prick, do you know that?" He turned on his heel and followed Daley from the room.

Daley had his victim's identity, now the investigation could accelerate.

It was just after ten and the Inspector was hungry. He had just heard from his right hand man, DS Scott, who was on his way from Paisley; already cursing the state of the rural roads he now had to navigate.

WDC Dunn, two uniformed officers along with Fraser and the bereaved Watson were now at the fisherman's home. Daley had to arrange a press conference, which he hoped would take place as soon as possible. In these days of twenty four hour rolling news, he realised that the press conference would go out live. However, in his experience, very few people watched these channels; much better to catch the main news programmes that ran in the early evening. He called the force Public Relations Office.

As it turned out, they had been geared up since the previous day, and had already arranged for the Press Officer designated to this case to contact the relevant news agencies. Daley groaned when he heard who the PR Officer was. Pauline Robertson; a woman with whom he had a long and tortured relationship.

Pauline had been a tabloid reporter at one of his first CID cases. In those days, before her damascene conversion to public relations on behalf of the force, she had been the scourge of Strathclyde Police, determined to uncover the corruption, injustice, and brutality that she was certain beset the organisation.

It was a younger Donald who, then in charge of 'A' Division CID, had persuaded her to take the job in Strathclyde's PR department: 'Fight the demons from the inside', he had implored her.

Of course, once she was tied down to a generous pension plan and an incremental salary structure, and the rest of the benefits attendant with a civil service, such as flexi-hours, job security, and six weeks' paid holidays a year, she appeared to lose her zeal for investigative journalism. She had however, lost none of her ability to rile Daley. He was under a lot of pressure here, and because of the isolated nature of the investigation, it would have a certain cache for the press. For now, he put the press conference to the back of his mind.

8

He had been up since three-thirty a.m. - so, on his way to Watson's home, he went back to the County Hotel to get a quick shower and change, and hopefully a bit of breakfast.

The smell of bacon and eggs and coffee greeted him like an old friend as he entered the hotel. He saw Annie busy at the reception desk as he made his way across the faded carpet.

"Morning, Annie - any chance of that breakfast? Say in fifteen minutes or so? I'm afraid I had a call out in the middle of the night."

"Aye, there wiz me, up wi' the larks cookin' bacon an' sausage, an a' the time the bird had flown."

"Sorry about that," Daley smiled at her, sheepishly. "You know how it is in my line of work - duty calls and all that. It's OK, I'll pick up a sandwich or something in the town."

"Indeed you will not," Annie was adamant. "There's naebody goin' tae say we canna treat oor guests right in this hotel. No, no' when I'm at the helm o' the cutter."

Happy that he was going to be fed, he bounded up the sweeping staircase and into his room. He had somehow forgotten that there was no shower in his room, so he immediately turned on both taps, and quickly drew a deep bath. He supposed that he bathed or showered a lot. He had picked up the habit as a young cop, finding the smell of the death and decay he frequently encountered followed him off duty. Bathing at night and in the morning seemed to banish the malodorous taint. He also found the activity invigorating. It was going to be a long day; he needed all the help he could get.

Feeling infinitely fresher, he took a clean shirt from the small chest of drawers, and subconsciously chose Liz's favourite tie. Somewhere in the back of his mind, he remembered that she would arrive this evening with the odious Mark. He sighed quietly to himself, what with the imminent arrival of Scott and his posse, Kinloch was rapidly becoming home from home.

He sat down to a hearty breakfast - full Scottish - from the menu. He knew that this artery clogging feast would do nothing for his waistline. However, he was suddenly starving, and devoured the meal sitting alone in the hotel dining room, with only the local radio station for company. It was being played over two large speakers attached to the wall above his head.

'*Police are still baffled by the discovery of a dead body jeest outside the toon,*' the voice was pure Kinloch. '*Noo - whoot is it Jamie?*'

'*Weel, I wiz jeest thinking, it wid be a strange kinda thing if the body they found wisna deid. I mean, whoot kinda polis investigation wid cover that?*'

There followed much muffled laughter. Daley reasoned that this station was most certainly not BBC Radio 4, however he had to admit, it did have a certain charm all of its own.

Lost momentarily in his cooked breakfast, and the hilarious banter of the *Jock and Jamie Show,* he reluctantly answered his mobile, which displayed Fraser's number.

"Sir, I think you better come over to Mr Watson's; there's been a development."

"Well, DC Fraser, you can tell me. What is it?" Daley sounded more impatient than he was, and he grimaced at his own brusque question.

"We checked Mr Watson's house phone; you know, for messages and the like?" Fraser was already sounding maligned.

"And?" Daley was chewing a particularly tasty piece of sausage. "Don't tell me she's been on the phone; this investigation's strange enough as it is without messages from the dead."

"That's the thing, sir; we tried 1471 to get the last caller - just as a matter of course - it was Mrs Watson's mobile number. Two hours ago."

Daley looked down at the remainder of his plate, and stuck his fork in the last sausage.

"Give me five minutes, DC Fraser." He masticated the last of the sausage.

Watson's home was not as he had expected. No low fisherman's cottage, or ill-kempt council dwelling. Rather, a pleasant bungalow in a small estate of about ten other properties, situated on a hill with wonderful views over Kinloch's harbour and the rest of the town from a large, treble-glazed, picture window.

The interior was conservatively furnished, with an expensive-looking 'Chesterfield' suite in dark red leather, a large glass-fronted cabinet, displaying various items in silver and crystal, an enormous coffee table sitting on a sheepskin rug, which itself was either artificial, or had come from a truly Herculean beast. A CD midi unit was perched on a small table to the side of an impressive gas fire, surrounded by a dark wooden fireplace. On the walls were a couple of Turneresque prints, and above the fireplace a well varnished ship's wheel. All of this bore testament to the occupation of the householder, who was himself recumbent on one of the armchairs, his leg shaking up and down in what Daley had already noted as a nervous habit. He was cradling a small silver cordless phone; his face bore an understandably puzzled expression.

"I mean, what now, Inspector Daley? It's her number, no doubt aboot that - look here." He propped himself up on one elbow, as he fished a mobile phone from the opposite pocket of his denims. After pressing a couple of buttons, he handed the phone to Daley, who read the screen which read *Izzy,* and displayed the same mobile number that he had just heard over the house telephone as last caller.

"As you know, Mr Watson, sadly this was most certainly not

your wife, and whoever made this call, and for whatever reason, I am sure will be able to shed at least some light on what happened to her. However, don't raise your hopes too high. The person who rang may well only have found her mobile. It's a common enough thing to call *home* from the phone's contacts list if you're trying to find out who the owner is."

"Oh, I hadn't thought about that." Watson looked towards Fraser, whose face was beginning the now familiar reddening process.

"Sir, I never really thought of that possibility either," he shrugged his shoulders, moving his weight from foot to foot, in an unconscious act of contrition.

"This is a positive development, Mr Watson. We will trace where the call was made from, and with a bit of luck, be able to trace the phone and the caller. Could I have a word with you please, DC Fraser?" Daley walked out of the house, with a nervous-looking DC in his wake.

"I'm sorry sir, I... Mr Watson... I thought for sure that the call was of importance - maybe from the murderer." He looked at his feet.

"It's important that we keep Mr Watson on-side, Archie. The caller may be our killer - who knows? We have to keep our suspicions to ourselves - understand? We'll have the so-called *gentlemen* of the press descending on us later, and be absolutely sure, they'll jump on any mistake or unintentional slip. They'll also wind up Watson, so we have to tread carefully. OK?"

"Sir."

"Consider yourself severely admonished." Daley now had a smile on his face. "My DS, Brian Scott is on the way: now there's a man who'll be able to show you the finer points of subtle police work."

As agreed, Watson was taken to his parents' house, a much more modest affair, set amidst a housing scheme situated about half a mile from the Police Station.

Watson's parents were typical of their geography and vintage:

Mr Watson senior, was of middle height and probably had the stocky physique of his son when younger, which now had matured into a sizeable girth, and jowly face.

Mrs Watson, in contrast, was stick thin and bird-like. She fussed over her son as the police officers were shown to their seats by her husband. She had clearly been crying and looked as though she had had little sleep.

After the introductions, Watson's father was the first to speak. "This is a terrible thing, Inspector - jeest terrible. I mean, whoot kinda person wid murder a bonnie wee lassie lake oor Izzy?"

"Don't even speak aboot it George," Mrs Watson wailed. "When I think o' whoots heppened…" She burst into floods of tears, "That lovely wee boy. What will we say to him, officers? He's mammy's deid." She sat on the edge of her chair, her legs and hands shaking, mirroring the nervous habit of her son.

Daley established that the boy was next door with the neighbours. He would have WDC Dunn speak to the child; she had been trained in child protection issues and would be able to couch her questions in a way most likely to gain a response from a boy of that age.

The Inspector recalled how a seven year-old girl had been a successful witness in a murder trial only a few months ago. He had interviewed the girl early on in the investigation, getting nowhere. A properly trained WPC had later been able to gently elicit pertinent information which eventually led to a guilty verdict. He was not going to discount any evidence from this poor kid.

"Could you tell me how your daughter-in-law was when she brought your grandson to stay, Mrs Watson?" The Inspector's question was gently couched.

"Jeest the same," she answered, doing her best to regain her composure. "Done up tae the nines, of course. She wiz obviously away oot that night; aye her skirt was half-way up her arse," she looked up, a look of determination on her face. "Sorry, Inspector. I jeest wizna happy with the way she…wae whoot she wiz daein behind my son's back."

"Mum." Watson was clearly reluctant for his mother to discuss his wife's behaviour.

"Mr Watson," Daley looked stern. "I need every piece of information that I can get." He then softened his expression. "Please let your mother speak."

Watson got out of his chair and walked out of the room. His father got up to accompany him, but Daley indicated that he wanted him to stay.

"I know this is difficult for everyone, but if we're going to catch the person who did this, I need to know as much as possible about Izzy's life - good and bad."

"She wiz a lush, Inspector; a lush and a tart." Mrs Watson jutted out her chin. "I wiz sick telling my son aboot her. She wiz nathin' but a common slut, an' she wiz leadin' him a merry dance - aye, fir maest o' their married life. I hated her. I'm sorry she's deid, but only fir because o' the wee boy." She looked Daley straight in the eye. Mrs Watson was clearly not as timid as she appeared.

"Margaret," her husband shook his head, "whootever she wiz, she's deid. It disna' dae tae talk ill o' the deid; especially when they're family."

"Aye, an' you were the wan that came back fae the pub every night wi' stories aboot her. No, she wiz no good, Inspector. No good at all. It wid be a lie if I telt ye any different."

"She wiz a stranger, Mr Daley," Mr Watson offered up as an apology for his daughter-in-law's conduct.

"A stranger - what do you mean, Mr Watson?"

"Jeest whoot I say, Mr Daley - she wiz a stranger - she wisna fae the toon. Nane o'us knew much aboot her. We soon found oot mind."

"What did you find out, Mr Watson?"

Watson shifted uncomfortably in his seat. He looked over to his wife, who was only too ready to come to his aid.

"She was from a wee village near Lochgilphead, Inspector. No' place anybody cares for, no' that I know of anyway." She had the same determined look on her face, which somehow masked her previously shattered countenance. "Her mother wiz notorious there too. Apparently she wiz sleeping around when she wiz nae mair than a lassie. Like mother, like daughter. She was a nurse here - I refused tae be treated by her. Aye, oor poor Michael pit his sows tae a poor market indeed."

"Do you know anything specific about her background? Did she have any trouble with old boyfriends, for example? We'll have to speak with as many people who had contact with her as we can find."

"Aye well, you'll be daein' lots o' interviewin' Inspector," Mrs Watson was adamant. "There nae shortage o' boyfreens, that's fir sure, past an' present. That's why oor son had tae go an' work away - he wiz affronted - jeest affronted. An' I tell you, Inspector, in a wee place lake this, nane o' your business is your ain, an' whoot they don't know, they jeest make up. No' that there wiz any makin' up needed as far as she was concerned." She sat back in her chair with a look of vindication, as though she had just managed to purge herself of a great burden.

For Daley, this turn of events was not wholly unexpected, though the scale of Watson's parents' obvious dislike for their daughter-in-law did come as a surprise. Watson himself had only given the merest indication that he suspected his wife of infidelity. It now appeared as though she was a serial philanderer.

"Janet Ritchie," Mrs Watson spat the name out. "Speak tae Janet Ritchie - that wiz her bosom buddy. Another tart: birds of a feather. She'll know a' aboot her carry-on, if anyone does."

Daley asked a few more questions. Izzy had not given any indication where she was going that night, or who she was going to see. She had assured Mrs Watson that she would be back the following afternoon to pick up her son, but when she had not appeared, Mrs Watson had put it down to her habitual tardiness, to which she had become accustomed. Only when hours became days, did she become concerned.

Apart from being constantly late, it appeared that Watson's parents were always expecting her to run off with another man. It was only when Mr Watson senior had heard about the murdered woman that they thought of alerting Michael.

With Janet Ritchie's address, Daley took his leave of the Watsons. He agreed with Michael Watson that it was best if he stayed with his parents for the time-being. Police officers were currently tearing his house apart in an attempt to find anything pertinent to the enquiry.

A request was made to the phone company with regards to the position from which the call from Izzy's mobile had been made. It would take a few hours.

He sent Fraser to find Janet Ritchie, and returned to the police station, where waiting for him was a disgruntled DS Scott, with a team of four Detectives, including one much-needed WDC.

"That fuckin' road's a nightmare. When you think you're getting here you're still miles away."

Daley decided it best to deflect his right hand man's obsession with the inaccessibility of Kinloch. He set the small team operation based tasks, including the preparation for the looming press conference. They were told to arrange to be booked into the County Hotel. This organised, he and Scott drove the few short miles to the crime scene, the bay where Izzy's body had been found.

Scott was impressed with the progress that had been made since Watson had come forward. On the way though, Fraser phoned to say Janet Ritchie was not at home or her work and hadn't been seen for a couple of days by her neighbours. The two detectives exchanged looks. It was possible that Isobel Watson might not be their only victim.

"Aye, it's a bonnie wee place right enough," Scott mused from the passenger seat of the car Daley had commandeered from Kinloch's ailing DS. "Beats walking up and down Back Sneddon Street for a living - eh?"

"You know my wife's arriving tonight - with my dear brother-in-law." Daley changed the subject suddenly.

"That cunt. Whit the fuck do they want?" Scott was, as usual, the soul of discretion. "I mean - you know - you're kinda busy the now."

"You know Liz. Anyway, we'll all be one happy family, even though we're far from home," Daley smiled at his DS.

"You couldna' hae a happy family wae that shite cloaking aboot. Mind you nearly hit him o'er the heid at thon barbecue? I wiz pissing myself - not literally of course," he added quickly, just in case.

Daley raised his eyebrows at that memory. "We'll see, Brian. He's out of his own environment, maybe he'll be less annoying."

"Don't fuckin bet on it compadre. If he fucks you aboot again, there'll be a reckonin'." Scott looked grim-faced from the window.

Arriving at Machrie Bay, Daley parked the car on the verge. As soon as he exited the vehicle, his senses were assailed by the smell of the sea. The sea was bordered by rough machair, fringed with yellow blossomed gorse bushes.

He often found the locus of certain murders incongruous with the act itself. For some reason, finding someone lying with a staved in head in a grimy block of inner city flats, seemed more appropriate than the body of a murdered woman being found at this idyllic location.

The sea was a deep blue; it looked viscous, as lazy ripples made their slow progress to the shore. High overhead, gulls and gannets dived and wheeled over the small bay. Not far from the beach, Daley could see a boat on which two men were hauling in lobster creels, supported by a cacophony of screeching sea birds.

"I think a wee word wi' those guys widna go amiss Jim - eh?" Scott echoed Daley's thoughts precisely.

The young cop guarding the locus pointed out just where the body had been found. Yellow chalk markings left by SOCO, were still visible on various rocks. On the shore, Daley kicked at a three-fingered fisherman's glove absently, as he and Scott took in the scene.

"Do you know these guys out on the boat, son?" Scott enquired of the young PC.

"Eh, aye, sir. It's Bobby Johnstone and his brother, Camel."

"Camel? What kinda name's that?" Scott wondered.

"They call him that because he disna' drink, sir. It's a wee bit unusual here for folk no' tae drink; especially young people. I don't even know his real name... just Camel Johnstone."

"Aye, very good. Well just you use your initiative, an' work oot how tae get them tae come oe'r here, we want tae talk tae them. Aye, an' it's sergeant, by the way, no' sir."

The constable apologised awkwardly, then made his way to the water-line stroking his chin as though deep in thought.

"See I telt ye, Jim, they're a' half daf..." He didn't get to finish his sentence.

"Bobby, Camel! Get yoursels oe'r here quick smart! The CID want tae talk tae you!" The sudden shout made Scott jump involuntarily.

"That's whit you call initiative, son? I could have roared at them myself," Scott was displaying the short fuse for which he was famous.

"Sorry si...sergeant - seems tae have done the trick though," he gestured over his shoulder to the fishing boat, where one of the men was giving a *thumbs up* sign with an outstretched arm.

"Great, son. Take the award o' *Polis o' the Year.* Noo amaze me mair an' find me an' the Inspector a cup of coffee. Aye an' don't be wakin' the dead while you're at it."

They watched as the fishermen attached an empty creel to a rope interspersed with pink buoys, then throw it back into the sea. So engrossed were they with this process, that they failed to notice that someone was heading along the sand in their direction. Not that is, until he shouted an airy greeting.

"Whit have we got here?" Scott tutted as the figure got closer. On closer inspection, he was a short, stocky man, dressed - somewhat bizarrely in a yellow oilskin jacket, and green water-proof trousers, tucked into red Wellington boots. He had thinning grey hair, which still bore witness to the fact it was once probably ginger, swept back over a pate reddened with the sun, as was the rest of his jowly face. He was unshaven, sporting grey stubble speckled with red. Daley put him somewhere in his late fifties to early sixties.

"I wonder whit they call him in Kinloch - Joseph, I shouldna wonder - he looks like he had a narrow escape fae a jelly bean factory." Scott was good with the public.

"Hello, sir, how can we help you?" He called out in a rather different tone.

"Good morning, gentlemen," the man said breathlessly in a well-spoken accent. "Allow me to introduce myself: Glynn Seanessy. I presume you are police officers?"

"Yes, sir," Daley got in before Scott could be sarcastic; "I take it you are aware of the reason we're here?"

"Oh yes, yes - most unfortunate - I never thought that something like that would happen here. I mean look around, it's glorious. So sad that someone should die here, in such an awful way."

"May I ask how you know how this person met their death, Mr Seanessy?" Daley tested the man.

"Oh well, you know, officers - Kinloch rumours - that sort of thing." Seanessy was blustering, clearly flustered.

"It's OK, Mr Seanessy," Daley lightened his expression. "In the short time I've been in Kinloch, I realise that there are few secrets."

"Oh, yes, just so," Seanessy laughed nervously. "It's just, I spend a lot of time on the beach and round about. You know, beachcombing, bird watching and the like. I'm afraid time's a bit heavy on the old hands now I'm retired; one's little pleasures etcetera. I'm sure you are well aware how it is."

"No, I'm not, bit I canna wait tae find oot," Scott answered, gruffly. "I'm counting the days until I retire."

"Ah yes, I imagine your kind of job is, well...very stressful."

"You could say that," Scott said dismissively.

"Well, of course. As I said, I spend quite a lot of time here, so I was wondering if I could be of any assistance? You know, local colour and the like. I'm afraid I haven't any more to offer than that. I wasn't here when the body was found - school reunion - a pain really, but nice to see the old faces." Daley could see that the *local colour* remark was amusing Scott, who was associating the comment with Seanessy's attire. He spoke quickly, again before Scott could comment.

"You were at school here, Mr Seanessy?"

"Eh - yes and no - the reunion was back in Cambuslang, where I grew up. But yes, in a manner of speaking," Seanessy had a nervous, halting manner, "I was a teacher at the local high school here - chemistry - pretty boring really. I'm afraid the stress got to me though; I took early retirement a couple of years ago. I live over there - love the sea - wonderful, don't you think?" He pointed back along the beach, to a small, whitewashed cottage, set back from the shore on a portion of hilly machair.

"A might chilly in the winter - eh?" Daley could see that Scott was anxious to get rid of the man.

"The body was found the day before yesterday. How long were you away?" Daley persisted despite the sarcasm of his colleague.

"Let me see," he mused, "five days in total. I was told about it this morning in the local CO-OP. An ex pupil on the check-out - she knew I lived near where the body was found - looking for gossip probably."

"So nothing suspicious in the few days before you left?" Scott this time.

"No. Nothing at all. As you can imagine, anything out of the ordinary here sticks out like a sore thumb."

For appearances sake Scott took a note of Seanessy's contact details.

"Well, thank you for your help, Mr Seanessy; we know where to find you should we require any - colour." Daley made it obvious that that was the end of the conversation, by turning round to look at the progress of the Johnstone brothers.

"Yes, quite; you must be busy men." Seanessy was apologetic. "I conduct the odd wildlife tour, if eh, you ever get time?" Scott gave him a withering look, Seanessy muttered a goodbye, and walked back towards his cottage in a blaze of colourful clothing.

"Fuckin' weirdo." Scott's uncharitable appraisal was no surprise.

"Are you trying for that PR posting again, Brian? Please

remind me not to recommend you."

"Oh that reminds me, Jim, I've got that letter from his majesty for you - nice envelope - looks mucho official. It's in the glove compartment o' that minibus. Remind me and I'll gie it tae you when we get back."

The Johnstone brothers made their way slowly up the beach. They were deep in conversation; a conversation that was getting heated.

They were both of middle height with sandy-red hair. Their builds however were quite different: one of them was stocky - muscular looking - with a broad, tanned face, while his brother was impossibly slim; his oilskins hanging off his slight frame. He had a sharp, intelligent look, and by the body language on display, was very much in charge. Both brothers had the fresh, weathered look, associated with those who spend long hours at sea. Daley recognised them immediately.

"Gentlemen, did you enjoy your trip to Glasgow?"

The brothers looked at each other, then the thinnest spoke. "Right, I remember you," he turned to his brother. "The plane, do you mind Bobby?" The thick set man, now identified as Bobby, scratched his head.

"I canna say I dae, but as usual you'll be right."

His brother looked at him sharply, and it seemed that the two may continue the heated discussion they were having on the way up the beach, until Scott intervened.

"Whitever, lads," he said dismissively. "Now you'll baith be aware that the body of a woman was found in this wee bay a couple o' days' ago. Now if yooz were on the plane with the Inspector here, I'm thinking that you'll no' have seen too much. How long were you away fir? - and when did you leave?"

Scott's ability to get to the point seamlessly always impressed Daley. He reminded him a bit of the men who helped at the fun fair when he was a boy. *The shows*: now there was a treat which every child looked forward to, in the days before a quick hop across the channel to Euro Disney, or a run to one of the many theme parks that had sprung up around the country, were possible.

Despite the obvious excitement of their young charges, these men looked thoroughly bored with life, spinning the waltzer, or manning the dodgems with something approaching a perfunctory manner. Scott gave the same impression, conducting the most serious enquiry as though he would rather be in bed, or in the pub - virtually anywhere else in fact. Daley had to concede though, this approach did get results, albeit in a gruff, distant fashion.

The man they now knew to be Camel answered. "We were up at the fitba' - wish we'd no' bothered - the game wiz shite."

"So you're Rangers fans, boys, eh?" At last, a smile from the taciturn Scott.

"Na," Bobby answered with a grin on his face, "I'm a hoops man - he's a hun." Scott looked bemused.

"But Celtic werena' playing this week. Did you just go fir the trip?"

"Na," the grin remained on Bobby's face, "we take it in turns: wan week we go tae Parkheid, the next tae the evil empire." At this his grin turned to a girn.

"Whoot he means is we don't suffer fae the same level of bigotry here as you lot up in Glesca'." Camel was clearly the more intellectual of the two.

"The next thing ye'll be telling me is that ye all go tae the same schools," Scott proffered under his brows, with a look of scorn.

"Aye we dae. Nae room for a' that sectarian stuff here, constable." It seemed that Scott had met his match. Camel was as adept at sarcasm, as he was with the intricacies of religious division within the West of Scotland.

"Sergeant, son - Detective Sergeant. You've still no' telt me when you left for the game. Just get on with it."

Camel's sharp features lit up with the smile that said *one-nil*. "Day before yesterday, on the efternoon flight. We get a hotel deal off the internet, check-in, get something tae eat, head tae the game…" His brother stopped him in full flow.

"I get pished, he helps me back tae the hotel and we come hame on the flight the next morning. That way, we're back in time for the creels. Nae worries."

"Do either of you know Izzy Watson?" Daley threw this question in unexpectedly amidst the banter. "Her husband's Michael Watson. He used to fish from Kinloch; works out of Dublin now - a local guy."

Some cases came to their conclusion on the back of a mere nuance - a gesture, ill thought utterance, a facial expression. Daley witnessed what he considered a contender, as the smile left the face of Bobby Watson, as he lowered his head and looked at his brother under beetling brows.

"Aye," this was Camel, "everybody knew Izzy - she wiz, well - very friendly." Some of the tension left Bobby's face at his brother's obviously flippant remarks.

"Friendly - in what way?" Daley acted as though he hadn't picked up on the implication of Camel's last statement.

"She wiz a whore. She wiz ay' wis gagging fir it, Inspector." Camel's smile was broad and supercilious. "It wiz a fuckin' shame fir Mecky, but whoot guy's gonna look a gift horse in the mooth - eh? She wiz a wee cracker."

Daley let the conversation drift. In the awkward silence that followed, he watched Bobby as he looked back out to sea, his face more serious than his brother, who simply looked at the two policemen with a fixed smile.

"You keep saying she was - why is that?" Daley's expression was blank.

"That's easy, Inspector: there's been a wiman found deid, an' there polis all o'er Mecky's hoose, aye, an' his mother's hoose tae. I'm a lobster fisherman, no' a polis, but I can still work that oot." Camel held up a mobile phone, his smile was again one of triumph. *Two-nil.*

"What about you, Bobby - how well did you know Izzy Watson?" The Inspector waited for an answer as the young fisherman's gaze remained on the sea.

Eventually he turned back to Daley and answered.
"She wiz a nice lassie. No' right wae the drink, but jeest a nice lassie, that's all," he shrugged his shoulders.

Daley noticed how uncomfortable the young man seemed. His

brother, on the other hand, left his face a mocking mask. The pair had very different opinions of Izzie Watson.

"You both seem very young to have your own boat," the Inspector changed tack. "I mean, can't be cheap - one of those boats - all of the kit." He gestured out to their boat now bobbing near the beach, the pink and orange buoys to which the fishermen's nets were attached were jostling with seaborne gulls further out in the bay.

"Oor faither left it tae us when he died," Camel yet again spoke for the pair. "I wiz twelve, Bobby wiz ten. Whoot's the point o' school when you've got a career oot here? We baith left the school as soon as we could, an' we've been at this ever since." His summing up of their lives to date had all the skill of a lawyer or journalist. Camel was a fisherman, but even at this brief meeting, Daley could sense that a sharp intellect was at work.

"What did your father die of?" Scott intervened. He and Daley were so used to working together, that their interview technique was easily intertwined, each man instinctively knowing what the other was trying to achieve.

"Whoots that got tae dae with anything?" Bobby was on the defensive.

"The drink," Camel blurted out, clearly also annoyed at the question. "He drank himself' tae death. Aye an' he's no' alone 'roon here."

"I see, is that why you don't drink?" Daley's question to Camel was direct.

"I can see how you got tae be an Inspector. Aye, that's how I don't drink. Noo if you don't mind, we've got mair creels tae dae..."

"Just one last question," Daley wasn't giving in at Camel's request. "When did you last see Izzy Watson?"

Bobby looked nervous, and tried to give a stuttering response; his brother though quickly hushed him.

"Last weekend. She wiz in 'Pulse' - you know, the Nightclub?" Daley bridled, that intonation had even reached Kinloch.

"What about you, Bobby? You don't seem as sure as your

brother." Scott was playing the game well.

"Aye, the same. I was with my brother the other night." Both officers noted his uneasiness.

"By fuck, Camel, fir a man that doesn'a drink, you spend a hell of a lotta o' time in pubs - eh?" Scott again echoed Daley's thoughts.

"There no' a lot else tae dae here - or has your nose fir shite no' detected that yet?"

Daley saw Scott's face change fleetingly, but he managed to keep his cool.

"You can gie me your addresses - aye an' the name o' the pubs you drink in - just in case we need tae speak tae you again."

The brothers' shared a house in Kinloch, and, as could have been predicted by anyone who knew of the partisan nature of pub-going in the town, spent their leisure time between *The Royal*, *The Douglas Arms*, and *Pulse*.

The two policemen watched as they waded out on to the boat, started the noisy diesel engine, and went about the business of lobster fishing.

"Someone's no' telling' the truth." Scott needed no confirmation from his boss denoting his full agreement.

The uniformed constable was walking slowly down the beach, carrying two styrofoam cups of coffee.

" Well done, son - mebe yer no' such a fuckin' idiot efter a'?"

The young PC smiled at the backhanded compliment. "Made them in the incident van up on the road."

Scott hadn't thought of that.

9

Back at Kinloch station, Daley was confronted with the prospect of the looming press conference. It was not that he was a particularly nervous performer, or that he was of the shy, retiring fraternity. No, rather he was tired of all of the experts who would generally mill around before, during, and after such an event took place, offering nebulous pointers and pieces of *useful* advice. Everyone it seemed, from the Chief Constable, down to the office janitor, became an expert when the bright camera lights burst into life and the gentlemen of the press arrived.

He and Scott had already recognised a couple of *red top* hacks as they drove through Kinloch. The town's bars would see a boost to their already burgeoning trade.

He resolved to change tack as far as the press conference was concerned. He had noticed that more and more of these affairs were being conducted by lower grade officers. It was high-time Scott got more used to the limelight. It would be useful experience for him, as well as being a relief for his immediate superior.

Normally, these events were organised by the Supt. Donalds of this world. They would sit by, faces the picture of gravity, as some poor DCI or DI sweated under the glare of television lights, answering the probing questions of inebriated journalists; always conscious of the dark ranks of their friends and colleagues marking the performance in the shadows; busy formulating an aggravating litany of 'handy hints and tips'.

Well, woe betides them today. He looked surreptitiously across the room at his DS as he poured through a mountain of paper and envelopes, trying to find the one that Donald had entrusted to him to deliver. Needless to say, the air was a particularly bright shade of blue.

"You know, I don't know where the fuck anything goes. I left the bloody thing in the glove compartment; I'm certain."

Paper and brown envelopes were piling up on the floor at his feet; two Paisley DCs looked on disinterestedly as they chewed on bacon rolls.

"Aye an' you pair can just get off your backsides an' get o'er here an' help me. You wid think we'd been livin' in that minibus fir three years, the fuckin' state it's in. We only got it at six this morning. Get cracking."

Daley decided that now was not the best time to tell Scott of his decision. Instead, he called Crichton at the mortuary.

After a few minutes on hold listening to Mendelssohn's Scottish symphony, Crichton's familiar tones jolted the Inspector back to life.

"You out for one of those fly puffs on that pipe, Andy?"

"As a feat of detection, that has a certain paucity, Jim - you might even solve a case at this rate. Now, how can I help you?"

Daley watched as Scott threw a banana skin at one of the DC's then answered. "I'm just wondering if you've had any luck with getting any identifiable DNA from those semen samples? - I could really use it just now."

"Well then you are in luck," the pathologist sounded bright. "We did extract successfully from all three. They're being compared with our database samples as we speak. Sorry I can't guarantee that we'll come up with a match - but a step forward - what?" His old-fashioned intonation amused the Inspector.

"What's the easiest and quickest way for me to get a DNA sample to you for testing? - bearing in mind where I am at the moment."

"In that part of the world Jim, we usually have the Force Doctors do the necessary. The chap down there's quite obliging," he hesitated momentarily. "Can't remember his name for the life of me. May I enquire, will this be a voluntary sample, or one you've managed to get from something?"

"No, just a suspicion," Daley was shaking his head, even though Crichton could not see him. "We'll get the sample one way or the other."

"In that case, my advice is to contact your man down there. Get him to call me first - some of these hick docs are a bit ham-fisted when it comes to this sort of thing. I'll keep him right."

Daley had no sooner put the phone down, when the door to the CID office burst open to reveal a short, middle-aged female dressed in a dark suit and jacket combo, which looked as though it was about to burst at the seams. Indeed, the jacket was so tight that it further accentuated her ample bosom into which her neckline plunged under a mostly unbuttoned, white blouse. Her hair, cut in a bob style, was obviously dyed as it appeared to be almost navy-blue in colour. A pale face was dominated by a bright red, lip-glossed mouth, and a pair of extra-large sunglasses that gave her the look of a malevolent, squat bug - which, Daley reckoned, was exactly what she was.

"Fir fuck's sake," was Scott's first, and probably predictable response. "I didna' know that they'd given you a long-range broomstick." The assembled DCs chortled heartily.

"And I didn't know that the Police were still employing deadbeat alcoholics."

Suddenly Daley wished he had taken the opportunity of speaking to his DS earlier. "Pauline, hello - I trust your journey was pleasant?"

The PR Officer grunted an unintelligible response, and stood in the middle of the floor taking in her surroundings. She had a large, leather bag over her right shoulder, while the wheeled suitcase which she had in tow now stood, precariously angled, at her side.

"I see you chaps have been able to replicate the usual standard of organisation, despite the change of venue." She was looking at the detritus that surrounded Scott. "Now, I'll need some kind of desk, in this…this shambles. Preferably as far away from him as possible," she pointed at the Detective Sergeant. "Please, no matter the circumstances, do not be tempted to bring anyone from the press in here, the state of this place would be headline news." Pauline Robertson, had, as usual, made her presence instantly felt.

"Aye well, just you remember, that while you're prancing aboot wae a' they poofs an' chancers, we're busy solving a murder. So keep your opinions tae yersel'."

Daley reasoned that there was no time like the present, and calmly invited both Pauline Robertson and Scott into his glass-walled office.

Once his proposal to make Scott the PR liaison offer was made clear, both Robertson and the DS sat in what could best be described as stunned silence.

"I must admit, this is not what I expected. Does no-one have anything profane to shout?" Daley's sarcasm was intended to illicit some - any, response.

Pauline was the first to speak. "I suppose with your new-found eminence, it would be pointlesss to argue."

Both policemen looked at her blankly.

"Don't tell me you don't know yet? I got the memo this morning before I caught the plane."

"Oh fuck, just get on wi' it. Has he got a Knighthood or something?"

"Nothing of the kind. So you really have no idea, *Chief* Inspector Daley?"

Daley took a second or two to assimilate the information, which was filled by Scott.

"Of course, that broon envelope 'His Highness' gave me. It must be your promotion; well done Jimmy boy," he said, somewhat irreverently as he stood to congratulate his colleague.

"Yes, congratulations I'm sure. I'm just pleased I was the bearer of such good news."

"That's another thing, Chief Inspector," Scott was being mockingly deferential, "how the fuck did she get doon in the plane, and I had tae suffer that fuckin' minibus fir 'oors on end?"

It was clear, as far as Scott was concerned at any rate, that very little had changed, and that an elevation to the rank of Chief

Inspector barely warranted a mention.

"Anyway, we better get a shift on. I've arranged this press conference for two p.m. at the locus. Nice day and all that; more chances of getting TV coverage." She gave both policemen a superior smile. "So, chop-chop, DS Scott. Most of the work is done, all you have to do is follow my instructions. Oh, can you read out loud?"

On hearing the beginning of Scott's expletive rich reply, Daley decided to leave the pair to organise the press conference unaided. He took a few moments to ponder his good fortune.

He had most certainly not expected to be promoted; ever, never mind now. He recalled Donald's assurance that he had something 'up his sleeve', with which to counter the waspish MacLeod. His promotion must have been it.

Promotion changed a lot of things. His operational status would change. He would be forced to pay more than lip-service to the bean-counting he so despised.

What about his working relationship with Brian Scott? He watched the combustible DS through his glass window, shaking his head, raising his eyes, and finger-pointing. Beneath all of the repartee, they made a good, effective team. Would this be their last investigation together?

And what about Liz? She constantly berated her husband for his lack of progress through the ranks. He knew she would be pleased; but would her pleasure be felt on his behalf, or on her own? He would tell her about it later; she was due to arrive in the late afternoon - with the odious Mark of course.

He didn't suppose that Mark Henderson would give a damn whatever rank he achieved. He saw all policemen as poorly-paid, unimaginative functionaries; careers spent trying to stem the tide of human degradation. Not unlike those who cleaned the sewers, or emptied bins; the only difference being they dealt with human effluent. They had talked about it late one night, when without an audience, and after a few Highland Park's, Mark had become almost human. The contempt he held for any kind of public service was obvious. He had told Daley that he could have done so much better in life; made so much more money - this would be bound to impress Liz. Patronising prick.

Daley stood with Macleod, who was stiff, as though he was standing to attention in his well-pressed uniform. The pair had exchanged a brief conversation earlier, when the Highlander had congratulated Daley on his promotion. It was clear he did not intend to call Daley *sir*, merely avoiding the need for its use by addressing him obliquely.

They were on the shore overlooking Machrie Bay, where the body of Izzy Watson had been found. Pauline Robertson had persuaded everyone that the beach was an ideal venue for the press conference; a location that would stick in the public's collective mind.

Fraser stood beside Scott, who was, in turn, flanked by Watson and Pauline Robertson. The sea fizzed in soft, white breakers on the shore at their backs. The ever present gulls performed complicated aerial aerobatics in the clear blue sky, their cries adding to what Robertson termed: *a visually memorable happening.*

MacLeod though, was unsure. "I've never seen anything like this in my career," he surveyed the scene with a disgusted frown. Television technicians set up lights, microphones and cameras. Around thirty reporters, representatives of both the electronic and printed media were present; they mingled on the beach in loose huddles, stood alone with mobile phones held close to their ears, or silently observed the scenery. One hack sat cross-legged on the sand typing furiously onto a small lap-top.

Daley's own mobile rang, and he could see MacLeod's face recoil at the ringtone as he stomped off.

"Jim, congratulations," it was Donald, gushing out of the phone. "Well deserved, well deserved indeed. I've had it up my sleeve for a while, you know. Just a case of persuading the powers-that-be that it was the correct course of action, etcetera."

Oh great, you're my new best friend. I owe you everything.
Daley nodded, unable to answer the Superintendent now in

mid-flow.

"Not too sure about this decision to let Scott loose on this press conference though, Jim," the voice had changed from one of warm congratulation, to that of doubtful caution. "I mean to say, he's not exactly what I would call the soul of discretion when it comes to contact with the public; never mind on television."

"Yes, sir, I…." Daley was cut short.

"However, on your head and all that - big responsibility now, Jim - buck stops here. Do you have anything worthwhile?"

Daley thought before he answered. A couple of Paisley DCs were currently questioning Bobby Johnstone, who had been asked to *volunteer* to attend the station. Daley had seen the young fisherman's face when he and Scott had interviewed the seafaring brothers at Machrie Bay earlier. His instincts told him that they were mixed up in some way with Izzy Watson. He didn't think either or both of them were murderers - but, you had to be sure.

Bobby was chosen, as it was clear that he would be a more malleable witness than his acerbic brother, Camel. He was waiting for news about this from Kinloch. He hoped, at the very least, they would manage to soften up Bobby. He would try again later; they had decided not to mention this in the press conference.

"A couple of leads, sir, nothing else. We've got the DNA of the men she had sex with, so here's hoping; my team are on it now. I just want to get this circus out of the way first."

There was a short pause at the other end of the phone, which was unusual. Normally Donald filled every available second of a telephone conversation with his own form of condescending brio. Alarm bells rang in Daley's head.

"Yes…," more hesitation, the Superintendent was playing for time. "I hear that your wife is on her way there. Do you think this is wise?"

The cause of his superior's uncharacteristically silent musing was now clear. Daley decided to meet it head on.

"Look, sir, I of all people should know that your network of informers is legendary, and I neither know nor care how you found out about this. My personal life is my own - murder investigation or not. In fact she is coming here on a totally unrelated matter. I hope you credit me with enough professionalism to be able to cope with members of my own family at close quarters while chasing a murderer. After all, sir, I do live with her back at home when I'm involved in investigations."

Donald hesitated again, but when he did speak, his tone was equally serious. "I've invested a great deal of my personal credibility to get you that promotion, Jim." Gone the honeyed congratulations. "And I know as well as you do, that when it comes to Mrs Daley you can be - well let's just say - impetuous. Don't be distracted by her, or your brother-in-law. I hope that is clear?"

As Daley muttered a sullen reply, the line clicked dead. He had to hand it to Donald, his intelligence network was second to none. More galling, was the fact that his concerns were at least partly justified. He was already put off his stride by her visit, and the presence of the despised Mark did nothing to aid the situation.

He silently berated himself for being so immature, and turned his attention to the beach, where proceedings looked ready to commence. Scott was pawing the sand with his left foot, like an impatient dog, while Pauline Robertson flitted amongst the assembled journalists and TV crews, imparting final words of wisdom.

Michael Watson now stood silently beside Fraser, the embodiment of misery. Daley felt sorry for him; when the full excess of his wife's lifestyle became public, he would suffer all over again. He knew how that felt.

At the signal from a TV Floor Manager, and an angry look in his direction from DS Scott, Pauline Robertson began her spiel to camera.

"Good afternoon, Ladies and Gentlemen, my name is Pauline Robertson, and I would like to welcome you to this press conference, on behalf of Strathclyde Police. I would also like to introduce you to Detective Sergeant, Brian Scott, who is part of the investigating team, and will be conducting today's proceedings. There will be a brief Q and A session at the end, as is customary; during which I would be grateful if you would address your questions through me. Sergeant Scott -", she gestured to the DS, whom Daley was pleased to note had buttoned his collar and straightened his tie just for the occasion.

Scott coughed and moved about uncomfortably from foot to foot; for a dreadful moment, Daley thought his hard-bitten colleague had lost his bottle, but after a particularly noisy clearance of his throat, he began.

"Aye eh - thank you, Pauli – Ms. Robertson," he coughed again, and then looked down at the clipboard he was holding, squinting at the paper which was reflecting the bright, afternoon sun. "I'm sure you're all aware that a body was found here - aye right here at this locus, the day before last," he consulted his notes. "Noo after a series of investigations by oor team, we've been able to identify the victim." he cleared his throat again. "She's is - or rather was, Mrs Isobel Watson, a thirty-one year old wuman residing in Kinloch."

So far so good, Daley thought. He was surprised just how nervous his deputy appeared. He also tried to remember a time when Scott had been in charge of such an event, and couldn't think of any. Sure, he had sat at Daley's right hand during press conferences in the city, but he hadn't had to speak. Maybe he shouldn't have ducked this. Scott continued haltingly with the more procedural content, such as dates and times, appeals to those who may have seen Izzy prior to her death etc.

Scott then turned to Michael Watson. "With me is Mr Michael Watson, who is the deceased's spouse. He would like to say a few words to you."

Watson's head had been bowed throughout Scott's pre-amble, and remained so for a few seconds after he had been introduced. Suddenly, to the clatter and flash of camera bulbs, he raised it. He had clearly been crying, and the dark rings around his eyes bore testament to lack of sleep. However, he stood squarely on the sand in front of the force background board, jutted his chin out, and began to speak. For the first time Daley saw him resemble his mother.

"Izzy wiz everything tae me an' oor wee boy," his accent was thick, and it was clear that the composure he was maintaining was a great struggle. "I jeest ask the person who did this tae come forward." There was a change in his expression; he lowered his eyes and the register of his voice, "an' am telling whoever did this wan mair thing. The polis will find you, and when they dae, I'll get tae you somehow and kill you wae my bare hands, ya bastard."

A number of things happened at once. Watson's next words were mercifully cut off by an alert Sound Engineer, camera flashes erupted into life and Pauline Robertson stepped hastily out in front of the stricken man. Assembled journalists and TV crews issued a collective gasp, and DS Scott looked directly at his boss, his face set in a rictus grin, that said, *oh no! - what the fuck have you let me in for?*.

Order was eventually restored, and the press conference brought to a sudden end. Pauline Robertson took Watson aside, while a number of the TV journalists gave their piece to camera, one in particular gesturing over his shoulder to where Watson was being consoled by the PR Officer, his body yet again wracked with convulsive sobs.

Fraser was standing stock still on his allotted position, looking left and right without turning his head. In the heat of the moment, he reminded Daley of a grotesque mime artist he and Liz had once seen in Paris.

Scott now, was making his way through the scrum of hacks, not without some difficulty. He looked as though his television demeanour was in great danger of slipping into his more habitual glare with a side dish of accompanying expletives.

As Daley pushed his way across the sand towards his stricken DS, he felt his mobile vibrate in his trouser pocket, having disabled the ring-tone for the press conference. He took the phone from his pocket, and grimaced as he read *Donald,* from the screen. He answered.

"Excellent. Well done to you all. That was more entertaining than these interminable soaps my wife inflicts on me every evening. I thought Brian Scott looked as though he had just been taught to speak - and as for the victim's husband, well..."

"The guy's under a lot of pressure, sir. I mean..." He was not given the time to make any excuses.

"You'll be pleased to hear that that little pantomime went out live on the BBC News Channel, as well as SKY, and some more of these dreadful satellite stations. You should have been up there, Jim. Scott was as much use as a ha'penny watch. You'll be hearing more about this - let me assure you."

With that, the line went dead.

Scott's mood was not good. He appeared from the scrum of journalists, policemen and members of the public, tugging his tie loose from an unbuttoned collar.

"That wiz a fuckin' nightmare, Jim man. I never want to have tae dae that again. Fir a start, I couldn't read a word off that sheet of paper 'cos o' the sun. And as for that Watson guy, he's no' the full shilling. Its nae wonder he's wife was on the flighty side..." Realising who he was talking to, he coughed diplomatically, and changed the subject. "Wiz that you on the phone tae his majesty? - I suppose he's plenty tae say on the matter. I'll be in fir a right roasting when I get back up the road."

"Don't worry on that score, Brian. The blame is squarely at my door as far as he's concerned."

As though he thought it impossible that things could get worse, he looked round to see Inspector MacLeod sidling up the beach towards him and the hapless Scott, his face alive with a smug grin. Daley reasoned that attack was the best form of defence. "Before you say anything Inspector, don't bother," the rank was emphasised. "We've got enough on our plate here without your petty shit."

"On the contrary, *sir*," that clearly stuck in the Highlander's throat. "I think the press conference was highly effective. I mean who's going to forget that; surely the whole point of such an exercise is to jog peoples' memory - no?" That said, he carried on up onto the road, where he got into a marked police car driven by a constable.

"Aye, fuck me, Jim, a nest of vipers here an' no mistake - is he

Norwegian? - me and the wife wir there on holiday two years ago - mind? He's a dead-ringer fir them." Scott lightened the mood just as Daley's mobile vibrated again in his pocket; this time it was the office. Camel Johnstone wanted to speak to him urgently.

10

Camel was sitting in one of the interview rooms with his feet up on the table, as Daley and Scott entered. Scott casually shoved the fisherman's legs on his way to his seat, nearly forcing the young man off his chair with the force.

"I don't know where you grew up son - likely in some fisherman's shack - but see where I come fae, you pit yer feet on the groon. Got it?"

Camel's sharp features accentuated the sneer. "Aye, whatever. Anyway, I came here tae talk tae your boss, no' you," his heavy-lidded gaze turned to Daley.

"Well make it quick, and make it good," Daley was in no mood for a game of verbal fencing with Camel. "And if you're here to plead a case for your brother, you can forget it."

"If you listen tae whoot I've got tae say before ye accuse my brother, ye might learn something." Camel was clearly agitated beneath his façade of bravado.

"We're all ears, son." Scott sat directly across from the fisherman, his arms folded, Daley beside him. The newly promoted Chief Inspector held his hand out, palm up, inviting Camel to speak.

"You might as well know, I wiz havin' an affair wi' Izzy Watson."

Daley and Scott stayed silent; a tactic they used automatically when someone was embarking on a confession. Often people, burdened by the information they were keeping secret, wanted some kind of confirmation that they were now absolved of the guilt that they felt. In short, if you interrupted a confessor confessing, the well could dry up, instantly.

"I must admit, I'd hoped fir mair o' a reaction." Camel was sitting with his arms folded, no trace of emotion on his sharp face. He clearly had come to say what he had to say, and that was all.

"So Bobby's not who we're looking for?" Daley kept his expression neutral. He had misjudged the younger brother's body language on the beach; either that or Camel was making a desperate attempt to save his sibling. Somehow, Daley didn't think so.

"Listen," Camel sat forward earnestly, "I know you guys will probably have evidence that I slept wi' her the day she disappeared, so why are we fucking about? This has got nothing to dae wi' Bobby. He just canna help looking guilty - he's ay'ways been the same. Jeest let him go; I'm yer man. I promise ye though: she wiz alive an' kicking when I last saw her." He looked directly at Daley with the unnerving, steady gaze that the policeman had first noticed on the beach that morning.

"So, if you don't mind, maybe you can fill us in on your little dalliance? Where and when did this act of passion take place?" Daley knew that the fisherman was telling the truth, on instinct. "Dalliance; I've never heard it ca'ed that afore. If you must know, I couped her o'er the bins at the back o' *Pulse*."

"Nae bother tae you, son, eh?" Scott sneered at Camel. "Forget romance an' a' that shite. Nice setting."

"They ca' it the 'honeymoon suite'." he leered. "It's no' Paris in the spring, but the owner turns a blind eye. An' well, you know how it is when passion strikes, boys - or ur yiz both too auld tae remember?"

Daley shot out of his seat, and slammed the desk with his clenched fist; an action that Camel was clearly not expecting, as he pushed himself quickly back from the desk, an open-mouthed look of astonishment on his thin face.

"I've had just about enough of your childish sarcasm, son," veins were standing out on Daley's neck. "A woman has lost her life, and a wee boy's lost his mother; never mind her husband, whom you *obviously* don't give a fuck about. Now, I'll give you another chance to answer our questions, this time with the tape on. Remember, son, before we start - right now, after your revelations - you're the prime suspect. So take that fucking stupid grin off your face and try to get yourself out of the mess you're in, or the only crabs you'll be catching will be off some lonely psychopath with a three day growth, and a life sentence. Get it?"

Camel, much chastened by Daley's outburst, went on to tell them more about Izzy Watson's life than could have been hoped for. It was apparently not unusual for her to arrive in the club with one man, then visit the *honeymoon suite,* with another.

It seemed as though her life was truly out of control; Camel assured them that she was addicted to crack and regularly snorted coke. She paid for this, he said, by acting as a sort of unofficial prostitute; drugs the reward for sexual favours. He had paid for his romantic interlude at the bins with a wrap of cocaine he had picked up in Glasgow. He also gave the officers an impromptu, if extensive, list of other men whom she had similar, ad hoc arrangements with.

"By fuck, Jim, beasts in the field doon here, eh? You wid think it was just a nice wee seaside toon, but there up tae their ears in illegal drugs and illicit sex. Oor lassie Izzy's been a bit o' a girl right enough." Scott shook his head, and looked thoughtfully at the floor. Daley knew his partner was sensitive to his domestic situation, and every now and again - purely because of his inherent lack of tact - would realise that he had said something that was too close to the bone, touching on the marital difficulties of his boss. He wished Scott would forget all about it; but the problem remained, silent and unspoken.

He decided to lighten the mood. "On the subject of wayward women, my dear wife will be winging her way here as we speak - or should I say rotating." he looked at Scott and smiled.

"Aye, so she will." Scott was still clearly embarrassed, so he decided to change the subject completely.

"It's been a long day, Brian. Will you liaise with the local guys, and get the rest of Izzy's paramours rounded up? I want to go for a walk for half an hour or so - clear my head, you know?"

"You do the right thing, boss. If anything exciting happens I'll bell you on the mobile. We'll need DNA fae a' these guys, so I'll bump it upstairs for his Lordship tae sort oot."

"Aye, do that, Brian," Daley was shrugging his jacket over his shoulders. "Get young Fraser to help you, he's up at Watson's. He's a good lad; nothing like old Davie, eh?"

"I can tell he's nathin' like Davie 'cos he's standing up. You go an' get your walk, *Chief Inspector.*" He slapped his friend on the back. "An' don't be goin' anywhere near that *Pulse*, or you'll catch something. I'll mebe take a wanner doon there later," Scott grinned.

They were back on easy terms by the time Daley left.

There was a large map on the wall of the CID office, which Daley had consulted when he first arrived. A short distance from the twin piers, there was a stretch of promenade running along the side of the loch towards its mouth. It was here that Daley walked as he mused on the progress of the case so far. The sky was still a cloudless blue, and the fragrance of honeysuckle mixed itself with the ozone from the bay. The ever present gulls emitted their habitual cackle, that somehow, despite its harsh nature, complimented the ambiance. The warm sun felt good on his face; if he hadn't been walking he was sure that he could have happily drifted off to sleep.

Izzy Watson's life had been complicated, and he was convinced that her lifestyle had contributed to her demise. There were though, nagging doubts at the back of his mind: he didn't seriously think that Camel had anything to do with her murder, but of course he couldn't be sure. The same he suspected, went for the other sixteen guys on the list that Camel had given him. They were all young lads out for a good time. Recreational drugs, shed loads of booze, fast women: yes; murder: no. The young people he had seen here didn't have the rough, world weary taint of their peers in the city, where casual, extreme violence had become unremarkable.

The gnawing of instinct continued in his head. He recalled the bunches into which her hair was tied, the red ribbons which stood out so incongruously on the crime scene images. Neither her, husband, in-laws, nor even Camel remembered her wearing her hair that way. Why had she suddenly changed her hairstyle? - and for whom?

Then there was Janet Ritchie. Despite having both CID and uniform officers look for her all day, they had turned up nothing. Nobody recalled seeing her or Izzy after their capers at *Pulse*. He had officers at the club now, questioning staff and customers. The owner was nowhere to be found. He lived in a flat above the premises that was as quiet as the grave. He had toyed with the idea of breaking down the door to the flat, but he wanted to take a look himself before he took this action. At the moment, CCTV tapes made on the night that Izzy had disappeared were being reviewed by two local DCs. *Pulse* was his next port of call.

On another level in his head, he was revelling in his surroundings. The loch itself was a generous C shape, about half a mile across at its furthest point between one side of the town and the other. On this side of the water, large Victorian mansions spoke of the prosperous times that Kinloch had seen when the sea was the world's highway. He had *googled* the town on the evening before his departure; and now he imagined the bay filled with small fishing boats, larger masted schooners carrying coal and whisky - the town's main exports - and the general hubbub that such a scene would generate. In the Second World War Kinloch had seen a brief revival, as the port was a strategic base for the Royal Navy. The deep, safe harbour provided a welcome retreat from the brutal exigencies of the war in the Atlantic. At that time the population of the town rose to a dizzy thirty thousand, the high water mark of inhabitation.

As with so many other communities in Scotland, the seventies and eighties had brought decline and despair. The fishing industry contracted to virtually nothing; the sea-coal mine which had tunnelled deep under the ocean near to where Izzy Watson's body had been found, closed. And, of course, attendant businesses suffered a commensurate demise. The thriving shipyard, that had once produced some of the finest fishing boats in Europe, was a shadow of empty, decaying buildings, located on the other side of the loch. The rise in the popularity of Speyside produced whisky saw all but one of the town's many distilleries demolished. It was the old story: confidence in the area drained away, smaller factories closed, shops shut, and people moved on. In their wake, a hard-core of individuals struggled to maintain the spectre of the thriving, happy community that once was.

Unexpectedly, a cloud passed over the sun, turning the loch from a shimmering blue, to an impenetrable grey. The hills, standing sentinel over the scene, seemed to gather in around their ancient charge. An unseasonable chill rent the air; the squawking gulls quietened; and looking back, the town took on a demeanour of drab foreboding.

In the distance, the distinctive alternating thud of helicopter blades hard at work began to sound ever volubly. Automatically, Daley turned his head to face the noise. A dot, growing steadily larger over the mound shaped island that sheltered the entrance to the loch, immediately caught his eye. *There may be trouble ahead...* the words and melody of Nat King Cole's song appeared in his mind, unheralded. The brain was indeed a complicated, if prescient, organ.

He was suddenly aware of somebody behind him. He turned to face the wrinkled visage of old Hamish, his features the same inscrutable mask the policeman had noted in the harbour master's office.

"Well now, Mr Daley," the old man's voice was a rasping whisper which sounded barely above the crescendo of the helicopter. "That's a day that's changing - eh?"

Hello, Hamish. You know the weather around here better than me, what do you reckon?"

The old man looked heavenwards and took his pipe from the pocket of the green oilskin coat he was wearing. "There a storm on the way. Aye, a storm, Mr Daley." He looked back at the

117

detective. "That'll be yer wife."

Daley looked up, the helicopter was now over the loch. There was writing along the side of the aircraft that he couldn't read at that distance; he squinted for a moment or two, but gave up. He opened his mouth to answer the old man, but he was gone - no sign of him in either direction. Chief Inspector James Daley shivered involuntarily.

He was walking back towards the town; there was still no sign of the mysterious Hamish. Daley reasoned that he had probably taken some unlikely route onto the gravel beach. In short, he didn't know.

He was passing a young mother with her baby in a pushchair, when his mobile started to ring. The girl smiled at him, her baby gurgling happily; he answered the phone - it was Liz.

"Hi there, darling, we've just landed - right in the middle of the town. Can you believe it?"

He had seen the helicopter lose height over Kinloch, and had supposed that there must be a landing platform somewhere in the town dedicated to that purpose. He knew that patients from the local hospital were taken to Glasgow by helicopter, if their condition was deemed serious enough, and briefly tried to imagine where such an aircraft could land, using his admittedly limited knowledge of the town's topography.

"Hello, Liz. Good flight I trust - I actually saw you flying over, I...," as usual she butted in.

"Good, Jim, good," her voice was distant, and he could hear someone talking in the background. "Listen: Mark wants to get settled into the hotel. We've a taxi waiting. Can I meet you later? I'm sure you'll be busy right now anyhow." It was amazing how understanding she could be when her plans suited him being elsewhere.

"Oh, good - where are you staying?" The halting dialogue of their phone calls remained unchanged.

"We're in some posh lodge about five miles out of town. Mark says he wouldn't like to rough it staying in Kinloch itself; he's been here golfing a lot, darling, he says the people are, well...

quaint." Liz giggled, no doubt prompted by her odious brother-in-law. "From where I am I can see a little bar; it overlooks the loch. Hold on I'll ask the taxi driver what it's called." There was a brief, muffled conversation with somebody who, judging by his accent could only be local, then Liz was back. "It's called *The Island* - the driver here says it's the poshest bar in the 'toon'." She tried, without success, to affect the accent. "So, just the place for you and I my love - meet you there, about six?"

"Well, I'll have to see what's happening - I've got something to tell you anyway, so I'll do my best. Will you be alone, I...," she interrupted again.

"Got to dash, this driver's getting himself into a bit of a panic - wants to get home, or something. See you at six." After the familiar sound of a prematurely terminated phone conversation, Daley slipped his mobile into his trouser pocket with a sigh.

He hoped that she would be alone, and he was silently furious that she was staying at Mark's hotel, and not his. He tried to console himself by reasoning that having Liz underfoot in the middle of an investigation would be a disaster, and that she was better off where she was. However, he had just assumed that she would be staying with him. He heard Donald's voice in his head, *To assume, is to make an ass of you and me.*

He banished thoughts of his wife and his superior from his mind and headed back into Kinloch. The town was quite busy, and looking at his watch he realised that being four-thirty, some people might be starting to leave work, or were heading home from shopping. However, come to think of it, Kinloch's Main Street always seemed busy.

It had been a very difficult and long day. He had time to take a look into the nightclub where Izzy Watson had last been seen.

Pulse was situated half way up Main Street. The windows were glazed with privacy glass, and remembering what Camel had told him of what went on within its confines, he wasn't surprised.

A small, brass plate to the side of the door, was all that announced the function of the building to the public. 'PULSE'

Licensed to sell alcohol and tobacco. Prop. P. Mulligan. It looked like the kind of plaque that might be found outside a private medical surgery, or an upmarket legal firm. He pushed at the large, black door and entered.

Pulse was all he expected it to be: an impossibly dim, windowless interior, allowing no natural light to permeate the gloom. A long bar with oversized beer fonts was the empty preserve of a jumpy looking barman, who hastened over to Daley in silent enquiry. A uniformed officer sat with his back to the Chief Inspector, watching golf on a huge plasma screen, located at the far end of a lowered section of the establishment, which formed an obvious dance floor.

Cluny, a loud-mouthed, but effective DC from Paisley, was talking into his mobile, and acknowledged his superior with a raise of his eyebrows. A local DC was sitting at a table on the edge of the dance floor, looking intently at a series of black and white images on a large laptop.

"Hello, sir," Cluny had finished his call quickly. "We're just going through the CCTV records. It's a long job, but we've got sight of the victim now, so we're taking it frame by frame. Anything new on the owner?"

"I was about to ask you the same question, Chick - he's not surfaced here then?"

"No, sir, not a peep from the flat. Do you think we should pan the door in now?" Cluny was, as usual, anxious to be at the heart of the action, an impetuous characteristic that had got him into numerous scrapes, but had also had its rewards on a - *fortune favours the brave* - basis.

Daley turned to the barman. He was a thin youth, probably still in his teens, with untidy fair hair, and a face full of spots. "Is it usual for your gaffer to be away all day like this? I'd have thought he would have plenty to do while it's quiet."

The barman made to speak, opening his mouth, without any words coming out. The detective realised he had a paralysing stutter.

"It's..ac..ac..ac... actual not that unusual," the last part of the

120

sentence came at the gallop. Daley recognised that he was using *actual* as a trigger word to help initiate speech, a common tactic amongst chronic stutterers. Start speaking with a word that was relatively easy to say, using it as a springboard for the rest of the sentence. One of his school-friends had been a stutterer - Colin Chiveney. He had found it virtually impossible to get words out, and commensurately he was a target for the ridicule of his peers. Daley had befriended him, and soon discovered that if they were alone, in relaxed surroundings and once they had got to know each other, Colin would begin to talk almost normally. Then, when anyone else appeared, the stuttering returned with a vengeance. He remembered the exasperation and embarrassment on his friend's face.

When he was in his mid-teens, Colin had formed a rock band; he was a talented guitarist, using the instrument to express in music what he found virtually impossible to do in conversation. It was then he had discovered something which - from his point of view - was truly miraculous: when he sang or spoke through a microphone, his stutter disappeared. Not only that, he found out that he had a fantastic singing voice. Nowadays he played the lucrative Vegas cabaret circuit, as well as session singing work. He was tanned, confident, and worth a number of million dollars. Only a trace of his impediment remained. The pair had kept in touch, and even though they occupied very different worlds, were still at home in each other's company.

"Take your time, son. I'm Inspector Daley," he still hadn't got used to his elevation in the ranks. "Do you have any way of contacting Mr Mulligan, other than those we have already tried?"

The barman looked at the floor, and the set of his shoulders changed, as though he was about to attempt some athletic feat. "Ac...ac...ac... actual if he doesn't answer his mobile, we...ca...ca...ca...," he shook his head in frustration, "actual we canna get a hold o' him." He looked mightily relieved at having managed to get all he wanted to say out.

"Ok, fine," Daley looked back towards Cluny. "I'll just make sure we have a warrant." He pulled his mobile from his jacket pocket, and rang Scott from speed -dial.

He wondered briefly how you could be a barman with such a speech impediment, and then reflected that most of the time in *Pulse*, no-one could hear to converse anyway.

"Hi, Jimbo - did you enjoy your walk?" Scott answered brightly.

"I'm at *Pulse*; have we got a warrant to break into the owner's flat yet?"

He heard a rustling of papers. "Aye just arrived fae a local JP a few minutes ago. Dae you want me to come down?"

"Aye, good idea, Brian - and bring one of those battering rams. My days of kicking in doors are over."

"Has your good lady arrived yet? One o' the boys said a helicopter landed on the green earlier; wherever that is." Scott's curiosity had the better of him.

"Yep, she's on her way to some posh hunting lodge with my brother-in-law. Nice for some, eh?" Daley couldn't see Scott raise his eyebrows on the other end of the phone. "I'm due to meet her shortly, so can we get a move-on?" He looked at his watch, then sent a brief text to his wife to tell her that he would be slightly late for their rendezvous at the *Island Bar*.

Peter Mulligan's flat was a bare, characterless place. There were no pictures on the walls, no framed photographs above the fire, no food in the fridge; in short, it was as though the dwelling was fully furnished, waiting for someone to move in.

This idea was reinforced by the scrupulous tidiness in the flat. Not a thing was out of place: the cushions sat plump on a white leather sofa in the lounge, which also boasted another easy chair, and a small, LCD TV. A chest-of-drawers in the bedroom contained the usual array of pants, t-shirts, jumpers, and shirts; though, in this case, they were all neatly folded and arranged. Whoever did the laundry had made sure that all of these garments could have quite easily come straight out of the packet. Even the bed was tidy. It reminded Daley of his time at the Police College as a young recruit. As with the army, beds had to be made to an exacting standard of precision, complete with *hospital corners* and wrinkle free duvet covers. Some zealots even ironed their beds once they had been made - Daley, not included. So it was with Mulligan's, any inspecting Sergeant would have found no fault with it. The clothes that hung in the wardrobe: coats, suits, jackets, and shirts all hung in ordered perfection - many of the garments were still covered in the polythene covers and marked with the logo of a dry cleaning firm.

There were no personal papers to be found; come to that, there was not one book, CD, tape, or newspaper in the whole flat.

"Something no' right here, Jim. I mean, whit kinda guy has a flat like this, an' at the same time allows lassies tae prostitute theirselves doonstairs in the yaird? It doesna' fit."

As usual, Scott had summed things up elegantly. Peter Mulligan would have to be found - as a matter of priority.

PART TWO

<u>Prologue.</u>

She wanted to be able to move her arms, but to her surprise she could not. She wasn't doing anything consciously different from at any other time in the rest of her life when she tried to make them move; they refused to obey her commands.

She could feel numbly though. She was cold, very cold; and she knew that the reason for this was being naked. She longed for her recalcitrant limbs to conform to her desire to get off the floor and pull the duvet from the bed around herself. However, nothing could instill even the slightest response from her body.

She was moving her eyes in a slow and random way; a bit like falling asleep as a child. She would get quieter, her eyes would roll, and her granny would lift her from the couch, and up the stairs to her bed. It was the only way she could get to sleep. Being left alone in a darkened room conjured up all manner of ghosts; the fears of an over -active imagination, her granny had said.

By the time her lids forced themselves closed, those fears receded. She benignly complied with her granny's wishes. It had been so long since she had felt that way.

Her heavy head had flopped forward onto her chest; she could do nothing to stop it. If she raised her eyes towards her brow until it was sore, she could just about see to the top of the bed. She studied the hand that hung limp over the side with complete indifference; though the blood that trickled down from the fingers and onto the carpet below held a strange fascination for her.

There was noise now. It was like listening to a voice from underwater - another memory from childhood - the swimming pool at school. The screams and shouts of her friends became quiet and distorted by the rush and gurgle of the water in her ears. Yes, that was what it was like now, though it was pretty certain that she was not under water. Something sparked in her mind. Water? Try as she might, the thought would not form.

Then something else: a change of sound and, out of the corner of her eye, movement - legs, booted feet. A dull prompting. Thoughts through cotton wool. The bed moving; a thud; more mumbles.

She had a life-sized doll's head when she was young. A blank canvass on which make-up could be applied, or the hair could be fashioned. Training, designed to turn fresh-faced little girls into painted, groomed and fashioned women. That head was looking at her now; though the eyes stared and the tongue lolled from the mouth. She could feel something dripping on her legs. Red rivulets ran down towards her feet, like drops of rain on a window. The head swung from straggled hair held by a black -gloved hand.

She could feel the blood on her legs. She could see the syringe sticking out of her arm, held there by the needle which was thrust deep into her flesh. She felt gloved hands under her armpits. The scene changed before her eyes, as she was half-dragged, half-lifted from the bedroom. She tried to focus on the mass of flesh, bone and blood on the bed, but she was pulled away too quickly. She felt her thigh catch on something sharp as she progressed across the floor.

More pain. Her face connected with a hard surface. A dull crack filled her head, as waves of agony consumed her. More mumbling. Something sharp in her behind.

A tightness in her chest: this was fear. She was frightened all of a sudden. Abruptly, a rush of noise made her flinch. The cotton wool filled world had gone. The voice - that horrible voice - so clear now.

She was in a kneeling position, pain from her knees as well as *her face.*

Then a flash of pain she could see as well as feel. Red agony: then blackness.

11

The bar was a one room affair. Two old men sat at the long counter, drinking whisky from small glasses. The proprietor - she knew because he had told her - was a looming presence behind the bar. He was a portly man, with a red face and a welcoming smile. She sat at a window seat, looking out over the loch and the road which led from the centre of the town to *The Island Bar*. 'O'er there', as her taxi driver had put it. Three fishing boats bobbed in the harbour, while a long low vessel was being loaded with what looked like logs from an orange crane standing on the faraway pier. The crane nearly matched the luminous orange of the top half of the life boat, moored not far away.

Mark had wanted to come too, but she wanted to speak to her husband by herself. She wanted to tell him how miserable she was, how much she hated living where she did; how long her days were; how undervalued she felt; how frustrating she found sharing a marriage with a man devoted to a career that could see him drop everything, at a moment's notice, in a rush to go and stare at another mutilated corpse, or try to drag the truth from a low-life scumbag who didn't deserve to draw breath.

She reflected what loneliness had done to her. Like almost everyone she knew, she had entered married life a starry-eyed optimist: the cottage in the country, the long walks, making love on windy nights beside a blazing fire. Being wholly possessed by someone, so utterly, that to identify where she ended and they began was an impossible, if hackneyed, spiritual quandary.

The cottage in the country was a dreary detached villa, in an equally dreary private estate, in the 'village of the damned'. Dozens of identikit women, living identical lives; all of whom looked the same, dressed the same, spoke the same, drove the same cars, and had the same withering ambitions. A good school for Jake, or Jed, or Perdita, or whatever other ridiculous name that was currently in vogue. Two weeks on a beach in the summer; weekend in Paris or Prague in the spring, and a skiing trip after Christmas. A new four-by-four every few years, and maybe even a move to a slightly bigger house, on a better estate, in a nicer area where the ambitions were essentially the same though more elevated. A public school, a more exotic holiday destination. A Porsche Cayenne, rather than a Volkswagen Toureg.

In short, people who would be born, grow up, and die, with nothing to show for any part of their lives, apart from a reasonably good credit rating, and a will for their progeny to fight over. Offspring, who would themselves embark upon an identikit, middle-class existence, while thinking themselves at the cutting edge of society.

"Would you like another drink? We're in a wee round up here - having a wee soiree - I'm on the bell. You're looking pretty lonely over there." The proprietor smiled gushingly, as one of the two old men turned round from his perch on a barstool, better to survey her.

"Jeest you stay where ye' are lassie. It's no' a soiree he's thinking aboot wi' you - is that no' right big George?" The old man had the bronchitic cackle of the confirmed smoker.

It was clear though, that Big George was not enamoured with his customer's opinions. His face darkened and he glared at the old man. "Yes," the word was an elongated preamble, "I thought when you lost your job and your wife left you, Dennis, you'd have learned to shut up - obviously not. Don't worry about him, darling - no," again the elongated word, this time as a link. "I like all my customers to be happy. C'mon up - we'll make an evening of it."

Just at that, the old man tried to manoeuvre himself around to face her again, however, drink or old age must have got the better of him, as, after cartoonesque flailing arms and desperate

128

grabbing of the bar counter, he fell backwards on his stool, his head narrowly missing the table where she was sitting.

"Don't worry, darling," Big George seemed unconcerned. "No - if I had a pound for every time I've seen him do that, I'd be able to close up for good, and not have to talk to a bar-full of drunks every day. Yes - is that not right Dennis?" He moved as close to the bar as his girth would allow and peered down at his stricken customer, who was, by this time, doing his best to get back to his feet amidst a torrent of bad language and abortive attempts at balance. "Hurry up, it's your round."

"Aye, but you said that it wiz your roon', Big Man." Customer number two looked confused.

"Yes - that's before he fell over and I realised what a fuckin' awful life I've got." Big George smiled at her and turned to the gantry, holding a small glass up to a large whisky bottle. "You'll be for another dram, Dennis?" That was in the form of a statement. Dennis, now back on his feet, muttered in the affirmative and fumbled in his pockets for money to buy the round.

She wondered idly just how many rounds Big George actually bought his drink addled customers.

Just then, out of the corner of her eye, she saw a tall, dark-haired, slightly overweight man wearing a suit, striding purposefully across the esplanade. Her husband, Jim Daley, was on his way.

The flutter in her chest was involuntary.

Daley entered the bar and stood, his eyes taking moments to adjust to the gloomy interior. Turning to his left, he spotted Liz sitting at a table near the window. He held his hand to his mouth in a drinking gesture, to which she replied with a nod, pointing at her wine glass.

"Pint of heavy and a dry white wine, please." Daley was aware that two elderly customers were appraising him from their perches at the bar. The large bartender reached under the counter for a glass, then made his way to the appropriate beer font.

"Don't tell me you're the lucky man who has the pleasure of that young lady's company?" The question was intrusive, but glancing at Liz he could see she was smiling, so assumed that she had been made welcome in this odd, little bar.

"Yes. I hope you have been keeping my better half entertained."

"Yes," the barman spoke as though Daley had just managed to get a particularly difficult question right. "Unfortunately, as you can see, I don't get the chance to look at many pretty customers in this establishment." He looked wearily at the two old men at the bar. "More like the chamber of horrors in this place; with a bit of *tapping* thrown in, of course. Oh, and naturally, hugely stimulating conversation, as I'm sure you can imagine." The sarcasm was palpable.

He handed over money for the drinks, telling the barman to put the change into the charity jar, which sat proudly on the bar counter.

"Thank you, sir, an absolute gent. I'm George, by the way," he held a meaty paw out over the bar for Daley to shake.

"Jim, Jim Daley - I take it my wife has introduced herself?" He looked back over at Liz.

"Liz," she shouted with a smile.

Daley took the drinks over to the table and sat down facing his wife. She was elegant as usual, wearing a tight-fitting, short-sleeved blouse, a pencil skirt made of faded denim - that looked old, but was probably brand new and had cost a fortune. The laces from a pair of Roman sandals, snaked up her tanned calves.

She observed him with her smoky-blue eyes; his dark hair was not as short as usual, while his top shirt button was undone, as was his habit. He looked tired, and she felt a sudden pang of sympathy - the desire to mother him. Instead, she lent over and touched his hand, looking up at him under her arched eyebrows.

"You look as though you've been up all night, darling," she stroked his hand absently.

"I have, well just about. I managed a couple of hours sleep last night. You of course, look stunning as always." He didn't know how she did it; even just stroking his hand made his pulse race. "Sorry I'm a bit late. Did you get my text? It's been one hell of a day."

"Darling; you work too hard. I've been telling you that forever. The Lodge is lovely, by the way; you must come up and have a gander."

He sat back in his seat, removing his hand from the table and from her caress.

"Aw - huffy bunny," she said, her bottom lip thrust out in an affected pout, "are you missing little-old-me?"

"You might as well know I'm not all that chuffed that you're staying with Mark and not me. We might be away from home, but there's plenty of the usual suspects here on this investigation - know what I mean?" He looked straight at her, clearly irritated.

"Oh, I might have known that would be a problem, I simply thought that you and the boys would be in the hotel in the town and you wouldn't want me there getting in the way. After all you are working - this is just a jolly for me."

Daley had now crossed his arms, and took a few moments to answer her, during which time he was looking out of the window at the loch, and the hills behind.

"You know I can't stand Mark, Liz. You must have realised that I wouldn't be happy, you choosing to stay in the lap of luxury with him, while I'm kicking my heels in the local flea-pit. Anyway, why can't he bring his own wife? How does she feel about you pair jetting about all over the place? - not good I'll venture." He grabbed the pint glass angrily, and quaffed a few mouthfuls.

"We are in bad trim," Liz was now sitting back in her seat, leaning on the wood-panelled wall; the smile had been replaced with a *been here before* frown of bored resignation.

"Liz, I can't stand that cu...," he remembered where he was, "...your brother-in-law, and he hates me; so why jolly all the way down here with him, when you must know that I'm up to my neck in a serious investigation? Sometimes I feel you're just trying to rub my nose in it - after all that's happened and everything." He looked pointedly at the floor, his head slightly shaking, as though he was reliving one of her infidelities in high definition.

"Because the chance turned up. Because I needed a break. Because Mark's a good laugh: for all sorts of reasons. You and I need to talk - really." She lent over and grabbed his hand, this time holding it tightly.

"If you've chosen right here, right now for my *Dear John* moment, don't bother," his face was starting to burn. "I wondered why you were so anxious to talk to me - you usually can't be bothered spending more than ten minutes in my presence - and that's in our own house."

"Me? Me not bother about you?" Her face was a picture of indignation. "I'm there for you all the time, but you're too busy staring at corpses, or trying to bring about the downfall of some old lag, or whatever it is you call them."

He looked away again, this time at a painting on the wall picturing a Scottish landscape, complete with braying stag.

"Let's keep this civil," he had lowered his voice, a sixth sense telling him that the other occupants of the pub were all ears. "I might have time for dinner or something later; this is not the time or place for one of our arguments. This town is the mother-of-all gossip holes, and I'm trying to lead a murder investigation, so I'm quite high profile." He looked at her pleadingly, willing her to understand.

"When are you not heading up some investigation?" Liz had no intention of keeping her voice down. "I remember my poor mother warning me what it would be like being married to a policeman."

"Please, not your mother again," he raised his eyes to the ceiling.

"Why not? - she was right: shit job, shit pay, shit life." She re-crossed her legs, folded her arms, and looked resentfully out of the window.

They didn't speak for a few minutes; time filled avoiding each other's furtive glances, and overhearing a conversation at the bar about some local who had managed to get his manhood stuck in his zip, and was only freed by an emergency flight to a Glasgow hospital, something George found hilarious.

"I've been promoted by the way," his voice was now almost a whisper.

"What?" he had her full attention now, even though her face was still a mask of anger.

"Promoted. I'm a Chief Inspector now; I only found out this morning."

She looked at him for what felt like a long time. She knew how he coveted career advancement, and how she felt guilty that it was because of her that he had appeared unlikely to get it. "That's wonderful, darling," her voice was even now, however she still looked troubled.

"I thought you would be pleased. It's what you've always wanted me to achieve. Remember Gabby at the tennis club, or Rachel at badminton? - well you can tell them your husband is a Chief Inspector now." He lifted his glass and glugged thirstily. "Do you want another?" He took her nod as an affirmative and went back to the bar.

She looked at him standing there; those were new trousers: dreadful, the backside was hanging down towards the back of his knees. She wished he wouldn't shop without her there. Somehow though, it was hard to change his level of sartorial elegance, clothes that looked fine in the shop, or catalogue, or on somebody else, immediately developed that *lived in* look as soon as he put them on. But he did have something - Jim Daley, her husband - exuded a raw sexiness that was beyond people like Mark, despite all of his success, money and style. He was more - she supposed - like mankind was intended to be, as opposed to the well-groomed, fragrant, slightly effeminate creatures that now inhabited popular culture and the imagined fantasies of women.

She smiled at him as he sat down, watching as he put both drinks down then pushed her wine glass across the table. "I am pleased for you, really. I'm worried what it means for us though - you know? I hardly see you as it is. Will this promotion make things worse?"

Daley looked distracted. "He's one cheeky bastard," he lifted his eyes and inclined his head to indicate that he was referring to George behind the bar. "He's asking if you and I can keep it down to a dull roar, says it's affecting his sensitive customers."

She managed to gulp down her wine before bursting into laughter. "Darling, you're a natural comedian - do you know that?"

He began to smile too; her laugh was so infectious, it was one of the first things he had noticed about her. Her eyes crinkled into mirth, transforming her languid gaze into a cheeky, sexy, mischievous grin. She had a dirty laugh too, at odds with her refined, smooth mien. As always, he felt the familiar tingle of desire when in her company. He laughed too.

They stood outside the bar admiring the loch and the hills beyond, their myriad shades reflected in the gently rippling water. Liz breathed in the scented evening air.

"It's so mild, I was quite cold at home, but it's as though summer's come early here," she looked over at Daley.

"It's because of the Atlantic drift. It comes off the Gulf Stream and warms up the coast. I don't think you'll see palm trees growing naturally anywhere else in Scotland - eh?" He pointed along the esplanade at three of the exotic trees, as their long green leaves ruffled in the gentle sea breeze.

"Hark at the old sea-dog," she gripped his arm. "I'll meet you later for a meal - what about eight at this County Hotel?"

"Better make it half eight. I'll phone and book in case they shut up shop; I probably won't make it until then. What are you going to do for the next hour or so?"

"Oh, probably go for a stroll. I can get a taxi back to the Lodge any time I want; Mark's opened an account with the taxi company… sorry." She noted that her husband's face had darkened considerably at the mention of her brother-in-law's name.

"Do you still love me, Liz?" that question came from nowhere.

She paused for a while, looking out over the harbour. "Of course I do, it's just - well - it's just that we can't go on living this way. I never see you. I'm lonely Jim - bloody lonely."

He stroked her hair and lent forward, finding her lips with his.

"Wow, it must be the sea air," she panted as they quit their embrace. "I must come here more often."

Just at that, the door to the bar swung open.

"Yes," it was George, "you'll be frightening custom away with all that - folk'll think we're a knocking shop." He beamed at the Daleys. "Hope I'll see you both again?"

"After the effect your little town's had on my husband, you'll have to fight me off," Liz laughed.

"Lucky swine," George gave Daley a friendly smile, "cheers now," he disappeared back inside.

"I liked him." Liz looked up at her husband.

"Me too."

They kissed again.

12

Daley felt light, as though some huge weight had been lifted from his shoulders. He often felt this way when things were going well with Liz; all of his doubts and insecurities about their relationship seemed to disappear. His irritation with people like Mark appeared worn down, rubbed until almost bare. Almost.

His mood was so good that he hardly noticed the walk up Kinloch's Main Street, and onwards to the Police Station. He eschewed the front door, where he saw a couple of familiar faces lurking about - two journalists from Glasgow. Despite his mood, this investigation was not easy: he had a murdered woman, her missing friend, not to mention Mulligan, the proprietor of *Pulse*.

As soon as he entered the CID room, Scott got to his feet and ushered him into the glass box that served as his office.

"We've got a lead on the missing wuman, Jim," Scott's voice was conspiratorial. "Well it's mair factual to say we've got two leads on the missing lassies."

"You're sounding very mysterious, Brian - come on spit it out; I'm in a good mood, so I can take it."

"Aye well, taking it and liking it are two different things, Jimmy boy, as we a' know." Scott rubbed his chin thoughtfully.

"What? You're speaking in riddles Bri, it's not like you - straight and to the point - that's what I expect from you." Daley was half joking when he said this, but he could see that something was troubling his DS.

"First of a', Janet Ritchie was spotted in Tarbert yesterday morning in a blue Audi A3 - that matches the make an' model o' the car driven by oor man Mulligan. That's only aboot forty miles away fae here - so they're either away on a jolly, or they're on the run. Wid ye no' think so yourself, James?"

"Let's take one step at a time, Brian. I'm sure people travel away from here for all sorts of reasons, and remember there's only one road out and one road in." Daley was encouraged by this progress, but wanted to keep things in perspective. He couldn't fathom why Scott looked so pre-occupied by this news. "Who saw them, somebody local I take it?"

"Aye," he retrieved his notebook from his inside pocket. "A Mr Allan, one o' oor boys spoke tae him in a door tae door a while ago. He knows the lassie 'cos she wiz at school wi' his daughter. He pulled up beside her in the car park, she geid him a wave."

"Did she seem OK - nothing unusual?"

"No, Jim - he said she smiled and waved. He didna' think anything o'it; but why wid he? I've pit an alert oot fir Mulligan's car, an a' ports an' airport notification - so no' so bad eh?" Scott looked at Daley with a forced smile.

"Progress indeed; but you're not telling me the whole story-Bri - what else is there?"

"It's aboot oor mutual friend, Inspector MacLeod."
Daley was suddenly relieved; he could take the childish behaviour of the recalcitrant Highlander now that the investigation was taking shape, and especially since he was now senior to him in rank.

"What's the little prick said now?"

"No' so much said - mair no' said," again, Scott looked evasive; however, the look on Daley's face encouraged him to carry on. "It's like this, Davie Fraser's boy - what dae ye' ca' him?"

"Archie - and he's Davie's nephew by the way," Daley corrected.

"Aye, nephew, whatever; when you went fir your wee jaunt he comes up tae me - sort a' quietly like, you know?"

"Yes, quietly. And?"

"So, he says tae me that he didna' want tae upset you wi gossip, but he thought he wid run it past me." Scott hesitated.

"Oh no, has somebody found out what happened between me and that horse; I never touched it like they said." Daley's habitual response to some imagined conspiracy.

"Shut up you - this is serious."

"Well spit it out then."

"Right - well apparently yer man MacLeod has been dain' the business wi' this Janet Ritchie; dirty auld bastard."

It took Daley a few moments to assimilate this information.

"So, let me get this straight, that wee shit MacLeod's been tupping this woman Ritchie who's twenty-five years' younger than him, and also a heavy drug user, and a sort of part-time prostitute?"

"That's the kinda thing, Jim - aye." Scott looked at his boss, waiting for the explosion.

Daley's response was a surprise; he threw his head back, and began laughing uproariously. "Brilliant Brian - just brilliant. That anally retentive arsehole's in the shit now," he continued laughing.

"I think that's what you call a mixed metaphor, Jim."

"Ask young Archie to come and see me would you? We'll nail the policeman formally known as Inspector MacLeod right now," the tears of laughter were spilling down his face. "Wait until I tell His Majesty; he might even forget the press conference."

Scott frowned as he went to find Archie Fraser.

"I know I should have let on earlier - when she was first mentioned in connection with the victim; but you know what it's like sir, loyalty and all that shit." Fraser looked at the floor; the revelation that MacLeod was having an affair with Janet Ritchie obviously weighed heavily on him.

"I do wish you'd told me sooner, Archie, though I don't believe that this will have any bearing on the case. I don't suspect weasel face of any crime, other than a spectacular lack of judgement. I'm going to confront him shortly. I won't mention your name if you don't want me to, though it would add some weight to my accusation. Are you absolutely sure that this is true, son?"

"One hundred percent, sir - he's been spotted by half the station. He thinks he's being very clever, meeting her on the West Beach where he thinks no-one's about. You know what this place is like - eyes everywhere - I got told about it first in 'The County.'" Fraser's colour was high; it was not often that a young cop got the opportunity to get his own back on a senior officer who had been tormenting him for nearly a year, though Daley detected no malice in the DC.

"OK, Archie, I might need a statement from you in the near future. Anyway, we've got more to be worrying about at the moment than Inspector MacLeod's peccadilloes - what are you doing at present?"

"I'm just about to go up to Tarbert with one of your Paisley guys, sir. We'll have a poke about and see if we can find out what Mulligan was up to there. Do you think he is a viable suspect, sir?"

"All we have on him at present is the fact that he's disappeared," Daley smiled, "and of course that he's friends with Janet Ritchie - but as we know, that doesn't make you a murderer. I want to find him - and the girl - pronto though."

"Ok, sir," Fraser got out of his chair, "if you're finished with me I better get on, DC Glavin's champing at the bit."

Daley watched Fraser leave the office; he rubbed his hands together vigorously. He had thought of calling Donald as soon as he had found out about MacLeod, but decided to speak to the Inspector first; he was a colleague after all, no matter how odious, and Daley had never been in the business of hanging other cops out to dry - not unless they deserved it.

He picked up his desk 'phone and called Macleod's internal number.

"Hello, Inspector MacLeod." This guy was formal, even in the office.

"Daley here, I want you to come and see me - as soon as possible please."

"What?" MacLeod sounded instantly irritated. "If you want

me to run to you like a lap-dog now you've got promotion, you can fuck off. I'm here getting some much-needed paperwork done. I'm still Sub-Divisional Commander here; if you want to speak to me you report to my office."

"I want to talk to you about Janet Ritchie; I'm sure I don't need to elaborate any further."

The line went dead, and within a minute, MacLeod appeared in the CID office and made his way to the glass box.

MacLeod sat down opposite Daley in the chair so recently vacated by Fraser. His face was ashen, and he bore none of the arrogant superiority that was his trademark.

"Whatever you've heard is not true." He looked darkly at Daley. "This place is a nightmare, if you've got any kind of status at all, they'll come crawling out of the woodwork to try and put you down - fucking bastards. They hate anyone who's not local - you wait, they'll have you in their sights too."

Daley noted that his voice was even more accented than usual, he hissed his 'S's like a spitting snake, his poison the vitriolic hatred of the people he was in charge of policing.

"It wasn't a local that informed me of your - relationship, it was a police officer, if you must know."

"That red-haired shite Fraser, no doubt," he muttered some curse in what Daley assumed could only be Gaelic. "I should have despatched him back up the road. He's totally unsuited to the CID. Just you wait until I get my hands on him." Veins were prominent on MacLeod's forehead, his fists clenched on the desk.

"You'll shut up and listen to me, MacLeod. I've not mentioned this to anyone other than DS Scott. Firstly, I want you to confirm, or deny that you have some kind of relationship with this young woman; then, if the answer is in the affirmative, I want you to explain to me what the fuck you thought you were doing, and why, when you found out that she was beginning to feature prominently in this investigation, you didn't see fit to come and tell me - like anyone with any sense would have done."

"It's not like you think, Daley - it's my business. Nothing to do with this investigation." He stood up, and was thumping the desk.

"Can a man have no privacy in his life?"

Daley got out of his chair too. "Sit down, MacLeod, and remember where you are." Furtive glances were already being cast towards the glass box.

Both men re-seated, Daley spoke again, in more measured but no less stringent tones. "I'm investigating a brutal murder of a woman, who was last seen in the company of her best friend, who has herself disappeared. I then find out that the senior officer in the town has been giving her one. You can forgive me for wondering where it will all end." He stopped and leaned back in his chair; a silent invitation for MacLeod to explain himself.

"You don't understand," Macleod's voice was no more than a whisper now, his head downcast.

"You're damn right I don't understand - don't give me 'the wife doesn't understand me' routine." Daley was beginning to get impatient.

Suddenly MacLeod raised his head, and looked right at the detective with his pale, blue eyes.

"She's my daughter, Chief Inspector." His head sank again.

Daley sat motionless for a few moments. MacLeod held his head in his hands, his fingers working over his balding head.

"May I ask you how you end up with a daughter in Kinloch? Apart from the obvious answer of course."

MacLeod raised his gaze; he looked resigned, tired and unhappy; Daley could see that he was on the verge of tears. There was something else here - something that he couldn't fathom. OK, it wouldn't be nice being in MacLeod's position having a daughter with such a chaotic lifestyle, however, it was not unusual for the children of police officers to go off the rails; one of his colleague's sons was doing time for serious assault, and Brian Scott's daughter had been involved in drugs when she was barely a teenager - no, there was something else here.

"I can see your mind working - I know you are a clever detective, Daley, so I don't intend to try and lie to you in any way," MacLeod's accent was stronger still, a sign that he was under pressure. The same thing happened to Donald when he was stressed; Kelvinside drawl soon took on the guttural twang of the Glasgow's East End.

"I can see that something is troubling you, Inspector MacLeod, if it's of a personal nature then I feel sorry for you, and I will do my level best to help you, as I would any colleague, but if, in any way what you are clearly holding back affects this investigation, I must demand that you tell me immediately what impact it is having, or going to have. I realise that you will have loyalties to your daughter, but this is a murder enquiry and she is the best friend of the victim. For all I know she may herself be in danger."

"Do you think I don't know that?" MacLeod shouted. "I do have some police experience myself, no matter what *you* think of me." He paused, again looking down at the table.

"I promise you, that I will do all I can to keep your name out of this, and that includes informing my superior - on my word, no matter what *you* think of *me*." Daley's voice was calm, whatever it was that Macleod had to tell him, he wanted to find out as soon as possible.

"As you are no doubt aware," MacLeod pronounced doubt as though it started with a 't', " my daughter is less than I could have wished for. Her mother and I were close when I was a young beat cop in Glasgow - she was a nurse in The Royal Infirmary." MacLeod was looking into the middle distance, reliving the past through his mind's eye.

"I got posted away - to Oban, I had never wanted to work in Glasgow; I was home-sick I suppose. Anyway, we lost touch - she had visited me on a few occasions, but she liked the city life. That's why I was so surprised to bump into her here, not long after I arrived. I hadn't set eyes on her for over thirty years."

"Obviously that wasn't the only surprise she had in store," Daley probed gently.

"No, indeed. She told me about Janet - not straight away you understand - after a while. She and our daughter barely spoke; she hoped that when I was introduced to her as her father it may bring them back together. Janet, I learned had always been a bit of problem, which is why her mother moved from Glasgow to a village near Lochgilphead when she was young. She thought that rural life may improve her." He looked at Daley. "They ended up here because of her mother's work."

"Do you have any children?"

"No, I don't," he said with no expression, anxious for MacLeod not to lose the thread. "It must have come as a real shock to you."

"I don't know what kind of man you are, Chief Inspector, but I had always wanted to have children - my wife is unable to you see," his gaze drifted again. "When I found out that I had, well I was thrilled, despite the difficulties it presented - we all have a past, do we not?" He looked frankly at Daley.

"Did you tell your wife?"

"Therein lies the problem - I didn't. I always meant to…but." He sounded choked, almost as though he might burst into tears.

"Go on," Daley was anxious to proceed, no matter how hard these revelations were for MacLeod, he had to find out if they were relevant to the enquiry; otherwise regardless of their nature, they were in essence, none of his concern.

"When I found out what a thoroughly detestable human being that Janet was, I couldn't bring myself to tell Mary, and possibly ruin our relationship too," tears were now in his eyes.

"How do you mean detestable, Charles?" Daley used the Inspector's Christian name by way of encouragement, letting him know that he sympathised.

"Och," MacLeod suddenly stood, the chair tipping over behind him. "She is all I despise in life: a drug addict, a whore, a fucking opportunist. It didn't take me long to suss her out let me tell you: a fucking chancer, prepared to open her legs for money or drugs. That's what the only child I have is like - you name it, crack, cocaine, speed - even this new *cat* stuff. She's a disgrace." He bent down and picked the chair up from the floor, setting it back on its legs.

"She might be a lot of things, but her record is pretty clean - nothing for three years. You'd have thought that someone with her

143

lifestyle would…" One look into the face of the Inspector answered his question before he had asked it.

"Yes, I have covered up for her - I know what you're thinking. She was blackmailing me; her and that bastard Mulligan. I've been a fool, Chief Inspector Daley - a fucking fool."

"How much have you covered up?" The tone of Daley's voice had risen considerably.

"Bits and pieces - turned a blind eye to soft drugs and some of the goings-on in that bar. Nothing serious; you know yourself, the whole world's mad with narcotics. I couldn't have stopped them even if I had the manpower and the courts behind me - which I do not."

Daley rubbed his face with his left hand. He felt as though he had been awake for weeks; this was the last surprise that he had expected this investigation to throw up.

"What form did the blackmail take? I'm assuming it was pretty bad when you went to such lengths to keep her sweet."

Silence.

"I'll ask you again, Inspector MacLeod - in what way were you blackmailed?"

"I want your word Daley, your word that this will go no further. I promise you that anything I have done has no bearing on this murder enquiry."

"And…?" Daley drummed the table impatiently.

"I had a brief affair - a fling, nothing more. My daught… Janet Ritchie found out. The usual stuff: threatened to tell Mary, call headquarters - bitch."

"Who did you have the affair with?"

"I've told you that I had an affair, is that not enough man?"

Daley stood, leaning over the desk propped up by his arms, fists clenched, in much the same way he had when he and MacLeod had first met.

"You've already told me enough to see the end to your career. I have never come across such wilful stupidity in my life. All you had to do was admit to your wife that you had an affair, and put a stop to Ritchie and Mulligan. You didn't have the balls - much better you tacitly condone illegal drugs and prostitution right under your nose. Tell me who you had affair with, or I swear to you I will pick up this phone and dial Complaints and Discipline myself right now."

When it came the revelation was enough to unsteady even the unshockable Daley.

"It was Izzy Watson. Izzy Watson," he said it again, as though this revelation had come as a surprise to himself. "Now you know; but I promise you, I had nothing to do with her death. You've got to believe me, Daley; please - for fuck's sake man, help me." MacLeod broke down.

"You've got a big heart Jim, I'll gie you that." Scott was shaking his head ruefully. "It was obvious the man wiz a snake, but I didna' expect he wiz turnin' a blind eye tae drugs dealers an' shagging prossies."

"I know it's a risk, Brian - but I don't think he's involved in this murder, no matter what a tit he's been. He's not to leave his house though - he has a pretty good motive after all, so I've stuck a car outside - just in case he thinks the unthinkable. There but for the Grace of God and all - you know?"

"I cannae imagine anyone wi' his experience being so stupid. So, he's reporting tae you twice a day until we get this sorted?" Scott looked at Daley with eyes ringed with dark circles.

"There's no way we can cover this all up, but we can try to get the murder solved, and then he can try to sort it out - can you imagine what Donald would do? End of career: full stop. No wonder he was so resentful when I arrived. What a mess." Daley rubbed his own eyes. It had been a long and very eventful day, and it wasn't over. He had to dine with Liz, though he felt more like crawling into bed.

"Get yourself back to the hotel, Brian - I'm meeting herself for a meal. Is everything OK here - nightshift and all that?"

"Aye, organised," Scott was shrugging on his jacket, "two o' oor guys, and two o' theirs' o'er night. Still no sign o' Mulligan or young Miss Ritchie, but they'll turn up - half the country's looking for them. C'mon you an' we'll maybe get a dram afore your good lady arrives."

The two detectives left Kinloch Police Office by the back door, walked through the car park, out of the side entrance and towards the County Hotel.

The bar was busy; Daley reckoned that the good people of Kinloch knew that most of the investigation team were staying at the hotel and there would be a likelihood of juicy gossip to be gleaned over a pint or two.

"The usual, big man?" Scott was already threading his way through the throng of drinkers at the bar, who looked on with the collective interest of a pride of hyenas.

"Aye, please, Brian, make it a large one." Daley looked for a table, and was amazed to find one - the same table he and Fraser had occupied the night before; it seemed like weeks ago to the fatigued Inspector.

"A pint o' heavy an' a large Springbank, hen," Scott shouted at the young girl who was behind the bar. *Expensive tastes,* he thought as he searched the back pocket of his trousers for his old leather wallet. A tall, thin youth was eyeing him from his seat on a tall bar stool.

"Ur you no' too wee tae be a polis?" The young man's words were slurred with drink, his half-closed eyes bearing testament to the fact, even if he hadn't opened his mouth.

"You're no' too wee tae get a belt in the mouth, you cheeky wee..." Scott didn't have time to add the expletive.

"Right - that's it, Hughie - oot; never mind your pint. I've warned and warned you aboot that gob o' yours, an' noo you've had the good sense tae wind up the CID. Well, hell mend ye!" A bustling woman had appeared behind the bar, and was now busy pouring the bemused youth's drink into a sink under the counter.

"On yer sel'," Scott directed this hearty appraisal at the new barmaid. "Can I ask you how you all know I'm a polis anyway?"

"I wiz watchin' you this efternoon on the telly, an' anyhow, you can ay'ways spot the rozzers - is that no' right, Mandy?" she turned to the younger barmaid, who acknowledged with a grunt as she was pouring a second helping of malt whisky into a small glass from a pewter measure, her tongue sticking out with concentration.

"My name's Annie. I'm kind o' chief bottle washer aroon' here. The drinks are on the hoose by the way - tae celebrate Mr Daley's good news." She raised a glass and her voice to the new Chief Inspector who was regarding the scene with mild surprise, and no little amusement.

"Allow you, Mr Daley - you've no' been here a couple o' days', an' you've got a promotion. They'll likely make ye Chief Constable if ye find oot who murdered that poor lassie."

"Trust me," Scott was now collecting the drinks from Annie's colleague, "that's no' goin' tae happen."

"Oh, whoot a peety," Mandy held her hand to her mouth. "Does that mean yiz are gein' up tryin' tae find the murderer?"

"No," Scott winked at Annie, "he's never going tae be Chief Constable."

He turned and made his way back through the revellers standing at the bar, the drinks clasped in front of him in a manner familiar to any drinker.

"Noo," Annie addressed no-one in particular, "I widna mind him pumpin' me for information." She let out a particularly filthy laugh. "Whoot are you waitin' fir Hughie - dae ye want it in writing? Get oot!"

"I see whit ye mean aboot them knowing all your business; I mean, how did she know you got promotion?"

"Because this place processes gossip better than Strathclyde Police; it's just a pity they'll not come forward with information about things that matter." Daley took a swig of his whisky and worked it around his mouth, better to savour the flavour.

"Ye can hardly blame them," Scott's voice was almost a

whisper, "wae that prick in charge doon here - I widna have much faith in the police either."

"That's another twenty pounds ontae the account, sir," the taxi driver was parking outside the County Hotel. "We had tae pick your good lady up doon at the point." He said by way of explanation.

"Don't worry," Mark's accent only hinted at being Scottish through his public school vowels, "there's plenty to go round my man." He turned to Liz, who sat beside him in the back seat, "is that not right, darling?"

"No it is not, I'm not his good lady," she addressed the rear view mirror, where she could see the driver's eyes, "and I'm not your darling, Mark - for goodness' sake, don't be winding up Jim; we got on fine today, don't spoil it." She looked from the taxi at the castellated frontage of the hotel. *Please don't,* she thought.

"He's just no' the player that Laudrup was," the detectives were having one of their habitual discussions on the relative merits of various *old firm* players.

Daley was about to answer when he spotted Liz and Mark entering the bar. His eyes were immediately drawn to the open neck of her shirt, revealing the cleft of her breasts; he had the familiar feeling - somewhere between feeling faint, and lifting off the floor. A number of the locals had noticed her too, and a couple of lads at the bar appraised her with what they thought was unobtrusive elbow-nudging.

She searched the bar standing on her toes, then waved at her husband when she spotted he and Scott sitting near the back of the room.

"Over here, Mark," she tugged at the sleeve of his Italian leather jacket as she made her way over to the detectives' table.

Scott eyed her progress. She was a beautiful woman, of that there was no doubt; likeable too, with an easy-to-talk-to, good sense of humour. He was sometimes very angry at her though, especially when he saw the negative effect that her actions sometimes had on his mate, Jim Daley.

A mate: he supposed that was how he saw the tall man beside him. They had first worked together eleven years ago, and had instantly hit it off. They had both been DS's then, and while Daley had risen - albeit painfully - through the ranks, he had reached the limit of his ability and ambition. He had joined the police to be a policeman, not some kind of diplomatic administrator, drowning in reams of unnecessary paperwork, having to meet quotas on this, and targets on that. No, being a detective sergeant was hard enough, and that's where he intended to stay; if he thought about Daley's sudden promotion at all, it was only that he was pleased for him, and that he hoped it would not mean their separation as a team.

Aye, she's bonnie right enough. He smiled as Liz sat on a small stool across the table from him and Daley. His expression changed as Mark took his seat - permanent sneer playing across the accountant's lips. *Cunt.*

Mark Henderson always looked the same to Daley: smug, arrogant, elegant, tanned, fit, tall - around the same height as the Chief Inspector himself - rich, good-looking; the superlatives just went on and on. He had the louche, easy manner of the upper classes, and would have looked much more at home at the Henley regatta, or standing by the Grace Gates at Lord's cricket ground, rather than here in the faded, rural splendour that was The County Hotel. His family were ancient - if somewhat minor - Scottish aristocrats; and it showed.

"Jim, my good man; how nice to see you again - especially in such…" Mark looked around the room with his permanent sneer exaggerated, " exalted surroundings." He looked at Scott. "And with your faithful retainer too - how touching."

"When can I deck this bastard, Jim?" Scott was smiling, but Daley knew he was deadly serious.

Liz intervened to change the subject.

"Brian, how are you? What a lovely little town this is, it's such a shame you're both here under such sad circumstances." She smiled her open smile.

"I wouldn't worry too much, Lizzie - some yokel bint from what I can gather," Mark was in fine form. "The taxi driver insisted on telling me all about it - an absolute bore if you ask me."

"I wisna' aware anybody wis asking you." Scott was up to the challenge.

Daley wasn't surprised that Mark had turned up, though this didn't stop the disappointment he felt. After a shaky start earlier that afternoon, he thought that he and Liz had been closer than they had been for quite some time. Maybe it had been the change of bar with its larger than life landlord, or perhaps just the change of scene. In any case, he had remembered all over again how much he loved her. He was determined to treat the appearance of his brother-in-law as a minor irritation.

"When would you like to eat, Liz?" He leant over the table and held his wife's hand.

"Asap," Mark said that as a word, "I'm bloody famished; any chance of a decent G and T before we partake in whatever swill there is on offer here?"

"Oh, Mark," Liz looked embarrassed, "I thought…"

"She thought she wanted tae spend some time wi' her husband, an' no' you hangin' on like the posh gooseberry fae hell - get it?" The smile had left Scott's face as he glared at Mark, who affected not to hear what he had said.

"How territorial these rozzers are, Lizzie," he got up from the table. "I'm for a large one - how about you?"

She managed to mumble in the affirmative as Mark made his way to the bar shouting impatient *excuse me's* to the locals who were obstructing his route.

Liz gave Daley an apologetic look.

"He just turned up in the taxi; I was walking down by the loch, the cab just appeared from nowhere. I can't work out how he knew where I was. He's been drinking most of the afternoon by the looks of things; that makes him more arrogant than usual."

"Which is quite a feat." Scott added quickly.

"Don't worry, Liz, I'll handle this," Daley had spotted the

formidable Annie pass en route to collect another pile of empty glasses - he called her over, and covertly whispered in her ear as she leant over him.

"Aye, nae bother - jeest you lee' this tae me." She stomped, purposefully off to the bar, holding what seemed like an unfeasible number of empties between the fingers and thumbs of both hands.

"What was that all about, darling?" Liz looked puzzled. "It hasn't taken you long to ingratiate yourself with the locals, I must say."

Up at the bar, Mandy was just about to relieve Mark of the cost of two large gin and tonics, when Annie appeared in a flourish of empty glasses.

"I'm sorry, sir," she addressed Mark politely, "I'm in charge here, an' it's my opeenion that you've had too much tae drink - so, I'll need tae ask you tae leave."

For an instant Mark looked astonished, as though presented with an amazing fact, or a chance encounter with a relative he had thought long dead; slowly though, the reality of the situation dawned on him.

"Listen to me, I'm a paying customer here, and I will not be spoken to by some…some bottom-feeder who neither knows her job nor her place. Now cut along out of the way while this little treasure serves me with my drinks." He seemed satisfied with this outburst, and beamed haughtily across the bar at Annie.

"Sir," Annie was now plainly furious, "I'll ask you again. Please leave the bar, you've had too much tae drink, and I'm no' prepared tae risk the licence of this estableeshment by serving you."

"You listen to me, you dried up old bitch…" he didn't get the chance to finish his sentence. Three large men stood up from their bar stools and crowded around him. The largest man - sporting the tattoo of a rampant lion on his meaty forearm - thrust his face so close to Mark's that he could smell the whisky on the man's breath through the haze of wine and gin he had, himself, consumed.

"You're talkin' tae my wife; noo dae whoot she says 'less I take you ootside an' gie ye a hammering ye'll no' forget. Got it? – arsehole." He poked a sturdy forefinger into Mark's sternum, forcing him to exhale involuntarily.

Mark opened his mouth to say something, but instantly thought the better of it. He turned on his heel, muttered something under his breath, and made his way, red-faced, back to Daley's table, leaving a chorus of coarse laughter emanating from the bar.

"Come on, Elizabeth, we're not staying in this dive to be talked down to by Neanderthals. Let's get back to the Lodge and get some decent service." He put his hand on Liz's shoulder.

Annie's refusal to serve Mark had been more entertaining than Daley had thought possible; he had to admire the gall of the man, simply expecting Liz to abandon her husband, and without protest, leave with him.

"Mark...I'm with Jim; we're having a meal..," she looked slightly flustered.

"In other words," Scott interjected, "dae whit the lady behind the bar asked you, and dae one before I have you arrested for refusing to quit a licenced premises when required to. Fuck off - tae pit it mair plainly."

Mark's face was like thunder. He hauled his jacket from behind Liz's chair making her jerk forward suddenly, almost knocking over her drink.

"Bad choice, Lizzie. Bad choice." He glared at her briefly, then slung his jacket over his shoulder and strode - somewhat unsteadily - out of the bar.

"An' don't come back," Annie shouted through the serving hatch which led out onto the corridor. "Noo, Chick, whoot are ye for?" She resumed normal service as though nothing had happened. "An' since when did you become my husband - dream on big man - dream on."

"It's at times like this you really hate the smoking ban." Liz was breathless as she made her head comfortable on Daley's chest.

"Bollocks, it's the best thing that ever happened." He was

stroking her hair absently.

They had eaten a shared meal of local lobster - which had been delicious - had a few more drinks, then headed up the grand staircase to Daley's room.

"I'll arrange for you to stay here with me, I'll get someone to pick your luggage up from the lodge tomorrow." When he didn't get a reply he craned his neck forward to look down at his wife, who was already fast asleep with her head on his chest.

He lent back, satisfied. They had eaten, chatted easily, and then made love. She had rejected Mark in an obvious way. There was a warmth between them now that had been absent for such a long time. She looked so beautiful as she lay asleep; her breath soft on his stomach. Despite his exhaustion and the length of his day, he felt strangely content.

He thought of Michael Watson. He was sleeping alone.

13

The light that streamed through Daley's hotel room window was of a distinctly more dull quality than hitherto. Liz was still sleeping soundly, despite the restless night that he had just experienced. He had been sound for the first couple of hours, after what had been a very tiring day; however, on waking in a cold sweat around two-thirty, he had drifted in and out of sleep: thoughts about the case, Mark, his promotion, the body of the young victim, Donald - all crowded in from his subconscious. This was something he was used to, especially during a difficult enquiry; usually though, he would consign himself to the spare bedroom at home in an attempt to disturb Liz - who herself slept fitfully - as little as possible.

Whether it was the sea-air, or the change of scene, he noted with pleasure that she seemed as serene as he could remember, her light-brown hair falling over the pillow framing the soft lines of her face; her long lashes exaggerated by the fact her eyes were closed. Her left breast was showing above the top of the duvet, displaying her brown and taught nipple. He remembered last night, smiling unintentionally at the memory of carnal pleasure.

A sudden gust of wind rattled a pane of the sash window; he walked over to it, moving the musty net curtains aside, better to see the street below. Even now, at six-thirty there were a few people milling about, most of them huddled into warm jumpers or buttoned-up coats and jackets; cars and buses motored up and down the street.

The weather had indeed changed. Looking up, he saw the sky

was mostly a light grey with small patches of blue visible. The wind was animating the scene, pushing the cloud along - a constantly changing vista.

Even the air smelt different: more about the sea, less of the land. The gulls cries, carried on the restless wind, echoed amongst the tenement buildings that lined the Main Street on both sides. Movement below caught his eye - Annie was crossing the street, waving enthusiastically at him. Shit. It seemed that looking out of the window in Kinloch was a spectator event. He hesitantly waved back, and then let the curtain fall back into place.

He gave Liz another admiring glance as he walked into the bathroom to draw a bath. Shaving amidst the steam he wondered where the investigation would lead today. He was sure that Mulligan was pivotal in the whole sordid business. MacLeod was merely a hapless accessory - a witless one at that - still, he couldn't afford to risk his own career in an attempt to cover up for the irascible Inspector. Things had gone too far, crimes - the most serious of all - had been committed. MacLeod could have at least done something to curb the drug-taking and casual prostitution that was conducted nightly in *Pulse.* He had shown little contrition during his confession the day before. Initially, Daley had felt some sympathy for him - *long lost daughter turns into newly discovered nightmare* - this had rapidly evaporated on discovering Macleod more concerned with saving his own skin, rather than atoning for his astonishing lapses in judgement as the area's senior police officer.

Liz slept on as he dressed, brushed his hair, and took a moment to appraise the product of his toilette in the full-length mirror on the front of the wardrobe. His belly was already doing its best to encroach over his waistband, and peer through the buttons of his white shirt. Maybe he would just have cereal and coffee for breakfast.

Scott was already at his borrowed desk within the Kinloch CID department when Daley arrived. He looked rough, with blood-shot eyes, tousled hair and the same shirt and suit he had been wearing the day before.

"Morning, Jim," he said throatily, rubbing his temples at the same time.

"You look as though you've been on the batter all night, Brian - did you go to a party after last orders?"

"No. Well no' really; the lassie behind the bar 'n me had a few drinks efter closin' time." He blinked his eyes and yawned copiously. "She's a nice lassie," he said through the yawn.

"Mandy, eh? You're a dark horse, Bri. I'd have thought she was a bit too young for you - I suppose you never know."

"Na, no' Mandy! She's a wee lassie for fuck's sake," he reached for a packet of cigarettes on the desk, then pushed them away realising again that he couldn't smoke in the office. "Annie - the manageress. Aye quite a character." His laugh quickly transformed itself into a very chesty cough, which he tried to banish amidst a cacophony of throat-clearing and snorting.

"You try to get that lung up and I'll get you a coffee," Daley walked out into the corridor where a rather superior drinks machine was located. To his further surprise, a bright-looking Fraser was walking towards him, the antithesis of DS Scott, in a crisp, white shirt under a newly pressed suit.

"I'm pleased to see my team are taking this investigation so seriously. Not even eight and my core men are already in place. Do you want a coffee, son?"

Somewhat predictably, Fraser began to beam red. "Eh - yes sir - tea please if you don't mind: white wi' two sugars."

Daley pressed the relevant buttons, fed in the appropriate coinage, and, as the first styrofoam mug began to fill, turned to the young DC.

"I want you to liaise with the nightshift and see what - if anything - happened last night, while I try to sober our intrepid DS up. You're looking pretty fresh this morning - my new tie too, I see," he smiled benignly at Fraser.

"No bother, sir. I'll get it back to you," he grinned blushingly. "Do you think we're getting close with this Mulligan guy?- it's all a bit suspicious - you know, him disappearing an' all. Nothing up in Tarbert last night. People know him because he goes in and out on his boat, but nothing new. Nobody's seen him since our last witness."

"You know him better than me, Archie. You must have come across him on your travels down here - no?"

"Yes and no, sir," he cleared his throat and moved nervously from foot to foot. "He wasn't exactly welcoming when I went in for a pint when I first came down here. No' really surprising, when you consider what's been going on in there."

"More of that later, Archie," Daley looked rueful. "He seems a bit of a mystery man, our Peter Mulligan."

Scott's head appeared out of the CID office, he spoke through a continuing coughing fit.

"It's some guy called Flynn tae speak tae you, Jim" - cough – "says he's the harbour master" - cough – "are you fir taking it, or do ye want me tae deal wi' it? Mornin' son," he turned to Fraser, "that's one hell o' a tie." He burst into another paroxysm of recalcitrant phlegm.

"Look after this man, Archie, while I attend to our caller - and bring in the coffee, will you?" he shouted over his shoulder.

Daley picked up the receiver from Scott's desk, "Good Morning, Mr Flynn, Jim Daley, how can I help you?"

"Aye gid morn' *Chief* Inspector, I hear congratulations are in order."

"Thank you, Mr Flynn - a surprise to us all let me assure you," he fell silent, hoping that Flynn had something more to say.

"Oh aye, tae the point, Chief Inspector, tae the point. I thought I wid let you know, there's been a report of a pleasure boat adrift in the sound, a passing yachtsman called it in to Clyde Coastguard a few minutes ago. If the identification number and description are correct, it's a boat belonging to a local man," his voice became hesitant.

"Very interesting, Mr Flynn, and I thank you for letting me know - but I don't see how this affects me - at the moment, at any rate?"

"Oh well, the cruiser, it belongs to a man named Mulligan -

Peter Mulligan. It's just - well you must have an idea what Kinloch is like now - I had heard you were looking for him."

Daley took a few moments to assimilate the information. "So, what do we do now, Mr Flynn? I take it this vessel will have to be checked out? Obviously I am interested..." He let Flynn outline procedure.

"The local lifeboat has been mobilised, Chief Inspector - would you like to have a police presence aboard? She'll be underway shortly."

"Oh yes, Mr Flynn - in fact, ask them to give us five minutes. Will there be room for three?"

"Aye, aye I shouldna' think that'll be a bother. I'll speak tae the Coxswain noo. See yiz shortly."

The door swung open as Scott and Fraser made their way through from the drinks machine.

"Sorry, chaps, I hope you have your sea legs on this morning. We're going for a sail, and we've got to rush."

"Eh, sail - whit are you on aboot noo?"

"C'mon, Brian. The very thing for a hangover."

The beverages were placed untouched on the desk as the three left the office for the harbour, Scott muttering a string of impressive oaths on the way.

The scene on Kinloch's second pier was one of organised chaos. Men in bright orange RNLI survival suits darted to and fro' with ropes, lifesaving equipment, unnamed boxes, and various pieces of technical equipment. The deep throb of a powerful diesel engine added tempo to the scene; even blocking out the omnipotent cries of the many gulls that gravitated to the harbour in search of provender from the meagre assembly of fishing boats.

Flynn was standing by the lifeboat on the quayside as the three detectives pulled up in the unmarked car; he was wearing a robust looking fleece with *Harbour Master* emblazoned in bold, gold lettering, over his chest.

"Gentlemen, gid morning. Yooz have picked a fine day for a sail. Hang on there, and I'll introduce you tae the coxswain o' this fine vessel."

Daley recalled how thick his accent was, and just how neat the harbour master was too; the white of his cap contrasting sharply with the gloom that had now descended over Kinloch, despite the continuing strength of the strong breeze.

He noticed also that Scott looked a pale grey colour, as he stared over the side of the quay onto the loch below; itself a more dark, impenetrable shade than in the last couple of days.

"All right, Bri? You're looking a bit green about the gills there," he slapped his old colleague vigorously on the back, inducing another coughing fit in the Detective Sergeant.

"Are ye sure you need me here, Jim? I mean, I'm sure I can be better employed back at the ranch - you know - cover for you?"

"No, don't worry, Brian. Just enjoy the trip. I've got a feeling about this."

"Well, if you're sure, boss," Scott said, whilst looking doubtfully at the restless water of the loch.

Fraser was on the phone to one of the DCs who comprised the day-shift investigating team. They were busy ploughing through the mountain of records, interview statements, CCTV footage and further, nebulous strands of the investigation which had - as yet - yielded little positive information. The young DC had been assured by one of the lifeboat crew that they were unlikely to lose mobile signal on this trip, and in any event, they could be contacted via the boat's radio system, or internet comms link should anything vital arise.

He felt a bit foolish. When Daley had asked him questions as to the character of locals, he had not been able to be much help. He clearly wasn't paying enough heed to the surroundings he found himself in. Sometimes Fraser felt that Inspector MacLeod was not merely torturing him with jibes about being hopeless and unsuited to his current position; perhaps he did lack the intuitive qualities necessary to be an effective CID Officer. He banished this from his mind, as he walked over to the DCI and appraised him of the status quo back at the station.

Scott eyed the whole situation with something more than

trepidation. He had drunk much more than was good for him the night before which was not an unusual occurrence. However, he was more used to assuaging his hangover with a greasy fry-up, followed by a couple of pints of coffee; certainly not taking to the high seas, an element on which he had never been comfortable. He knew enough about the sea to realise that the agitated quality of the waves here in the harbour were likely to be superseded by much less tranquil waters when they reached the sound. He stroked the stubble on his chin as a seagull, swooping low over the assembled throng, deposited a large watery shit on the shoulder of his jacket.

He turned to his colleagues, who were already in the first throes of mirth. "If any of yooz says this is lucky, I'll stick my toe up yer arse." Moments later he saw the funny side himself, laughed and strengthened his resolve ahead of his impending nautical odyssey.

A rotund, ruddy-faced man appeared, sporting the grey and orange RNLI survival suit, augmented by a peaked officer's cap, similar to that worn by Flynn, though adorned by the RNLI insignia, as opposed to an anchor and chains.

"This is John Campbell, coxswain of this fine vessel," Flynn was effusive. "Born on the seventh wave – eh, Johnnie?"

Ignoring this warm introduction, Campbell held out his hand. "Which one of you is DCI Daley?" They shook hands and swapped introductions, Scott somewhat less enthusiastically than his superior. "Ah, young Fraser - I hope you're still working on your court technique - poor effort the last time we met, don't you think?"

Both Daley and Scott looked confused, Fraser explained: "As well as being lifeboat coxswain, Mr Campbell is also a local lawyer."

"C'mon old chap - Managing Partner of Campbell, Hope and Mason - Solicitors, Notaries Public and Estate agents. Though since the demise of poor Stuart - Mason that is - the property side of our business is sadly on the wane. Now would you chaps slip on these waterproofs and lifejackets - he indicated to a crew member carrying an armful of garments - and we'll make haste to sea, don't you think?" With that he breezed off, shouting a request to another member of the crew, who hurried off to do his master's bidding.

"I'd expected some auld sea-dog tae be daein' the job; this guy's mair like a coxcomb than a coxswain." Scott was clearly unimpressed.

"You know, you never cease to amaze me," Daley addressed his DS who was still trying to remove the bird dropping from his jacket with a piece of white serviette, the name *County Hotel* emblazoned upon it. "For a man who never reads a book, where do you find words like coxcomb?"

"Well that, Jim, would be telling." Scott winked.

Flynn, clearly put out by Campbell's dismissive attitude towards him spoke up. "Aye, in days gone by, the lifeboat wiz manned by fishermen. Usually the auldest skipper got the job o' coxswain. Generations o' families served afore the mast. No' noo," his face spoke volumes. "As ye know, there's precious few fishermen left, and o' those that are, wid rather be in the pub during their spare time than hanging aboot, on-call, for the lifeboat. Peety, really." He stared into space wistfully.

"Whit next - lawyers taking tae the sea? I'll tell you this, I've never been impressed wi' a solicitor in my life. I hope he knows whit the fuck he's daein'?" Scott's question was querulous.

"Oh aye, he knows whoot he's daein' a'right, he's an officer in the RNR tae. The Royal Naval Reserve," he answered their blank looks at the acronym. "The trouble is, nooadays being on the lifeboat's mair o' a middle-class thing; lake a badge o' honour. A' these posh buggers have yachts, an' they're a' jostling fir a place on the boat. Wan o' the toon's ither solicitors is involved tae, he's the deputy cox. But believe it, or believe it no', they'll no' sail on the boat thegether. It's a wile carry-on right enough." He shook his head in apparent disbelief.

"Right, gentlemen - let's be having you - on and out, on and out." Campbell was bellowing from the open bridge of the vessel.

"I'm no' goin' tae enjoy this one bit." Flynn was helping Scott clip his lifejacket on as Daley and Fraser bounded up the iron gang-plank. "Na', no' in the slightest."

The bridge of the lifeboat was much more high-tech than Daley had expected. Two black seats with high backs, that wouldn't have been out of place on the space shuttle, dominated the front of the cabin, with its windows - complete with large windscreen wipers - facing straight ahead. An impossible array of dials, levers, LED readout screens - large and small - along with two oversized computer monitors, faced John Campbell and his deputy, who were - Daley assumed - responsible for steering the boat. Behind them, on a lower seat facing the side of the craft sat another crew member, staring at a huge monitor, which to Daley's untrained eye, was displaying similar geographical notation to that he had seen in the harbour master's office.

The three police officers, thoroughly out of their comfort zone, held on - somewhat unsteadily it must be said - to chunky, black handrails, which were dotted randomly around the bridge. Other members of the crew moved about the vessel with the easy gait of those accustomed to the rolling, undulating nature of sea craft.

"As you can appreciate, gentlemen," the coxswain's voice was amplified via loudspeakers built into the bridge, "we are unable to ramp up the power until we're out of the harbour area and clear of the loch. As soon as we pass the island there," he gestured airily with one hand; "we will be able to take her up to forty knots plus." he smiled to himself.

"Aye, just fantastic." Scott mumbled; his face was now bordering on a shade under lime green.

Daley leant forward, peering out of the bridge windows; the island at the mouth of the loch looked like an oversized bread roll. He could see that the water beyond looked choppier, and suppressed a smile as he sneaked a look at his DS, who was clinging manfully to his hand rail.

"Now, from the position reported earlier this morning," Campbell's voice boomed out from the loudspeakers, "I reckon that it will take us around thirty minutes to locate the craft. I must warn you that the weather is deteriorating somewhat, and once we get beyond the island, it might get a tad rough, so I may have to ask you to take a seat and get strapped in. I'll see how we go."

They were now level with the island. Daley could see what he thought was a sheep grazing halfway up what appeared to be a sheer cliff; he shouted to Campbell.

"Too much time spent in the city, my good man. That sheep's a mountain goat. Ancient beasts you know; probably introduced to this area by the first hunter-gatherers; fascinating - run wild now of course. Ah - hang on chaps - tally ho!"

Campbell pushed a large lever located in front of him. The tone of the engines changed, indeed, they could now be felt through the steel floor of the vessel; the prow of the lifeboat rose into the air as the trim altered, and they began to pick up speed more rapidly than Daley thought possible at sea. Of course, his experience of the ocean was mainly confined to the Clyde steamers of his childhood, plus the odd channel ferry, or trip on Mark's sailing yacht; the feeling now was much more exhilarating, even though the boat was now bouncing through the waves, shaking up those onboard like ice in a cocktail shaker.

He saw Campbell lean over to the man beside him, who began to unbuckle his seatbelt.

"As I expected, the swell here's a bit lively - Gareth here will help you into the chairs behind you, and get you strapped in. The last thing I need is a lifeboat full of injured bobbies."

The shorn-haired crew member helped them into the seats located just behind the bridge in a wide corridor. As he strapped Scott in, Daley noticed the DS whisper in the ear of the life boat man, who smiled and disappeared, only to return a few moments later with something that looked like a small cardboard potty, the type which would be provided for elderly patients in hospital.

Scott contemplated the receptacle for a few seconds, then retched copiously into it, splashes of vomit dotting his orange lifejacket.

Fraser, sitting next to him, wrinkled his nose in obvious distaste, leaning away from the stricken detective, in case he too benefited from the return of last night's over-indulgence. The smell of stale alcohol suddenly filled the vessel.

"Fuck this," seemed an adequate summation of events as far as Scott was concerned, as he wiped his face with a large paper hankie provided by the attentive Gareth.

"You all right, mate?" Gareth's English accent was discernible through the general hubbub.

"I'll tell you when I'm back in Paisley, son," was the pallid policeman's reply.

The engines suddenly quietened, and the lifeboat slowed perceptibly. Daley turned in his harness - as much as was possible - looking towards the bridge; Campbell was unbuckling his ample seat belt.

"Unscheduled stop, gentlemen." He said as an aside to the three trussed Policemen. "Have you met Hamish, our local seer?"

"Oh, yes," Daley nodded vigorously, "I don't understand, what does he have to do with all this?"

"He's just waved us down - so to speak. I'm just going to have a word with him; he's got a day-sailing working boat, keeps his hand in with crabs, shellfish and the like. Do you want to come up top and see what he wants? It won't take long - he's a good old buffer - knows much more than people think."

"Of that I have no doubt," Daley was struggling to unfasten his belt. "I'll come with you."

Scott was rubbing his forehead with his left hand, still looking deathly. "If yooz don't mind, I'll jist stay here an' try and stop my small intestine from ending up in a bucket."

"I'm OK, sir," Fraser was still keeping a reasonable distance between himself and the DS. "I don't want to abandon a colleague in his time of need."

The DCI released himself from the bonds of his safety belt, and followed Campbell up a small gang-plank and out onto the deck. Light drizzle brushed his face, the sea was a deep grey colour, and he could see a bank of darker sky to his left, just above the horizon. The water lapped noisily against the sides of the lifeboat, as a much smaller vessel chugged slowly towards them amidst a blue pall of diesel fumes; it looked like a large rowing boat, onto which a square-built wooden cabin had been incongruously grafted, the registration number KH 213, was painted in peeling black letters on the prow of the craft. Hamish's head popped up from above the cabin canopy, his tanned face distinctive under a well-used Breton cap.

"Ahoy there, Hamish!" Campbell shouted from the bow of the lifeboat; "what can we do for you?"

The engine fumes from the venerable vessel caught Daley in the back of the throat, and momentarily he thought he might retch - he swallowed and took a deep breath, allowing the nausea to pass. The sensation of movement on the lifeboat was much more pronounced than he had experienced at sea hitherto, and he was glad that Liz's presence in the County the previous evening ensured that he hadn't over indulged.

Hamish threw a coil of rope at the lifeboat, which Campbell caught in the casual manner of the accustomed sailor.

"Mornin' Meester Campbell, Chief Inspector; how'yiz daein'?"

"Fine, Hamish, fine," Daley noticed how Campbell, despite being a Scot, pronounced the name with a flat vowel, in the way of the Scottish upper-classes; an unconscious imitation of their social peers south of the border. "More importantly, what can we do for you, old chap?"

For a heartbeat Daley thought that the old fisherman wasn't going to answer, indeed, he wondered if he had heard the coxswain. Slowly though, he turned his head, and seemed to be sniffing the air.

"Aye - there something' no' right, Meester Campbell; can ye no' smell the taint in the air?"

Campbell raised his head, as though he too was about to carry out an olfactory assessment of the gloomy morning; he stopped though, thinking better of it.

"What do you mean, Hamish? None of this mystic stuff. Have you seen something? We're here to find a small cabin cruiser that's been reported to be drifting unmanned off Thomson's point - have you spotted it at all?" The enquiry was kindly put, but emphatic.

"No, no, canna say that I have; but ye don't need tae see the moon tae know It's there - dae ye noo?" Hamish flashed the huge, beaming smile that Daley had first noticed in the harbour master's office.

"Eh - what do you mean exactly?" Campbell looked confused.

"It's a black day, that's a' I'm saying; ye can feel it in the air," he raised his head and sniffed, as though illustrating the point. "Aye, an' the weather's fair comin' in tae." He turned to Daley. "I'm wulling tae bet you'd still rather be cuddled up tae that lovely wife o' yours in bed - eh, Chief Inspector?"

Daley was stuck for words; however, Campbell saved the day. "Well, we have to get on Hamish, and judging by that sky and the weather report we've just taken off the satellite, you would be well advised to head back to Kinloch now - I don't want to be diverted to come and rescue you - what?"

Daley-who admittedly had little knowledge of the sea-borne etiquette - thought Campbell was being a little high-handed. However, he should have realised that the old man would have a response to this.

"I've spent mair time on the wan wave than you have experience on the sea; aye an' I don't need any fancy statalite neither," he was clearly annoyed.

"I will leave you to be the judge of that, but don't say I didn't warn you. Come on, Chief Inspector, we'll get back under way, and leave this old sea-dog to his tricks." Campbell waved perfunctorily at Hamish and stomped off towards the bridge, with Daley following in his wake. The detective turned round to bid Hamish a farewell - the old man was standing proud at the wheelhouse of the small boat, his hand raised in a one-finger salute.

"No' you, meester Daley. No, no' for you."

Daley was being strapped back into his seat as he heard the loud chug of Hamish's boat, as he sailed away from the lifeboat and towards Kinloch.

Their vessel was soon ploughing through the waves; from what Daley could see through the bridge windows, heavy rain had started to fall, and the yawing motion of the boat indicated that the sea was much more restless than it had been when they left Kinloch harbour.

Presently, Campbell's voice came, loud over the intercom. "By my reckoning, gents, it will take us about another ten minutes to reach the last known location of the vessel we are looking for - however, such is the fickle nature of time and tide, we are already on the lookout for her. As soon as we find anything, I'll give you a shout, and then you three will come into your own, so to speak."

Scott shouted over to Daley, "I wisna expecting tae be chasing the wreck o' the Hesperus when I got up this morn," he still looked bilious. "First that fuckin' press conference yesterday, noo this - it's a bit like that Japanese game show; you know the one where they stick scorpions doon their troosers and suchlike. Aye an' before you get any ideas, you're no' pitting any dangerous insects anywhere near me, never mind my troosers."

Their collective mirth was stopped in its tracks by a sudden slowing of the engines and Campbell's voice over the tannoy. "Gentlemen, we have reached our objective."

Daley, now used to the workings of his seat harness, managed to release himself, and walked forward to the bridge of the lifeboat, where Campbell had a radio microphone to his mouth. "Vessel, Russian Gold, this is Kinloch lifeboat - is there anyone aboard?"

Daley could see no movement on the vessel - a small cabin cruiser - he looked at the coxswain, who tried again.

"Russian Gold, if you can hear me please show yourselves. We are making ourselves fast to your port side, and will board unless we receive confirmation that all is well, and that your vessel is appropriately manned - over."

Again, nothing. Daley gave Campbell a questioning look.

"OK, Chief Inspector, we have fulfilled our legal obligations; there is no response from the vessel and we are now at liberty to board, as I feel that she may be a hazard to other shipping. Charlie, signal my intent to Clyde Coastguard, please." His crew-mate busied himself on the radio, while Campbell extricated his considerable bulk from his seat.

"So, how do you want us to proceed, Mr Campbell? This is still your domain after all. Though I would ask you and your crew to disturb as little on or in the boat as possible, in case it turns out to be a crime scene."

"Of course, of course," Campbell sounded somewhat impatient. "By the same token, I must ask you and your officers to follow my instructions as far as gaining this vessel is concerned. We'll get you some more suitable footwear for a start."

The ever-helpful Gareth appeared with what could best be described as a selection of bright yellow Wellington boots, all of which had a sturdy variegated sole designed to afford grip on the decks of rain-slicked boats. The three officers picked out the most appropriate sizes, donned the boots, and followed Campbell out on deck.

The sky was a lowering grey, and although the sea was not showing itself in angry breakers, the swell was making the thin line of the horizon skew in an alarming way. A light drizzle had already coated their waterproofs; Scott's hair had been pushed back from his face, and was now standing in salt and pepper spikes from his head, Fraser was looking at the grey water between the two vessels, as three lifeboat men - one of them now on the deck of 'Russian Gold' - secured ropes between the lifeboat and the cabin cruiser.

"I would prefer if I took the lead, Chief Inspector - I am technically in charge of both vessels - unless, of course, something happens that should ensure that I relinquish that charge. The lads will secure both vessels as soundly as possible, however, I should warn you all that getting down onto her deck will be tricky in these conditions. Are we good to go, gents?" He looked at the three detectives, who showed various degrees of acknowledgement, Scott - unsurprisingly - looking the least willing.

The main problem was that the cabin cruiser was a much smaller vessel than the lifeboat, which meant that each man would have to be lowered from boat to boat, as well as across a gap which - regardless of how well the lifeboat crew had made their lines - changed in width and height quite rapidly.

Campbell explained: "I'm afraid that we can't lash her right to our side, as we'll end up doing damage to both vessels - do you follow?"

Daley nodded.

"What I recommend is that you watch me, and then try to replicate what I do." With that he made his way to the lifeboat's safety rail, stiffly hefted his left leg over its short height while leaning on a stanchion, then with equal lack of poise, repeated the process with his right leg.

"Now," Campbell said hesitantly, as he stared at the gap with obvious concentration, perched on the narrow ledge between the safety rail and oblivion. "One judges the pitch and roll," he leant forward, hand outstretched towards the grim-faced lifeboat man below, "and... off!" He jumped clear of the lifeboat, whilst making a desperate attempt to grab the hand of his crew-mate below.

Unfortunately, he had misjudged his jump, the rapidly rising swell having propelled the smaller vessel upwards, towards him more quickly than he had anticipated. Despite the valiant attempts of his colleague to arrest the fall, Campbell's large bulk hurtled onto him with some force, ending with both lifeboat men writhing on the deck clutching various parts of their anatomy, to many grunts and oaths.

"Fuck me," Scott eyed the scene with a furrowed brow, "I'm no' in a hurry to replicate that - if that's the best he can dae, how the fuck am I goin' tae manage?"

"Are you OK, Mr Campbell?" Daley enquired of the stricken coxswain, who was now being helped to his feet by his unfortunate crew-mate.

"Ah - harrumph," he brushed himself down. "Well, you get the general idea - who's next?" He looked up at the policemen.

Jim Daley was not one to shirk the responsibilities of rank, so he stepped over the rail, positioned himself on the ledge, and looked down at the ever-changing gap; it reminded him of the 'penny-falls' he had played at the fair when he was young. Trying to calculate the optimum time to insert a two pence coin in order that it would fall at the back of the pile, prompting the outpouring of financial reward. He had always been quite good at that. He held his hand out towards the crewman and took the leap of faith.

Daley had always prided himself - despite his size - on being relatively graceful; he was a good dancer and golfer, and motor skills picked up during these pursuits saw him land, two-footed onto the deck, while at the same time gripping onto the proffered hand of the lifeboat man. He breathed out in silent relief.

Fraser managed the jump with some aplomb, judging the rise and fall of the vessels relative to each other perfectly; he landed on deck sure-footedly, barely requiring the assistance of the crewman.

Next, Scott: Daley caught him muttering something about Fraser being more like Rudolph Nureyev, as he concentrated on the job in hand.

"Are yooz ready?" he turned to Gareth, who was giving advice at his side; and then, without warning, he jumped - not the exaggerated stride that the others had executed with varying degrees of success, but a full blown spring - head first - towards the smaller boat.

He landed - probably somewhat fortuitously - on the large bulk of the coxswain, and for the second time in a couple of minutes, the corpulent solicitor struggled on the deck of the cruiser, Scott on top of him muttering a sentence devoid of anything but expletives.

"Well done, Detective Sergeant Scott; you reminded me a bit of a Rangers striker there - beautiful dive."

Campbell, now back on his feet again, gave the remaining crew on the lifeboat the thumbs up, and started surveying the deck of the cabin cruiser. "Typical of its class, Chief Inspector. This is the flying bridge, so to speak," he gestured at a level above the main deck, which housed a large wheel, and was bordered on three sides by a slanted windscreen, giving it the look of an expensive open-top sports car.

"Now here," he pointed at a low door located on the base of the bridge, "is the access to the lower cabins - heads, bunks, galley - that sort of thing." He pushed at the door with the toe of his sea-boot; it swung open with a high pitched squeak, to reveal a precipitous set of steps with a handrail on both sides leading to the inner cabin, which was out of sight.

"Be my guest, officers," Campbell made a sweeping gesture with his outstretched hand, as though showing them into his own home.

Daley grabbed the rails and gingerly lowered himself down the steps, the unfamiliar sea-boots making his descent difficult. Already though, a sixth sense - brought on, no doubt, by years of police work, was telling him all was far from well.

A few steps on, he realised why.

The body of a woman was slumped forward on hands and knees over a table which was - in nautical fashion - secured to the floor. The corpse was kneeling on an upholstered bench that served as a dining chair, and was also screwed down. She was naked apart from a bra, which had been torn in two, but still hung from her shoulders by its straps. Daley noticed her hair was tied back in a pony tail with a thick, white bobble.

The cause of death was sickeningly obvious. The handle of a stout, wooden walking stick protruded from her anus, and had been inserted there with such force, that a huge amount of darkening, congealed blood was visible down the backside and legs of the victim, and also in pools on the bench and the cabin floor below. At a rough estimate, Daley reckoned that the walking stick had been forced almost two feet into the body of the dead woman.

"Only police officers down here, please," Daley shouted. He didn't want Campbell and the crewman to see, or trample over the gruesome scene with their big sea-boots.

"Have you found something...what the fuck?" The familiar

voice of Scott; now just behind his boss.

"Careful Bri - Archie, come down here, will you?" the DC was descending the stairs.

Fraser looked at the woman's body, and then he and Daley edged around the pool of blood on the floor to look at her face. Her head was left-side down on the Formica table, her eyes were wide open in an expression of abject horror, more dark thick blood issued from her mouth and pooled on the table.

"Sir, that's Janet Ritchie." Fraser was as white as a ghost.

"Are you sure, son?"

"Yes, no doubt." He turned away from the scene, desperately trying to swallow down the gag reflex.

"Go back up and get yourself a breath of air," Daley nodded to the DC. "See if you can get a mobile signal and let me know. Don't tell our lifeboat friends anything right now, or news of this will be back in Kinloch before we've had a chance to speak to the office. OK, on you go." He watched Fraser make his way back up top.

"Fuck, Jim, some mess," even Scott - the hardened detective - was shocked by the level of violence on display.

"I've a feeling there's more, come on, Brian." The two Detectives walked towards a slim wooden door, set in a wood-effect wall. Daley took a hankie from his pocket, and turned the handle.

They found themselves in the sleeping cabin. On a double bed with raised, wooden sides, lay the body of a man, stripped to the waist. His left arm had blackened as a tourniquet had been applied just above his elbow; a large hypodermic syringe was still attached to his forearm, its needle thrust deep into the darkening flesh. Peter Mulligan.

It was not the first time either of the officers had attended a heroin overdose victim: the man's bowels had voided, and his head lay in a pool of his own vomit; the normal physical manifestations of a body, desperately attempting to rid itself of the poison destroying it - in this case - to no avail. A raw, black gash ran along the neck of the victim. The corpse had clearly been decapitated,

172

then the severed head put back in place, as a macabre resolution.

"It doesna' get any prettier, Jim," Scott held his hand over his nose, "what are these marks?" He pointed to two marks on the victim's chest, where the man's chest hair had been singed away, leaving small, brown burns to the skin.

"Taser," Daley bent down low over the victim, without touching the cadaver. "He's been tasered. I was at a tactical weapons course a few months ago - they asked for volunteers; you know that bastard Phil Anderson from the Crime Squad?"

"Aye, that prick."

"Well, they asked for volunteers, so he stuck up his hand and they tasered him. After he recovered - which by the way took the rest of the day - he had two wee marks exactly the same as this on his stomach where the electrodes had attached themselves. Our man here's been tasered, then the overdose has been administered; I'll take any bets on it."

Scott peered over the corpse. "They're no' long deid - either o' them. Whit dae you reckon, Jim - a few hours, eh?"

"Something like that; late last night maybe." He stood up, almost hitting his head off the low cabin ceiling. "We'll have to get forensics down here pronto, and secure the crime scene. How the fuck do we do that out here?"

"Can these bastards in the launch sail oot the Clyde? I've never heard aboot it if they have."

"I'll have to get a hold of the supreme leader - he's going to love this. Give Fraser a shout, Bri; see if he's managed to get a mobile signal."

Scott ascended the steps cannily, only to be met by coxswain Campbell at the top.

"Just what's going on, Sergeant? - this boy won't tell us anything. I have a right to know; after all I'm still in charge of this little party. So come on, spill the beans. If its legal consequences you're worried about? - remember I'm a lawyer."

Scott looked at him unimpressed, "The *boy* you are referring to is a detective constable, and your being in charge has just come tae an' end. Have you got a signal, Archie?" He called over to

Fraser, who, still looking green, was making his way towards them from the stern.

"Aye comes and goes a bit, but it'll do."

"I have a satellite comms link back on board - you can use that, but first you must tell me what the fuck's happening." Campbell was doing his best to sound emphatic.

"This boat's noo a murder scene," Scott suddenly looked weary. "For the time being however, I don't want anyone from your lifeboat phoning hame tae tell the missus - is that clear? The Chief Inspector will take charge from here," Scott looked to the heavens, the weather was deteriorating, his face was already soaking and the cabin cruiser was beginning to pitch and roll alarmingly, despite now being tethered at both bow and stern to the much larger lifeboat. "What's the likely forecast, Mr Campbell?"

"Grim, Sergeant. I've just had an alert from Clyde Coastguard - we've got a storm warning. I strongly advise we tow this vessel back to Kinloch before it becomes a Herculean task. Do you understand?"

Scott went back below.

"The weather's getting bad, yer man says we've got a storm on the way, he's advising us tae head back tae Kinloch wae this little boat o' horrors in tow. What dae ye think, boss?"

Daley thought for a moment. It was unlikely that there would be anything to be gained by maintaining the vessel in her current location; even from his limited knowledge of these matters, he realised that evidence would be placed at risk with a storm brewing.

"OK, Brian, tell him to make arrangements to tow us in as soon as possible. I'll need to get a hold of Donald, and we'll have to get Flynn to find us a berth somewhere on the harbour where the whole of Kinloch can't see what's going on. We'll have to have somebody down here for the duration too." Daley was working through the processes.

"Young Archie says he's got an intermittent signal on the blower; Campbell's got a satellite phone." Scott shrugged. "Your

174

call, James."

He chose the satellite phone on the lifeboat, and after another undignified scramble from one vessel to another, made the relevant calls.

Flynn, back in Kinloch, assured him that *Russian Gold* would be away from prying eyes on the second pier where the lifeboat itself was moored, though on the other side of the construction, near to its end, which was closed off to the public for health and safety reasons. The harbour master told him that the Royal Navy sometimes used that berthing for dignitaries coming ashore from warships moored further out in the loch. There was nothing structurally wrong with the quay and the health and safety notice was merely a ploy. *Anything to keep the locals at bay,* the dapper harbour master clearly had hidden depths. He also promised to provide plastic sheeting with which to cover the boat, helping to preserve the crime scene.

With that in mind, Daley, having failed to get a hold of Donald despite numerous attempts, alerted the forensic department; they were going to send a helicopter to Kinloch within a four hour window.

As an afterthought, he contacted the PR department; after the disastrous press conference, he would have to grasp the nettle and face the cameras himself. The brutality of these killings, plus the link with the existing enquiry, would ensure that this would be a national story.

He rubbed his eyes wearily; he was still standing on the lifeboat bridge, while her crew prepared to tow *Russian Gold* back to Kinloch. The sea was swollen, but steady. The storm that Campbell had predicted had not materialised, though the sky to the west looked dark and foreboding; not unlike the detective's mood.

One murder could be anything: a personal vendetta, revenge of a cuckolded partner - or, as was often the case - pure bad luck on behalf of the victim; being caught up in a whirl of fatal circumstances, without premeditation. The brutal killing of three people with close personal ties was another beast entirely. Ritchie and Mulligan had not just been killed, they had been slaughtered. It was not impossible that sex had been the motivation, however, even in this sordid world, the level of violence shown in these murders was exceptional.

There was also a cold, clean, professional feel to what had taken place on the boat, which chilled Daley to the core. These murders could be the work of one, very sick individual, or clear warnings sent out by organised crime; signals that did not require too much interpretation. The connections to drugs and the underworld were already there.

"OK, Chief Inspector, we're ready to get under way," Campbell was at his side. "Let's hope the weather holds." He gave a few orders, and the deep throb of the powerful engines trembled back into life through the deck onto the edge of hearing.

14

"Can you tell us how the couple on the boat died, Chief Inspector?" The reporter held a large microphone to his face, with what looked like a dead hamster affixed to the end.

"No comment, at the moment." Daley was flustered, and not just by the reporters that swarmed around him as though he was a hunted celebrity. No, he was furious that within an hour of their arrival at Kinloch with the cruiser *Russian Gold*, the press had begun to descend on the town's police station. Someone had talked. The reporters were all aware that two bodies had been found on the vessel, and they were pressing Daley to confirm that they were those of Janet Ritchie and Peter Mulligan; which - because he had not had the chance to contact the next of kin - he steadfastly refused to do.

To make matters worse, Superintendent Donald was on his way, alongside a Senior PR Consultant. At least, Daley reasoned, Donald would - in his usual fashion - attract the attention of the press like bees to honey.

Because of the unwanted media attention, they had been forced to close the large gate which guarded the rear car park at the station. The gate creaked open enough to allow Daley and Scott entry, leaving the three constables who had the unenviable task of closing it again, to their business.

"Bunch o' bastards," Scott intoned just within earshot of the reporters. "Some bugger on that lifeboat must have spilt the beans. My money's on that pompous arsehole Campbell - what d'you think?"

"I'll set our beloved leader on him; that'll give him something to get his teeth into, and keep him out of our hair." Yet again, he hadn't had the time to have anything to eat since breakfast, and his stomach was groaning balefully; lunch time had come and gone.

"I'll be trying tae stay oota' his way efter that press conference yesterday; it seems like a hundred years ago now." Scott looked reflective as Daley punched the security code into the door entry system.

"Sir," a young constable met them inside. "Inspector MacLeod is inside asking for you - he's – well, quite upset."

Daley winced at the questioning intonation. "Where is he, son?"

"He's in his own office - demanding to see you the minute you get in."

"Tell him tae stick it up his arse," Scott spat out at the suggestion.

"No, it's OK; I'll go and see him in a minute. Tell him I'm on my way, son, will you?" Daley turned to his DS. "Remember, Brian, Janet Ritchie was his daughter."

Daley knocked at MacLeod's door, and turned the handle. Scott was right, it did seem much longer since he had first met the odious little Inspector; in reality it was only two days.

MacLeod was sitting behind his desk, his uniform replaced by a garish golfing jumper, replete with a large diamond pattern on a pink background; he looked tired and drawn, and had none of the brash confidence so evident when they first met.

"I'm sorry, Charles, I've not had a minute since…"

"It doesn't matter - not now. Lord knows, she was hardly without sin herself." His sing-song highland accent was strong. "Did you know, Chief Inspector, my father was a minister in the Free Church?"

"No, I didn't."

"He was ashamed enough of me," he looked directly at Daley. "I drank, smoked, liked women; all of the things he hated most. I had to get away from him and his moralising. That's why I joined the police." He looked out of the window, down onto Kinloch's main street.

"He died fifteen years ago. I wasn't there, in fact I had only seen him a few times since I joined up; but he left me a letter." He opened one of the drawers in his desk, and took out a pale blue sheet of paper covered in what looked like faded fountain-pen ink. "Aye, no wonder you're looking. One page; one page from my dying father." He put on his glasses and started to read.

"You have been an affront to me, to my church, and to my beliefs. Mark my words, as ye sow, so shall ye reap. You too, Charles will feel the shame that I have felt - and the pain. You are, and have always been, a wicked man. May the Lord forgive you." He looked up, removing his glasses. "Not much of a goodbye - eh?" there were tears in his eyes. "I wondered for years what he could mean: when I met my dear daughter, I knew." He looked back at the desk, a shrunken figure, his tears falling on the bitter epistle sent by his dying father; his only daughter brutally murdered, in the place he thought of as a personal dominion.

Daley stayed silent for a few moments, not least as he didn't know what to say. "I'm sorry," was all that eventually seemed appropriate. He knew that he would soon have to tell the broken man in front of him of the horror involved in his daughter's death; for now though, he decided to leave it. He got up to go; to leave MacLeod alone with his thoughts.

"If you could indulge me for a short while longer, Chief Inspector. I know you are a busy man, but I have something to say that you need to know," he rubbed his eyes with the forefinger and thumb of his right hand. "Janet and Mulligan were involved in the supply of drugs. Even though I turned a blind eye as you know, I still investigated the matter; quietly, so to speak. I know what you're thinking," he was responding to an incredulous look from Daley, "but please, hear me out."

"OK," Daley sighed heavily. "You'll appreciate that I have my Super on his way, as well as a triple murder to solve, with precious little to go on."

MacLeod nodded his head. "The drugs were coming from the

Baltic states - on a fishing boat from Latvia, to be precise."

"Hence, *Russian Gold*?"

"Aye just so, just so. The pattern was regular: Mulligan knew I was getting wise to him, so he berthed the boat at Tarbert - sailed from there. Then the Latvians got a taste for the high-life. They started to come into port themselves - drink and women - you know." MacLeod stood. "I may have been misguided, but I did what I did for all of the right reasons; in my head at any rate."

Daley again found it hard to feel angry with the Inspector. He cast a pathetic figure. "You must know that Donald will destroy you for this?"

MacLeod nodded absently. "No pension, no job - who knows, maybe even a spell inside? Shame, affront and pain. Do you see? My father was spot on." He paused, "The boat - from Latvia, it's due in tonight, well the early hours of tomorrow morning. I've checked with Flynn, the harbour master. She's called *Koba*; but be careful, Chief Inspector, from what I know about these men, they are ruthless, ex Russian military and KGB. For them, fishing is merely a hobby."

Daley stood, "I don't suppose you'll tell me how long you've known this?"

"You suppose right. Here, take this, I'll not be needing it." He threw his warrant card at Daley, who made no attempt at a catch, stepping over it as he left MacLeod's office.

"I canna believe that man; I mean whit can ye say? He knows aboot the supply o' drugs by the crew o' a foreign fishing boat - aye, intae his ain community - an' he does nathin' aboot it. Do you think he wid have ever taken any action?" Scott looked at Daley in apparent disbelief.

"Who knows, Bri? But I don't think we have to look too far to find out how the purchase of *Pulse* was funded. I've got the forensic accountants coming down to audit everything. It kind of makes sense now - you know - the way his flat was; impersonal, nothing in it; sterile. I very much doubt that our man is even really called Peter Mulligan; there's certainly nothing to identify him in his effects."

The two fell silent for a few moments. The case was proving far more complex than they could have ever imagined: they now had three murder victims, investigations into prostitution, illegal drug-taking and possession; and - if that was not enough - international drug trafficking. Daley was sure that false accounting and money laundering would be added to that list once the accountants had done their work.

Needless to say, any chance that Daley could cover for MacLeod was now impossible. The Inspector would be lucky to keep his liberty, never mind his job. He knew he would have to be straight with Donald, whose arrival was imminent.

"So run it past me again, Jimmy. We're going efter these Ruskies tonight -right?"

"We've got the drug boys and tactical firearms en route; but we're still leading. Any of this could compromise the murder enquiries; they still take priority."

"Whit if His Highness decides different? He might want tae pap this off tae special branch; aye, or take the reins himself."

"Come on, Brian, how long have you known the man?" Daley smiled. "Of course he'll be in notional command, which goes without saying; but he'll never let go of this. It's another brilliant opportunity to shine in a big way. He'll leave us alone too, just in case there's a fuck-up and we end up with nothing. That way he can wash his hands of it and hang me out to dry. If we succeed, he steps in as the guiding light, and before you know it he's an ACC. QED."

"A whit? Anyhow you're right, I dunno whit I wiz thinking aboot; the hangover's still dulling my heid." Scott busied himself tidying his desk. "The last thing I need today is lecture on how 'a tidy desk reflects a tidy mind'. Its OK fir him, he's got a battalion of wee lassies lifting an' laying everything fir him; if you pardon the pun." He picked up a piece of A4 paper, and after squinting over it for a few seconds, rolled it into a tight ball, and despatched it neatly, into a metal wastepaper basket.

Daley looked out of the window and down the Main Street.

The grey skies and rain had given Kinloch an entirely different feel. The tenements now looked grim and foreboding, their dark, slate roofs slick with the downpour, seemed to huddle in on the street itself. Daley had been impressed with the buzz about the town, but with the change of weather, the pavements and road were virtually deserted; only the odd brave soul dashing out from cars to purchase essential items from the shops that lined the street. From where he was sitting, Daley could see a bored looking shop assistant surveying the dismal scene, arms folded, from her position at the window of the large jewellers that was the nearest shop to the police station, which - under the lowering sky - stood like a grim sentinel on the hill overlooking Kinloch.

It was now mid-afternoon. He intended to wait for the arrival of Donald and the drugs and firearms units, and formulate plans for the arrival of the Latvians. Both he and Scott could carry firearms, and he had spoken to the station's armourer - who was also a shift sergeant - who had shown him the small selection of weapons available. They had taken two side arms, and an automatic rifle; Scott having to have his firearm holder's certificate faxed from headquarters, because - as was habitually the case - he was not carrying the document.

Daley picked up his mobile from the desk, and pressed *one* on the speed dial.

"Hi, darling, there seems to be a lot of excitement - you OK?" Liz's voice oozed from the phone.

"I'm sure you know about as much as me. Are you in the hotel?"

"Oh no; Mark arrived an hour or so ago - he's flying back tonight." She paused in time to hear Daley sigh. "Don't worry, darling, I told him I was staying. We're just having lunch. I'll be back at the hotel about four. Is that OK?"

"Sure - sure," Daley hesitated. "Listen, Liz, things are pretty full-on here; maybe you would be better going back up the road - I mean…"

"Don't be silly, Jim, after last night, I'm staying put." He could picture the wicked smile which was at this moment - no doubt -

playing across her face.

Her voice became serious. "I really feel we got somewhere last night - you know - I remembered why I married you - why I love you. Do you understand?"

He felt his heart soar. "Yes, I do understand, and I feel the same. I'll try to make it down to the hotel about five or so. I don't know how long we'll have this evening, but I'll explain it all to you later - OK?"

They said goodbye; and as he put the phone in his jacket pocket, he realised that they had suddenly made progress with their relationship. This was a chance to heal things - amidst all of the chaos. All it had taken was a fading seaside hotel, a murder, and this place - Kinloch. There was indeed, something in the air.

The arrival of Donald was, if anything, more of a virtuoso performance than even Daley had expected. Three cars sped up the rain-swept Main Street of Kinloch; windows blacked out, the front vehicle sporting a flashing, blue police light and warning siren. The Prime Minister could not have made more of a splash.

A splash literally; as the rain and gloom that enveloped the town became ever worse, drenching policemen, the public and press alike. So bad was the downpour, that a press conference, to be held in the early evening, had to be cancelled as the wet weather was playing havoc with the satellite up-links. In short, a feeling of impending doom was all pervasive - well almost.

Superintendent Donald, after the most brief of briefings with his DCI, commandeered the wretched Inspector MacLeod's office, called on the senior sergeant now nominally in charge of the Sub-Division, relieved him of this onerous responsibility, and took full control of both the Sub-Division and the triple murder enquiry, quoting *forces of extreme circumstance,* as legitimacy. A well-groomed, watchful PR man never left his side, whispering into the great man's ear at every opportunity.

Amazingly, one of his first actions was to seek out DS Scott and envelope him in a manly bear-hug. Much mumbling of *don't worry about yesterday,* and *watch a master at work,* followed by a hearty slap on the back, and an assurance that Scott was a pivotal member of the team; and - in a stage aside - *regardless of his deficiencies in PR, and as a human being in general.* This brought a sycophantic outburst of mirth from his PR guru, who reminded Daley of a cross between Tony Blair and Goebbels, such was his slimy mien of slickly disguised threat.

To Daley though, behind the closed door of MacLeod's office, he was less sanguine. With even Goebbels banished, Donald came straight to the point.

"Needless to say, Jim, we have a situation of the utmost seriousness on our hands here," he looked heavenward, hands steepled in front of his face.

Daley actually wondered if he was in fact in prayer, but decided that even the consultation of the Almighty would be deemed unnecessary by his glorious boss.

"A bloody bear-trap for us all." Suddenly the mask was slipping, as he took the back of his hand to a tartan mug bearing the ledged *Clan MacLeod,* propelling it against a wall and breaking it into three neatly proportioned pieces. "That little bastard; as far as I'm concerned, you can take the Highlands and all that's in it, and stick it firmly up his arse - I'll do it personally."

"Here's me thinking that all we have to do is send you down here to solve some dispute amongst the bottom-feeders who inhabit this God-forsaken place, identify the murderer, and bag the plaudits and a little piece of empire at the same time. We'll all soon be working for *The Scottish Police Force*, the way things are going. And a right bun-fight it'll be too," he stared into the middle distance.

"What have we got now? A corrupt senior police officer, an international drug smuggling ring, as well as a brutal, sadistic murderer who takes pleasure in perpetrating the most unimaginable horrors. All life is here; or death, more appropriately." He looked past Daley and out of the window onto the almost post- apocalyptic scene outside. "I can tell you this, James; we better hope we can round up these Lithuanians tonight and tie up all of the strings, or we'll have Special Branch on us like a ton of bricks. The customs and the drugs boys are already getting territorial about all this, to say nothing of the crime squad."

"They're Latvians, sir."

"What?" Donald looked at Daley as though he was surprised by his presence.

"They're from Latvia - the guys on the fishing boat tonight."

"Well, whatever," Donald drew in a deep breath and pursed his lips. "Whether they are Latvians, Lithuanians, or Spanish Hermaphrodites, we'll have to nail their arses to the wall, or we'll be going down the same road Heelan' Laddie's embarking upon, as we speak." Two discipline branch officers had been despatched to interview the disgraced Inspector. "The Ruskies will be at home here at any rate; can't be any grimmer in The Gulag than it is in this dump, that's for sure." At that, a gust of wind splattered a flurry of torrential rain against the office window.

"You're not seeing the place at its best, sir. This weather: it's quite nice when the sun's out." Daley smiled neutrally at Donald, secretly enjoying the discomfort his superior was feeling at being involved so closely in such a complex investigation. "What's the form for tonight - I know the support unit's on the way."

"Oh, yes." Donald took some notes from his desk. "We'll have a team of six armed men from the unit, two representatives from Customs, and a DI and a DC from the Drug Squad, along with a dog of some description, and I presume a handler, to search the vessel once we have subdued these bastards. Even the fucking Royal Navy's involved now: tracking the fishing boat. They reckon they'll get in here about 0330 hours, if they carry on their current course and speed. The Navy are going to block the head of the loch in case they make a break for it or something. Though just quite how they would effect an escape in a fishing boat, I'll leave to your imagination. We could of course, have done all this at sea, but we want to find out if they meet anybody here, or en route."

"There's something bothering me, sir." Daley's face was serious.

"Bothering you? The whole fucking thing's bothering me.

What is it?" There was more than a trace of the old shift sergeant in Donald's tone.

"These guys are out on the high sea; they've been up around Skye, yes?" Donald nodded his head. "So, if we are working on the premise that one of this Latvian gang was responsible for our three murders, how does the fact that they are miles away when at least two of the murders were committed, factor in?"

"Hit man; or one of their party sent here ahead. Could be an associate, or even someone involved with this Mulligan character; the possibilities are endless. Anyhow, I'm certain that these Russians - or whatever they are - will unlock the door to the riches of the truth," he noticed the confused look on Daley's face. "Hanson, my PR man came up with that. Good, don't you think?"

"Truly inspired, sir. I better get on; is there anything else?"

"No, Jim, off you go and get organised. We'll have a strategy meeting here at 0100 hours - unite the various agencies. You'll be Officer Commanding - under my auspices of course," he smiled beneficently.

"Of course, sir. Of course."

The forensic teams had thoroughly swept *Russian Gold*. Only a small quantity of cannabis had been found, which strengthened the uneasy feeling that was gnawing away at Daley.

If they were out on a drugs run, who were they meeting? The Latvians were nowhere near Kinloch at the time. It didn't make sense. Unless of course, they were involved with some other supplier. Who knows? - they may just have been running away, though Daley doubted this scenario.

Like Izzy Watson, the body of Janet Ritchie contained evidence of more than one sample of semen. Whether they came from the same partner had yet to be verified, however, Daley was almost certain that would be the case. Collecting and identifying samples was one thing, matching them to suspects, was another.

Something he could not define was shouting at him, like someone trying to make himself understood from a great distance; the odd word, or part of a phrase could be made out, but offered little in the way of understanding.

That he was missing something, he was sure. The question of what, was perplexing his subconscious; distracting him during conversations, or when trying to work through other problems. He needed to step back - if only for an hour or so - to get some perspective.

With forensics doing their job, and while the rest of the team were involved in the daily grind of the investigation, he decided he could make some time to meet Liz. Scott opted to go to his room for a sleep, ahead of the late night raid on the Latvian fishing boat. They had agreed that Daley would wake him around ten, when they would go back to the station and prepare.

Daley had led many raids; mostly on the homes of suspected drug dealers, or murder suspects. He once had to stop a train with a passenger on board whose suitcase was filled with cocaine; he had never though, had to perform this task aboard a boat.

He worried about the character of the Latvians. MacLeod had made no bones about the fact he reckoned them tough. In Daley's experience though, anyone who came from an area anywhere near what was the old Soviet Union, was suspected of being either ex KGB, or Russian Special Forces. More often than not, they turned out to be gangs of opportunists, desperate to escape the grinding poverty of the Balkans, or Caucuses, or wherever, formed up into a gang, the like of which he had more than ample experience. The possibility that something more sinister lurked on the fishing boat en route to Kinloch, was a possibility. He hoped that they had the firepower to cope with any eventuality.

The two detectives cadged a lift to the door of the County Hotel, despite its proximity to the station. The torrential rain was now thudding off the road and large puddles were forming in potholes; a blocked drain spilled filthy water into the gutter. At the bottom of the street, Daley could see that the loch was near to the edge of the pier, meaning a high tide, swollen further by the deluge.

"See ye later, boss - and mind don't forget tae gie me a shout at ten." Scott waved idly as he made his way up the sweeping staircase.

Through the hatch, Daley could quite clearly make out the tinkle of his wife's laugh. He found her sitting on a tall bar stool, her long, tanned legs shown off to their optimum effect by a short denim skirt, and a pair of tooled cowboy boots. Her white blouse hugged her trim figure, open neck showing off the promise of her ample breasts. Daley's smile was pure reflex.

She took a few moments to notice him, so engrossed in conversation was she with a tall, dark-haired figure, leaning on the bar, a small glass of whisky clutched in his large, veined hand.

"*Chief* Inspector, I hope you don't mind me passing the time of day with this bonnie wife of yours. Aye, it makes an old cop's heart glad," he smiled at the detective.

"Good evening, Mr Bain. Be my guest, I'm used to men finding my wife excellent company." He grimaced slightly at this as it sounded more terse than he had intended, and was glad to see Liz effect a mock pout in response.

"Why don't you have all of these funny stories about your time in the police, darling? Lachie's been keeping me company; can't do anything else in this weather." She grinned magnificently.

He bent over her, briefly kissing her forehead. "What do the good people of Kinloch do in weather like this, Lachie?"

"Drink mostly; mind you, it doesna' really matter what the weather's at for that to happen." His highland lilt - in contrast to MacLeod's - was easy on the ear, something to do with the tone.

Daley bought them a drink each: gin for Liz, a Talisker for Lachie and a pint of seventy shilling for himself. With the operation to coordinate in the early hours, he had decided to limit himself to two pints of beer. He was secretly pleased that Scott had opted for a lie down, as he reckoned that his wayward DS may have found it difficult to resist a *hair of the dog,* such had been the severity of his hang-over, and the nature of his day's work.

They sat at the table near the back of the room that Daley had grown strangely accustomed to during his short stay in Kinloch. The bar was quiet, with only Mandy making herself busy re-stacking newly washed glasses onto shelves behind the bar. A log fire spat in the grate near their table, which - along with the dark wood panelling and low lighting, gave the place a cosy, mid-winter feel. A sodden customer entered the room, shrugging off a heavy waterproof jacket which seemed to gush water like an open tap. He was ushered back into the corridor by a fussing barmaid and instructed to hang the offending garment over an old, iron radiator. Daley looked on as steam rose from the coat, while its owner ordered up a half pint and a whisky chaser, rubbing his hands together vigorously in an attempt to set his circulation to rights.

"You certainly have abrupt changes to the weather here, Lachie - it was like summer yesterday, and now its feels like winter again." Daley put his arm around the shoulders of his wife, who nestled closer to him.

"That's the thing, sir; the joys of living on the mighty Atlantic seaboard."

"Please, Lachie - Jim; you're a civilian now, I hear enough of that at work."

"Old habits die hard. Ye'll find oot yersel', one day. Anyway that's half that's wrong with the job these days, no-one has any respect anymore," his face was thunderous, but soon broke into a smile. "We had an old meenister on Barra when I was a boy - Wee Free of course - I think I'm getting more and more like him every day." They laughed.

It was strange how hypnotic a real fire could be; all three of them stared blankly into it for a few moments, until Liz broke its spell.

"Oh, weather depending of course; I'm off on a photography trip tomorrow, out into the wilds."

Liz had studied photography at university, and had her work exhibited on a number of occasions. Her parents though, disappointed that she hadn't opted for law or medicine, actively discouraged her, and, disheartened by poor sales and distracted by becoming a policeman's wife, she gave up, consigning her beautiful and expensive Lecia 35mm camera to the back of a cupboard, where it had stayed. The rise of digital photography, with its instant results, had re-ignited her passion for the subject. Now, armed with the Nikon *Coolpix* Daley had given her for Christmas, she had produced some stunning results, mostly land or seascapes.

"I noticed an advert on a card in the newsagent's window - you know the one in Main Street?"

They both nodded.

"Well, this guy does escorted wildlife trips, especially for photographers, birdwatchers - that kind of thing. I hope to bag some wildlife images. Anyhow, I gave him a bell earlier, and we're heading out tomorrow about ten; weather dependent of course." She held up both of her hands with fingers crossed.

"Is it that wee bugger Seanessy?" Bain looked inquisitive.

"Oh yes, I take it you know him?"

Daley was only half listening to the conversation, the weight of the enquiry was heavy on his mind. He did though, catch the name Seanessy.

"Is that the guy that lives in the cottage by the beach, near to where - well, where we...?"

Bain nodded. "Aye, an unfortunate man in many ways he is too." Bain's *S's* were elongated by his Highland accent.

Daley was surprised at this; he had found Seanessy to be a harmless eccentric - nothing more.

"He had a bit o'a hard time when he was teaching up at the school."

"Oh, in what way?" Liz was all ears.

"Och, the kids used to give him a hard time - nothing malicious you understand."

Bain went on to tell them that his daughter had been taking her exams when Seanessy arrived at the school as a young chemistry teacher. He had an awkward, shy manner and was excellent fodder for a classroom full of adolescents, who could spot an insecure teacher at a hundred yards. Despite himself, he was prone to allowing his eyes to wander to the plunging neckline of female students, who - girls being girls - made sure their blouses were unbuttoned to the absolute limits of decency when they went to get their work marked.

"They would all piss themselves watching this poor bastard clocking their tits - oh, eh, pardon me" he looked embarrassed at Liz.

Liz was not offended. "I'll have to watch myself tomorrow - best wear a polo neck," she laughed.

"We got a complaint about him once; I went up to talk to him at the school. I felt sorry for him really. Some wee lassie accused him of touching her up - nothing in it."

"Oh?" Daley looked at Bain questioningly; he didn't want Liz tripping about in the middle of nowhere with the local pervert.

"Och, something and nothing," Bain's lilting voice was hypnotic. "We had a complaint from a town councillor, so we were obliged to take it further. It turned out that he had been married, but his wife buggered off with a colleague; they had a young daughter too. I don't think he ever saw the wife again, at any rate."

"Oh, the poor guy," Liz intoned.

"Anyway - out of the blue a few years ago, his lassie turned up - in her twenties by this time. She caused him all sorts of problems - drugs, drink - you name it. She buggered off after about a year or so. Not before she relieved him o' bags o' money, right enough."

"Wayward daughters seem the order of the day down here," Daley said absently, gazing into the sparking flames of the fire.

"Sorry, darling?" Liz touched his face with the back of her hand.

"Nothing, just miles away that's all," he smiled warmly and kissed her fingers.

Bain carried on, seemingly oblivious to the scene of marital bliss. "A couple of years ago he found out she died. Aye, in some squalid flat somewhere in Edinburgh. Drugs of course; I think he took it badly. He's one of these do-gooders who think they can change the world with a bit o' kindness. He brought her back, and buried her here," Bain swilled his whisky. "Can I be getting you both another?"

They both said yes, and the older man got stiffly to his feet, proceeded to the bar with his hands folded behind his back and waited for Mandy to serve another drenched customer.

"He couldn't be anything else but a cop, could he, darling?" Liz was studying Bain's stance.

Daley nodded. It was true: once you had been in the police, or had been involved in any meaningful way with it, spotting other policemen was easy - even ones like Bain - long retired.

"What a sad story about Mr Seanessy - poor guy."

"Just you keep your hand on yer ha'penny, darling and wear that polo-neck." Daley grinned as she punched him playfully on the arm in faux anger.

Bain suddenly turned around. "Spunky - that was his nickname - aye, Spunky," he chuckled, turned back, and ordered the drinks.

They spent some time discussing the changes that had taken place in Kinloch since Bain had arrived in the late seventies. It appeared that locals had a fierce loyalty to their town, and despite the remoteness of the place, thought there was nowhere like it; a kind of relationship to home and hearth that had all but disappeared elsewhere. This didn't surprise Daley, who had rapidly developed an affinity with the area.

Like everywhere else in Scotland, alcohol and drug abuse took its toll, and in the words of Lachie, *things hadn't changed for the better.*

Daley wasn't sure how many times he had heard this legend trotted out. Every generation throughout history must have looked upon the behaviour of their progeny with a leery eye. Things weren't perfect by any means; however, the town had a kind of bonhomie, surely extinct in many communities in the twenty first century.

"Having said all that, I wouldn't like to live anywhere else in Scotland," Bain drained his whisky. "Aye and it'll be even better when you get this little mess cleared up - eh? It's all that people will talk about out at the airport; I even heard that the army were on their way to sort things out. Anyway, folks, I've enjoyed your company - hope I'll see you again," he got up stiffly. "The best of luck to you tonight, *Chief* Inspector." He winked at Daley, gave Liz a big smile and then left, assuring them that *mince and tatties would wait for no man.*

Later, in the dining room, Liz asked him what was happening that evening.

Daley paused. "I can't really talk about it - I'm not trying to be difficult," he shrugged. "Nothing you're not used to." He raised his eyebrows in contrition.

"All I'm concerned about is you," Liz looked earnest. "I don't know what it is, I've just got a feeling in my stomach - do you know what I mean?"

Daley did, but decided that reassurance was the best policy. "You know me - belt and braces; and anyway, I've got Brian with me. What could possibly go wrong?"

She smiled, but the strain on her face was clear. The rest of the meal was a quiet affair.

15

Tick. Tick. Tick. The wall clock in the CID room was loud; or maybe the tense atmosphere just made it appear so. It was, though, quite audible before the meeting of the various agencies involved in the looming raid on the Latvian registered fishing boat, *Koba*, began.

Representing Strathclyde Police: Superintendent Donald (Chair), DCI Daley (O/C), and DI Paterson, who was in charge of the Tactical Firearms Unit to be deployed at the raid.

The Customs were represented by a wispy-haired Ulsterman called Tommy Shanks, whose thin, angular face bore a constantly pained, disgruntled expression, as though being in the Kinloch CID office in the early hours of the morning was absolutely the last place in the world he wanted to be.

The Royal Naval Frigate *Sirius'* Security Officer, Lieutenant Philip Carter, had just arrived via helicopter from the warship that was still trailing the Latvian vessel at a discreet distance.

Flynn, the Harbour Master sat nervously at the end of the table, the sharp creases in his shirt the only testament to his neatness, now that he had had to remove his peaked cap, and his well-pressed trousers and shined shoes could not be see under the table.

Donald, as Chairman, was the first to speak.

"Welcome, gentlemen, and my apologies for dragging you all here at such an uncivilised hour. However, as you no doubt can appreciate, we are facing a tricky set of circumstances.

Here we go, thought Daley, as his boss consulted an

impressively large pile of typewritten notes.

"We know from our friends in the Royal Navy," he smiled at Lieutenant Carter, "that the *Koba* is heading for Kinloch, and on current estimates should arrive at the harbour between 0330 and 0400 hrs. We will, of course, be in position well in advance of this time." He discarded the top sheet of notes. "Now we all know the challenge: we are reliably informed," he looked uncomfortable, "that this fishing boat is a regular visitor to the port, and that her crew is involved with the supply and distribution of illegal drugs."

At this, Shanks sighed volubly. "I think we're all aware why we're here Superintendent. I think it would be more appropriate at this time to discuss who should be leading this operation. This is clearly a matter where we at HMRC take precedence." He waved his hand at Donald in an imperious way that Daley reckoned he may regret, as he looked back at his boss.

Say something about the Superintendent: vain, posturing, arrogant - yes, absolutely; ill-prepared, easily dominated, malleable - never.

"I had hoped we could run this operation in an adult, non-partisan fashion; I see that is not going to be the case," he removed his spectacles and glowered at Shanks. "While I do not deny HMRC have every right to be involved in the due process of the operation, the non-availability of support personnel, combined with lack of infrastructure in this area, excludes the possibility of command." Shanks cleared his throat to speak, but Donald carried on, unabashed. "We came by the information about this boat as part of an enquiry, which now concerns the brutal murder of three individuals. We have good reason to believe that an individual, or individuals aboard *Koba,* could well be involved with these events, if not directly responsible. Therefore, this operation will proceed as it began: Police led." he slapped the flat of his hand on the table to emphasise the point.

Shanks, though, was still not content. "Firstly, I find it highly irregular that you have chosen not to inform us from whom, and from where this information came, and also - perhaps more crucially - when? We were only contacted in the late afternoon;

however, it has been brought to my attention, that you received the tip-off this morning. Had we been contacted then, we would now be in a position to have the correct infrastructure in place. Do you follow, Superintendent?"

It had been a long time since Daley had seen Donald go red in the face with anger, not since his make-over from being a crude, gruff, overweight shift sergeant, in fact.

"You listen to me," he pointed his *Mont Blanc* fountain pen at the Customs Officer. "I am overseeing a triple murder investigation a hundred and fifty miles from my headquarters, an investigation which contains much sensitive and restricted information, as well as the possibility of a number of serious crimes. Too many cooks spoil the broth, in my experience. Do you really think I am about to hand over the reins at this crucial phase to an organisation more at home slouching about bonded warehouses, or getting my taxes wrong? If you are not prepared to go along with the command structure of this operation, you can fuck off - it's going ahead with, or without you - clear?"

Daley saw the young Naval Lieutenant lower his gaze to the table in an effort to conceal his obvious amusement, while Shanks managed to look more waspish than ever. After a moment's pause, he made a dismissive gesture with his hand, then folded his arms as a silent indication he was now in reluctant acceptance.

From then on, the meeting progressed in the way Daley expected: Donald firmly in charge and making all of the decisions.

Basically, the whole process was simple: the Navy would track the Latvian fishing boat by radar into the harbour, while keeping an open communication link with the land-based authorities; themselves in position around Kinloch's second pier, to which the two access roads would be closed - just in case one of the good citizens of the town was out for a stroll at that time. The Navy would then send an armed security team in a *RIB* to seal off the loch should the Latvians somehow get wind of what was going on, and try to make a break by sea; admittedly hard in a craft that could barely do ten knots.

"We'll have ten marines on the *RIB,* Superintendent," Lieutenant Carter oozed confidence and professionalism "just in case things get a bit tasty on the ground, so to speak - nothing your men can't handle I'm sure," he smiled at Donald. "We don't have any Intel on this particular vessel; however, some of these ex-Soviet gangs can be ruthless. If required, we should be able to deploy in three to four minutes; it'll mean giving away our position, but that won't matter once the trap's sprung - eh, gentlemen?"

He reached down, picking up a blue holdall from his feet and lifting it onto the table. He unzipped it and took out what looked like two very large two-way radios. "These chaps are satellite enabled comms devices," he looked around the table. "They're intuitive: if the radio signal goes down or is blocked by defensive tactics etc., they'll open up a local satellite channel with the Command Unit. In this case, *The Sirius.* I suggest that the ground O/C," he handed one of the devices to Daley, "and the overall Ops Commander retain these units notionally." The assembled police officers nodded in sage agreement. "Of course, I'll be shadowing you closely, Chief Inspector Daley, so you might choose to give me control of comms - for Naval communication at least."

Daley was impressed with the competence shown by the young Naval Officer. He hadn't really appreciated just how often the RN was now involved with crime enforcement issues, especially those involving drugs or armaments. Carter pointed out that international terrorism sourced a huge proportion of their funding from the sale of narcotics; the well-worn drugs route from Afghanistan overland into the former Soviet Caucuses region was a favourite. The defence of the UK coastline was the historic role of the Royal Navy; to them, the trade embodied the Armada of the twenty-first century.

Scott was standing in the office car park smoking. Daley gave him a brief summary of the meeting, while the pair stared up at the night sky, now a blanket of stars. The weather had taken a turn for the better, though the night temperature was only four or five degrees.

Being city boys, they weren't used to seeing the firmament because of the amber glare of light pollution. Daley remembered his grandfather's passion for the heavens. On their trips away from Glasgow, he had shown him the different constellations, explaining how they moved across the sky; most of which he had now forgotten, though he thought he recognised certain patterns.

"I think that's Taurus, Bri - just there, to the left," he pointed at a section of sky.

"Na, na - that's the Bear, Jim," Scott was thinking. "Or maybes the Plough - och, I'm no' sure. I wis brought up in Maryhill fir fuck's sake; the nearest we got tae stars wiz when Thistle wir playing the 'Gers at hame - you know whit I'm sayin' - or some bastard stuck wan on ye at the dancing."

Nevertheless, they stood, silently rooted to the spot for a few more minutes, with only the click-flare-click of Scott's gas lighter to break the spell. This was done more effectively when the security door swung open to reveal Superintendent Donald, swathed in an expensive, black overcoat.

"You won't get any answers up there, lads," he said through a mouthful of food. "We depart in an hour, so we better press on with this general briefing; all the chaps are ready," he stared up at the sky. "Ah, The Big Dipper - wonderful sight," he mused.

Scott looked dubious. "It's the Bear, is it no'?"

Donald shook his head. "Don't be ridiculous, Brian," he adopted his habitually haughty look and walked back towards the door.

"Aye whitever you say, boss," Scott said in a loud whisper so Daley would hear. "Fucking Roger Moore, noo."

"It's Patrick, Bri," Daley enlightened his DS they made their way to the briefing.

"Eh?" Scott was already disconnected, stubbing out his cigarette in a flurry of orange sparks.

The whole team now consisted of the crew of the Royal Navy *RIB*, a seven strong Police Tactical Firearms Unit, four armed CID

Officers, plus six uniforms and a DC, charged with keeping the public away. Not that the townsfolk should be a problem considering their intention was to keep the matter as low-key as possible, using the element of surprise as their salient tactic.

Still, Daley had a heavy heart. Those involved in action on the pier were kitted out with the latest bullet-proof body armour over their civilian clothes, and had each been provided with a reinforced steel helmet by the firearms unit, which Scott was refusing to wear. The DCI though, was still not entirely happy.

Sure, they had enough firepower to effect a small revolution, and had more Support Unit Officers on their way from Glasgow to deal with any possible aftermath. Somehow though, he felt there was an element out of kilter; something he had missed.

He had discussed this with Donald, who had immediately deployed his *arm around the shoulder* approach, assuring Daley that *everything would be fine*, and hinted that he felt that the DCI's fears were merely down to the added responsibility of a more senior rank. He would *get used to it.*

Daley though, had learned to trust his instincts; and he was finding it almost impossible to rid himself of the leaden feeling of impending doom.

I'm just getting too old for this, he lectured internally, as he shouted for a bit of quiet from the room full of police officers. Body armour was being strapped on, helmets secured, weapons being checked just one last time, and the radios and secure mobile phones being used by each officer individually, monitored for serviceable quality, battery level, and the like.

"We all know how we want things to progress," he was projecting as though on stage. "Our first priority, as always, is our own and the public's safety - please bear that in mind. I don't want anyone to be too shy to speak up if they feel that something is wrong, or draw my attention to likely problems." At this, he looked at Donald, who seemed engrossed by something on his Blackberry.

"We embark in five minutes, so good luck, lads. Now, Superintendent Donald will say a few words."

Despite thinking that his boss was not concentrating, no sooner had the invitation to speak left Daley's mouth, than Donald was on his feet addressing the assembled personnel, or *Unit*, as Donald now insisted on calling them. At his side, the waspish Shanks looked straight ahead, expression absent from his face. Daley pondered how he and the much maligned Inspector MacLeod would get on; they seemed very similar in nature. Daley doubted though, how Shanks could possibly plumb the depths of unprofessional behaviour shown by the Highlander.

Scott was struggling with a strap on his body armour as - Donald having completed his hackneyed pep-talk - saw the room now emptying into the three personnel carriers that would transport them all to their drop-off point, behind a row of buildings located in front of the harbour. A tactic designed to conceal their arrival from any sea bound vantage point.

"This fuckin' thing reminds me o' the ski-jacket she bought me last Christmas - mind I telt ye aboot it?" Daley always admired the *sang froid* of his DS, under almost any circumstances, constantly distracted as he was by some seeming triviality. "I says tae her - fuck me, you'd need tae be Harry bastardin' Houdini tae get intae the thing, never mind get oota' it."

"I never knew he had a middle name."

"Who?"

"Houdini."

"Aye very good, *sir*. Can ye no' make yersel' useful, and strap me intae this contraption, in case Ivan the fuckin' Terrible wants tae take pot-shots at me?"

As Daley was securing the recalcitrant strap, he saw DC Fraser making his way across the floor; not trained to carry a firearm, his job was to oversee the uniformed constables who were to be involved in sealing off the pier from the rest of Kinloch. He was wearing a dark-coloured ski jacket.

"Tell me, Archie, did you have any bother getting into that jacket of yours?" The young detective's answer was obscured by a stream of invective from DS Scott.

The night was now cool rather than cold, and stillness had

descended upon the sleeping town, as the *Unit* emerged from three vans, now parked nose to tail behind the local ships' chandlers.

Daley took a deep breath that smelt and tasted of the sea, which itself looked as black as ink, reflecting only the amber glow of the few lights bordering the harbour. In the distance, he recognised the peeling bell as that of the yacht pontoons; the mournful tolling adding an air of melancholy to the scene.

Quietly and efficiently, those involved in the operation gathered around the Chief Inspector, who, after a few words, sent them to their relevant positions. Radios were to be used only in emergencies, to keep the frequency clear for command and control purposes, and each officer was wearing a *hands-free* earpiece, so that no command could be missed.

Donald and Shanks remained in the station control room, gaining an overview of the operation by monitoring radio traffic, and CCTV images from the town's system, now trained on and around the second pier. Though Daley was in charge of the operation on the ground, Donald had reminded him that should the necessity arise, he would have no hesitation in taking direct command from the control room: *Not that that was likely to happen,* he had assured his DCI.

Fraser and his uniformed colleagues, were positioned to the north and west of the second pier - the only road access points. Instead of the regulation fluorescent jackets commonly worn at night by police officers, they wore plain, black waterproof jackets. Not being in the front line, and only responsible for crowd and traffic control, they did not wear the bulky bullet-proof vests. Fraser himself was stationed in the doorway of the last shop on the Main Street before the harbour, keeping a watching brief on the street and the two roads which converged near the piers; he too was wearing an ear-piece, with a voice activated mic.

Daley, Scott, and Lieutenant Carter positioned themselves at the side of the ships' chandlers, in a narrow lane between it and the next building, a two storey office block. The Firearms Unit was placed at strategic points at the head of the pier, making sure no-one would be able to make a break for the roadway. The four

DC's who accompanied them were wearing bullet-proof vests under black jackets with discreet police logos, their heads adorned by the navy-blue helmets reminiscent of those worn by German storm troopers during the Second World War, and tonight by everyone apart from Scott, who claimed that it made him feel claustrophobic.

The tolling sound of the pontoon bell continued undisturbed, until only those with the sharpest hearing discerned another noise; a light, but regular thud, reminiscent of a generator hidden in the basement of a house.

At 03:42 precisely, Carter's radio burst into life; even with the volume low, Daley could make out what was being said.

"*Sirius* calling Carter. Over," the voice was clipped and precise.

"Go ahead. Over," Carter spoke quietly into the mouthpiece.

"Please note that our quarry has entered the loch - our Alpha unit will shadow in approximately five. Over."

"Roger. Out." Carter whispered into the radio, and then to Daley, "The marines are Alpha unit, in case you haven't guessed."

Daley nodded, and Scott raised his eyebrows, as he removed his sidearm from the shoulder holster concealed by his jacket.

"Fucking sure I'm no' facing doon half o' the red army wi' jist my baton – whether they're retired or no'." His features were set in a determined expression.

The thud of the diesel engine grew louder, and to their left, they could see the fishing boat was making slow, but steady progress up the loch, bright arc lighting hanging from the rigging.

"It's a pity that dug couldna' get here - it wid have been the very dab on that boat - supposing they're carrying drugs." Scott was referring to a sniffer dog, which until an hour ago, had been plying it's trade at a huge drugs raid in Glasgow, and was now in the back of a van driven by its handler towards Kinloch.

"Can't be helped, Bri; with these cuts, we're lucky we can still feed the dogs we have, never mind get any more. Here, you take this; and don't point it at me for fuck's sake," he handed Scott the Koch automatic machine gun, as Lieutenant Carter looked warily on.

The vessel was now less than four hundred yards from the pier. The Latvians were regular visitors to the port, and knew exactly where they were going to berth, after contact with Flynn, whom they had spoken to by radio earlier in the day. Despite this, the dapper little harbour master was sitting nervously in his office, ready to be of assistance.

"DCI Daley to all units." He spoke using the hands-free throat mic.

"On my mark of three initiate strategy *F* foxtrot."

This entailed DI Paterson illuminating the fishing boat with an enormous searchlight set up by his team. At this, he was to shout, through a loudhailer, instructions; in what he had been reliably informed was Latvian by the Force Translation Department. The firearms team would board, then secure the vessel accompanied by the DCs, who were also equipped with side arms. The marines aboard the *Alpha RIB* would speed into the harbour proper under full power to assist where, or if necessary.

Daley knew that the moments following the trap being sprung were likely to be the most dangerous. However, he took comfort from the professional conduct of Paterson and his fellow officers, as well as the reassuring presence of Carter's Marines, and the indomitable Scott.

He could now see the fishing boat manoeuvring around the end of the pier towards her pre-designated berth. He would wait until the last minute to give the order; waiting until the ropes were secured to bollards, and the engine began to die. His men were well concealed from even the crew member of the fishing boat who would have to jump onto the pier to secure the ropes. So far, so good.

The tone of the engine lowered, and he could make out the foreign voices of the crew as orders were barked into the cool night.

In the instant before he pressed the button at his lapel mic to give the order, he thought he heard another distinct noise, high pitched and buzzing. However, unable to hold back for fear of confusion, he gave the go-ahead,

"Three, two, one - GO, GO, GO!" Almost as he said the words, he saw the bright searchlight on the pier illuminate the scene, and the sound of raised, familiar voices rend the air.

As always with these situations, everything happened in a blur of noise and adrenalin. He took off down the pier, closely followed by Scott and Carter, the latter giving instructions through his radio to his marines to speed into the pier as soon as they could.

Two tactical officers with automatic weapons were kneeling on the pier, fore and aft of the vessel, their weapons pointing towards the crew, who were standing on board with their hands placed on their heads; apart from the rope man, who was already being handcuffed - none too gently - by a Paisley DC.

The bridge of the fishing boat was illuminated, and he could see the man whom he assumed was the captain clearly standing at the window, his hands aloft, as police officers poured onto the vessel. The crew was being subdued easily, no doubt fearful of the consequences of making a wrong move whilst being watched by a dozen heavily armed men.

Flynn had told them that the crew usually comprised of six men, though occasionally, that number could vary up or down. He watched as Paterson bounded up the gangway to the bridge, followed by two of his men. The figure on the bridge turned his back to the window, and hastily put his hands on his head.

"DI Daley to Paterson. Over. Update. Over." Daley was breathless, quietly cursing his unfit state; DS Scott was beside him, his automatic weapon raised menacingly.

"Standby." This from Paterson.

From his position in the charity shop's doorway, Fraser had a clear view of both piers and their environs. He was slightly put out that he wasn't involved in the raid proper, but reasoned that his lack of firearms training and consequent inability to carry a weapon, was the main factor. He found it hard to believe that in all the time he had been in Kinloch, these serious crimes were going on under his very nose. He had not suspected *Pulse* to be the den of iniquity it had proven to be, despite visiting the establishment many times. Again, he felt the gnawing doubts as to his suitability for a career as a detective eating away at his confidence. Was it possible that men like Daley and Scott had started out their careers in such an inept way? He couldn't think it likely; nor could he contemplate a future like that of his uncle, an unfulfilled drunk, whose only boasts were contained within the confines of some hostelry and from the bottom of a glass.

He worried too about his personal life: the police was not a job conducive to social interaction with the opposite sex. His only proper relationship - with a girl from school - had ended abruptly when he had joined up. He was no longer available to go out with their mutual friends at weekends, or felt uncomfortable if somebody lit a joint etc. She accused him eventually of always having secrets, and being obsessed with his new job. She didn't realise he was just being subconsciously assimilated into the world he had chosen. A journey she was not willing to accompany him on. Her name was Tina, and try as he might, he could not seem to conjure her face in his mind, nor bring back the warmth in his heart that she had - once upon a time - kindled.

Just then, he saw movement; a figure was slouching along the short distance between the pontoons and the east pier. *That's not right.* All of the vessels moored at both piers and the pontoons had been cleared earlier under the excuse of the discovery of an unexploded WWII mine. He knew where all of the Operational Officers were - something was wrong. He thought about alerting Daley, but reasoned that the interloper was most likely some inebriated yachtsman, inadvertently left aboard his vessel during the clear out. Still, the man was about to stray into a very dangerous situation. Fraser stepped out of the doorway.

Daley could see four men on the deck, now in various states of detention by police officers. There was clearly one man on the bridge, and the crewman on the pier, now lying prone with his hands cuffed behind his back. That made six.

"Bridge secure. The captain's taking me into the body of the vessel - he says crew accounted for. Over." At that, a scruffy man made his way, gingerly, down the gangway from the bridge, his hands on his head, preceded by an officer walking backwards in front of him, gun trained upon the Latvian. Behind, also wielding a weapon pointed in his direction, came another tactical officer, himself followed by DI Paterson.

The man from the bridge was shouting in broken English. "We are fusherman - land fush - no problem. We have no problem - no?" He looked around, bemused at the sight of his crewmates, most of whom had assumed the prone position.

They were wearing an assortment of torn oilskins, old jeans, filthy jumpers, and baseball caps; in truth, apart from their swarthy complexions, they would have passed for any of the fishermen Daley had seen since being in Kinloch. Back on deck, DI Paterson stood behind the captain as he opened a door on the side of the superstructure of the vessel, which clearly led into the body of the fishing boat.

Daley looked warily at the side of the boat, then decided he would have to make yet another nautical leap of faith; he grabbed the gunwale with both hands, arms stretched out over the inky void between the vessel and the pier; judging the rise and fall, he heaved himself up, managing to get one leg over the side then propelling himself in a rolling motion onto the fishing boat deck, to the sound of tearing fabric.

"That's another pair o' breeks away, Jim," Scott grinned from below, as the DCI, dignity barely intact, got back to his feet.

Within two minutes, Paterson's head poked around the door leading to the lower deck.

"It would appear that we have the all-clear, sir. No sign of a seventh crewman."

No sooner had the Inspector uttered these words, than a distant crack sounded over the harbour, closely followed by another; it took no expert to recognise the report of a firearm. Instinctively, all heads turned to the likely genus of the shots - the east pier, some seventy metres away.

"Code twenty one - man down, man down; repeat man down!" The voice over the radio was panic-filled; Daley recognised it was one of the young uniformed cops. He was also aware of Carter yelling into his Navy Radio, as what sounded like an aircraft sped between the gap in the two piers.

More shots.

Daley jumped back onto the gunwale of the fishing boat, paused for a moment then jumped down onto the pier, coming down so quickly that he had to take a couple of fast-paced steps forward, like a poor gymnast's dismount, to stop himself from falling. Scott was at his side; together they made for the short length of promenade that separated the twin jetties of the harbour.

"DCI Daley to DC Fraser - position please, over?" Daley shouted breathlessly into his throat mic.

No reply.

"DCI Daley to any unit stationed at the..." he had to pause to gulp down air, "...bottom of Main Street with DC Fraser - come in. Over?"

Ominously, still no reply.

Daley - though his lungs were bursting with exertion - was desperately trying to piece together what had happened. Paterson and his men had appeared to have the situation entirely under control; crew rounded up and a search of the vessel with the captain complete. Then he remembered the high pitched noise he had heard just before giving the order to spring the trap - *a small boat.*

Scott was ahead of him now and getting further away despite being the older man.

Suddenly his earpiece burst into life.

"Firearms being discharged; officer down," the voice in his ear was distant, the speech a rush of fear and adrenalin.

"DCI Daley receiving... more details; which officer," he swallowed more air, "is down?"

Silence again, though, from the corner of his eye, he was aware of the movement of black figures heading rapidly up the jetty.

Scott had reached the top of the pier with Daley following;

then, without warning, he felt a weight land on him from behind, and momentarily his world went black.

His first instinct was to fight; he didn't feel fear, only the desperate need to get whoever, or whatever off his back.

"Stay down, man - stay down!" The voice was loud in his ear; he recognised it as that of the young Lieutenant.

Shouting now: urgent and insistent, like two people trying to make themselves understood across a busy street. Then, for a heartbeat, silence, followed by a blood curdling yell and the deafening gutter of automatic gunfire.

Daley felt a hand with fingers spread wide weigh hard on the back of his head, pushing it down into the pavement. He felt the pressure pushing him down ease; he was aware of someone at his side, also on the ground, getting to his feet. Looking up he saw Carter standing over him, offering a helping hand up, while talking urgently into the large radio.

"Jim, Jim - get over here," this was Scott, standing about twenty metres away at the head of the east pier.

Daley pulled himself to his feet with the help of Carter's outstretched hand, nodded his gratitude, and hurried over to his DS. He saw the look on Scott's face; there was blood on his hands.

"Brian, have you been hit, how…?" He followed Scott's line of sight. On the ground a few feet away he could see someone lying on their back, legs wide apart, like a tired man who had just flopped down onto a particularly comfortable bed. Two men in dark clothing were standing around the recumbent figure, a third kneeling. He walked over.

On the breast of the black jacket, a deeper, blacker, slick stain had spread; at its heart, a gaping, dark hole - around which the blood was already congealing - shone beetle black, under the acetylene light. The body was motionless, head turned to the side as though in repose, not flat against the cold concrete. Even under the ethereal orange glow the face was devoid of colour, features standing in sharper relief - a strand of red hair curled onto the pallid forehead.

Archie Fraser was dead.

16

In all of his career, Daley had felt nothing like the pain - the burden of responsibility that now enveloped him. He stared, transfixed at Fraser's corpse; all that life and promise extinguished. Worst of all: it was his fault.

Often Daley - who had stared at many corpses - pondered as to whether any residue of consciousness remained after death was a medical certainty. Could the brain still perceive, be aware, even though the heart had stopped beating?

As a young cop he had stood at points duty in Glasgow city centre during the run up to Christmas. Shoppers hurried to and fro clutching bags whose logos spoke not only of their likely contents, but also something of the individuals carrying them: a tall, patrician figure with a small paper package bearing the name of an exclusive watch manufacturer; the teenage girls bundled together like an amorphous entity, as they, arm-in-arm, giggled their way down a decoration festooned thoroughfare, their bags proclaiming the latest and most trendy emporia; a whey-faced middle-aged woman bearing the stark, monochrome receptacle of the wares of the cut-price shop.

On and on they came: wet, cold, happy, sad, chattering, silent, fat, thin, bald, hirsute; man, woman, child - the whole world was here - or so it seemed. All caught up in the whirl of yuletide preparation.

So large were the crowds, that policemen were stationed at every pedestrian crossing in the city centre in a vain attempt to keep some kind of order. The one was subsumed by the heaving mass that was the many; an entity in its own right.

Red man stop: green man walk; the principle was simplicity itself. And, just in case the visually impaired, or just plain stupid should happen along, a shrill, insistent beep provided audible indication of when it was safe to cross. This though, proved too difficult a concept for many. Pitting their few pounds of frail flesh and bone against the hard, heavy edges of hurtling traffic, pedestrians regularly took insane risks in a festive game of *chicken*. A game that the overwhelmed policemen - mostly those wet behind the ears - who stood for nine hours at a time, were trying to prevent.

He was standing at one of Glasgow's most dangerous crossings, now long consigned to the city's history.

An attractive blonde girl waited dutifully across the road in the company of a phalanx of fellow shoppers, watching the red man, who stood out against the gloom of the dull December day. In his mind's eye he could still see her in every detail: her faux fox-fur jacket, short, to her waist, her tight blue jeans tucked into her knee-high boots.

Then things happened in slow-motion. The crowd of shoppers began to move, like the wind rippling over a corn field. The girl stumbled forward, as though she had been pushed. To his left the giant tri-colour of yellow, white and green that was a Corporation bus hurtled into view amidst the mechanical growl of a diesel engine and sigh of air brakes. A teenage boy pushed past the pretty girl, looking neither right nor left. He had a blue sports holdall thrown casually over his shoulder and the red of his hair nearly matched that of the amber of the traffic signal.

He was unlucky. He stopped when he saw the bus. He was halfway across the road and the shock of seeing the vehicle hurtle around the corner prompted the moment of indecision that killed him. The driver slammed on the brakes with a banshee wail, too late though to arrest the tonnage of the vehicle, which smashed the youth into the roadway with a soft thud. The front wheel of the bus crushed his skull, bursting his brains out of his head like a neatly squeezed pimple.

Daley looked down at his polished right boot and the white and red pulp that was dashed across it and up his trouser leg.

He had never forgotten the feeling of unreality that he had experienced during and after the incident; something he had never encountered before - or since - until now.

He was sitting back in the office now, trying to piece things together.

By what could have only been pure luck, a small dingy had set out from the rear of the fishing boat, out of sight of the assembled police officers, moments before they sprung the trap. The high pitched noise that Daley had heard had been the whine of the tiny outboard.

Scott reckoned that the crew member in the dingy was using the arrival of the larger boat to deflect attention from a proposed clandestine meeting with a third party. He had moored his small boat at the pontoons, and was then disturbed by the noise created by the raid. In an effort to escape he had stumbled upon the tragic Fraser, whom he shot twice at point-blank range through the chest, just before the marines, who had spotted the dingy through night vision equipment, had a chance to speed into the harbour. It was they who had killed the Latvian. Sadly, too late for Archie Fraser.

It was a good theory; but something about it didn't ring true for the Chief Inspector. There was too much chance involved. And, in his experience, chance was a rarefied commodity.

Why didn't I make him wear a bullet-proof vest? Daley was asking himself over and over again. The answer was simple: no-one had expected Fraser, nor any of the uniformed officers manning the temporary road blocks to be in any danger.

"The question is, who was this guy expecting tae meet? If it wiz Peter Mulligan, then we can hardly put them in the frame for his murder," Scott waited for his boss to reply, but got no response.

"Jim, you canna go on blaming yersel' - nane of us could have predicted that." Still no reply.

Scott tried a different tack. "You fancy a coffee or something?" On seeing the blank look on Daley's face, he decided to get him

211

one anyway, touching the DCI on the shoulder on the way past in a typical example of restrained W*est of Scotland male* sympathy.

Police officers had been sent to Fraser's parent's home in Glasgow, and Daley had resolved to call them once the news had been imparted; a task he was most certainly not looking forward to. He couldn't get the sight of the broken figure lying on the pier out of his mind. If this was the price of the promotion he had so coveted, it was far, far too high.

He was aware of the door being opened, and didn't bother to look up as he assumed it would be Scott. In fact, it was Donald.

"I know you are devastated - naturally. Though I barely knew the boy, it's an obvious tragedy." No response.

Donald walked over to the window. Though only half past five, the sun was beginning to light up the town's Main Street; the gulls, crows and a myriad of other birds were contributing to the morning cacophony, which today somehow, seemed so inappropriate.

"This may not be the best time, Jim," the Superintendent talked in low tones, "but for some time now, I've had the notion that your eye was off the ball - that you were distracted." He turned to look at the DCI, whose head was still firmly in his hands. Undaunted, he continued. "Under these extreme circumstances, and if you have no objection, I have decided to take operational command of this enquiry." He raised his eyebrows in an expression that demanded some kind of answer.

Daley felt the wheels in motion, the buttons were being pushed, and despite being fully aware of it, could not resist.

"So you swan in here with your platitudes and your empty sympathy," Daley was leaning back in his chair, but looking anything but relaxed. "Let me tell you something: for some time now I have thought you to be a thoroughly detestable man; vain, arrogant, and most certainly and absolutely unsuited to running an investigation of this nature. Your whole career has been predicated on the hard work of others. And if you think I'm going to hand the reins of power over to you, so that you can stumble along to no conclusion, then blame me when you turn up fuck all - you can reconsider. There are four people lying dead, and I don't care if I have to leave the job and become a private investigator, I'll solve this case. Understood?"

Donald stood in silence for a few moments looking back out of the window. He then turned on his heel and walked towards the door. "OK, DCI Daley. This time you have it your way. But, remember this: a young man gave his life to this cause - don't let him, or me, down."

He stared at Daley for a few seconds, then left, closing the door firmly behind him.

Daley ran his hands roughly through his own hair. He knew that he had just been in receipt of the proverbial *kick up the arse* he needed to galvanise himself back into action. He picked up the phone from his desk and dialled the nightshift custody sergeant's internal number.

Donald was now in the car park. He reflected ruefully on the night's events. He would have to get a couple of hours sleep, then face the inevitable press conference. The death of a young police officer - particularly under these circumstances - was bound to create yet another feeding frenzy. He certainly would not be leaving it to Daley and Scott; neither of them had what it took to appear competent in front of the media. Daley always looked fat, unfit and careworn, while his DS more resembled the criminals he was trying to apprehend, than the highly effective - if unorthodox - detective he was.

Donald had always found Jim Daley a man brimming with contradictions: a talented sportsman who had let himself go, early, to seed; such a volcanic temper, in a man who was frequently paralysed by over-sensitivity; a quick, intelligent individual, who could - as again today - be easily manipulated. Above all, one of the best police officers he had ever worked with.

Donald was in no doubt as to his own talents. He had always found the endless grind of a major investigation too much to bear; he quickly lost sense of objective, and became bored with the exhausting schedule of fact, procedure and the eternal sifting a grain of truth from a beach-full of lies. No, he knew that his talent lay entirely within his ability to make people bend to his will; the casual comment or harsh word that would send them into a flurry of productive activity. He smiled to himself as he got into his car, smoothed back his hair in the rear-view mirror, then turned the key in the ignition.

The persistent bleep of her husband's alarm clock was enough to rouse Liz from her slumber. She had asked Jim to set it for her, as she wanted to be up and about in plenty of time for her wildlife/photography trip with Mr Seanessy.

From what she could glean through the parchment coloured net curtains, the day looked like a huge improvement on the previous twenty-four hours or so; a return to a glorious spring, in fact.

She stretched and yawned. Still lying in bed, she looked at the bedside table and smiled at the sight of Daley's *Patrick O'Brian* novel and the fact that it didn't matter where in the world the couple found themselves, his side of the bed always looked the same; identifiable by his particular choice of reading material and ever-present radio. He actually pined for the BBC when he was abroad, and would go to extreme lengths in an attempt to receive the *World Service*, no matter the destination of their holiday.

She laid her head on his pillow, breathing in his very essence. The last few days had been a return to when they were first married. Despite the responsibilities of running a murder investigation, her husband seemed more at ease with her than he had been for a very, very long time. She supposed that being away from home and hearth threw people together more; exposure to the unusual reinvigorating interest in each other. Anyway, regardless of the reasons, the renaissance in their relationship was most welcome.

At times like this, Liz was afflicted with gnawing feelings of guilt; like the drunk waking up in the morning remembering acts of intoxicated stupidity from the night before. The litany of her infidelity often played, without summons, in her head. This, she reckoned, was a moving record of her own inadequacy, an admonition on her need to feel wanted in the most primeval way; as though the closeness of sexual intimacy would banish the demons of loneliness and insecurity that haunted her, as her husband - the man she truly loved - immersed himself in yet another impenetrable case.

The knock at the door was quiet but urgent. Preferring to sleep naked, she reached for Daley's jumper, which was to serve as an impromptu dressing gown.

"Hello - just give me a second," she called to her visitor. The reply she received was indistinct, however she discerned the voice of a woman. She pulled the jumper over her head, took a quick look in the long mirror, running the tangles of sleep from her hair and tiptoed across the cool floor to the door.

"Oh, Annie, how are you? Did I book a wake-up call? Sorry, I didn't remember, Jim...," the look on Annie's face made her stop what she was saying. "There's something wrong - oh no - is it Jim?" She felt the panic strike at her heart and stomach, making her legs feel weak.

"Don't worry, Mrs Daley." Annie's face was pale and the look of uncertainty she bore was out of place with her habitual mien - in Liz's brief acquaintance anyway.

"Annie, please tell me - what's happened?"

"I'm jeest telling you whoot a' the gossips are comin' oot way jeest noo," she was in the room now, and had closed the door. Liz sat down heavily on the bed, the knitted garment at her knees. "There wiz some kinda' polis operation last night - doon at the quay - did Mr Daley tell you?"

"I knew something was happening. Listen Annie, if its tittle-tattle you're after, I never discuss my husband's work with anyone, and in any case, I probably know less than you do." Liz could feel herself becoming annoyed. She liked the genial hotel manageress, but was in no doubt as to the major part she played in the dissemination of local gossip.

Despite a hurt look, Annie chose to continue, the words tumbling from her mouth in her hurry, in an effort to justify her visit. "I'm jeest here tae tell you, that everyone's sayin' that a polis got killed last night - I wisna' sure if you were awake or no', I...,"

Liz darted to her jacket that hung over the back of a chair. She managed to fumble her mobile from the inside pocket despite the trembling of her hands. She tried hard to focus on the screen: no messages, no missed calls. She began dialling a number, then realised it was the number of Daley's office in Paisley.

"What's the number of the Police Station here, Annie?" That was spoken with the intonation of a command. The local woman gave Liz the number, then she thought again and called his mobile. *I'm sorry the person you are calling is not available, please try later or...*

She didn't wait for the neutral message to reach its conclusion; she dialled the number that Annie had just given her, and - in what seemed like eternity - the call was answered. "Kinloch Police Office, Desk Sergeant Williamson. Can I help you?"

She could hardly get the words out. This was the scenario that had been in the back of her mind when she first met, then fell in love with Daley. Only two years ago, one of his colleagues had been shot during a drugs raid. Liz had visited his widow, who sat in an arm chair, behaving entirely normally, save for the fact she refused to believe her husband was dead, convinced he was playing out an elaborate hoax - a wind-up - so loved by police officers. "Can I speak to DCI Daley please? It's his wife."

The pause at the other end of the phone was excruciating; then, somewhat hesitatingly the voice again. "Yes, I'll need to put you on hold, I'm not sure that he's in the office at present." The line clicked onto a musical *hold* sequence - Queen's *Seven Seas of Rye.*

"Hi, darling, I'm sorry I haven't had a chance to..."

"Fuck!" she swore loudly. "Fuck, Jim; I've been at my wit's end here." Suddenly her mouth went dry, and no more words would come out. She felt as though something was trying to make its way from her chest into her throat. She started to sob convulsively.

"Liz - what's wrong; are you OK?" Daley sounded really worried, "Where are you?"

She did her best to master the spasm of tears. "I've just... just been told a policeman was killed last night, I thought...," this all came out in a rush, ending when her throat again came to an aching close.

Daley raised his head to the ceiling, massaging his temples with his free hand. "Listen, Liz, I can't say anything about what happened last night. You understand; it's been hard, OK?" He heard her trying to collect herself. "All you need to know is I am fine; the danger is over."

"Yeah," she managed to squeak in reply, "oh thank God."

Daley knew - despite all of her faults - Liz had a deep faith; not structured, or formal, just a basic faith in God, the supreme being - entity - whatever suited best. He knew she prayed every night and he realised that her words came from the heart and were not some casual blasphemy.

She felt her breathing ease. Annie was sitting beside her on the bed, arm around her shoulder, she felt comforted by the other woman's closeness.

"All I need to know is that you're safe and are out of danger; surely you can at least give me that?"

"I'm fine, really, and the danger has passed. I have a lot on, Liz. I'll call you later, by that time things will be a lot clearer. Please try not to worry. Aren't you going on your photography trip? - at least it's not pissing down." He heard her sob break into a nasal laugh. Calmer now, she told him what she had heard, and how fear had gripped her heart.

Daley steered her enquiries away from the incidents of the previous night, Liz herself realising that it was something he was unable, or unwilling to talk about.

"I could come up - see you for a few minutes." Liz's voice was now almost normal.

"I'd love that, but I can't - not just now. Things are going to be really full-on over the next few hours. Just enjoy your trip; and I promise that I'll keep my phone on - even if it has to be on silent. OK?"

They ended the call expressing mutual love. Liz tossed her

mobile on the bed and hugged Annie in silent thanks for just being there.

As Daley put the phone down, Scott was emerging through the door looking grim.

"The Captain of the boat is ready tae be interviewed, boss. Vassily, is his name - Vassily Demienov. He's an arrogant bastard an' all. What's the plan?"

Daley went back to massaging his temples, and stayed silent for a few moments. He felt real anger. Every time he stopped thinking of something specific, Fraser's big, open face filled his mind's eye. Every time he thought of something specific he felt his bile rise; the familiar lifting feeling he had when about to lose it.

"You and me, Brian; the emperor's gone for a lie down. Let's nail this bastard."

His face was blank, devoid of emotion. Scott though, knew that inside, his friend was struggling to keep a lid on his hot temper, which he would have to try to ensure did not boil over.

In silence, the pair made their way down to the interview rooms, passing an open doorway, through which they saw a young WPC, in floods of tears, being comforted by her colleagues. The left corner of Daley's mouth began to twitch involuntarily, and his eyes narrowed.

Vassily Demienov was sitting back, his ample frame filling the chair and also the interview room with the strong stench of fish, and the fainter odour of stale alcohol. His hair was dark and greasy and he had a two or three days unshaven growth of beard. His hands were clasped across his plaid shirt, which strained to contain his bloated belly. He looked as though he was in his early sixties, though he had assured the desk sergeant he was ten years younger. In short, he was obviously no stranger to hard living.

He appraised the detectives with bleary eyes as they entered the room. Scott went over to switch on the tape machine, but Daley asked him to wait. He took his seat and leaned into the desk that separated him from the Latvian.

Before he could speak, the fisherman began waving his hands. "I have been here for over an hour, and I have had no coffee, or tobacco," his accent was strong, like the classic movie interpretation of a Russian voice. "Before I say anything I want to be fed and I want a cigarette."

Scott saw Daley on the point of combustion, so spoke up, "You, my friend are in Scotland now: if you'd told us you were a transvestite, we'd have sent out for a dress, or if you told us you were a heroin addict we wid have filled you full o' a substitute to stop your cravings. Fuck, we'd have got you a picture o' Stalin if it wid help you cooperate. But I'll tell you this: you've mair chance of flying tae the moon right noo, under yer ain steam, than lighting up a fag in a polis station. Let me assure you, I know - I've tried."

Daley's face remained expressionless. "I want you to tell me all you know about the man who killed my officer. I don't want any shit. I'm most certainly not in the mood; you won't be seeing one bite of food, or anything else until you do - clear?" He looked the captain straight in the eye.

The Latvian raised his eyebrows, then unclasped his hands, letting a long, continuous sigh issue between his lips.

"Meester, before you try to bully or threaten me, I will tell you this: I was in the Soviet army. I've been interrogated by the KGB and the FSB. I've been made to stand in a barrel of freezing water for two days, then thrown back into a cell covered in my own shit and piss. I have had my finger nails pulled out; I've even had electrodes taped to my balls. Let me assure you: there is nothing that you can do that will scare me."

"You've obviously no' been tae the Stewart Street CID office," Scott quipped, silencing at a look from Daley.

"We have your boat, Mr Demienov," Daley's voice was steady but still contained menace. "So far we have found nothing aboard, but I know why you and your friends were here. So, unless you're willingly to help me, I'm sending the vessel to our Revenue and Customs, who will take it apart piece by piece, then hand you it back as a lorry full of wood. Do you understand?"

Scott was impressed, he knew Daley was furious, devastated at the loss of Fraser, however, he was still managing to conduct the interview without exploding, and judging by the look on the fisherman's face, had located his soft-spot.

It was his turn to lean forward. "You are the one that does not understand - how could you? Living here where you are even paid not to work, given houses, food put in your belly by your country." Demienov was clearly an emotional man. "My whole life is in that boat - it is my home as well as my place of business." He sat back in his chair and stared down at his stomach. "In my country, we don't have people like you to defend us against the…" he uttered an unintelligible word in his own language, "I think you call them parasites."

"Explain." Daley was to the point.

The fisherman flung his arms in the air again. "If I want to land my fush, if I want to repair my boat, if I want a visa from the local magistrate to allow me to leave home waters - all these things must be paid for."

Scott, was sitting beside his boss, now he took his turn for a question. "We've a' got to pay - everybody, everywhere - whit makes you any different?"

"We don't pay a nice man with a briefcase in a government office." He put his head in his hands. "In the West, you think we have been liberated since *Perestroika:* you are wrong. This is why I leave Moscow," he was getting agitated. "In the old days of the Soviets, if you kept your head down, and put a few coins in the right pockets, you could get on with your life. I moved to Latvia - who cared about Latvia? I bought a small boat and started to fush. Do you not see? There was law and order; like you have here. Now - well now it is different."

"Give him a fag, Brian."

"Whit - fuck me, there'll be smoke alarms an' a' sorts goin' off. Are you sure, gaffer?" He didn't need to ask twice. He produced his cigarettes from his pocket, and flicking open the packet, offered one to Demienov, who grasped it desperately with filthy, sausage fingers. Scott lit the cigarette with his *Zippo*, then slid a metal wastepaper basket over to the man with his foot, to serve as an ash tray.

"Go on please, Mr Demienov."

"I am sorry for your loss; but it is not my doing. We are just fushermen. The man who is dead - I only know him as Kirov. We land him at certain places, he moves things about, he picks things up," Demienov shrugged his shoulders.

"What things?" Daley asked

"I never ask. Where I come from, it is better sometimes not to know."

"You can guess though - I can tell already that you are not a stupid man, Mr Demienov."

Daley studied the Latvian, going through the same mental processes that he always used when trying to form a picture of someone from whom he was attempting to extract information. People lied to the police: that was a given. Even seemingly upright, responsible citizens would find themselves guilty of at least the sin of omission when faced with any kind of questioning. Mistrust of the police ran as deep in Govan, as it did in Vladivostok; only the methods of investigation varied.

He had already decided that Demienov was in essence an honourable man, placed in an impossible situation. Daley was sure that the skipper was completely aware what Kirov - if that was the man's real name - was up to, however, he was powerless to do anything about it. As if reading his thoughts, the Latvian spoke again.

"Every time I come to your country, I hear complaints from people: 'it's too cold, I pay too much tax, the TV is rubbish, the beer is expensive, I can't afford a new car.' The list is endless, Mr Daley. People should come to my country and find out what it means to have a complaint. Do you understand me?"

The fisherman rubbed his debauched, sallow face, looking back at the officers through weary eyes.

"I have always dreaded this day," he sighed deeply, like someone carrying a huge burden. "You hope and pray that you will get through it, that they will leave you alone. But, in your heart you know that one day luck will run out, and everything you have worked for will come tumbling down." He narrowed his eyes, "A man is dead, a man from a strange land, who I don't know. It is my duty to help you; I am only too sorry that it has taken me so long to come to my senses; be brave enough to do the right thing. I hope you can understand this, Mr Daley?"

Daley nodded silently.

17

Liz waited outside the hotel. She could see that the bottom of the Main Street was cordoned off with a mixture of blue and white police tape, and the yellow *do not cross* variety. She shivered involuntarily, still feeling sick about the dead policeman.

Seanessy had arranged to meet her at ten, and he was already fifteen minutes late. She didn't consider this an auspicious start, but had managed to entertain herself by wondering just who the many people who had said - 'good morning, Mrs Daley - fine day,' - were, and more importantly, how they knew who she was?

She was perched on a broad granite window sill belonging to the hotel, and was - for her - dressed in a sensible way for someone who was about to go in search of the native wildlife: stout walking boots over thick socks, a pair of navy-blue *Ron Hill's*. She also had a heavy fleece, which she was presently carrying, as the weather had returned to the balmy conditions of the early part of her visit. The tight-fitting, open-necked t-shirt she wore, bore not only testament to her love of designer clothing, but also of the curve of her breasts, and her slim figure. Her hair was pulled back in a pony tail by a white bobble to keep it out of her eyes when she was using her camera. A pair of expensive sunglasses were propped on her head, while over her shoulder she had a backpack, specially designed to hold her camera and long lenses, along with her water and sandwiches, which Annie had insisted were made for her before she left.

Liz leaned her head back, feeling the warmth of the sun on her face. It felt hardly possible that this was the same country as yesterday, never mind the same town. The driving rain and strong winds of only a few hours ago, had given the place an entirely new aspect, and she much preferred today's conditions. Gulls soared in the blue sky, while the smell of the sea filled her nostrils. A cold hand grabbed her heart when she thought of the policeman lying on a mortician's slab, his days of feeling the wind on his face over for eternity. She removed her sunglasses and the hair bobble, then shook her head ardently, feeling the strands of hair over her face, banishing the nag of mortality she felt.

She was fixing her hair back into the pony tail, when an ancient Land Rover drew up in front of her on the road. The driver leant across the passenger seat, and after some difficulty, managed to wind down the window.

"Mrs Daley, I presume - sorry I'm a tad late - hop in."

Liz took the rucksack from her shoulder, and grabbed her fleece in the same hand as she opened the passenger door to the Land Rover, which creaked alarmingly. "Good morning, you must be Mr Seanessy - Liz Daley. Pleased to meet you," she held out her hand for Seanessy to shake.

Her guide seemed slightly flustered, gripping her hand weakly. "Oh I say, I wasn't expecting anyone as attrac…," he paused, "…I mean as young as yourself. I get a lot of retired people on my trips you see; all a bit like me - too much time on their hands. You can put your bag at your feet if that's comfortable enough. We'll take a drive to the car park at Machrie, then get the map out and try and find out the best places to take you. I'm so glad that the weather has improved."

Liz cast her eye over Seanessy, as he struggled to wrestle the stick into a forward gear. He was wearing a green waterproof jacket, though there was no obvious sign of rain. Liz had hers in a neat pack strapped around her waist. He was also wearing a pair of light-grey jogging bottoms that had seen better days, tucked into green Wellington boots, onto one of which was placed what looked like a puncture repair, more commonly seen on a bicycle tyre. His hair was plastered with some deliberation across his forehead, typical of a man who was going bald. He was unshaven rather than sporting a beard and she noticed a trace of faded red in his short sideburns. The whole vehicle smelled vaguely of fish, and an ancient mobile phone slid backwards and forwards across the dash board, depending on the direction of travel.

She began to wonder whether or not she had made the right decision in making the trip, but reminded herself of the pleasantness of the day and the possibility of snapping some great images of the local flora and fauna; something she hadn't done enough of recently.

"Would you like a mint?" Seanessy took a paper bag from the recesses of his waterproof, and offered it to Liz.

"No thanks," she said, feeling slightly queasy at the smell and also the thought of consuming something of such dubious provenance. "I had a big breakfast," she smiled.

"Ah yes, I'm afraid I rather skip breakfast as a rule - always starving by this time of the morning." He managed to steer and extract a small handful of mints from the bag, which he proceeded to place awkwardly into his mouth, missing with one, which rolled down his jacket and onto the floor of the Land Rover, destined to be lost amongst the detritus there. "We'll be there in five minutes," Seanessy mumbled through a mouthful of mints.

The deal was simple: in return for immunity from the further prosecution of him and his crew, Demienov would undertake to tell Daley all he knew about what the gang, who had inflicted themselves on his vessel, were doing and had done. This would include those whom he knew them to be in contact with, local drop-off points and any information he had with regards to their operation and structure within Latvia.

Daley knew that there was no-little risk involved with an agreement of this type. He could not be sure that Demienov was not part of the organised crime gang who had targeted Kinloch, nor could he be sure that anything the fisherman said would be of any value. However, he was working on the instinct, which throughout his career had worked better than any of the bookish philosophy he had acquired in training.

He would have to set the ball rolling by putting the proposition to Donald, who would then get authorisation for such a deal from the very top. He was desperate to bring those behind the murder of Fraser to justice. Despite the actual culprit lying dead on a gurney at Kinloch hospital, he felt, ardently, that the venal organisation behind him was still a cancer feeding on all parts of society, that must be eradicated.

He did not however believe that the Latvians were responsible for the three other murders he was investigating; it was that instinct again. On reflection, the gnawing doubt had been there before the raid took place. Was it merely his self-preening arrogance that had led to the death of Fraser? Should he have handed the whole operation over to the customs or the drugs squad? Certainly, he had been massively encouraged by his boss to retain charge of a situation of which he was not the architect.

He now had four murders on his hands; probably at least two distinct investigations. Why was he so sure that the murders of Watson, Ritchie and Mulligan, were disconnected from the drug smugglers who had killed Fraser? He couldn't be sure. According to the Royal Navy, the Latvian fishing boat, was nowhere near local waters when Mulligan and Ritchie were killed; they could have been murdered by accomplices of the gang, but Daley thought this unlikely.

"Apart from *Pulse*, and the involvement with the Latvians, Bri, there's some connection we're missing." The two Detectives were sitting in Daley's glass box, having left Demienov to sweat it out in the Kinloch cells. Donald was due back in an hour, and Daley was desperately trying to find something to justify his approach to the various deaths.

"I know what you mean. Why wid the Ruskies come intae port here if they'd jist killed their mates? They must hae known that we'd have found the bodies by that time, Jim," Scott said, swirling the coffee in his mug.

The DNA of all of the Latvians, including the dead gunman were being tested, along with the local DNA testing of all the regular male customers of *Pulse*.

Daley's phone gave its internal ring. "Sir, there's a Davie Fraser on the line to speak to you." The WPC's voice was strained; she had made the obvious connection.

Liz and Glynn Seanessy were standing in the Machrie car park studying an ordnance survey map spread over the bonnet of the Land Rover. He had donned a pair of old-fashioned, thick glasses, and his hair was now flying up in strands from his head in the light sea breeze.

Already, on a rock in the small bay, Liz had spotted a colony of common seals basking in the spring sunshine. The sea made the air fresh and new, and with the sun on the back of her neck, she was beginning to enjoy her trip - despite her unusual guide and the state of his transport.

"I thought we could try up here first," Seanessy was pointing at a location on the map, with a very chewed pencil. A small ridge was located behind the bay, from which, not only could good panoramic shots be taken, but also there was the possibility of spotting a pair of golden eagles that were nesting not far away. Now there was an image that Liz would love to capture.

Seanessy poured over the map, then scratched at his behind absently, only stopping when he noticed the curl of disgust on Liz's lips.

"Eh - sorry… I'm afraid I'm not so used to company these days; especially of the female variety."

Liz noticed that his ears had become very red. "I'm the one who should be sorry, I'm too used to nagging my husband when he does things like that. Go on, scratch your arse whenever you want." They resumed their deliberations.

"I canna believe it, Jimmy. He wiz a good lad, ye know? A bit o' a lassie when it came tae the bevy; but a good lad a' the same." Davie Fraser sounded frail over the phone.

Daley was holding the receiver to his ear with one hand, while massaging his brow with the other. "I know how you must be feeling, Davie. I've not even been able to phone his folks yet.

Everything's just been…," he didn't get time to finish.

"Well that wiz kinda why I wiz phoning, Jimmy." Davie Fraser still used the diminutive he addressed Daley by when he was a young probationer. "They've had that prick Donald on the phone; Mary's quite upset."

"How do you mean?" Daley could feel his hackles rise.

"Och, you ken that one. It wiz a' *noble sacrifice,* an' *for the greater good,* stuff. He's forgettin' I kent him when he wiz a two shilling bully fae the slums. Fuck me, ye wid think ye were talking tae Tony Blair noo the way he goes on."

There was a sudden silence on the end of the phone. "You there, Davie?" Daley stopped rubbing his forehead, and started doodling with a pen on the large pad on his desk. Speaking to bereaved relatives was arduous at the best of times, even more so when you shared a past with them.

"I'm sorry, Jimmy," Davie Fraser said, his voice breaking. "I had a lot o' time fir the boy - like a son tae me - ye know? I mean look at the state o' me noo, I can hardly walk the length o' myself, an' I know it's a' cos o the bevy. I'm a fuckin' waste o' space; the boy wiz worth somethin' ye ken?"

Daley agreed, but said nothing.

Liz and Seanessy were scaling the ridge which overlooked Machrie Bay. The climb was steeper than it had looked from the car park, and she could already feel rivulets of sweat running down her back. She wondered how Seanessy must be feeling; he was still wearing a waterproof jacket and now looked extremely hot. Despite this, he kept up a commentary on the visual pleasures of their trip: they had already seen a numberless quantity of seabirds, small mammals, and plant life, about all of which Seanessy seemed to be well informed.

"Ah look, a heron. Beautiful bird, would you not say?"

"Yes, they're so majestic in flight," Liz replied.

"Yes, they only nest in two places in the world: here, and the African savannah - incredible, isn't it? I've always thought of them as a little bit of Africa here in Scotland." He peered at the bird through a pair of dishevelled binoculars hung around his neck.

After much exertion, they reached the summit of the ridge. Before them at this elevated height, lay the full panoply of the vista. Immediately below, arable farm land gave way to rough, patchy machair, then on to the sandy bay, fringed by the white, breaking waves of the restless Atlantic. In the distance, the dark loom of islands of the Inner Hebrides were in plain sight.

Liz looked to her left, training her small, up market binoculars on what seemed like the closest landmass on view. "Which island is that, Mr Seanessy?"

"You are right to say it is an island - technically that is. However, it is a much larger one than the others." He had the perambulatory way of explanation, peculiar to the avid enthusiast. "That is the wonderful island of Ireland."

Liz looked again, amazed at the proximity of it. "Wow, I can see a car - look over there to the left - it's quite clear."

"It's only twelve miles at the closest point; not far from where we are looking at the moment, in fact. That's the coast of County Antrim."

The pair continued to take the view in for a few minutes. Magnified, the Irish coast looked blue, a light house flashed white every few seconds, wavering through a heat haze.

"Of course that is still the UK we are seeing; but look there - to the right - do you see in the distance, a faint shape?"

"Yes, quite clearly," Liz's binoculars were obviously more powerful than her guide's.

"That's County Donegal, in the Republic, a foreign country to all intents and purposes now; where my grandfather came from actually. We haven't strayed far as a family really."

Liz breathed in deeply, the mixed scent of land and sea was heady in the spring heat. "If you don't mind, I'll get one of my lenses out and try and get a few shots of the Emerald Isle," she said fumbling in her rucksack, and eventually removing a suitably expensive-looking piece of equipment.

"Be my guest, we've got all day," replied Seanessy.

She looked up and smiled in response, but his gaze was cast far away, his face expressionless. She busied herself attaching the lens, found her small, portable tripod then looked around for the best image.

Daley had just received a report from the pathologist: still no matches for the unidentified semen samples found on both Watson and Ritchie's bodies. They would have to consider extending the sample group criteria from the local community. Action like this was always controversial, people became worried about a *big brother* state.

Forensic examination of Mulligan's cabin cruiser, *Russian Gold*, had proved more fruitful however. SOCO, had found a number of fibres not belonging to the vessel or victims; more work was being done.

Scott arrived back in Daley's glass world to let him know that Donald had arrived back in the office after his *doss*, as the irascible DS had termed it.

He walked along the corridor to what had been MacLeod's office to find Donald sifting through a mountain of detritus which had been deposited on the hitherto immaculately kept desk.

"It's you, Jim," Donald had been caught off-guard, and looked flustered at the DCI's arrival.

"Just getting down to some investigation of my own," he intentionally furrowed his brow, to indicate sincerity, which always had the opposite effect. "Hopefully find what else this Highland rascal was keeping hidden. He's coming in later for an interview with discipline and myself. I wouldn't mind a few lines from you on what took place between you and he - say in the next couple of hours?" The tone of the question belied its status as a command.

"So you're basically rifling through his drawers." Daley's statement was flat - just the way he felt.

Deciding to ignore his subordinate, Donald changed tack. "I've spoken to young Fraser's parents; thought I would take some of the weight off your shoulders." Donald raised his eyebrows, looking, no doubt, for an expression of gratitude from Daley.

"I know," was his only response.

"They were upset; as is to be expected."

"I'm going to call them myself, this evening."

"I'm sure there isn't any need; I think I have covered our response to the tragedy adequately. They'll get a letter of condolence from the Chief Constable, and of course the First Minister." Donald smiled with satisfaction, as though, in his mind, the intervention of such exalted figures more than compensated for a dead son, lying in a mortuary drawer.

"Please ensure that no-one else talks to them before I get a chance to; enough damage has been done already." Daley was emphatic.

"Meaning what, exactly?"

"Meaning I've talked to another close relative, who thought that your call was shit, that's what."

Donald put down the silver Quaich that he had been examining and looked Daley levelly in the face.

"Whatever it is that is eating you, please excise it by bouncing it off your halfwit DS, not me. I have still not forgotten that we have a growing number of unsolved murders, with no solution in sight. Neither have I lost sight of the disaster that was the last press conference that you and that fuckin' idiot presided over. If you've come to chastise me, think again, and get your head back into the job in hand." He picked the Quaich back up again.

"I need to extend the local DNA sample," Daley ignored his boss's outburst. "Every man in the area between sixteen and forty. Is that possible?"

"Oh yes, it's possible - but is it desirable? These 'human rights' things are a pain in the arse. Endless paperwork and...," Daley intervened.

"The Latvian skipper wants to do a deal on behalf of himself and his crew, in return for information about the drugs supply here," he stood up. "I'll need an answer to both of these questions within the next hour." He turned on his heel and left the office, slamming the door in the process.

Liz had managed to capture some good images, including a baying stag, a hare, some fantastic landscapes; even a distant, yet clear shot of a golden eagle, soaring high over the escarpment.

She had enjoyed herself, though her guide had seemed to become more and more introverted as the trip had gone on, despite her frequent attempts at small talk and idle chatter. True to her nature, she decided to ask why.

"I hope everything is OK? - sorry if I've been blithering on. You must be so used to this wonderful scenery, it's such a novelty for me."

Seanessy looked blankly at her for a moment, as though he had been thinking deeply.

"I'm so sorry. Been a bit off-colour today. I can't help thinking about these dreadful murders. I hear a policeman was killed last night; that's the local gossip anyhow," he suddenly looked embarrassed. "I'm not fishing for information or anything; I mean I know who you are. I hope you don't think…," he mumbled, looking on in contrition.

"Yes, it's OK. It must be such a shock to everyone, especially in a quiet little place like this," she decided to change the subject. "You were a teacher here, weren't you?"

"Yes indeed, served before the mast for much longer than I care to mention. I always wanted to be a scientist. You know the type of thing: research at Oxbridge; a comfortable life as a Don. Not to be, I'm afraid," a shadow crossed his face.

"You can't complain about where you live now surely, this is absolutely glorious. You somehow never think that places as beautiful as this exist in Scotland. Do you know what I mean?" Her husband would have criticised the inflection in her voice.

"Yes, I suppose I have much to be thankful for," he looked dreamy, as though preoccupied by distant thoughts.

"Wow!" Liz's shout made Seanessy jump. She was looking excitedly through her binoculars. "I think I've just seen a whale out in the bay - surely not."

Seanessy took a look in the same general direction, just as the creature ejaculated another telltale plume of water from its breathing hole, the body then arching through the water like the sea monsters of legend.

"A minky whale if I'm not much mistaken; they're the most common of the genus here, though we occasionally get others. I've seen a couple of Orcas, but that was further out, from a boat."

"You have a boat?" Liz took her excited gaze away from the whale.

"Well no, not exactly; I have a loan of a small vessel from some local fishermen should the need arise. Helpful for spotting the more unusual. I bagged a Manx Shearwater recently - the world's most travelled creature, you know."

"That's fantastic. I would love to see a killer whale, or a Manx Shearwater come to that. I have a friend who works as a picture editor for a wildlife magazine. I'm sure he would be interested if I could get decent images of unusual specimens like that - kick start my career again," she looked wistfully for the whale.

"Tell you what, if you're interested, I'll try to get the use of the boat tomorrow - if the boys aren't using it; unofficially you understand. I'm not licensed to conduct nautical tours, neither is the boat for that matter. I do have a maritime certificate though - just don't tell that husband of yours," he grinned nervously.

"I think he has more than enough to worry about than me getting a jolly on a boat. That would be fantastic if you could manage it. I'll pay the going rate, of course.

"I'm sure we'll work something out to our mutual satisfaction, Mrs Daley." He gazed at her as she scanned the bay for another sight of the whale. Holding the binoculars made her t-shirt ride up, displaying her flat, tanned stomach.

Daley and Scott were discussing just how easy or not, it would be to round up all of the target male group for DNA samples to be taken: not, was the general consensus they reached.

For Daley, it was all a bit like wading through treacle at the moment. He couldn't get Archie Fraser off his mind, and there was nothing worse than being preoccupied when trying to fathom a difficult enquiry.

"I'm the same as you, gaffer," Scott was chewing gum to stave off his nicotine withdrawal, incurred by the strict no-smoking policy in the Kinloch office. "But if it's no' the Latvians that are responsible for our three murders - then who?"

"I want to take another look at all the CCTV footage," Daley stroked his face, and realised that he was badly in need of a shave. "There must be something we're missing around the time she left *Pulse*. How did she get from Kinloch Main Street to the bay at Machrie? I'm sure there must be a clue on it - somewhere."

Scott looked at his boss wearily. He knew the man inside-out. He could see how badly Daley had been affected by the young detective's death, and how horrified he was - they all were - by the violent way that he, and the other three victims had met their ends. He also knew how this determination was most likely to manifest itself: painstaking re-working of all possible evidence, re-examination of all potential witnesses, those close to the victims - anything that would be likely to churn up a vital clue to break the case.

It was quite unusual to have this amount of forensic evidence, and for it to have made so little difference. Yes, they had managed to expose an Eastern European gang doing a roaring trade in narcotics in this isolated community and who knows where else, plus a morally corrupt police Inspector; that though, was not the point. They had failed to come near to solving any of the three, original murders, and to compound this failure, had managed to lose a youthful colleague in the process. In short, Scott knew it was time to burn the midnight oil; time for his boss to become unbearably intense, in an effort to solve the crimes.

"Dae ye want me tae send oot fir pizza?"

Daley smiled wanly; not for the first time, his DS had read his mind.

The Land Rover was hot and stuffy inside when they opened the doors. Liz could again smell the fruits of the sea gone bad, inside.

The old diesel engine rattled into life, then they began the short drive back to Kinloch. Though she was tired, she was in high spirits. The little excursion had seen her capture some good images, and now couldn't wait to get them downloaded onto a PC and *Photoshop* them into saleable work. She felt a sense of pride that she was, once again, doing something positive; something she knew she was good at; something to make it worthwhile getting up.

"I hope seven's not too early for you? I have to fit in with when I can get the boat. It's a bonus that we can sail from Kinloch, it'll take about an hour and a half to get to where we want to be for your shots. However, it's a stunning sail, especially if this weather holds."

Seanessy changed gear, and Liz noticed how the sun had burned the back of his hands into an angry red, matching his forehead, unprotected by his receding hair. "I love being up early - and thanks for today, it's been lovely. I'm so looking forward to tomorrow. What do you think the chances of bagging an Orca are?"

Seanessy turned his head to talk to her. "Good, I would say. It's the right time of year and conditions; they tend to come a bit nearer into shore during the better weather. Our friends the common seals get a bit lazy in the sun - take their eye off the ball - before you know it: BANG!" He shouted and thumped the steering wheel, making Liz jump. Your Orca is a highly intelligent creature, you know, they've developed a number of really effective strategies with which to capture prey."

I would have thought that swimming as fast as possible and having big teeth was all that was required." Liz was now admiring the scenery from the Land Rover's passenger window.

"A good start, but not enough for these killers," Seanessy chuckled. "Do you know, that sometimes they hunt in pairs close to the shore. Recently - in Sweden I think - a woman was walking her dog along the beach and spotted an Orca about fifty yards off the shore, jumping from the water and doing tumbles - you know, the way they do in these dreadful Florida shows?"

Liz nodded for Seanessy to continue.

"Well, of course she goes a bit closer to the water's edge to get a better look, she stops, and then from nowhere, another killer whale launches itself out of the water, onto the beach, grabs the dog, pulls it from her grasp, and waddles back into the water, quick as you like."

"Really?" The story made Liz shudder.

"Oh yes. To an Orca you see, a dog and a seal look much the same, I suppose. They use that strategy all the time with seals. The poor things get mesmerised by the antics of the Orca doing tricks and forget to look out for his mate slinking through the shallows with murder in mind. Good, eh?"

Liz silently resolved not to walk too near the sea again.

The flickering images on the screen were from the five CCTV cameras that covered Kinloch town centre. The detectives had seen better quality footage. It was monochromatic, however, mainly in sharp focus, which made a significant difference.

Daley was desperately going through all he knew about the deaths in his mind: they were friends, and moved in the same social circle. They all used illegal narcotics, and were involved in the purchase and distribution of same within the community. And lastly, they were all dead.

Mulligan was from Glasgow, where background work by colleagues in the city, had shown him to be a petty criminal with two charges of shoplifting, three breaches of the peace and a minor assault charge against his name. Hardly a *Mr Big* in the fetid world of organised crime. However, he did associate with a few *players*; men whom police knew to be at the heart of Scotland's criminal underworld. Unfortunately though, coming from the housing scheme that he did, almost everybody qualified under the *associates* banner, so numerous were the criminals from that area. Certainly, no direct connection could be found between Mulligan and any existing crime family; how though, he had managed to fund *Pulse*, was still unclear. Daley was amazed that Mulligan was indeed his real name. The forensic accountants were busy going through his fiscal life with a fine tooth comb.

18

The atmosphere in the County bar was so oppressive that Liz decided to retreat to her room. She was not in the mood to answer questions about the death of a policeman the previous night; not least because she knew less than her interrogators. In any event, she would never have dreamt of being so indiscreet concerning her husband's work.

The ever faithful Annie, seeing her plight, had supplied her with a menu, large gin and tonic and told her to give her a call whenever she wished a top-up, or an evening meal.

"I've no' seen any o' the polis at all today - apairt fae a' the vans an' suchlike, ga'in up an' doon the street." Annie imparted with her habitual brio.

Settling down in her room, Liz tried to call her husband, but his phone was off. She left a message, then attempted to numb her mind with gin and the tail-end of afternoon TV.

She was marvelling at the prices of barn conversions in East Sussex, when her mobile intoned its best approximation of an old-fashioned callbox ring.

"Hi, darling," she could instantly detect the strain in her husband's voice. "Sorry I've had the mobile switched off all day - been checking it though. How was your trip?"

She proceeded to blab on about her photographic ramble with Seanessy, anxious for him not to feel he had to make mention of the death of a colleague.

Ultimately though, during a brief lull in her tale, Daley interrupted.

"Keep this to yourself for the moment," he sounded like a policeman, something she rarely pictured. "It was Archie Fraser who was killed last night - you know, the red-haired lad who was in the bar the other night?"

She suddenly felt cold. Yes, she remembered Fraser, very tall, slightly awkward; she had watched him look at Daley, and she could tell that he held her husband in great esteem by the way he hung onto the older man's every word.

"Oh, I'm so sorry," was all that seemed appropriate to say.

Though the call was brief, she was glad that he had taken the time to speak to her. She sensed the determination and tiredness in his voice, but noted that this was nothing unusual when he was on a major investigation. To her, it seemed that Daley could survive on hardly any sleep for days on end when the hard yards were being covered. She knew him well enough to know that he would be mentally scourging himself because of Fraser's death; re-enacting the whole incident in his mind, trying to isolate what had gone wrong - what he should have done.

He went on to tell her how he was going to come down to the hotel around eight, to get a bite to eat and a couple of hours sleep. If he could manage that. She had strongly advised he stay away from the bar, and take up Annie's offer of room service. After a pause, he agreed.

They were taking it in turns to examine the CCTV footage. Scott was at the screen now, with WDC Dunn assisting, her sharp eyes, and local knowledge adding perspective to what was being displayed. They were doing three-quarter of an hour shifts at this job, as it was literally, an eye-watering task.

Daley was in his glass room, brooding, thinking and calculating - not a mental count of numbers - more a studied equation of probability, combined with chance and vested interest.

Someone had left a car magazine on his desk, that he was flicking through idly, like an existential *aide memoir*. Why had he not made it clear to Fraser and his team that they were only present to keep the public at bay and observe? Unarmed, he should have made it crystal-clear that intervention was not in their remit. How had the Latvian known to jump ship when he did? The Navy had been monitoring their radio and internet traffic for a period of hours before the operation was conceived.

He turned over a page on which the Jaguar *XF* was being displayed in all its smooth-lined, polished magnificence. It was then he knew the answer.

Flynn's car was outside his building on the pier, so Daley and Scott made their way along to his office. A strained looking Flynn looked slightly wide-eyed at them when he answered the door.

"Good afternoon, Mr Flynn. Can we have a word?" Daley was business like in his manner.

"Well - eh - of course. I was just going home; long night and all that. It won't take long, will it?" He sounded unsure.

"Oh, I don't think so," said Daley, who watched the harbour master visibly relax.

The office was in its habitual state of untidiness, though there was no sign of Hamish sitting at the antiquated desk. The computer screen was still displaying the updating satellite weather map, beside it lay a half-eaten fish supper, still in the paper wrapping. The enticing smell of fish and chips made Daley's stomach rumble.

"Dae ye mind if I hae a chip?" Scott looked at Flynn with arched, enquiring brows.

"Of course not, be my guest. You might as well finish it off, I've lost my appetite after last night's - well, I needna' tell you." He looked at the floor, stroking his neat beard.

They all stayed silent for a few moments. The events of the previous night were still viscerally real.

"I thought I would bring you this." Daley handed Flynn a magazine. It's got the new Jag XF in it." He smiled at Flynn.

"Thanks, Mr Daley, thanks very much," there were beads of sweat on Flynn's brow. It was only then that Daley noticed the smell of alcohol on his breath.

"Been having a wee dram, Mr Flynn?" Scott - as he often did

- seemed to hone in on Daley's thoughts.

"I wisna goin' tae drive gents, if that's what you're worried about. In fact, I wiz about tae call my wife tae come an' get me."

"How much did you get for your scallop boat?" Daley's question came from nowhere.

Flynn now began to look very nervous, his eyes flicked between the two detectives.

"I don't understand, why would you want tae know that?" Flynn's voice was wavering in tandem with his resolve.

"Eight and half thousand, I was told. Not a huge amount - eh?" Daley's voice was flat.

"No, the trade around here's not what it wiz. It gave me an' the wife a wee lift though," Flynn spoke quickly, his accent thickening.

"The car that's sitting outside; what's it worth new? Forty-five, fifty K?"

"I, well I had saved up - you know, I…"

"Why did you do it? - You're a decent man. You have a good job and a nice house; why did you get involved with people who spread poison and misery?" Daley was standing in front of Flynn, dwarfing him in his swivel chair.

"I don't know whoot ye mean," he shouted, panic in his eyes.

Something inside Daley snapped. He hauled the dapper harbour master out of his chair by his collar and tie, and pulled him towards his face.

"A young man died because of your actions last night," flecks of spittle were on Flynn's face. "*You* tipped off our Latvian friend. *You've* been working for these scum - watching their backs, seeing they had a safe harbour - you little bastard." Daley threw Flynn through the air, he landed beside the old desk, hitting his head against a corner of it, making him yelp in pain. Daley moved towards the whimpering harbour master, but before he could strike him again, Scott pulled him back by the shoulders.

"That's enough, Jim. Fuck's sake man, this isna' goin' tae bring the young fella' back."

Daley was shaking with fury, but he managed to contain

himself, Scott's intervention clearing some of the red mist.

"Tell me how you contacted him? Now!" he shouted, Scott still holding on to him - just in case.

Flynn sobbed, the pristine collar of his white uniform shirt was now stained with blood coming from a wound on his head, sustained when he hit the desk.

"Mobile," he whispered through his tears, "I called a mobile number."

"Get the cuffs on him, Brian. I need some air." Daley left the office, slamming the door on his way out, then leaving the building. He breathed deeply at the salty air, leaning on Flynn's Jaguar. He looked inside the vehicle through the dark, privacy glass, at the leather seats and the walnut finishing, the creamy luxury of the interior. He cursed: the owner of that car had cost Archie Fraser his life. *Was that all it was worth?*

Flynn was taken back to the office by Scott, who had called a van.

Daley had another port of call. James Newell, who ran the RIB hire business from the pontoons. Daley had seen the vessel glide into the loch and despatch a handful of camera wielding tourists safely ashore. The area had been cordoned off for most of the day after Fraser's shooting; not that there had been much to find out, though the relentless master that was procedure, had to be followed.

Two men were still working aboard the boat as Daley made his way down the pontoon. He noticed that the bell was silent in the still air, and remembered its baleful reports through the operation the previous evening.

One of the men was probably in his sixties, though both were tall and thin with dark hair; no doubt they were related. Daley placed the younger man somewhere in his thirties, though trying to estimate the age of anyone between the ages of twenty-eight and fifty seemed to be an increasingly difficult task these days. He pondered absently if this was something to do with his own advancing years, then dismissed the idea.

The older man on the boat eyed him under his brow and over a pair of half-moon glasses.

"Can I help you?"

"Are you James Newell?"

"Yes, and I take it that you are Chief Inspector Daley," Newell smiled. "This is my nephew, Rory," he had seen Daley look at the other man. "He's up from the smoke for the summer to get some air in his lungs and to work out what he wants to do with his life now the bank have dispensed with his services - eh, Rory?" The younger man nodded.

Daley was invited aboard and he took Rory's offer of a hand up, over the side of the craft. He felt as though he was viewing himself from above, like a hackneyed death scene from a hospital drama and was angry with himself about losing control with Flynn. For someone who dealt with death as part of his daily life, the murder of Fraser had had an unexpected effect. That, combined with the heavy tiredness he was experiencing, left him feeling that his mind was wandering; like being in a meditative trance he had often thought. In these periods, he often had the inspiration that led to solving a case. Hope sprung eternal in the policeman's breast.

The three shook hands, observing polite introduction. Newell himself had an easy, patrician manner and had Daley not known that he was an ex-naval captain, he probably would have guessed; that or a senior civil servant, at any rate.

"Wedded to the sea, Inspector, that's me. Anyhow, what more could a man want than to ply his trade in such a beautiful part of the world - despite the hostility of some of the locals? I suppose that you've already come across that?" He looked to the detective for an answer.

"Not really, Mr Newell. They are a very interested body of people in my experience, but I haven't come up against anything malicious yet. Apart from the very obvious, of course."

Newell shrugged his shoulders. "That's probably because they see you as being from the same stable - what?" He went on to tell Daley that even though both of his parents had been Scots and, having been born in Glasgow, so was he. His accent and manner had marked him down as an Englishman in Kinloch. A posh one at that.

"I'm not in the least bothered, of course, though some of these plebs can be quite unpleasant. Water off a duck's back for me after being caged up with a submarine full of hairy submariners for months on end; and let me tell you, that breed don't suffer from the reluctance to speak out, that inflicts the rest of the service. I'm sure that I don't have to tell you anything about man-management."

After what had really been a round of pleasantries, Daley informed Newell that what he really wanted was any kind of rota, or ship's log covering the period of the murders.

"I'm not accusing you of anything, Mr Newell, it's just that I have to cover all my bases. I already know about the movements of the fishing craft, but you and the rest of the visitors to the pontoons are still a bit of a mystery."

"Well worry no more, sir, as you've probably heard, I am involved in the company that owns this pontoon. We keep records of all our visitors; well the honest ones at any rate."

"The honest ones?"

"An unwritten rule of the sea. If you moor somewhere, you do your best to find out to whom your harbour dues are paid. I'm not here day and night, so sometimes we get - let's just call them yachtsmen - who come in out of the weather late in the evening and upon the arrival of a better morning, bugger off without parting with a penny. They are, I am glad to say, in the minority."

It turned out that Newell had an office in the upstairs of the same building on the pier that housed the harbour master. The three men made their way back there, Newell promising that he would give Daley the register of vessels that had been moored at the pontoon during the relevant period.

Rory hadn't said much, so when his uncle went to find three coffees from the communal machine in the corridor, Daley took his chance to quiz the younger man.

He asked if Rory had known any of the victims; the detective thought he was being unhelpful when he did not answer this question immediately. After a long pause, he spoke.

"I did know one of the dead people," he looked intense. "If the stories I've been hearing are right?" Rory had the same patrician mien as his uncle, he sat languidly on a metal chair, with one foot resting on a small table.

"What stories would these be?" Daley stayed low-key. Why could no-one answer a straight forward question in a similarly straight forward way? This question had haunted him throughout his career.

"The cop who got killed last night - I knew him. If it's the guy I've heard about, of course." He continued to stare at Daley, his expression unchanging.

"I'm afraid I can't comment on that incident at the moment. Anyway, I was referring to the murders of Janet Ritchie, Izzy Watson and Peter Mulligan."

Rory Newell snorted derision. "I don't know why you're bothering to waste time on people like that. As far as I can tell they're scum of the earth, like most of the rest of this sorry shithole. I liked Archie though - good bloke." He stared at Daley again.

"Why did you leave the bank, Mr Newell?" As the policeman had planned, that had the desired effect; a shadow of annoyance passed over Rory's face.

"I wasn't aware it had become a police matter," he managed a weak smile, but Daley could sense his anger.

At that, Newell senior arrived back, clutching three styrofoam coffee mugs in his long-fingered hands. He handed the beverages around, then took his seat behind a small desk, on which were placed a lap-top computer, a telephone and a leather-bound *Roberts* radio.

"Is that an original?" Daley gestured at the radio.

"That set, Inspector, has been with me for forty-two years, and has been around the world at least four times. My guilty pleasure - addicted to Radio Four - now I've managed to settle down in the one place," he smiled.

"Though why the fuck it had to be here, no-one knows." That was said under his breath by his nephew, who was looking at the ceiling.

"Do you like the radio, Mr Daley?" Newell continued as though Rory had not spoken.

"Oh yes, a little passion of mine too. I just got my hands on a *Grundig Party Boy* recently, though like you, I still prefer *Roberts*. Owned by the Japanese now - how things change."

All three sat in silence, as though contemplating the consequences of a classic British radio brand being owned in the far-east.

"I'm sure you don't need me, Mr Daley. I've got to get back home; get on-line and see if I can find a real job, back in civilisation," Rory stood suddenly.

"I take it you are under forty, Mr Newell?" Daley questioned the younger man.

"Thirty-four," his uncle didn't give him a chance to reply.

"In that case, I would like you to volunteer at your earliest opportunity to go to the police office and have a DNA swab taken. Every man resident in the area will be taking part." He smiled at Rory.

"If I must, do you think you may have your man, officer?" He sneered at Daley. "OK, Uncle Jimmy - heading off to the hacienda. Goodbye, Inspector Daley. I'll attend to provide my swab tomorrow; if that won't hinder your investigation too much. Ciao." He left the small office.

"Don't let him wind you up, Mr Daley. I'm afraid he's very like my late brother: stupid. He had a good opportunity at the bank, but blew it. He tried for the Navy you know, didn't get a sniff, of course." Newell looked into the middle distance.

The two men discussed the pontoon and the Newells' movements and activities around the time of the murder of Izzy Watson. It turned out that they had been to County Antrim, acting as aquatic transport for a film crew making a documentary about the Giant's Causeway. The weather had caused a few problems, so they had to stay longer than intended.

"Flynn was in charge; nominally of course. As usual, he was too keen on chewing the fat with his fishermen mates than checking on my pontoon. I wonder where he is? His office is in darkness. It's an early dark, even by his standards."

"Was your nephew with you on this trip?" Daley changed the subject.

"Look here, Mr Daley, I am fully aware of how aggravating Rory is, but I can assure you he is no murderer. Beneath the swagger he is quite shy; certainly not outgoing - definitely not violent. His wife buggered off with one of his best friends just before he lost his job; tried to top himself," Newell looked at the ceiling in the same manner that his nephew had, only moments earlier. "That's why he's here. I hope you understand: and yes, to answer your next question, he was with me the whole time."

Newell went on to show him the list of craft berthed at the pontoons around the time of the murders. He decided to take the register with him; Newell reluctantly agreeing to use a temporary log in the meantime.

He was aware of eyes on him, that primeval sense that man long ago forgot how to use properly. Even through the limited vista of the bar serving hatch, the good citizens of Kinloch strained to get a look at the detective who had just arrested a well-known member of the community. Annie shouted a brisk *hello,* as he turned right before the reception, then up the faded elegance of the staircase.

The steps always felt strange, or so Daley sensed. They were less deep, wider than normal stairs, so consequently, those ascending felt as though the effort being put in was not commensurate with their progress. Maybe he was just tired.

In fact, he was shattered. He had little sleep the night before due to the fatal operation they had carried out against the Latvian vessel. He was hungry and his heart was sore - not in the sense of stress, or medical pain - sore as it represented the gauge of the soul; the prism through which was viewed all he felt, saw, heard, and sometimes subconsciously assimilated during his lifetime.

At this moment in time, he couldn't remove the image of Archie Fraser from his mind, and the empty feeling of guilt that accompanied it. Some people were destined to strive all of their lives for betterment, the march towards greatness of the truly ambitious: but at what price? Had Daley been a mere bystander - an operative, put in place by another during the raid against the fishing boat? No. Of course, he would have felt sad at the demise of any fellow officer. No doubt he would have said a silent prayer of gratitude that the man lying on the cold tarmac of the chill jetty with a suppurating hole in his chest, was not him. However, therein lay the difference. He was the man who had put Fraser in the place that eventually led to his death. He was the man who had played so carelessly with a young life that it was lost forever. For that reason, he felt none of the unspoken relief of one spared tragedy. He wished he could turn time on its head and swap places with the young detective. With his long experience he would never have exposed himself to harm, the way Fraser had so selflessly done. In the event that harm had come his way then: so be it. There would have been no-one to blame but himself and fate. There would be no pathetic, ashen -faced ghost, ready to fill any absent thought, or tortured dream.

He found the door to his room locked and before he could fumble the key from his pocket, Liz opened it. She was wearing his favourite jumper, which was pulled in at her waist by the loosely knotted tie. She was more tanned than when he had last seen her, and he suddenly remembered that she had been on a photographic trip. He tried to speak, but finding words so hard to come by, and the mere presence of her so intoxicating, he fell into her arms. Automatically, he began the anxious search for her lips. They kissed passionately. When he pulled away, he could see disappointment flicker across her features. He pulled the woollen garment over her head, deliciously, revealing the contours of her naked flesh framed by the drab room. A loose wisp of hair fell over her face. They fell on the bed, and made the frantic, desperate love, of those spared the terminus of death and free to carry on the chancy journey of life.

19

It was five in the morning, when Daley was roused from a fitful sleep. He had agreed to be back at the office around six to give Scott a break and some much needed sleep.

He switched the alarm off as quickly as he could, but to his dismay, Liz began to stir.

"Get back to sleep, Liz, its only just after five. Duty calls, I'm afraid."

She sat up, her breasts displaying magnificently over the duvet. "No, it's OK, it's an early start for me too. Mr Seanessy's taking me out on a boat he scrounged from somewhere. Oh, I promised him I wouldn't tell you, I don't think it's strictly legal. You know, licenses and suchlike; if I can get a shot of an Orca, he can have stolen the *Ark Royal* for all I care."

Daley processed this information through his newly alert brain. "As long as he is competent at sea. How far out are you going?"

Liz yawned mightily, arms outstretched; a *V* shaped arrow of tan pointed to the cleft of her bosom, and recalled the neck of the t-shirt that she had been wearing the day before, as well as the fine, warm weather.

"Huh," she completed her yawn, "I'm still tired - exhausted actually." She smiled mischievously at Daley, who was looking at his reflection side-on, in the wardrobe mirror.

"Do you think I've lost a bit of weight?" He drew in his stomach to exaggerate the effect.

As soon as he had opened his eyes, the gloaming of sadness had shaded the prospect of another day. Thoughts of Archie Fraser again crowded his mind. He was anxious not to show Liz how much he had been affected though, which was one of the reasons that he would have been happier to see her sleep on.

"Yeah, I think you have - a bit. You know I just love you as you are anyhow, don't you?" She looked up at him.

He smiled. She was heartbreakingly beautiful. He had often wondered if it was only him that could see her the way she really was. If, to others, she was somehow just another good-looking woman. He often thought about that, but managed to reason that this was most likely how the world kept turning; was there really *Someone for everyone*, as the song said? What song was that anyway?

"You're far away, darling," she looked somewhat bemused.

"No, just thinking," he said knotting his tie.

She was silent for a few moments, then, "I'm so, so sorry about Archie - but you can't blame yourself - it's not as though you, or anyone come to that, can legislate for something so horrible."

He felt a sudden buzz of anger; a feeling with which, he was very familiar. "Please don't go there today, Liz."

She bridled at his brevity. "That is your problem, Jim," her lip was petted. "You bottle every feeling or emotion up and then when your head can't hold any more hurt or worry, you hit out. It's always been a problem in our marriage, you know?"

Not that fucking intonation. He was adjusting his collar and trying hard to keep quiet.

"And this is another thing - a perfect example: I talk, and you say nothing."

The dam broke. "You talk about what *you* want to, and when *you* want to," he knew he was raising his voice, however, he was in no mood to be lectured; not today, not by her - not by anyone - come to that. "And when it comes to freeing emotions, we all know how you liberate those." He snatched his jacket from the back of the chair, and patted the pockets looking for his mobile and keys.

Liz lay back on the bed heavily, staring for a few moments at the ceiling. "You know, I thought we were finally getting over this," she paused, her face a picture of resignation.

That brief silence afforded Daley the perfect opportunity to administer his argumentative coup de grace. "Liz, just shut up please. Just you do what you always do: go and have a good time; enjoy yourself. Whatever. I've got to try and solve the deaths of four people, of whom, one was not only a fellow police officer, but in my care. How could a dedicated pleasure seeker like you ever understand the burden of that responsibility?" Not waiting for an answer, he opened the door, exited, then slammed it shut, by way of punctuation.

Still on the bed, Liz held her head in her hands, and sniffed back her tears of frustration.

WDC Dunn met Daley as he walked into the office. He saw she was hesitant, and realised that his expression was thunderous, as he had been contemplating the argument with Liz during the short walk from the County Hotel.

"Yes, DC Dunn, how can I help you?"

"Something and nothing sir, concerning Izzy Watson."

"Right now, I'm interested in anything, what do you have?" Daley ushered her into his glass box.

It turned out that Izzy Watson had been brought up - in the main - by her grandmother, now in her eighties and living in a retirement home in a small village about fifteen miles outside Kinloch.

"Why are we only finding out about this now?" He was puzzled that despite the thorough nature of the investigation, they had managed to miss the victim's closest blood relative.

"It was Mrs Watson senior that mentioned it to me last night, sir. You had already left for the evening, and I didn't think it significant enough to get you back in. DS Scott told me when you were due back this morning so..." she broke off what she was saying, not wanting to tread on her boss's fragile mood. "According to Mrs Watson, the old lady has some kind of dementia; they didn't think we would want to talk to her."

250

"Aye," Daley was already distracted by two enlarged CCTV images on his desk, "and you know what thought did, DC Dunn. Get me her details please, and give the home a call. We'll have to get somebody up there to see her. Where's DS Scott, by the way?"

DS Scott was in the station's grandly named audio visual room. He had spent the night pouring over hours of CCTV footage, looking for anything that didn't appear right around the time that Izzy Watson had gone missing. Just after three o'clock, as his spirits were flagging, he had a small breakthrough. At eight twenty- three on the evening of her disappearance, Izzy, had been caught on the camera walking up Kinloch Main Street, arm-in-arm with Janet Ritchie. As they were about to cross the road to *Pulse*, they stopped. Just at the edge of shot, a headlight, and part of the front of a vehicle could be discerned. The two women had turned around and Watson, breaking away from her companion, headed towards it. She was out of shot for no more than thirty seconds, returning to her friend, then entering the bar. Strangely though, instead of proceeding back up the street past the camera, the vehicle seemed to reverse out of shot. Scott had spent the whole evening trying to find a trace of it from other locations, but had come up with nothing. The poor CCTV coverage in Kinloch, had been further exacerbated by two of the cameras being out of action. In short, the vehicle had just disappeared.

The door swung open revealing Chief Inspector Daley, carrying two mugs of coffee.

"I take it ye saw the pictures on your desk, boss?" Scott was scrolling absently through CCTV footage.

"Yes, a breakthrough, do you think?"

Scott played Daley the sequence showing Izzy Watson. The Chief Inspector took it in, then asked to see the clip another couple of times.

"At last, something to get our collective teeth into, Bri. You're computer skills are fairly coming on by the way, I'm impressed." He took another slurp of his coffee.

"Aye, one o' they young geniuses showed me whit tae dae last night. I'm bloody cross-eyed looking at it, but as you say, it's a start." The pair watched the clip again, almost frame by frame.

"Apparently Izzy's old granny lives in a care home near here, and we've only just been told. Great, eh?"

"Aye, that WDC wiz tellin' me. The woman's no right wae us though, is she?"

"You never know, we'll take a trip to see her later. In the meantime, we'll concentrate on this motor," the headlight and the corner of the wing of the vehicle was frozen, tantalizingly, on the wide screen. "Get some of these young boffins to e-mail it to forensics; hopefully they'll come up with something by the way of make and model at least."

Liz sat in the dining room of the hotel, at a small table-for-two. It was early and the large room was cold. She could hear a distant radio playing - probably from the kitchen.

The girl who came to take her order looked about ten years old and had a sullen, disinterested demeanour. No doubt having to go to work at this time of the morning was not conducive to smiles and good cheer she reasoned. However, a little civility never went amiss. She was constantly amazed by the number of people working in service industries who seemed to be totally unsuited to the task. There was nothing worse than arriving at a restaurant for a much awaited meal, only to discover you were being served by some bored looking waiter or waitress, counting down the clock until it was time to finish. She had first witnessed that phenomenon as a child. A travelling fair came to the small town near where she lived every Christmas. The thrill of a ride on the waltzers was always tempered by the vision of a spotty youth, standing with one hand in his pocket, looking into the middle-distance while spinning a carriage full of screaming kids around.

She stirred her coffee absently. The fight with her husband had - as usual - put her off her stride. She was now starting the day with a heavy heart; something she had done far too often during the course of their marriage. She forced herself to look forward to her nautical outing.

"Here' yer bacon an' eggs." Liz marvelled at how the young waitress managed to run the words together, while being able to judge exactly how hard to throw the plate so that it landed on the table and not on her guest's lap.

The e-mail had been sent to forensics, then Daley had sent Scott back to the hotel for a sleep. To begin with, his deputy had been reluctant to leave, but was persuaded to at the promise he could return at lunch time, when they would both visit Izzy Watson's granny, to see if anything could be gleaned from the old lady.

"You know me, Jim, two 'oors or so does me. I'll see ye at wan." He donned his jacket, fished in his inside pocket for cigarettes and lighter, then headed out of the door.

Daley played the clip again. The front of the vehicle was straight up and down. He began to wonder if it was some type of van, quickly resolving not to waste too much time on the project and leave it to the experts.

He also decided to have a *team meeting*, as Donald termed it. It was an opportunity to refocus minds. He sat at his computer and began typing out the course of the investigation as he had seen it. He thought he would begin the meeting with a short silence in memory of Archie Fraser. The vision of the white, lifeless face he had seen on Kinloch pier, would never leave him. He felt sorry though that he had let his emotions at Fraser's death cause another eruption within his marriage. He pulled his mobile from his pocket, and clicked on her name on his contacts list.

Her mobile rang, but by the time she had searched through the cavernous, cluttered space, that was her insanely expensive handbag, the ringing stopped. She searched missed calls, and discovered that it had been her husband. Instinctively, she made to call him back, then changed her mind. He had behaved like a prick earlier, so she wasn't inclined to forgive him - not just yet, anyway. He could sweat it out a little longer. She had finished her breakfast, deliberately not returning the forced smile of her sullen waitress as she left the dining room.

She ascended the stairs, then once back in the room, filled her rucksack with the items she would require during her boat trip with Seanessy. A camera, lenses, bottled water, a small pack of paper hankies, travel make-up kit (essential), mobile phone and a case to keep it dry, and a large bar of chocolate she had purchased the day before, were all stuffed neatly into the bag. She recalled Jim arriving home from a fishing trip to Oban absolutely freezing, so resolved to tie a thick jumper around her waist. Looking out of the window, the sky was already blue; she could feel the pane had been warmed by the early morning sun. She looked forward to a lovely day trying to capture a digital image of an Orca.

She felt a pang of guilt at not answering his call, then decided to ring him when she was waiting for Seanessy outside the hotel. She left the room closing the door on the latch behind her.

Daley discovered that the images of the vehicle from the CCTV footage would not be analysed until later that day, as the unit was in the midst of another enquiry. It was now after seven, and he took the short walk to Macleod's office in the hope that, by this time, it would house Superintendent Donald.

Sure enough he was hailed by the familiar *Come,* when he knocked on the door.

"Jim, come in, come in. You're an early bird today." Donald was particularly bright and breezy, which immediately rang warning bells in Daley's head.

"Now, first of all, I take it you want something from me?"

"I would like to get forensics up the road to get a move on analysing some CCTV footage that we've identified as being of possible interest." His answer was flat. He sensed that Donald was on the verge of another announcement.

"I see, how significant is this evidence, do you think?"

"If you take a trip along the corridor, I'll show you - could be pivotal."

"I will, but first I must tell you that events have forced me to reconsider the tenet of the investigation."

"In what way?" Daley could feel the mist descend.

"I'm bringing in the National Crime Squad. We'll have a meeting of course, and I'll remain in charge over all, however, operationally speaking, we may have to reorganise a bit."

"Which really means that you have no faith that I will solve these crimes," Daley was keeping a lid on his temper.

"Not true Jim, not true at all," Donald was on the defensive, so Daley readied himself for a large dollop of honey, the habitual salve. "As you well know, we have four murder investigations running concurrently, investigations that may, or may not be connected; and one of which, is the murder of a police officer. Add to that a major narcotics enquiry, with foreign involvement, Well, we're swamped, Jim. You're not the only police officer under pressure from above here; maybe now you've been elevated in the ranks, you'll come to appreciate the delicate position I find myself in from time to time." He looked steadily at Daley, as though underlining what he had just said.

Daley played with a pen between his fingers, he was silent for a few moments, then, when he decided to answer, surprised himself with the level tone of his voice. "I'm not concerned with the drugs investigation - if the squad want to take that on it's fine - we're probably too emotionally involved anyway. I want to remain at the head of the Izzy Watson investigation though, as well as those of Ritchie and Mulligan. They were definitely carried out by the same person, or persons. We know there is a sexual element to the murders, as well as a level of brutality that is unusual. We haven't had much luck with forensic evidence yet, but I'm sure this CCTV footage is a breakthrough. Will you move things along with it up the road? Or are you content for the squad to trample over everything before we take action on this?"

Donald passed his hand over his slicked back hair, disturbing its hitherto shining perfection. Daley hadn't considered that his boss could be under the same pressure of scrutiny that he felt; he always supposed that Donald was too smooth an operator to be troubled by the highest echelons of the force. He thought he even detected strain on the face of the Superintendent.

"Sometimes, Jim, this job just gets to you - to us all," he sighed volubly. "Yes, I'll give them a kick up the arse," he stood up from his chair. "On the subject of the crime squad, I'm afraid I cannot commit myself. They won't be here until this evening; and if it's worth anything, they've been forced on me." He removed his uniform jacket from a coat stand in the corner. "Come on, show me this CCTV stuff."

They left MacLeod's office and headed for the CID suite.

Liz was surprised to find Seanessy's old Land Rover already parked outside of the hotel, as she walked out under the faux balcony, and onto the street. She pulled the stiff door to the passenger seat open, stepped in and sat down, arranging her rucksack and camera on her lap with one hand while searching behind the seat for the safety belt with the other.

"Good morning, Mr Seanessy - on time today," she smiled at her guide.

He seemed to force a smile in return, but said nothing. Liz noted immediately that he was wearing different clothes. His ad hoc assortment of multi-coloured waterproofs had been replaced by new-looking, combat style gear. The filthy Wellington boots he had worn the day before, discarded in favour of up-market hiking boots.

They drove down the Main Street, instead of stopping at the pontoons as Liz had expected, they followed the road around the head of the loch, passing the shuttered *Island Bar,* en route.

"I thought we'd be leaving from the pontoons?" Liz asked Seanessy.

"No." He seemed preoccupied. "Too much police activity there after the shooting. They've moored the boat round here, out of the way. Kinloch's forgotten pier, old, but still just about in use."

He stopped the car at the head of a small jetty adorned with emergency fencing and warning signs - *Keep out - Danger, Unsafe Structure.* The pier itself looked old and tumbledown, a large section of it appeared to have fallen into the loch; as though a giant mouth had taken a large bite at the central portion. Seanessy, however, seemed untroubled.

"Oh, don't worry about these signs." He could see Liz reading a warning notice doubtfully. "Needs a bit of attention; but the main reason these notices are everywhere is that the powers that be are in league with the owners of the pontoons. There's nothing to stop this place from being used, but it doesn't suit them. Fishermen use it all the time." He held out his hand to help Liz out of the Land Rover, his good humour apparently quite returned. Liz paused for a moment, but decided to place her faith in local knowledge. She jumped out of the vehicle removing her rucksack and camera bag. She could see only one vessel moored by the jetty, an old fashioned clinker built fishing boat, replete with a small wheelhouse, contained on a single deck. The vessel reminded her of the lobster boats that she had been taken trips on when her family holidayed in Cornwall, as a child.

She followed Seanessy towards an old iron ladder positioned over the edge of the pier, leading down to the boat. The tide was low, so the descent down the ladder looked long and precarious.

"Best foot forward, Mrs Daley. Nothing to worry about. We better get going if we want to take advantage of the time we have." Seanessy stood at the top of the ladder, adopting a beckoning stance. "I'll take your kit if you want, less cumbersome for you getting down - eh?"

Liz handed him the rucksack and camera bag, and kneeling down, slowly placed one foot on to the ladder behind her, beginning her careful descent onto the small craft.

"I agree with you, Jim. This could be a break, at last," Donald handed Daley the images printed from the CCTV footage. "I'll put a rocket under those lazy bastards up the road. Oh, by the way, if you're not going to charge this Camel Johnstone, we'll have to let him go. We've held him as long as we can."

Daley didn't want to admit that he had forgotten all about the fact that Camel was still in custody. So much had happened in the last thirty-six hours or so, the young fisherman's incarceration had completely slipped his mind. He didn't think for one minute that

Johnstone was guilty of anything apart from questionable morals and minor drugs offences, he would have had him released before now if had remembered. It was clear that even though he had sex with Izzy Watson prior to her death, he had not been the last to do so. Their tryst had taken place at *Pulse*, when she had been very much alive.

"I'll attend to that directly, sir."

"No, you have enough on your plate as it is, Jim. I'll deal with it." Daley was almost staggered by this unheralded generosity of time and spirit.

"Sir, we've also discovered that our original victim - Izzy Watson - has an elderly grandmother residing in a nursing home not far from here. It's worth a shot, even if she has some kind of dementia."

"In this case, we need to clutch onto any proverbial straw, no matter how tenuous that straw may be." Their business concluded, Donald left.

Daley reflected how changeable the man was; when you expected him to be at his most obstructive, he would surprise with unlooked for support, or even just a helpful word. Maybe Donald did feel the loss of the tragic Archie Fraser every bit as keenly as he did? Maybe there was just no fathoming the man.

After a few hairy moments, Liz managed to get on board the boat and decided to occupy the rear of the vessel, where there was a narrow bench seat, and where her view was only partly obscured by the small wheelhouse. Seanessy made his way, heavily, aboard; as he descended the ladder she could see that the soles of his boots were brand new, unworn. He was wearing a large backpack, which sagged from his back indicating that it contained something or things that were heavy.

When he was safely on the deck, he removed his rucksack, placing it in the wheelhouse. He had brought the large rope that had secured the boat to a bollard on the jetty on board with him, and the craft began to drift, slowly from the structure. She noticed that he had made no attempt at conversation, however she put this down to the early hour; in any case, she was more than happy just taking in the beautiful scenery of the still loch. The sun was already full in the sky. Although the smell of seaweed was strong, it bore none of the taint of diesel fumes redolent of the two main piers, which she could see facing her across the blue, oily water. The cries of seabirds soared with them in flight; she watched as a swan made serene progress up the loch not far from the vessel, its serpentine head moving slowly to and fro taking in the sights and sounds of the watery environment.

Though the bay was mirror-like, Liz was aware of a slight swell, which saw the vessel rise and fall against the static pier. She shivered momentarily as the sun was obscured by a small, white cloud, perhaps foretelling the temperature out to sea would be less balmy. She drew the zip of her fleece up to her neck, just as something landed on the deck beside her with a light thud, making her start slightly.

"Put that on please," Seanessy's request was polite, but perfunctory. She noticed that he had hardly made eye contact with her since he picked her up. She resolved though not to let his mood detract from the prospect of an exciting day on the water, with the possibility of capturing images of killer whales. She picked the lifejacket from the deck and intuitively put it on and adjusted the relevant straps and buckles until it was a comfortable fit.

Seanessy was in the wheelhouse. It reminded Liz more of the potting shed her father had built at the bottom of their garden, rather than anything maritime. She watched as he bent down and lifted a little trap door on the deck, then, not without some effort, managed to fire the noisy engine into life. Clouds of smelly blue fumes puffed from a thin, iron chimney which emanated from the gunwale and was strapped with metal bands to the side of the wheelhouse.

Seanessy made his way back towards her. "Have you managed to secure the lifejacket properly?" Without invitation he pulled at the collar with some force, almost dislodging Liz from her bench seat. "That'll do," he said flatly, "we'll get under way directly."

He turned and made his way back to the wheelhouse, where he patted at the rucksack that lay at his feet underneath the ships wheel. He then pulled at the various knobs and levers necessary to propel the vessel forward. Liz reasoned that whatever he had located in the bag must be important, as the action seemed to be subconscious, not unlike someone automatically patting their jacket to make sure they were carrying their keys prior to leaving the house.

The tone of the engine changed, and slowly they made their way out onto the loch, and the open sea beyond.

Daley had WDC Dunn arrange for him to have a pool car. He had decided to make the short journey to visit Izzy Watson's grandmother by himself. He doubted whether the old lady would be of much help, as she was - by all accounts - in the early stages of some type of dementia, however he was too long in the tooth to realise that lip service, at the very least, must be paid to her possible part in the enquiry and that you never knew what seemingly meaningless piece of information could solve a case. He kept on repeating this mantra as he looked again at pages of interview notes taken by the rest of the team. He decided to do this for an hour or so until it was late enough in the day to go to the retirement home.

Dunn arrived back with the car keys. "Sir, James Newell is at the front desk; he says he wants to talk to you urgently."

Daley asked for Newell to be shown through to the interview suite. He held back for ten minutes or so, working on the old cops' premise that the longer someone had alone to think about something they wanted to get off their chest, the more likely it would be for them to be honest. He left the CID office and headed for the interview room.

Once out of the loch and out into the sound, the breeze became more chilly, and the sea much more restless. They were sailing almost parallel to a road which threaded its way amidst a backdrop of fir trees and small, white sandy bays. Liz was reminded of holidays in the Greek islands. Come to think of it, she had been reminded of various vacations ever since she had arrived in this magical little place. Despite the undulation of the vessel, she was not feeling in the least sea sick, however she was irritated by the small funnel which was belching acrid smoke out into the cool, scented air.

Seanessy was positioned behind the wheel. He had looked back at her a couple of times, slightly inclining his head in a gesture that she supposed was one of reassurance, or merely checking that she had not fallen overboard. Suddenly, from the corner of her eye she detected movement. To her left the grey arch of a porpoise shadowing the boat was unmistakable. Liz fumbled into the rucksack at her feet, removing her camera from its bag, while checking the environs of the position she had last seen the creature.

"Have you spotted something?" Seanessy was making his way along the deck towards her.

"Yes, it's a porpoise, I think. Any chance of us stopping for a short while, so that I can try and get a couple of steady shots?" She held up the camera by way of illustration.

Seanessy looked at his watch, then shrugged his shoulders; presently the engine noise died away, the narrow funnel's issue ceased. Only the lap of water on the side of the boat was audible. Liz struggled to align her camera with the area she felt it most likely the porpoise would reappear. She focused on the water, taking her eye away from the small screen to check her surroundings. Seanessy looked steadily at her, showing none of the interest or excitement that he had on their trip the day before. His moods were beginning to remind Liz of those of her husband.

James Newell was standing with his arms behind his back, looking at the painting on the wall of the 'family' interview room. He turned on hearing Daley's arrival.

"Chief Inspector, thank you for finding time to see me. I suppose I could have let your desk officer deal with this, however, I thought that you would be interested yourself."

"Interested in what, Mr Newell? - please take a seat, by the way," he gestured to an easy chair, onto which Newell duly sat.

"My nephew has *done a bunk*, I suppose you would term it in the vernacular; buggered off I prefer to call it - and taken my *RIB* into the bargain. I'm the last person to tell tales Mr Daley. I must admit though, that I find his behaviour very strange, especially in the light of recent events. And of course, I want my livelihood back. Bloody inconsiderate as usual, he's supposed to be up here trying to find something to do with his life, not carry on in ever more ridiculous ways." Newell was plainly irritated, raising his eyes to the heavens as his jaw worked furiously.

"I will have to investigate this as having a possible connection to our other on-going enquiries." Newell nodded, "I'm just making you aware, that's all. Do you know if he submitted to a DNA test?"

"Oh, I have no doubt that he did not. He is and always has been irresponsible; his father should have given him a kick up the arse years ago, instead of forking out a small fortune on public schools and university courses he never had the gumption to finish." Newell drummed his fingers on the table and Daley could easily visualise the naval captain that he had been, frustrated by some incompetent rating.

"How much fuel was on board, or would he have had access to before he left?"

Again Newell raised his eyes, this time though as an aid to calculation. "I suppose enough for around a hundred nautical miles or so - she wasn't full, and he must have taken off well before the pumps opened up on the pier. So yes, his radius can be no more than a hundred nautical miles, maybe even slightly less than that."

Daley thought for a moment. "How fast does your vessel go, Mr Newell?"

"Forty-five knots in the right conditions, just over fifty miles an hour. That doesn't sound much on land, but I can assure you that it is quite fast enough on the water."

Using rough reckoning Daley appreciated that Rory could be

anywhere from the North of Scotland, Irish Republic, Wales, to the North of England. This was a complication, but yet it could prove a vital link in finding the killer or killers he was looking for. "Who exactly was Rory friendly with here? He must have had some kind of social life."

"Mainly local fishermen, or the odd tourist he would go out for a drink with after we had been on a trip. I'm afraid that there is little here on offer for someone with Rory's tastes."

"What do you mean by 'tastes'?"

Newell stayed silent for a moment, during which time he looked as though he was considering whether or not to say something.

"Please, Mr Newell, this is no time for misplaced family loyalty, let me assure you."

Newell rose from his seat, and took a few paces over to the opened window. "All of my life, Chief Inspector, I wanted to have family - settle down - you know the type of thing. However, being a sailor for so long, family life was never possible; never quite the right time." He turned to look back at Daley, who was surprised to see tears in the retired naval captain's eyes. "I have always looked on Rory as the son I never had. Brought him home toys and the like from my travels, took him to the zoo, camping - that sort of thing. I really don't know what happened to him. He was such a nice little boy."

"Meaning what? I don't have time for riddles, Mr Newell. If you have information for me you really must tell me now."

"Drugs, Chief Inspector. Rory's life has been ruined by drugs."

20

Liz's attempts to capture a shot of a porpoise had presented her with problems she had not hitherto considered. Despite having a camera with all of the modern stabilisation technology money could buy, the yaw of the boat meant that trying to focus on one of the creatures and stay upright, was virtually impossible.

She mentioned this to Seanessy, who far from being put out by her problems, showed the first signs of genuine interest he had all day.

"Now I think I can help you there. Just around the coast, about a mile off Machrie Bay, there's a small outcrop of rock; a glorified skerry really, and the very devil to get into, but an ideal spot for capturing footage of porpoise, orca, and suchlike. I mean, you're both off the sea, and on it at the same time." He smiled affably at her. "There's even a lobsterman's cottage there - handy for shelter or brewing up a cup of tea. I've used it a few times, quite dramatic really. You have the feeling of being at the power of the ocean," his eyes took on a distant look. "I keep a few creels there; just a hobby you understand. It will take us about an hour to get there - if you would like to go that is?"

Liz considered for a few seconds. The island skerry sounded fascinating, and as far as capturing any decent material from the vessel was concerned, she felt she might as well forget it. "How long do we have, Mr Seanessy?"

"Oh don't worry, my dear - as long as we want. I've had a word with the fishermen, I don't think they intended to do much today. A bit tied up with other things you might say," he smiled benignly.

"Well, if that's the case, let's go for it." She began to put away her camera equipment, as Seanessy made his way back to the wheelhouse of the small craft. Within seconds the noisy engine was belching clouds of black, pungent smoke as they chugged their progress through the blue of the mid-morning. Liz looked down at the sun's dappled reflection on the rippled wake of the vessel. She raised her head to see Seanessy smiling back at her from the wheelhouse. *Thank goodness he's cheered up,* she thought, as they slowly rounded the point.

Daley was about to leave the office in order to visit Izzy Watson's grandmother, when his phone rang. He instantly recognised Camel's long vowels.

"It's my brother, Mr Daley - he's fucked off. The boat's gone too - aye, along wae oor stash o' money. I canna believe the little prick."

Daley took some quick details, then told Camel to sit tight. He took a mental note of directions to the fisherman's home, deciding that he would take a look around there prior to making his way to the retirement home. He felt guilty, as it was obvious that Camel's brother had disappeared whilst he had languished in custody. The feeling was soon lost.

As soon as they had rounded the point, the sea had become quite choppy. Liz was actually feeling quite nauseous, but was trying to keep this fact from Seanessy, who kept turning round from his station at the wheelhouse to ensure she was still all right. The air had become more chilled too; gone the pleasant, spring warmth, to be replaced by spume-flecked breeze with a more salty edge.

She hadn't seen anything more in the way of maritime creatures, however, the number and variety of birds she had spotted was far in excess of what she could have reasonably expected on land. As she mused idly about this, a small ringed plover landed on the gunwale of the boat, head darting anxiously before it took off again. She swallowed back the bile in her throat, focusing on getting to the small island and the photographic opportunities it would offer.

Daley sat in the lounge of Camel's home. It contained none of the opulence he had witnessed in Michael Watson's well-appointed dwelling. An old sofa and two, unmatched easy chairs occupied the centre of the floor, around the dual focuses of an elderly TV set, and coal fire, the surround of which would have been familiar to anyone brought up in a Scottish council house during the fifties and sixties. A drop-leaf table under the window was adorned by bits of old netting, a dented plastic buoy and a copy of the *Rangers News*.

"Sorry aboot the mess," Camel announced as he bent down to pick up a discarded sweater from the floor. "Oor old-yin works two jobs, startin' at five in the morning cleaning offices, so she's no' feeling too much lake hoose work when she gets hame." He looked at the policeman apologetically.

"Do you never think of doing some yourself?" Daley asked in return.

"Aye right," Camel grinned back. "I'm happy enough wae things lake this. We live here, it's no' a veesitor's centre."

Deciding not to contemplate the state of twenty-first century Scottish male domestic reasoning, the Chief Inspector sat down in the easy-chair, indicated by his host.

"How long have you lived here?"

"Ay'ways." Camel's reply was to the point. "I telt my mither we should hae bought the place, she said we couldna' afford it. So it's still a council hoose. Shite, eh?" Camel shook his head ruefully.

"So; Bobby?" Daley had heard enough about what passed for domesticity in the Johnstone household.

"He's fucked off, Inspector. Simple as that."

"How do you know this is a permanent situation, and not that he's off on a jolly somewhere?" Daley was processing the fact that this was not the first time in the day that someone had 'fucked off'.

"He's taken his clathes, oor boat, and all oor savings - oh aye, he's no' comin' back." Camel's face was pale with anger. "An' see if he does, Mr Daley, ye'll be investigating another murder. Know whoot I mean?"

Daley took Camel at his word. He detected no dissemblance, no attempt to confuse or divert. Families could be impenetrable - usually so in a murder investigation. Sooner or later however, little fissures would appear, built up resentment would break down the walls encompassing the *united front*. Daley had never been family oriented. He had a brother he never saw and a sister he couldn't stomach. Both of his parents were dead and any aunts, uncles, or cousins were best left to their own devices. Indeed, his cousin Malky was currently serving two years at Her Majesty's Pleasure for theft and assault. Who needed family? His mind alighted momentarily on Liz and the fight they had earlier.

"Can I see Bobby's room, please?" He refocused on matters in hand.

Camel lead Daley up the threadbare carpet of the staircase. The smell of stale tobacco predicated itself on an under-lying stench of fish. The young fisherman swung open the first door on the left-hand side of the landing, gesturing Daley into the room beyond.

In many ways the room seemed more suited to a much younger person, a child in fact. Football posters adorned the walls, on top of wallpaper which was a print of some cartoon character the policeman did not recognise. An old chest of drawers sat in one corner of the square room, an empty drawer open so much that it pointed towards the floor and looked in imminent danger of falling. Against the opposite wall stood an equally antiquated wardrobe, one door of which lay wide open, revealing a bare interior. Beside a single bed draped in a duvet with a football print cover, sat a flimsy looking bedside cabinet. Daley opened a small drawer located on the top of the piece of furniture: it was empty save from three black plastic hoops, about the size of a large bracelet, though nearly an inch thick. Daley picked one up and on examination found that the collars could be closed by means of two metal press studs at the ends.

"What are these?" he asked Camel, who was still standing outside the small room with his arms folded.

"Jeest fastening braces for the creels," he sighed. "Helps attach them to the rope wae'oot havin' tae tie mega knots." He was clearly uninterested in the items.

"Why would your brother have them here in his room?"

"How dae I know? Probably jeest in his pockets or something. Whoot aboot it?"

Daley picked one of the collars up. "I hope you don't mind?" he said to Camel as he put one in his pocket.

"Aye, whootever," was the fisherman's reply.

"I can see that he's cleaned the place out. You didn't have any idea he was going to do this?"

"No, mind you, I wiz kinda tied up at the time," Camel sneered.

Daley ignored the reference to the young man's incarceration and continued to cast his eye over the room.

"Does your brother have many friends?"

"Same as anyone."

"But you would say that you and he are close - like best friends in fact?"

"Suppose so. We're brothers, Mr Daley, we're stuck wae each other." He looked around. "Well, no' noo right enough." He gave Daley a wan smile.

"What about girlfriends?"

"What aboot them?"

"Has Bobby had many?"

"Are you tryin' tae say he's some kind o' poof or something?"

"No. I'm just asking if he's had many girlfriends. I thought that was quite a simple question for you to understand." Daley's face suddenly took on a thunderous expression.

"Aye, OK, don't gie yersel' a heart attack. He's had a few."

"But not as many as you?"

"He's no' got the patter. Anyway, whoot's this got tae dae wae anything?"

"Just wondered. You do think he's quite awkward with women

though." That was a flat statement from Daley.

"He's no' the most confident guy, Mr Daley. If you had a faither lake oors, you widna' be very confident neither."

"Was he hard on you?"

"He used tae get drunk an' beat the shit oot o' us. If that's whoot you mean by being hard, well aye, he wiz." Camel looked straight at Daley, tears welling up in his eyes.

"Does your brother know Rory Newell?" Daley enquired.

"Aw - if this is the queer thing again, you can fuck off," Camel answered angrily.

"No," Daley said, then paused. "It's just that your brother doesn't strike me as the type of lad who does things on his own. He needs someone to give in a nudge, point him in the right direction - you, for example."

"Are you sayin' that Rory Newell pit this in his heid?" Camel looked as though he had made his own connection. "I telt Bobby tae stay clear o' that bastard. He's a right dope heid - aye, an' a fucking smart arse, tae," he said, more forcefully.

"Did he listen to you?" Daley observed Camel, who was now looking out of the window.

"Na, no' a' the time. We're brothers, Mr Daley, we spend a lot o' time wae each other - we fa' oot, tae - dae ye know whoot I mean?"

"So, when he's not got you to tell him what to do, he relies on Rory Newell, is that it?" Daley probed again.

"Mebe, I don' fuckin' know," Camel said, quietly. "Dae ye really think this bastard Newell has pit him up tae this?"

"Well," answered Daley, looking around the room one last time. "If he hasn't, somebody has."

The swell was heavy now. To Liz, it felt like being tossed in a blanket, as in some childhood game. She had been told that keeping your eyes on the horizon should help; a bit like *spotting* while doing turns whilst dancing or ice-skating.

As she squinted into the distance, and contemplated on asking Seanessy to turn the vessel back home, she spotted what looked like a sliver of land to her right. Just as she had realised this, Seanessy turned in the wheelhouse and gestured to her to look at the small island.

"That's us there - won't be long now," he called over the noise of the sea, wind, and echoing cries of birds. "Be able to get a cup of tea at least," he turned back to his steering duties, his mood quite transformed from the taciturn silence of earlier.

Men, Liz thought, as they began to turn in a slow, undulating arc towards the island.

He thought he had it; the break he had been looking for. The plastic collars in Bobby Johnstone's room. That's all it took.

He drove the car back into the town centre, stopping outside the County Hotel. In less than a minute he was hammering on Scott's room door.

"Aye, a' right, a'right. Is there a fire or some fuckin' thing?" Daley could hear his DS shouting from inside. With the rattling of a chain and the click of a lock, the door swung open.

"Here wiz me expectin' some wee blonde. Come in." Scott looked bleary-eyed, but Daley was sure that he would forget his tiredness soon. His bed was unmade; Daley said nothing, merely throwing the collar on to the bed sheet.

"What the fuck…?" Scott yawned, picking the plastic ring up off the bed. It took him a few seconds, then it clicked. "Well done, Jamie boy. This matches the marks left by the restraint on Watson's leg. Where did you get it?"

"In Bobby Johnstone's bedroom; looks like we might have missed the obvious from the start. Rory Newell was reported missing this morning. Now Bobby's done a runner too; what's the bets Newell's with him. What do you think?"

"Aye, could be. It's certainly a bit o' a coincidence that the two o' them disappear at the same time. And this thing," he held up the collar, "well, whit's your plan, boss?"

There was a small, impromptu jetty on the ocean side of the island; an ancient looking thing that looked more tumbledown than their departure point from Kinloch. The tell-tale florescent bobbing of small, spherical buoys indicated the location of lobster pots, held within a shallow bay which opened out quickly into the Atlantic proper. Starting at the head of the small pier, a dirt track led some fifty yards to a low fisherman's cottage, the walls of which had once been white-washed, but were now a wind-blown grey colour, contrasting with the rust-red of the corrugated tin roof. The cottage was framed by a hillock behind.

"Wow!" Liz was impressed. "From the sea you wouldn't know this place was here."

"Yes, it's an interesting natural feature." Seanessy was uncoiling rope from the deck now. "Been here a long time, hardly ever used now. All of the pots here are mine. Not a good enough yield for the commercial fishermen."

"So you just kind of turn up here?"

"In a manner of speaking. If there was any fisherman serious about this little nook, I daresay that I'd never have come here," he was shouting above the noise of waves washing onto the small, shingle bay. "I bought a small boat from an old seadog I met when I first came here. Boat lasted one season; it was him who told me about this place," he gestured over his shoulder. "I daresay most of the young chaps hardly know it's here at all. So the price of a worthless vessel, was more than made up for by finding out about this little idyll." He coiled the rope up, then handed it to Liz.

All systems go at Kinloch police office. The Royal Navy, Coastguard and the police's own Marine Division were now deployed in an effort to find James Newell's *RIB*, that contained - so everyone reasoned - Rory Newell and Bobby Johnstone. Daley found it hard to believe that the mild-mannered Johnstone brother was a cold-blooded, sadistic killer, or that he was somehow involved in international drug smuggling. Much more likely that he had been coerced by the louche Newell, replete with all his city sophistication and desire for the 'high' life.

Scott's face was a mask of concentration as he passed on details of the craft and possible occupants to yet another of the interested parties. Air searches were being initiated using an RAF helicopter, normally used for air-sea rescue. The coastguard were aware of what was going on, but under instructions not to let it be generally known what was afoot, in case Newell and Johnstone should get wind that the search for them was most certainly *hot*. The Navy was moving three ships which had been on exercise in the area over the last few days onto the trawl. In some ways, the land-bound police officers felt somewhat impotent, however they were at the centre of operations; radio traffic from all of the relevant agencies was pouring into the control room at Kinloch, which had been entirely seceded to the operation. Superintendent Donald sitting proudly at the hub of the effort.

Indeed, Daley had been amazed as to the speed with which this had been achieved. It was little over an hour since he and Scott had returned to the office with the news that Newell and Johnstone were prime suspects for the murders of Watson, Ritchie and Mulligan. Daley knew that Bobby Johnstone had an alibi for the time that Izzy had disappeared, however, the boys had been in Glasgow for little over eighteen hours, and accurately assessing the time of death had been difficult because of damage done to the corpse by the sea.

Daley opened the door into interview room one. James Newell was nursing a mug of coffee, staring into space.

"As you have been informed, Mr Newell, we are now actively seeking your nephew to help us with our enquiries regarding the recent murders, of which I'm sure you are aware." Daley took a seat opposite the retired sea captain.

"How very like a policeman you sound, Mr Daley," Newell placed his coffee onto the table in front of him with no little resignation. "However, I appreciate your candour; though I still find it impossible to believe that Rory has been so…" his voice tailed off.

"I want to go back to your trip to County Antrim. Are you absolutely sure Rory was with you all of the time?" Daley was unbuttoning the collar of his shirt, which was beginning to feel like a noose.

Newell thought for a moment. "Despite my nephew's feckless nature, Chief Inspector, he was not without his attractiveness to the opposite sex. Of course, when they got to know him properly things became very different. You saw him though: tall, well set up - a certain languid charm I suppose."

Daley said nothing, merely nodded at Newell to continue.

"He struck up a 'friendship' with one of the film crew." Newell indicated the parenthesis with a gesture. "At night, she and he were out and about. A couple of drams and off to bed for me; he was more adventurous."

"Did he use the *RIB* alone when you were there?"

Newell looked at the table, as though he was reading something. After a while, Daley thought that he had decided not to answer the question. Suddenly he looked up.

"Yes, as a matter of fact he did," his brows arched, making him look suddenly amazed.

Despite the warmth of the day, Liz still felt a chill. She supposed that being on this tiny outcrop of land was much the same as being on a boat. Such a small area of ground would be unlikely to retain any significant heat from the sun. It was by far the strangest place she had ever visited. A dank, fetid air hung about the island. She felt as though she was seeing the sky through a lens, like being enveloped in some gigantic glass bubble.

"On a stormy night, this place is quite memorable," Seanessy was standing closer to her than she had expected. "Normal for the sea to spray off the little pier and onto the windows of the cottage. I find it thrilling - dramatic. Do you know what I mean?"

Liz thought for a few moments. She had always been comfortable at sea - on a boat. She had often tried to imagine what being in a lighthouse in a storm would be like: all at sea, yet still on land, no matter how tenuous that land actually was. It must be the same here, though instead of a well-built phallus which had weathered generations of all the sea could throw at it, you had a broken down fisherman's hut. Liz marvelled at how the corrugated iron roof had endured even the most benign of metrological conflagrations.

"Do you often stay overnight here?" Liz addressed Seanessy over her shoulder.

"Only when I feel the need," he looked into the middle distance. "A bolt hole. You know how it is? When one needs peace and quiet to get things done. Away from the pressures of the world, so to speak." He gave Liz an unprepossessing smile. "We'll have to walk around here a bit to get a more panoramic view for you," he stomped off in his new boots.

All bases were covered. *As well as they can be at any rate,* Daley thought. He was trying to think himself into their heads. If these killings had been motivated by drugs, then why the ramped up level of violence? After all, these men were no hardened criminals bent on sending messages of fear to those who would oppose them. He had found Newell an arrogant prick yes - a sadistic killer? And he had much experience of their mien. No. Bobby Johnstone had looked like a lost boy rather than an individual who could perpetrate such horrors.

The salve that eased these concerns was the usual: logic dictated that the disappearance of the two men was just too coincidental for them not to be mixed up in the killings. The access to boats, involvement in the casual sex and drug taking that epitomised a section of Kinloch's youth, as well as acquaintance with all of the deceased, looked like a coalescence of circumstances that could not be ignored. There could be no others here who seemingly fitted the profile.

Donald was consulting the Force Psychologist. Daley was trusting his instinct - and yet. And yet, he had doubts; and what was more, so did his grizzled Detective Sergeant. Scott was not behaving the way he did when the end of a difficult case was in sight. He had none of the insouciant brio of a policeman, who, faced with insurmountable odds, had got to grips with a needle of a problem and found a solution within the haystack of possibilities.

Daley knew how he felt.

"Sir, it's the old folks' home for you," WDC Dunn poked her head around the door of his glass box. "They called my mobile for some reason. I suppose that's the number I gave them as a contact. Will I fling them a deafie?" The young woman seemed as though a great weight had been lifted from her shoulders. The death of Archie Fraser was still a raw and barely believable experience that bore down on all of the investigating officers. The revelations about Newell and Johnstone promised resolution and respite from this: a chance for all to move on. She smiled at Daley as she waited for an answer.

"No, tell them I'll call back in a few moments. Thank them please, and tell them 'I apologise' for not appearing when I said I would." He resolved to go and see the old lady, if only as a courtesy. It saddened him that the old were sidelined in the way they were; an exclusion imposed by those who had misjudged the rapid passage of time, and the onset of their turn at being elderly.

Scott appeared back in the glass box.

"It's a Land Rover in they photos from the CCTV, Jim," he enthused. "They're trying tae pin doon the colour up the road, but they reckon it's an older model, maybe late nineteen-eighties, early nineties. I've asked a couple o' oor boys tae see whether Newell or Johnstone has anything like that. What dae ye think the chances are?" There was doubt in his voice.

Daley mulled over this news in his mind. This was a rural area, so it made sense that the numbers driving that type of vehicle would be higher than back in the city. The reality of course was that even if they pinned down the identity of the Land Rover's owner, it was still uncertain as to whether he was involved with the crimes, or was merely engaging in conversation.

"Who knows, Brian? Whoever owns that vehicle, I want to speak to him. We're treading water here anyway; everything's happening out at sea, so we've nothing to lose - eh?"

"Na, you're right again, compadre." Daley loved the way Scott would manage to append so many designations to him in the course of a day; in so many different languages too. "A' this sitting aboot's makin' me jumpy, anyway. I'll go an' gie the lads a hand." He left Daley alone again in his glass world.

Liz was sitting on a rock scanning the horizon. She had seen nothing of interest since they had arrived on the island. Stoically, she considered this typical; not losing heart was the key.

Seanessy was in the shack working at something with a hammer. She was aware of him peering over the small rise that lay between where she was observing and the dwelling, from time to time. She supposed this was by way of checking that she hadn't been swept out to sea; though the possibilities of being overwhelmed by this millpond were few indeed. As - sadly - were the chances of being able to photograph anything mildly interesting. She slipped a piece of chewing gum into her mouth. She was starting to feel hungry, however, her rucksack was back at the shack where Seanessy had stowed everything to keep them 'safe' as he had said; though safe from whom, or what she didn't know. She decided to give it another fifteen minutes or so.

"Yes, I'm so sorry I've not had the chance to call in yet - things are always cropping up, as you can appreciate." Daley was on the phone to the retirement home. "Yeah," he said in answer to a question. "I should be with you within the hour. Thanks again for your patience." He put the phone down. The wheels of the machine were cranking along here. He checked for his mobile in the inside pocket of his jacket, shrugged the garment on, then tried to find the keys to his pool car.

Seanessy hastily exited the cottage as she walked past the head of the small jetty, the water lapping, lazily against the boat.

"Feeling a bit peckish," she shouted to Seanessy. "Time for a bite of lunch. My backpack's in there, right?"

"Don't worry… I'll get that," he said hesitantly. Liz was only a few yards away now.

She shrugged her shoulders. "OK, I'll take a seat on the jetty - thanks." She watched as he went back into the small building. He appeared to squeeze himself through the doorway, as though something was preventing the door from opening fully. *Strange man,* she thought.

"Aye, well you make sure you don't get up tae any nonsense wae them auld folk. They'll fleece ye at a hand o' dominoes." Scott was busy writing a report of his involvement in the case so far. They had what was thought to be a sighting of Newell's *RIB* off the Ayrshire coast, thirty minutes earlier. The trail however, had gone blank. Daley had spoken to the officer in charge of the search aboard the vessel. He was of the opinion that, working on the assumption that the men knew they were being pursued, hiding along Scotland's rocky coastline was quite a simple task. The sailor was convinced though, that time and patience was the key to flushing out the suspects; waiting until they broke cover, on land or sea. After all, they both had to eat, and the craft would need to be refuelled somehow.

Daley was well used to the waiting game - every policeman was. It was bred into the very bones of the profession. He surveyed the scene in the large CID office. Radio traffic involving the searchers at sea was being monitored by a feed through loudspeakers on the wall. Intermittently, Donald could be heard offering words of advice, or making hackneyed enquiries. Daley was convinced that this was merely for show and that he was determined to appear at the heart of the chase, even though desk-bound in Kinloch. All of the radio transmissions were being recorded as a matter of course, and Donald was making sure his involvement was to the fore - or appeared to be at any rate.

He left the office. Momentarily, he considered telling Donald where he was going, but soon realised that to be a fruitless exercise as his superior was too busy in the pursuit of glory via the Royal Navy and the deep blue sea.

He walked across the car park and got into the Ford *Mondeo* pool car. After a quick glance at the map, he drove the car through the gates of Kinloch Police Station, waving to the young cop who had saluted him. *Only salute a uniform son,* he thought as he drove down the town's Main Street, turning left at the harbour. The memory of Fraser's lifeless body oozing blood and gore flashed to the front of his mind's eye. He gripped the wheel tightly, doing his best to banish the vexatious image.

Liz sat at the edge of the water on a small rock that was ideally suited to the job of an impromptu chair. She was eating a breakfast roll filled with smoked salmon and cream cheese, made by the redoubtable Annie, while watching Seanessy, who was removing a coil of rope from the boat. He looked up at her; though she couldn't reason why, she swore he looked furtive. She was startled by a sharp sound to her left, and turned around to discover a gull hovering over a whelk that it had dropped on the ground to break its shell.

Seanessy passed her on his way back to the cottage. He smiled. "Running repairs, you know. Have to take every opportunity to get these things done when the weather is right." He hurried back up the rough path, as Liz pondered what running repairs could be effected in the shack using so much rope.

The glint of the sea suddenly dulled as a cloud passed over the sun. Liz shivered involuntarily; she noticed the goose pimples on her forearms and untied the fleece from around her waist, standing to put it on.

The road to the retirement home was winding, narrow, but very scenic, hugging the coast, dotted with little bays resplendent with pure, white sand. The ground on the other side of the road rose through a thick forest of pine trees, replete with little clearings occupied by houses, or the entrance to forestry tracks. He had discovered a *Sting* CD in the car's player: *Every Breath You Take* was the current track playing. His thoughts turned to Liz. He remembered dancing with her to the song in a nightclub in Paisley. He tried to work out how many years ago, he failed. It seemed like a lifetime - strangely, someone else's lifetime. The world was so different, so changed in the last few years.

The signpost read 'Firdale'. Daley slowed down at the 'Thirty miles an hour' signs, and started looking for the home. WDC

Dunn had given him rough directions; he passed a church on his right hand side, then a prefabricated building he presumed served as the village hall. By his reckoning, he needed to take the next right. He did.

The road narrowed; speed bumps stood proud of the highway at regular intervals. Triangular warning signs depicting a couple of bent figures using walking sticks, bore the legend *Slow - Elderly People*. Daley reflected on the indignity of old age in British society again, as the car rumbled over the last speed bump towards a set of large, wrought iron gates.

Excitement on the Skerry as Liz spotted movement in the water to her right, coupled with the grey flash of wet flesh arching through the waves. "Mr Seanessy - we've got a bottlenose! I think," Liz called to her guide as she put down her binoculars, and bent down to find the dolphin on her camera, already rigged to a long lens on a tripod.

She heard a muffled voice coming from the shack, while looking up from the camera to the sea, hoping for another sighting of the creature to enable her to get her bearings and grab some images - maybe even a spouting of water. She scanned the scene with her naked eyes; then again, almost in front of her and about thirty yards from the small island, the dolphin could be seen plunging through the waves. She bent down aligning the camera to that area of water just as the dolphin appeared again. With her left hand, she pressed the button of the remote camera device, hearing the camera whirl into action. She reflected how she missed the days of old fashioned cameras, listening to the shutter's rapid fire when set to automatic. The sound just wasn't the same now, the experience somehow lessened.

She was aware of footsteps behind her; she felt Seanessy was restless and distracting, she was trying to concentrate hard on the area of water where she had last seen the dolphin. Then a strange noise - humming - like one of the old fluorescent lights everyone had in their kitchens in the Seventies. She stood back from the camera in order to examine the source of the sound. *Typical for something to go wrong with the equipment just as I'm about to...*

The thought was left unfinished. She felt a sudden pain in the small of her back, like a sting from an insect, or the prick of a needle. A split second later her body began to convulse in pain; pain the like of which she had never felt before. She was falling but could do nothing to save herself. Her limbs would simply not obey her mental commands - even her eyes were blurred, her vision shot through with sparks and flashes. She fell to the ground heavily. At the same time her world went black.

Daley was led down a carpeted corridor by a young care worker, who chatted amiably as they walked. She told the detective how hard they worked to let residents feel that they had their own space in the home; each had a patio door leading out onto a communal garden, which they could access at any time of the day or night, unless of course they had medical problems, where this was inadvisable.

"Mrs Sneddon's a fine old woman," she intoned this with a more sing-song accent than prevailed in Kinloch. "A bit confused at times, because of her condition, you understand, but otherwise really nice and friendly." She looked rueful. "It's so sad to see them getting worse - you know, kind of losing who they are. That's a terrible way to end your life - don't you think?" She looked at the policeman, her face tinged with sadness.

Daley answered in the affirmative, recalling how his own grandmother had gradually lost her sense of self after three massive strokes. He would go to visit her with his mother every Sunday in the *Geriatric* ward of the local hospital. Not a pleasant, bright place like the one he was walking through now: cold, smelling of antiseptic, age, and shit. Rows of old people in various stages of decline lined the sides of the ward in metal framed beds, each with a small bedside cabinet, on which a tray and a plastic glass were placed, as well as the meagre possessions they were permitted to retain. Everything was impersonal, stripped of any kind of homely familiarity. Those who were lucky enough to be visited regularly by friends and relatives, boasted vases of fresh flowers by their beds; many though, lay alone day after day, often too ill to make the short walk down the corridor to the toilet, having to suffer the indignity of shitting in a cardboard potty, with only curtains pulled hastily around the bed for privacy. He could remember how sometimes the nurses would neglect to close those drapes sufficiently; the look of shame on the face of one old man, as he squatted on the bed trying to go, his hand held by an impatient nurse, her lip curled in distaste.

He would always come away from this melancholy place with the vague impression that those, like his grandmother, who had lost so much of themselves, were the lucky ones. Not for them the parade of indignity, as they lay alone watching the large clock on the wall inexorably tick down what remained of their lives. Where there was no sense, there was no feeling, as his mother often said. She used to cry though - every Sunday - before they arrived, and as they left.

This place was so different. Paintings lined the walls of the corridor, local scenes, or the familiar paint and crayon creations of children, all adorned with names and ages. Three easy chairs were placed at intervals along the corridor, beside small book cases filled, in the main, with popular romances, or well-known thrillers.

The nurse stopped at a door marked with the number ten and a small name plate that read *Mrs M Sneddon*, she cleared her throat and knocked on the door lightly. "Madeleine, it's the policeman I was telling you about," she turned the handle, opening the door and poking her head through the gap. "Ah, you're decent - is it OK for Mr Daley to come in?" A muffled answer saw the young nurse open the door wide, then step back to let the detective enter.

A thin, old lady sat in a high backed chair, with a woollen patchwork rug over her knees. The room was bright and airy, containing, as well as the chair the woman was seated on, a narrow couch, coffee table, modern television and a unit consisting of drawers, and a glass display cabinet. Had it not been for the high bed in the corner, it could have been a sitting room in any house. French windows, slightly ajar, looked out onto a garden, which given the time of year, was reaching full bloom. The scent of newly mown grass and flowers filled the space with a glorious aroma. A door to his right was marked *toilet*. No stink of shit, or lack of privacy here.

"Hello, Mrs Sneddon," he remained standing, despite the nurse's indication that he should sit on the couch. "Do you mind if I take a seat?"

"Na, son, be my guest," her voice was thin and crackled with age; her accent Glaswegian, not the long vowels of Kinloch.

He sat down, looking out of the French windows. "Lovely view you have here, Mrs Sneddon," he smiled at the old lady.

"Aye, no' bad, no' bad. Ca' me Madeleine, by the way, son," she smiled a toothless grin in return.

"Would you like a cup of tea or coffee, Mr Daley?" The nurse was hovering behind Madeleine's chair. Daley noticed a mini kettle and some mugs placed on a tray on the cabinet.

"Yes please - coffee if you don't mind. It's the only thing that keeps me awake, Madeleine. Do know what I mean?"

"Ye canna' beat a nice cup o' tea, son. No, I love ma' tea - dae I no' Maggie?" She lifted her head towards the back of her chair. "Make sure you gie the constable wan o' my special biscuits noo," she held up a bony finger by way of making her point.

Daley saw that the nurse was about to correct her about his rank, so shook his head to indicate that it didn't matter.

"You know why I'm here, Madeleine?"

Momentarily she looked confused, then realisation spread over her face. "The wee lassie - whit's her name - och," she shook her head in frustration.

"Isobel - Izzy," Daley helped her.

"Aye, right enough - Izzy," she shook her head again, and looked at him with a resigned expression. "I hope yer no' going tae tell me she's been plunkin' the school again. She's a wee rascal, so she is."

Daley knew through his telephone conversations with staff, that they had told her what had happened to her granddaughter, but that the old woman didn't seem able to accept or retain the information. He hadn't expected to glean much from his visit, however, he hoped that maybe Mrs Sneddon would be able to give him some background, and in any case, he had felt impotent back at the office.

Maggie the nurse handed him a mug of coffee. "Do you take sugar?" She smiled.

"No, milk only," he patted his stomach by way of an explanation, "watching my weight."

"Away wae ye,'" Madeleine looked animated. "Yer a braw lookin' young man, right enough," she let out a cackle, then coughed asthmatically. "A' these skinny malinks ye see the day. Sure the constable's just lovely, Maggie?"

"Oh, very nice," she gave Daley an embarrassed smile. "You'll take a biscuit though?" She offered him a tartan tin, containing small, shell-shaped biscuits. "You like them because they've got the same name as you. Eh, Madeleine?"

They chatted about the home, Madeleine telling him how much she liked the place. Daley took a couple of the biscuits, recognising them from his trips to France. *It could never be said that Jim Daley didn't like a biscuit.*

He looked around the room as he took the first sip of his coffee. Behind the glass doors of the cabinet were some framed photographs; mostly black and white, though some in colour looked like old school class photos.

"Would you mind if I took a look at some of your photographs, Madeleine? Is there one of Izzy?"

"Aye, son, be my guest. She's in a couple right enough; though how they managed tae get a photo o' her at the school, I'll never know," she shook her head again. "She's never there".

Daley got up awkwardly from the couch, mug of coffee in one hand, the remaining biscuit held in his mouth. He walked over to the cabinet, removing the biscuit as he went.

He scanned the pictures from left to right: an old, black and white posed image of whom, he presumed, was Madelaine as a young woman, bore a strong family resemblance to her granddaughter. There was another of two men wearing flat caps, and what looked like football scarves giving thumbs up to the camera, one smoking a pipe. Another grainy image of a young man in a Second World War army uniform. The two more modern photos were at the end of the line. He had dipped his biscuit in his coffee and had just taken a bite when his heart sank. He was so shocked that he dropped what remained of the biscuit on the floor.

It was a typical school photograph. A group of about twenty children, some sitting, some standing, flanked by a teacher. Seated at the front, arm-in-arm, sat two girls, one looking side on at the other, both laughing. The girl in profile had her hair up in a white pony tail, she was laughing heartily. The other girl was pretty, she stared at the camera, her dark hair tied into two bunches by red ribbons, only slightly faded by the age of the picture. They were young, but instantly recognisable: Janet Ritchie and Izzy Watson. On the left hand side of the class photo stood the teacher. He was wearing what looked like a green jacket, a white shirt and an orange tie, knotted badly and hanging askew over his paunch. His hair was red and brushed in whisps over a balding pate. Despite the passing of years, Glynn Seanessy was unmistakable too.

Daley thrust the mug onto the cabinet and reached for his mobile phone in the inside jacket of his pocket, pressing '2' on his speed dial. The nurse looked on with no little alarm.

The call was answered. "Brian, we're wrong. It's Seanessy and he's got Liz."

Daley was in his car now. He drove hastily towards the gates of the retirement home, the small stones on the driveway popping under the car's wheels. He felt the same sensation of disorientation that he always experienced at times of extreme stress: his face was hot and sweaty, a sinking feeling in his stomach, accompanied by vague nausea. In short, he felt as though he was on some kind of hellish rollercoaster, unable to do anything to stop the feeling of falling, spinning out of control. At times like this he spoke to himself. *I must focus, take the overview*

- *stop being subjective.* Amidst all of this self-counselling though, his heart was heavy, beating in his chest like a leaden stone.

For some reason, he remembered the day his mother died. She had been ill for a long time, and when the hospital had contacted him to say that her condition had worsened during the course of the previous night - being used to such calls - he hadn't hurried to her side. He had taken time to shower and have a quick lunch before he left. The look on the face of the nursing sister when he had eventually arrived required no articulation. His mother was dead. In the infinite universe of time, he would never see her again.

He dragged his mind from these melancholy reminiscences, and tried desperately to concentrate on the matter in hand. He was surprised just how hard he found it to concentrate, such was his current plight. *Liz.* For some reason he couldn't recall her face to his mind's eye. All he could visualise was the hideously violated body of Janet Ritchie, sprawled across the table of *Russian Gold.*

His mobile rang. "Jim, where are you?" This was Scott. The sound of his voice managed to somehow strengthen his resolve.

"I'm just heading out of Firdale. I'll be with you in twenty minutes or so, I hope." He checked the time on the dashboard clock.

"No, listen, Jim," Scott's voice was insistent. "We know what boat he's in - it's the Johnstone boys', they lend it tae him for sightseeing." Daley remembered the small lobster boat with the for'ad cabin he had seen at Machrie Bay. "We just found that out when we were trying tae get a number on Bobby Johnstone. That's not all," Scott sounded breathless, even excited. "That vessel was sighted about three hours ago near a wee island ca'ed Abb's Skerry. I got a hold o' Camel, he says that yer man Seanessy has some lobster pots in the bay there. There's a run doon fisherman's cottage tae - dilapidated apparently - but he remembers Seanessy askin' fir the boat tae take some wood and stuff o'er there tae dae some repairs. Are you still with me, Jim?"

"Yes, I think so - what's the plan, Brian? I'm desperate here." Daley could hear the plea in his own voice.

"I've got Camel wae me. He thought maybe Bobby had taken the boat, he forgot tae mention Seanessy sometimes uses it. We're just waitin' for the lifeboat tae get under way..." Scott was about to continue, until Daley interrupted.

"So I better get a shift on," Daley had stopped the car at the side of the road, but was now taking off again.

"Na. Stop!" that was an order from Scott. "You're nearer where you are. Camel says tae get yersel' doon tae the harbour at Firdale and get someone tae take you oot tae this place. He says there's a wee shop on the quay an' they'll sort ye oot. OK, Jim?"

Daley was already turning the car in the middle of the road, heading back into Firdale.

"I'll bell you when I get to the pier, Brian." He threw the mobile on the passenger seat, and gunned the car towards the village harbour.

Liz opened her eyes. She couldn't remember anything for a few seconds, such was the pain she felt. Trying to get up, she realised that she could not move her arms. She fought the urge to scream, trying to control her breathing. It was so gloomy she could barely see. Diffused light was coming through a tiny window, curtained by what looked like a filthy hessian sack; the room reeked of damp fish, and a chemical smell.

Managing to turn her head, she saw that her arms were spread either side of her, each tied by the wrist to a rusty metal headboard. What looked like a large belt encompassed the bed and her lower limbs, leaving her only able to move her head forward by craning her neck. A cold shaft of fear pierced her mind, almost making her cry out. She fought the impulse. Her whole body was sore, she could see her pulse in her eyes. *What the fuck has happened to me?*

Her eyes were assailed by bright light, as the door to the shack swung open.

Daley drove too fast through the village of Firdale. He remembered looking at a map of the area before he had left the

286

office, so he knew the village was spread along a main road which led down to the harbour. His mind was a riot. He was trying to think like the detective he was, but could not get the image of a lifeless Liz from his thoughts. He had seen so much death - so much gruesome death - that it had become his default response. When he heard of people he knew personally, dying, he automatically pictured their greying corpse on the gurney at the mortuary, chest roughly sewn up by a course attendant after a post mortem. He heard himself whimper as he steered the car down an incline, the sea now visible through buildings and trees.

At the bottom of the hill, a road forked off to the left, whilst ahead, two small boats were tied up alongside a short pier. He stopped at a grey building with a corrugated iron roof, replete with a venerable *Esso* sign. He got out of the car, and seeing no-one about, entered the shop through a creaky wooden door, bell ringing above his head as he did so.

The shop was like Aladdin's cave: shelves of groceries lined two walls, whilst the floor space in the middle was taken up by items as diverse as a large box of cabbages, and a small outboard motor. In the dim light he could see an array of wares hanging from hooks from the ceiling, including a child's mountain bike, a spade, mop, and a camping stove. The emporium smelled like those he had visited with his grandparents when on holiday in the west coast: hard to define, yet a heady mixture of detergent, fruit and vegetables, engine oil and polish; though these were only the scents he could readily discern. At the end of the crowded space sat an old-fashioned counter, glass-fronted and framed in stout oak, the varnished wood worn bare in places by age and much use.

"Can I be helping you, at all?" A disembodied voice seemed to come from somewhere behind the counter. Suddenly, an elderly man stood up. He was wearing a faded barge cap and a thick, dark-blue fisherman's sweater, which he rubbed his hands on absently. "I've lost one of my bloody contact lenses again and I can't see bugger all." His voice had much more of a Highland quality than that of Kinloch, like the young nurse from the care home. "You'll have to come a bit closer. I like to see the colour of my customers' eyes, before I ask them to part with their money."

Daley approached the counter, fishing in the inside pocket of his jacket for his warrant card. The man took a step back at this, as though he was expecting the detective to produce a firearm from his pocket.

"It's OK, sir. Detective Inspector Daley," he flourished the I.D. "I have to ask you for your help, I'm afraid."

The shopkeeper examined the warrant card, squinting through one eye with his other closed. "Aye well, I'll have to be taking your word for it officer. You could be Rechie Kray for all I can see at the moment." Daley noted how he pronounced the letter jay as a 'ch' sound - like MacLeod he realised.

"I have to get access to a boat - and someone to sail it come to that. We have a very serious situation at Abb's Skerry; I take it you know where I mean?" Daley was doing his best to present a calm façade, while underneath his heart was thudding in his chest.

"Abb's Skerry, eh?" The man scratched his head under his cap. "My grandfather used it for creels; I didna' think anyone did now though. Would you be having a cup of tea, or something stronger perhaps? You seem a bit overwrought."

"Listen, Mr - I'm sorry I don't know your name?"
"Munro, Anda Munro. Say your piece, officer. I'll help you if I can," he realised Daley's change of demeanour indicated something serious was afoot.

"Thank you, Mr Munro." Daley gave him a brief summary of what was happening, leaving out names, and the fact that the person who was in dire danger at Abb's Skerry was actually his wife.

"A dreadful carry on, all together. I knew there were problems in Kinloch - aren't there always - but this is serious stuff indeed. C'mon with me and I'll see what I can do for you," he lifted a hatch at the end of the counter, the polished brass hinges squeaking in protest, stepping out into the body of the shop, then replacing the heavy hatch gingerly. "Very nearly took my head off with this damn thing a number of years ago; I'm ready for the bastard now though." The bell rang again as the pair opened the door and left the shop.

"Under normal circumstances, I would be able to take you there myself, unfortunately our boat is beached at the moment; my brother has her over at McConachie's slip."

Just great. Daley thought to himself.

They headed for the edge of the pier. The water was low, the tide, according to Munro, was on the turn. Daley thought he recognised one of the vessels, but wondered how he could. A cloud covered the sun, turning off the glistening sparkle of the harbour and casting a distinct chill over the Chief Inspector. He was desperately trying to keep things together; his mind though, kept up a loop of visceral images - horrible murder scenes he had witnessed. *Please stop.*

A face appeared from the small wheelhouse of one of the vessels; a low, old-fashioned looking craft that looked in much need of repair. Hamish, his leathery face quite unmistakable, grinned at the two men above him on the pier. "Aye, m'boys, fine day for it. No?"

"Ah, Hamish," Munro adopted a slightly wary tone. "This man is a police officer, his name is…"

"Mr Daley," Hamish removed the pipe from his mouth. "And how can I be of help tae you the day?"

Munro turned to the policeman, his hand cupping his mouth. "He has the sight, Chief Inspector," he said querulously. "Sounds like a damned fool half the time, but mark my words, he's as wise as a bloody owl." Munro looked back down to Hamish with a forced smile.

"Hello, Hamish. I need your help. This is really urgent…" Daley looked imploringly at the old fisherman, as Munro turned towards him, surprise etched across his face.

"I take it you are acquainted with this reprobate already?"

"Oh yes," said Daley. "Our paths have crossed quite a few times in the last few days." He suddenly remembered his arrest of Flynn, and knowing the men to be friends, wondered how the old man would react to him. "I need you take me to Abb's Skerry."

"Aye." Hamish's response was concise, if nothing else.

"You'll be reimbursed for your fuel, and your time of course," Daley said, for want really of something else to say; already planning his best route down onto the vessel.

"You better get aboard, Mr Daley. It'll take us aboot three quarters of an hour tae get there, wae steady steaming you understand." He moved to the side of the boat, offering his hand up to help Daley onto the boat.

The policeman eyed the jump with trepidation, however time was of the essence. He leant forward, grabbed onto Hamish's meaty hand and jumped down the three or so feet onto the craft, which lurched to the side as he landed heavily on the deck.

"I'm thinking you're built mair for the land than the sea, Mr Daley," Hamish announced in a puff of smoke as he sucked on his pipe before disappearing into the wheelhouse.

"All right, Mr Daley. I wish you safe passage," Munro shouted from the pier. "I'm afraid you're stuck on this bucket. The fishing fleet - such as they are now - are all at sea, and there's no sign of anyone aboard this vessel here," he nodded at the boat tied up next to Hamish's. "Is there anything else I can be doing for you?"

"No thanks, Mr Munro," Daley said, then changed his mind. "Would you be able to lend me some kind of jacket or something?" He remembered his trip on the lifeboat and the chill he had felt whilst at sea, despite his survival suit.

Munro disappeared back into the shop for a few moments, returning with a red garment wrapped in a clear plastic bag. "An excellent sea-going fleece, Mr Daley," he threw the package at the detective. "Water-resistant an' everything - a snip at a hundred an' twenty pounds. Do you have the cash on you, or will I open up an account?"

"An account please, Mr Munro. We are in a hurry." Daley said flatly.

"Aye, very good," Munro smiled back proprietarily. "I hope you have a life jacket for the Chief Inspector, Hamish?" he enquired cheerily.

"Why?" Hamish's head poked from the wheelhouse. "What

will it cost if we have to buy one fae you? - a thousand pounds no doubt. Don't you be worrying Anda Munro, you've made all the money you will today out of us. Now get back in your shop an' keep countin' yer fortune; and think on forbye, there nae pockets in a shroud." Hamish was moving nimbly around the small vessel for a man of his age, he had clearly realised the urgency of the situation.

Munro's hasty reply was drowned out by the loud rumble of the boat's engine firing into life in a cloud of blue, pungent smoke. The shopkeeper untied the rope that was securing the craft to the pier from a stubby, silver bollard, throwing it coiled onto the deck at Daley's feet. "God speed to you, Mr Daley," he shouted loudly to be heard over the engines, waving languidly as the small boat turned from the pier, heading out of the harbour, into the open sea.

Just as they neared the mouth of the harbour, Daley's mobile rang.

"What's happening, boss?" Scott's voice was loud and clear despite the rattle of the boat's engine.

Daley informed his DS that he had found a vessel and was now en route for Abb's Skerry, a journey that Hamish reckoned would take just under an hour.

"Aye, well you'll be there before us," Scott sounded rueful. "The weather is closing in; some kind of sea-haar. It's not safe for the helicopter, and we're waiting for the lifeboat. She's towing a boat back into Kinloch. The upshot is, I'm not sure when we'll be leaving. Mind you, I'm told it'll only take aboot an' hour when we do get underway, given they can get any speed up if the weather closes in."

"I want to have armed officers on the boat, Bri," Daley was trying to visualise what he was about to face without thinking of Liz, a task that he was finding virtually impossible. "I'll have to work things out on the hoof."

The answer from Scott was garbled, they had just left the mouth of Firdale Bay and the mobile signal was going, rapidly. He could make out Scott's plea for him to be careful, then the connection was broken. He checked the screen: *No Signal* was emblazoned across it.

"Can I use your radio, Hamish?" Daley shouted to the sailor.

"Well, a wee bit tricky, Mr Daley," Hamish rubbed his chin with a grimace.

"Meaning?"

"I'm no' big on people interfering with my movements - there' a'ways somebody tryin' tae tell you whoot tae dae o'er the airwaves. Dae ye ken, Mr Daley?"

"You mean you've no radio, Hamish," Daley stated in resigned tones.

"No," Hamish was being canny, "we've got wan - its jeest no' workin' very weel, at the moment.

Great. Daley stared ahead. What was that saying he had first been made aware of in anger management? *We are where we are.* How apt.

In the distance, he could see where the blue sky ended. It was as though a giant wad of cotton wool had been left on the horizon; there was no way to discern where the sea ended and the sky began. Daley remembered his history, when sailors were genuinely afraid they would sail off the edge of the world. If anything had happened to Liz, this would indeed be an apt metaphor.

21

Seanessy leaned over Liz, his face in her's. His breath was rancid; she could count the individual blackheads that populated his bulbous nose. The shack had become very gloomy inside and despite her predicament, she reasoned that the weather outside had changed - clouded over.

"What are you thinking about, whore?" Flecks of spittle sprayed into Liz's face, her stomach churned in revulsion. She remained silent. "Wondering what is going to happen to you, I've no doubt," Seanessy grinned manically, displaying an uneven mouthful of yellow teeth. "First, we're going to have some fun, you and I. Fun. The kind of fun you would never have with someone like me. Look at me, you bitch," he grabbed her chin, pulling her face in line with his. She had to blink his spittle from her left eye.

He leaned back, taking something from his trouser pocket. She gasped as he leant back forward, a Stanley knife brandished in her face. "You're like them all. Young or old you're all the same - eh?" His eyes looking as though they were on stalks, bulging, the pupils mere pinpricks. "Nice when you're little girls: happy, funny, pretty - all you want to do is play at being mummy," he snarled, still holding her chin so that she couldn't move her head. "Then you start to bleed, and we all know what you think about then. Time for a change, pretty one." In one swift movement, he let go of her face, grabbed the neck of her t-shirt, and slit it open with the sharp knife, revealing the white of her bra which contrasted with her tanned skin. He grabbed her left breast and began to knead it through the undergarment.

Liz closed her eyes tight shut. This was her - every woman's - worst nightmare. She tried to move her arms and legs - she was held tight. For the first time, she realised what was going to happen: she was going to suffer, then she was going to die.

Daley massaged his temple in the way familiar to him when he was under extreme stress. The weather had indeed changed. Within fifteen minutes of leaving Firdale, they were seemingly engulfed by a thick, impenetrable mist. He could barely see from one end of the boat to the other; the scene, that had seemed wide-open and infinite, had now been reduced to a patch of dark, almost black, oily water; hardly a ripple on the surface now. The strangest thing was the lack of any noise. No squawk of gulls, rush of wind, or crash of breakers onto the shoreline. Nothing; like being enclosed in a constricting bubble of life afloat on a silent ocean. Despite the expensive fleece, he shivered with cold. Only the noise of the engine was present, and even it appeared deadened, like listening to the old generator his father had kept in the garage during his childhood, when regular power cuts were a matter of government policy.

"This will slow us up a wee bit," Hamish's voice at his shoulder made him jump. He turned round to face the old sailor, the smell of pipe smoke taking the place of the stench of diesel, any tang of the sea now strangely absent.

"How the hell do you know where you're going, Hamish?" Daley gestured at the lowering scene with an outstretched arm.

"It's no' a case o' jeest knowing where you are, Mr Daley, mair feeling it," his face creased into its habitual slit-eyed, parchment smile. Daley looked at him doubtfully. Despite the desperate nature of the situation, the older man remained utterly unhurried - serene almost.

"You do know what's at stake here, Hamish? This is more than a case for me now. If he harms her…" The rest was implicit.

Hamish sucked on his pipe a couple of times, and just when the detective thought he was not going to answer, he spoke. "In life,

Mr Daley all we have to hold ontae is the certainty of death," his eyes were bright-blue, and at their most piercing. "If she's deid you'll know - even if she's in pain, you'll know. But I'll tell you this, Chief Inspector, if a' you can dae is picture her lying deid on a mortuary table, then deid she'll be - aye, as sure as ye killed her yersel'," his gaze was steady and unflinching. "That Inglish playwright wrote aboot there being mair things on heaven an' earth; well let me tell you: it's no' jeest heaven an' earth, it's in the mind tae." He removed the pipe from his mouth, still staring at the policeman, and casually tapped it on the hull of the boat. Such was the stillness, the fizz as the spent ash hit the water was plainly audible.

Hamish turned on his heel, heading back towards the wheelhouse, as Daley looked back out to sea. He thought back on making love to Liz on the bed in his hotel room. The warmth, the smell, the very touch of her filled his senses. Suddenly he felt a calm resolve, as though he had been emboldened by the old fisherman's words.

Liz was aware of a thumping noise on the wall of the shack, which made Seanessy stop what he was doing and listen. She was breathing heavily, and despite herself was crying silent tears of fear and humiliation. Her tormentor had sliced into her bra' exposing her breasts, which he devoured visually as one would the serving of an expensive meal, actually salivating at the prospect of having her.

He's going to rape me. Her mind was still working, though in a random, intermittent way. Subconsciously, she was calculating the possibility of survival. The sickening realisation that while others knew that she was on the boat trip with this man who had turned out to be the monster of her worst nightmares, nobody knew where they were going and certainly not that they were on this strange island.

Seanessy stared at her for a few seconds more, then abruptly left the shack. Absently, she was aware of a dull thud. Her situation precluded speculation as to its source; instead, she pulled, tugged and strained desperately at her bonds, a cause she knew to be futile, though she knew she had to try something - anything - to remove herself from this hell.

The door creaked open again, the leering figure of Seanessy framed in the doorway.

"Very appropriate weather, don't you think?" He walked towards the bed. "Even if that brave, arrogant husband of yours and his grubby little sidekick have managed to realise what's happened to you, they'll never find you in this - well not now anyway." Instead of looming over her, he sat down awkwardly at the end of the bed. Liz could feel the thick strap that held her legs fast loosen slightly as his weight made an impression on the filthy mattress. She jerked her leg, hoping that she could free herself. To no avail: Seanessy caught her limb with both hands, so tightly in fact, that she cried out in pain. "You're going nowhere, Mrs Daley. Time you had a little rest, I think," he fumbled in the pocket of his jacket. "Now, I have things to attend to and it will be better for both of us if you spend some time out of harm's way." He flourished a hypodermic syringe, removing the needle cover and squirting some of the fluid within into the air. "This will help you get some sleep - keep you fresh so to speak," his searing grin revealing rotting yellow teeth. "Not many bonuses to being a chemistry teacher - apart from knowing the effect of particular substances on the human body."

"You mad bastard," she heard herself say this as though she was listening to a recording of her own voice.

In one quick movement he leant forward, grabbed her pinioned arm, feeling along her forearm with his fingertips. "Ah, the joys of being thin and fit, Mrs Daley," he smiled at her affably. "Never hard to find a vein when you need one." He thrust the needle into her arm.

Liz felt a wave of nausea, rapidly followed by an overwhelming tiredness. She slipped out of consciousness.

Seanessy waited a few more seconds, then slapped her gently; the strong sedative had an almost immediate effect. He began to untie her bonds, all of the time taking in the curve of her breast under her ruined shirt. Again, he began to salivate.

Daley crabbed his way towards the wheelhouse. "Any idea how we're doing, Hamish?" He looked on as the doughty skipper raised his head and seemed to sniff the air. They had been on the water for forty minutes. Daley had no idea where they were, and was not encouraged to see the paucity of instrumentation available to Hamish; from what little he knew of life afloat, he could discern no radar, no clever electronic device that may help them navigate through the enveloping gloom.

"Did I ever tell ye aboot my grandfaither, Mr Daley?" Hamish addressed him with his level gaze.

"No, I don't think you did," his heart sank at the thought of some hoary old tale, but recognising that this man held the key to saving Liz and that they probably couldn't go any faster, decided to listen to the story with as much enthusiasm as he could muster.

"Don't be worrying," Hamish displayed his habitual talent of reading others' thoughts. "I can talk an' navigate at the same time." Daley smiled despite himself, and nodded for the older man to proceed.

"He was a fishermun, lake myself, you unnerstan," Hamish took a draw from his pipe. "He volunteered for the Russian Convoys - a hell o' a thing tae volunteer for if ye ask me - but there ye are, he wiz a'ways a thrawn auld bugger," he sniffed the air again distractedly, Daley waiting patiently for the yarn to continue.

"Tae cut a long story short, they were sunk by a torpedo in the Baltic. My grandfaither an' a few others managed tae scramble intae a lifeboat afore they froze tae death. Jeest a widden boat wae a pitiful sail an' an even mair pitiful sack full o' basic rations, maist o' it ruined by the sea," he fixed Daley with his piercing blue eyes. "Nae such thing as a compass - na', nor radar eithers - the auld fella' navigated them safely tae the shore - aye safely tae the shore," he repeated, "jeest wae whoot he had up here." He proceeded to tap his temple with his right forefinger.

Daley raised his eyebrow. "Some feat, Hamish. I hope you

have the same talent," he smiled encouragingly at the old man. "I suppose he went on to sail on more convoys?"

"No. He didn'a," Hamish shook his head. "Unfortunately hee's instinct fir the shore didn'a run tae jeest whose shore wiz whose, if you get my drift, Mr Daley." The detective looked confused. "Ended up he'd sailed them right intae German waters; aye right intae the hands o' the Nazis themselves." Hamish looked at his fingernails, a look of regret on his tanned face. "Spent the rest o' the conflict in a preesoner o' war camp." He paused for a few moments, then looked up with a beaming smile on his face. "Still an' a', Chief Inspector, things could have been worse - they could a' hae been drooned." He pursed his lips, signalling, Daley thought, the pride he felt in his grandfather's nautical prowess. The policeman said nothing, peering desperately through the fog.

Suddenly his mobile burst into life, the theme from the *Sopranos* somehow amplified by the lowering mist.

"You'll be getting' a signal fae County Antrim," Hamish announced with a nod of his head, as Daley fished in the pocket of his fleece for the phone.

"Brian - what's happening? We're ploughing on, but this fog's a bastard."

"We're jist aboot tae leave, Jim," Scott's voice was surprisingly clear, and again raised Daley's spirits. "We should be at the island in about an hour, or a bit longer, yer man tells me - it's doon tae the weather. Where are you?

"Eh," Daley looked back at Hamish, "kinda hard to tell at the moment. Just get going mate."

"Don't worry, boss," Scott could hear the desperation in his friend's voice. "We're going tae sort this oot - trust me." Daley could hear voices in the background. "I'll need tae go Jamie - keep the faith man." Daley smiled at the use of the phrase his DS normally kept for footballing purposes; especially if Rangers had a bad game.

Seanessy held the knife in front of his face, examining the blade carefully. It shone, polished by the sharpening process.

Things hadn't gone as well as he had hoped - they never did - in his experience. People refused to fit into his idea of how things should be, how life should be conducted. He drew a finger gently along the blade, drawing a bubble of blood, which turned into a small drip. He watched as it spattered onto the dirty wooden floor with a barely perceptible tap. He wondered idly how long it would take for his life to drip away at this rate of flow. He knelt down over the recumbent, unconscious figure, taking the back of the knife in both hands. He positioned the knife onto the middle of the neck, just touching the white skin; immediately a red line of blood streaked across the length of the implement, an involuntary twitch began in one of the muscles on the bare shoulder. He pushed down, his full weight behind the blade. Blood spattered his face, hands, chest and trousers. The body underneath him shook in the spasms of death throes. Another gush of blood then a snap. The eyes opened, but the light behind them was already gone.

Without warning, Hamish shut off the engine in the small boat. Daley turned to see him listening, his head cocked to one side, eyes closed. "Can you hear that?" He asked the policeman, as he removed something from his pocket.

Daley listened intently, but could hear nothing other than the dull lapping on the side of the boat, and a distant hissing noise. He clambered over to see Hamish holding a small compass in a wooden frame up to the light. "Thank goodness, for a minute there I didn't think you had any instruments to sail by at all." Daley looked hopefully at the old fisherman.

"Been with me noo for over fifty years; my first skipper gave it tae me. Handy when you're caught up in a pea-souper lake this," he sniffed the air, eyes closed again. "From now on," he said in a much more quiet voice, "ye might conseeder speaking a bit mair quietly." He nodded into the gloom. "We're no' far off the Skerry."

Daley peered over the prow of the vessel. He could see nothing, no shadows, or breaks in the water - nothing to indicate they were nearing land. "How do you know Hamish? I can't see anything."

"Aye, well you see," the old man mused. "Whoot you're no' takin' intae accoont, is the fact that ye need tae use a' yer senses - no' jeest yer eyes. Dae ye no' hear that swish in the distance?" His voice was barely a whisper.

"Yes I can," Daley closed his own eyes, better to hear the hissing noise he had detected a moment ago.

"That's the surf drawing off the shingle bay at Abb's Skerry; either that or we're on the coast o' Islay, which wid be a bugger indeed. I canna stand Islay." he smiled his crinkly smile at the detective.

Daley's heart leapt into his mouth. If Hamish was correct, he was within a few yards of Liz; he said a silent prayer of hope that she was there and still... still alive, he shuddered. "How, or should I say where do we land, Hamish?" He whispered in return.

"Noo that's a metter o' tactics. I kinda' thought that wid be your concern, Mr Daley."

Daley thought for a few moments. He had to get onto the small island, but he didn't want to alert Seanessy. This was not an easy operation to visualise: firstly, he couldn't see the lay of the land, and secondly he had no manpower apart from himself and his ferryman, whom he could not put at risk.

"I'm no' blaming you fir the harbour maister, Mr Daley," Hamish whispered apropos of nothing. "I knew fine he wiz up tae something - the big car an' a' the fancy holidays. I wid never hae pit him as a drugs dealer though - no not at all," he shook his head in disbelief.

"I'll not even ask you how you know that, Hamish," Daley admonished his nautical guide. "We've other things to worry us at the moment. The lifeboat won't be here for at least another hour, and if we can get onto the island unseen, we'll have the element of surprise in our favour. At the moment, that's all we have in our favour. How well do you know this place, Hamish?"

Hamish squinted back at the Chief Inspector, rubbing his nose with the back of his hand, while sniffing hugely. "This place hasna' been used regularly since before they had engine power. In the old days, when ye had tae sail or row - whoot wae tides an' winds an a' that - ye could be stuck here for a good while. It's a great place tae get the big lobsters though, the deep sea kind. They shelter in the wee bay; much bigger than the wans nearer the shore..."

Daley interrupted the tale. "I'm sure that's all very interesting, Hamish, and if we get through this, I'll buy you a bottle of the best malt whisky there is and you and I can talk about it until the cows come home. At the moment though, I really want to catch a murderer and save my wife's life." He had raised his voice at the beginning of that statement, but recalling Hamish's warning, his voice was back to a whisper by the end.

"Noo, if I'm right, we're at the back o' the island. There's a wee inlet - nae mair than a pond ye unnertsan'." Hamish was holding his hand to his mouth in a conspiratorial manner. "We can lakely pit in there - under cover o' the wee hill - yer man'll no' see ye fae the cottage; unless o' course he's no' in the cottage an' on top o' the hill, in which case..."

"Right, Hamish," Daley stopped him in his tracks. "We'll - I'll - just have to take my chances." He looked back into the fog. "I don't suppose there's much chance of this clearing soon? I can't see it will hold up the lifeboat too much, though - all that equipment they have at their disposal. Looks like they could get to the moon and back."

Hamish took his pipe from the pocket of his dungarees. "Aye, nae bother for them, Mr Daley. No' so funny fir the vessel comin' in the other direction wi'oot a' the gadgets. No. Campbell will no' be able tae make headway wae any speed in this jeest in case he hits something." He struck a match on the bulwark of the vessel, cupping the tiny flame expertly in his meaty fist as he applied it to the pipe, whilst making a noise not unlike a fish out of water in an effort to set the tobacco aflame.

"I'll say this for you, Hamish, you're not scared to give anyone bad news - eh? Get me as close in as you can; I'll just have to make it up from there on in." He slapped the old sailor on the shoulder. "You better put that pipe out, you can smell it at two hundred paces."

"Aye, maybe your right, Chief Inspector." Hamish took the pipe from his mouth and tapped its upside down on the side of the boat, its glowing contents disappearing with a tiny hiss into the sea. "I'm letting her drift in - the swell's in oor favour. Hopefully yer man'll no' hear a thing, an' I can manage tae steer her where we want to go. I want you tae keep an eye oot on the bow - my eyes are no' whoot they used tae be. Jeest raise yer hand if ye see any sign o' land, an' we'll take it fae there."

Seanessy didn't like the way things had gone; not that things hadn't gone wrong before. No, this time it was different: he had been forced to kill before he had the chance to exploit the situations he had created - all of the careful planning and subtle persuasion involved in luring someone unsuspectingly to their death had been spoiled. Like cooking the perfect meal, and being able only to eat half of it.

He looked across the small bay. It would take keen eyes to spot the headless corpse submerged beneath the still water, one of the legs attached to a large weight by a rope and a rubber cuff around the ankle. It had taken him a long time to work out the best way of disposing of a body. They could be killed at any time of course, then kept relatively fresh, or at least kept from polluting the air with the foul stench of decay, by employing this method.

He cursed himself for the mistake he had made with the body of his first victim. The cuff had not been strong enough to hold in the swell. He had searched the small coastline of the skerry to see if the woman had been washed up on its rugged shore; but to no avail. It had led to a pathetic attempt at extortion and more death. In a way he had enjoyed the torturing and killing that day, despite the unexpected nature of the circumstances. He had resolved then and there to be more spontaneous, less deliberate as to the identity of his victim - that was how he had stumbled upon the policeman's pretty wife; rather she had stumbled upon him. The improvised nature of the situation had added an unexpected frisson of excitement to her capture. Yes, things had gone wrong, however, the world was an uncertain place and it didn't do to be so concerned with the perfect symmetry of a well-executed plan.

He smiled at the memory of how dismissive the big detective and his common sidekick had been of him when they met. *Dismiss me now, gentlemen.*

The air was beginning to clear. Slowly more of the bay was visible. It was time to put the next part of his plan into action. He picked up the bag of tools at his feet and strode back towards the shack. First he wanted to fix the corrugated iron roof of the lean-to at the side of the cottage, where he stored his fresh meat. He fished inside the bag, bringing out the nail gun he had brought especially for the task.

The boat edged forward on the swell, Daley peering into the grey mist. Gradually, he thought he could see shadows, he turned, lifting his arm as Hamish had instructed; the old man made his way for'ad.

"We're close tae the shore, Mr Daley," he whispered. "Better prepare yersel' fir a wee bump - here can ye try and fend us off any rocks wae this," he held up a gnarled looking oar to the detective. "Shouldna' be much o' a bump in this sea, and mebe we'll be lucky an' get right ontae the shingle. That's whoot I'm aiming fir, anyhow." He made his way back to the tiller as Daley kept watch intently on the bow, the oar poised.

Without warning he could see something ahead - a bay - with large rounded pebbles. Again, he held up his arm, looking round at Hamish, who nodded enthusiastically back. Even though they were not under power, the beach seemed to be rushing towards them at some speed. Daley braced himself against the gunwale for the inevitable impact.

As it was, they seemed to slide onto the shingle, like a car suddenly moving across a gravel drive, the noise was sudden and brief. They stopped quickly, the vessel lurching to one side as they came to rest. Daley looked down, to see that they were three quarters of the way beached, the stern of the craft still in the water. Without reference to the old man, he laid his impromptu fender carefully at his feet, and jumped over the side of the boat, levering himself over the bulwark of the vessel as though he was clearing a fence. He landed heavily on the shale with a dull crump, nearly toppling over, though he just about managed to keep his feet. As he looked up, Hamish was looking at him from the deck.

"Now you're in charge, Mr Daley," he whispered. "At the top of that little knoll you'll get a grand view of the whole island, just about. If you can see for the mist that is, though I think it's clearing."

"Thanks, Hamish," Daley's voice was equally quiet. He hoped that he hadn't alerted Seanessy. All of this, of course, presuming this was where he had taken Liz. Daley's heart was pounding. "I want you to stay here, Hamish. If you see the lifeboat, tell them what's happening." He turned to face the small hillock, dropping to his hands and knees.

"Very good, Mr Daley," Hamish whispered as he watched the detective scramble up the hill, crouching so that he wouldn't appear silhouetted against the skyline should Seanessy actually be at the cottage.

Seanessy loaded the nail gun. The lean-to at the shack was his larder; it was the place he kept his dead meat - for meat was all they became - and it was the place he did his butchery. He had killed his first victim there; he had killed there only a short time ago.

He looked at the door to the outhouse. The big padlock was lying on the grass where he had left it before securing the corpse in the bay. *No need to lock it now.*

An old wooden ladder was propped up against the wall. He decided to secure it before attempting any repair to the roof. He placed the nail gun on the grass beside the padlock, then put his foot on the bottom of the ladder. The rungs were worn, but not dangerous; he pushed down on it, ensuring that the ladder gained purchase in the rough soil, adding to its stability. It seemed firm, though he decided it would be best to climb to the top, just as a test, before he had to alight with his tools. He climbed carefully, noting that the mist was indeed clearing, as there was a tiny patch of blue showing through the gloom.

Daley gained the top of the hill; his trousers were already torn at the knee - one of his new pairs too, he mused. He cursed his lack of fitness: his legs were stiff and his back ached after having to climb the small incline. He couldn't recall ever being so nervous. He tried again to force thoughts of Liz to the back of his mind; it was impossible. The mixture of rage and fear he was experiencing was like a completely new emotion; he had thought himself immune to such flights of visceral feelings. All of his senses appeared intensified: the ground smelt richly of wet earth; the tang of the sea was so sharp in his nostrils that he could taste it. The swish of the swell falling back off the shale beach behind him sounded like distant thunder, over the pounding of his heart in his ears. Then he saw him.

Seanessy looked across the slanted corrugated iron. Two large nails had come loose in a recent storm causing a bulge between the roof and the top of the wall, through which rain had poured, leaving part of the earthen floor within the construction damp and cloying. The roofing material was old, but still thick and robust. He passed his hand over it, deciding the nail gun would make short work of the job. He paused briefly, then made his way back down the old ladder.

Daley watched the man scale the short ladder and examine the roof. He was literally only fifty yards away; the proximity made Daley hold his breath.

He recognised Seanessy, however, he looked different compared with the time he and Scott had encountered him on the beach. He seemed more stern, dark - evil in fact. Daley analysed this as being his gut reaction to the horrors he had perpetrated. He was still fighting to keep thoughts of Liz at bay. He now knew for certain she must be here. His chest ached with fear, he had to wipe beads of sweat from his brow.

What am I going to do? He was alone; he had to get to

Seanessy and subdue him, but at the same time not put Liz in danger. He had thought through alternative consequences, however he had to keep a clear head and be optimistic, a mantra, he realised, he had picked up from Donald.

He watched as Seanessy descended the ladder and went into the little side building. Taking a deep breath, still crouching, he scrambled over the top of the hill, and began to slip and slide down the muddy slope. He was heading for the rear of the cottage, all the time keeping his eyes on the building in case Seanessy would appear. He reasoned that he had the element of surprise, and that the retired teacher would be no match for him physically. He had to slow down, shortening his stride as he reached the back of the dolorous cottage, minimising the thud of his footfall.

He reached the back wall of the building, leaning against it in order to catch his breath, which he drew as silently as he could. *Please God, let her be in there. Please God, let her be safe.*

He was filthy from his clandestine traverse of the hill. The walls of the cottage were cool and damp, the salt smell of the sea here replaced by a fetid air of age and decay. Looking up he could see a small patch of blue sky - the mist was beginning to clear - he began to make his way slowly along the wall, the opposite way he had watched Seanessy disappear. He could hear no sound, nothing to indicate that Seanessy was busy inside - that he was inside at all - come to that.

He edged to the end of the wall. He paused, gripping the corner of the stonework with his fingers. He could hear nothing, so decided to be bold and craned his neck around the corner.

He could see the bay now. There was no sign of Seanessy. He stood at the side of the cottage motionless; he was consolidating his progress. If Seanessy had seen or heard him, he must surely make a move. There were tools strewn about the front of the building, and amongst them Liz's rucksack. His blood suddenly ran cold. All of the emotions he had been fending off welled up inside. He now knew that this man - this monster - had her. He tried to apply all of the lessons he had been taught in anger management to stave off the blinding rage he was now feeling;

ultimately though, he knew this to be a futile task. He was getting past the point of caring about the consequences, his only goal - saving his wife - was all that was important.

Distantly, he heard a high pitched whining, and in the split second he turned to face the direction of the noise, he saw a figure, arms outstretched holding something before it. He just had time to lift his arm to protect his face when the flash of something caught his eye.

His head felt as though it would explode as he felt something hitting his arm. Instinctively he fell to the floor. Taser: they had been shown how to use the weapon on a CID course. He had seen a colleague volunteer to be shot with one, and the effect he was feeling now was unmistakable. He landed heavily, banging his head on the sparse grass, feeling his chest start to convulse as he tried to breathe. Agonisingly he couldn't, his lungs would not inflate, as though he was held tight in a massive fist. He saw a figure loom over him. Seanessy. His body arched as his torturer triggered the weapon, sending the crippling voltage along the wires now embedded in his arm. His right hand spread involuntarily, as though he was forcing his fingers to span, the pain excruciating.

"Now, now, Inspector Daley, I had expected so much more from you." Seanessy looked down at him. "Your air-head wife, yes: an easy conquest. I had thought you were going to be an altogether tougher nut to crack." Daley heard the whine beginning to rise in pitch again.

He felt a certain surprise; despite the pain and convulsions he was suffering, he had remained conscious, and was fully aware of what was going on around him. Also, he could move his leg. He knew the whining noise was the weapon rearming another charge. With all of the strength he could muster he managed a shallow breath, and struck his leg out catching Seanessy on his knee, knocking him backwards.

With huge effort he managed to force his right hand to work. This arm was trapped under him the way he had fallen, which meant - fortuitously - that hand was only inches away from the wires inserted into his left arm. He strained, little bursts of light exploding in his vision. He remembered that he had bought the fisherman's fleece in Firdale, and that its rubberised coating had somehow dissipated the voltage of the taser. He tore the wires from his arm, then leaned desperately on his right arm, determined to be able to stand and face his attacker.

Seanessy looked suddenly panicked. He had fallen backwards and had dropped the weapon, which was squealing now on the ground beside him. He was groping at a small pouch that was attached to the waistband of his trousers, while at the same time trying hard to force himself off the floor with one arm in much the same manner as Daley.

The detective managed to get to his knees and with the very last strength he had left, forced his large frame forward on top of the older man, who still struggled with the pouch. The policeman's effort and the shock of his bulk landing on the other man made them both gasp simultaneously. Daley felt his muscles loosen, the enforced cramps the taser had initiated were fading; though he still knew his body was not entirely his to command. He managed to force himself up enough to straddle his opponent.

He could see the panic in Seanessy's eyes. Daley lifted his arm, ready to send a fist into Seanessy's face. "Where is she, you sick fuckin' bastard?" It was almost as though someone else was shouting. As his fist connected with Seanessy's face he felt a sharp pain on the top of his left thigh. Looking down he saw a hypodermic syringe sticking proudly from his leg. He tried to lift his arm to dislodge it, but could not. He saw a smile spread across Seanessy's face, blood trickling from his mouth. Then he lost consciousness.

22

He came round suddenly, like someone being thrown into a pool of cold water when asleep. Strangely though, he was unable to move. He could feel - he knew he was being dragged - he could see the blue of the sky showing through the evaporating haze of mist, but despite every effort he could not move so much as a muscle. Without warning he was thrust roughly to the ground, his head bouncing off a hard surface. Whatever he was drugged with dulled the pain, however his eyes still pricked with the tiny lights he associated with being hurt.

Seanessy's face was in his.

"I thought a city boy like you would appreciate drawing his last few breaths of sea air," he was grinning at the detective, a wisp of sparse hair flopping over his eyes, his face lobster-pink with freckles. "Oh, and you might like to take a last look at that wife of yours." Daley felt himself being pulled up by the hair. He was facing a tiny harbour, they were on what he could only presume was a kind of pier.

"Look down there, Chief Inspector," he felt his head being thrust forward; a brawny hand clasped the back of his neck. The water in the bay was clear, the burgeoning sunlight reflecting off the sandy bottom. Daley fought to focus his eyes; there was something else, something in the water. It was a body; he recognised arms flailing in the gentle swell, like restless seaweed on the tide. He couldn't see well, the drugs had made his sight blur; he could see enough to recognise that the body had no head. He retched, unable to expel the vomit from his mouth, he coughed, almost choking. He felt himself being flung back onto the hard surface of the pier, banging his head again, the force sending spew splattering from his mouth. He felt very confused for a few seconds; images of the floating corpse, Liz's face and Fraser's body lying lifeless on the pier at Kinloch, all flashed before his mind's eye.

A shadow loomed in front of his face again. The words were hard to understand at first, but gradually he began to make them out as his head cleared from the battering it had just taken.

"I have her head, you know. It's back at the cottage. Do you want me to get it?" Snot was flowing from Seanessy's nose, insanity written all over his features, now somehow morphed into those of a demon. Liz was dead. Daley could hear his own scream - half anger, half fear - as it echoed around the bay.

"I was made a fool of all of my life by idiots, people who were not fit to lick my boots." Seanessy's rage was palpable, even through Daley's, drugged, diminished senses. "I had to stand in front of classes of imbeciles, trying to impart some knowledge to them as they called me the most awful names and laughed at me," he was breathing heavily. Daley could smell the tang of the sea mixed with the stench of his own sick. "And the haughty bastards - like your wife for instance - teasing with their low necklines and tight jeans; all the while repulsed by someone who was their intellectual superior - superior in every way. Even my own daughter had been transformed into one of them: useless, ruined with drugs - profane." White spittle was showing at the corners of his mouth. "Now they're all dead; and soon, very soon, you will be too."

Daley saw him reach behind. The silver flash of a large blade filled his field of vision; the implement was like an old butcher's machete, polished bright with sharpening. It had two improvised handles at either end, covered with electrical tape: it was a hand-held guillotine.

He struggled to make his limbs move, to do the least of his bidding: nothing. Having come into contact with so much violent death in his career, he had always wondered how the victims felt;

did one's life really flash before your eyes? - or was the fear of imminent death an all-encompassing, visceral experience, to the exclusion of everything else? He knew that the drugs were affecting him - the fact he couldn't move bore witness enough to that. Now that he knew he was going to die, he felt a strange detachment as far as his own experience was concerned. What hurt, what gnawed away at him inside, was the thought of his beautiful wife having met with this grim fate. He had failed her as a husband, as a human being, and even as a police officer.

He stared up at his executioner, silhouetted against the patchy blue sky. He could smell the stench of stale sweat mix with the freshening smell of the sea. Seanessy was straddling him, the heavy knife held between two hands, like someone about to force down an old-fashioned explosive detonator. Beads of Seanessy's perspiration dripped onto Daley's new fleece. Seanessy licked his lips, which Daley noted absently, looked dry.

"I'm not in the habit of dispatching conscious victims, Mr Daley," his voice was hesitant with nerves. "I thought it important for you to feel the pain of death for both you and your pretty whore of a wife." He leant back on his heels, raising the blade in front of his face. Daley tried again to move, but could only feel the very tips of his fingers claw gently at the rough surface of the pier. This was it, he was going to die. Seanessy took a deep breath.

The scene seemed to dim suddenly. There was a noise - a metallic snap - followed by a dull impact, like the sound of an axe biting into a damp log. At the same moment, the sun glinted a shaft of light through the clouds of dispersing mist, picking out Seanessy's face in grim detail. His right eye had exploded in a shower of blood and gore, replaced by a bright, sharp metallic point. He didn't scream - didn't even move - his mouth gaped open letting a torrent of blood ooze over his bottom lip and down his chin. Still upright, straddling the detective, he dropped the blade, which landed heavily on Daley's chest, causing him to exhale sharply, as though he had been punched. The sharpness of the implement saw it bite into Daley's new jacket, though its oblique trajectory combined with the rubberised nature of the garment, made only the merest nick on the policeman's skin. Slowly, like a building being demolished, Seanessy's lifeless body fell forward, his forehead catching Daley on the chin. Above him now, another figure was silhouetted against a now blue sky: Hamish; in his meaty fists a nail gun.

"Aye, I'm sorry I let things go so far, Mr Daley, it's jeest you'd said that you'd be taking care o' everything. I wisna sure whether or no' ye had a maister plan on the go, that I couldna' fathom. I take it ye need a hand?" He smiled down at the recumbent police officer, his eyes their familiar slits in his parchment face.

"Get this bastard off me," Daley managed to whisper through his mouth, clasped semi-closed by immobile jaws. "He killed Liz," he felt a sob emanate from his throat.

Hamish rubbed his chin. "No he didn'a," he said staring down at the stricken officer. "She's up in the cottage - spark oot mind ye - but she's no' deid. I checked her pulse myself." He walked to Daley's side, and sticking his boot under Seanessy's body, kicked him aside. A loud klaxon sounded. "Here' the cavalry, Mr Daley - as much use as a ha'penny watch." The large orange and blue lifeboat was entering the tiny harbour.

23

Daley had never attended so many funerals in such a short space of time. Judging by what had been found in Seanessy's cottage, they were lucky not to be attending many more. Pictures of schoolgirls from throughout his time as a teacher in the local school adorned the walls, their faces circled in red marker. The smiles of the two dead girls were almost obliterated by thick black crosses. They had been the unlucky ones; or was it merely that the others had been lucky?

A criminal psychologist reckoned that Seanessy had bottled up his resentment over many years; the dam simply bursting when he retired. It seemed likely that his hatred of the mocking adolescents had been heightened by the debauchery and premature death of his own daughter. Whatever the truth was, it had died with Seanessy on Abb's Skerry.

Izzy Watson's funeral was first. Her widowed husband Michael, had shaken him by the hand, his blond-haired son hanging on to his father's trouser leg. The child looked wary - sad - as though he grasped something of what was going on. Daley mumbled the usual platitudes, hoping he was showing the correct level of empathy. In truth, he had spent every day thanking God that Liz had survived her ordeal at the hands of the deranged Seanessy. For her part, she had insisted on accompanying him to the burials of the other victims as a show of solidarity with them and their families; as well as unspoken offerings up of thanks for her delivery from evil. Daley looked at her now. No signs of the torment she had gone through, bar a small scratch on her cheek, even now fading under the adroit application of foundation and the brief passage of time. His heart swelled with love and relief, though she was still quiet - not the same spark in her eyes. He supposed that it would take time for her to completely recover: if indeed she was ever able to recover from such trauma.

Then, the next day, it was Janet Ritchie's funeral. MacLeod was at the service, accompanied by two prison officers. He had been remanded in custody after a speedy investigation by the discipline branch, instigated by Superintendent Donald, who himself was present at this service. Daley was sure that he had only attended to see MacLeod's shame, however decided to say nothing. Officially, Daley was still on sick-leave, however, he had been keeping in touch with Scott and the rest of the team who had remained in Kinloch tying up the loose ends of the Seanessy case, while beginning a serious investigation into the drug-smuggling ring responsible for Fraser's murder.

He found his mind wandering to the circumstances surrounding the killing of the affable, young DC. In fact, he found it hard to think about anything else.

He was back in the CID office at Kinloch. It was the morning of Bobby Johnstone's funeral. He had been the headless corpse, floating in the tiny bay of Abb's Skerry. His head had been recovered from the lean-to shed attached to the shack, where they had found Liz, unconscious, naked, but alive. The lean-to had looked like a butcher's shop, and it had been obvious that the young fisherman had been killed that day, most likely as Liz lay next door.

"It's like wading through custard here, Jimmy," Scott was chewing on an egg roll, the yolk of which was steadily progressing down his chin. "There's nae doubt aboot it, they're a tight-knit bunch doon here an' no mistake. Still, I've no' had tae go shoppin' wae the wife fir nearly three weeks," he shrugged, then cursed as a large dollop of tomato ketchup landed neatly, in the middle of his tie. Daley remembered Archie Fraser, and unusually, could think of no witty aside.

He had spoken to Camel briefly after the service, offering him his condolences. The normally chirpy young man was withdrawn and sullen; to be expected perhaps, however, he was still under investigation for his purchase and use of illegal drugs. It was obvious that he saw Daley as the enemy as well as the man who had failed to save his brother.

Daley was about to leave the office when Donald appeared, apparelled in his best uniform, a vision in sharp creases and gold braid.

"Can I have a word with you, Jim?" Donald was affecting his most gushing smile.

"I suppose so," Daley looked at his watch. "Liz is down at the County having a drink with Annie and the staff. We'll be driving up the road soon."

"I will only take up moments of your time." Donald already had Daley by the arm, steering him towards the door, his smile positively unctuous now. "Quick chat, then you can hit the road."

They walked in silence along the corridors of Kinloch Station, entering the office that had once belonged to the disgraced Inspector Macleod. He gestured silently for Daley to sit in the 'visitor's' chair, while he removed his cap, placing it carefully on an arm of the coat-stand.

"Now," he said, wearing an expression of great empathy, "how are you both getting on after your - well - ordeal?" He leaned forward in his chair, and for a brief moment, Daley thought he was about to grab his hand in a gesture of sympathy.

"You know how it is, sir - taking a bit of time. Liz is doing well. She's my priority at the moment." He left a pregnant pause in the conversation by way of emphasis.

"Absolutely. You do the right thing," he stroked his chin, a thoughtful look on his face.

"If you have something to say, sir, I would appreciate that we get on with it - as I say - I have to take the long road home." Daley looked at his superior with an even expression.

"Quite so, Jim, quite so." Donald opened a file on his desk.

"You've been off sick since the incident?" he looked at Daley who nodded. "Mmm…" more chin stroking. Just as Daley was about to interject, he closed the file and patted it in a gesture of finality; something coming to an end, Daley thought. "I'm going to be blunt, Chief Inspector." *Oh, Oh,* articulated through Daley's brain. "I cannot afford for an asset like your good self to be idle for much longer. It's the usual madhouse up the road, and you are fully aware of the extra manpower we have had to divert here." He raised his eyebrows as Daley nodded silently, fully aware that an announcement of some import was about to be forthcoming. "I want you to spend some more time down here - let's call it a temporary transfer," he smiled guilelessly.

"Ah, at last we have it, sir." Daley threw his head back in disgust. "I fully realise that we are pushed on all fronts, however I'm not about to up sticks and leave Liz on her own at home, while I become the friendly neighbourhood sheriff, in perpetual residence at the County Hotel."

"As usual, Jim, you are jumping to conclusions; strange for such a gifted detective." Donald stood, giving the impression of an edict from on-high. "And as far as your accommodation is concerned, I am quite prepared to rent a home of your choice - within reason of course - with the expectation that your wife will accompany you on your - let's say - mission, here." More smiles and raised eyebrows. The deed was done.

Abba's *The Eagle* blasted from the car's speakers as they drove parallel to a truly stunning seascape. Islands showed blue above a darkening sea; the light was beginning to fade and change colour as the evening progressed.

Liz had said very little since they had left Kinloch, her husband anxious to find the best time to articulate Donald's idea. He really had no clue as to how she would react; a notion that he had made clear to his superior. She had suffered the worst moments of her life near Kinloch. He didn't know if he should ask her at all.

"Are you OK, darling?" She was playing absently with a strand of hair. She smiled. "I need to run something past you, Liz."

Shades of purple adorned the sunset that was now framing the distant isles.

24

Donald was behind the wheel of his new Audi. It was top of the range, and paid for - in most part - by his generous police car allowance. He was wearing his No.1 uniform, complete with white gloves, and service medals.

The church where Archie Fraser's memorial service had been held, was only thirty minutes from his home in the leafy suburbs to the north of Glasgow. He was enjoying the familiarity of the route, as well as child-like pleasure at driving this car - his new toy. The humid clamour of a cloudy, July day was expelled from the vehicle by the highly efficient climate control system, and he luxuriated in the music of Beethoven's Ninth Symphony issuing from the car's Bose speakers. He had spent a very long time listening to classical music, trying to develop a taste for something he saw as a social necessity. After many months of struggle, he had now come to prefer this sea of sound and emotion to the noise made by the prog-rock bands he had so admired in his youth. Like everything else in his life, he had worked hard at it and now he could impress those who travelled with him by being able to name the music being played on Radio 3 or Classic FM, long before the presenter had seen fit to enlighten the audience. He was particularly fond of Beethoven, though he was currently developing a taste for Wagner as well.

His attempts at learning a foreign language were coming along well too, as were his piano lessons. He had made it plain to the tutors of both subjects that he wished to gain only a fundamental knowledge of their subjects, enough to be understood in this new tongue, and to be able to play a simple piece that would be easy to learn, while sounding impressively difficult to the untrained ear. His progress on both fronts made him smile.

The smile quickly disappeared from his face as his mind scrolled back over the cool reception he had received at Fraser's service. The late DC's mother had refused to shake his hand; he reflected how like her son she was, with her faded red hair, and awkward manner.

One man who had needed no introduction was the lad's uncle; though even he had been shocked by the ruined figure Davie Fraser had become. The ex-cop sat motionless in his wheelchair during the whole service, his emaciated body leaning to one side, his white shirt so contrasted by the orange of his skin. Indeed, he had brought to mind Donald's own father, who had killed himself with drink: the same jaundiced complexion brought on by a rapidly failing liver. They could do more these days; though why bother in Davie Fraser's case, he knew not. He thought that his ex-colleague would have been better employed asking the minister to reserve himself a funeral slot, rather than his slurred attempts at insults. It wasn't his fault that the nephew had as few brains as the uncle, walking into a highly dangerous situation wide-eyed and ill-prepared. Why should he reproach himself for the failings of others? After all, he couldn't hold the hand of every cop under his command; the job required common sense. To his mind, Archie Fraser had displayed none.

He had been momentarily diverted however, by the fetching figure of Liz Daley. How it was possible for her to look so sexy in her plain black dress and small hat - he did not know? She bore little signs of the traumatic experience she had, so recently, been through, apart from perhaps being a little more pale than normal. He had read the report on her ordeal with great interest. Though he refused to admit it to himself, he had been aroused by her plight, trying to picture how she would have looked, chained, naked to the filthy bed on the bit of rock that was Abb's Skerry.

The sight of her lumbering husband brought him back to reality though. He was wearing a suit that looked at least two sizes too small, his paunch plain over the taut trouser band. He still bore faded marks of assault on his chin, and carried himself stiffly, the cause of which were the muscles he had torn trying to fight the effect of the taser gun as its voltage held him rigid. Donald admired his skills as a detective - even his humanity - however, he still saw the DCI as being weak-willed; unable to come near to the potential he undoubtedly possessed. One look at his thickening waist line, was enough confirmation.

He turned the car into his street, then drove the further few yards to his large, Georgian home. The pebbles on the driveway crackled under the eighteen-inch alloy wheels, as he drove up the driveway and parked at the side door of the house. The exultant soar of the orchestra was suddenly silenced as he turned off the car's ignition.

He was about to open his door and leave the vehicle, when he heard his mobile ring in one of the bottom pockets of his uniform jacket. He removed the phone and noted the name on the screen with a raised eyebrow.

"Good afternoon, Sergei. I can only imagine that you have an urgent reason to contact me this way." A frown spread across his face as he heard the familiar bells of the small, Latvian town tolling plaintively in the background of the call.

The End.

ABOUT THE AUTHOR:

D. A. MEYRICK

After a varied career, including spells in the police force, studying politics, working as a manager in a distillery, and sales and marketing director in various businesses, D.A. Meyrick decided to realise a lifetime's ambition by writing his first novel.

He lives on Loch Lomond side with his wife, Fiona and cats.

Whisky From Small Glasses was published in November 2012 as both an Original Paperback and an E-book.

He is already hard at work on the next of the DCI Daley Kinloch series of novels, which will be published in 2013.

Good Deed by **Steve Christie** is a fast paced crime novel that captures the reader from beginning to end.

The gripping story of Good Deed rattles along relentlessly, leaving the reader breathless but enthralled. Good Deed introduces a new Scottish detective hero, DI Ronnie Buchanan, who is certain to quickly attract a legion of fans.

The events crammed into Good Deed take Buchanan from his base in Aberdeen on a frantic journey around all the major Scottish cities as his increasingly deadly pursuit of a mysterious criminal master mind known only as Vince comes to a breath-taking climax back in Aberdeen.

"The pace of Good Deed is exceptional and unremitting. It is the kind of book that demands to be read in one sitting, but most readers will be so breathless as the saga unfolds without pause that they will need occasional rests before eagerly returning for more."

Good Deed is Steve Christie's first novel. Based in Edinburgh, the good news is that he is already hard at work on the follow up to Good Deed, which will also feature Ronnie Buchanan. Ringwood is confident that both Steve Christie and Ronnie Buchanan are names that will become very familiar to all lovers of quality crime fiction.

Good Deed can be purchased on *www.ringwoodpublishing.com* for £9.99 excluding p&p, or ordered by post or e-mail for the same price.

The e-book version is be available for £7.20 from the Kindle Book Store or Amazon.co.uk

Torn Edges by **Brian McHugh** is a riveting mystery story linking modern day Glasgow with 1920's Ireland.

When a gold coin very similar to a family heirloom is found at the scene of a Glasgow murder, a search is begun that takes the McKenna family, assisted by their Librarian friend Liam, through their own family history right back to the tumultuous days of the Irish Civil War. The search is greatly helped by the discovery of an old family photograph of their Great-Uncle Pat in a soldier's uniform.

The McKennas quickly realise that despite their pride in their Irish Irish history. With Liam's expert help, they soon learn that many more Irishman were killed, murdered, assassinated or hung during the very short Civil War than in the much longer and better known War of Independence. And they learn that gruesome atrocities were committed by both sides, atrocities in which the evidence begins to suggest their own relatives might have been involved.

Parallel to this unravelling of the family involvement of this period, Torn Edges author Brian McHugh has interwoven the remarkable story of the actual participation of two of the McKenna family, Charlie and Pat, across both sides of the conflict in the desperate days of 1922 Ireland.

"Torn Edges is both entertaining and well-written, and will be of considerable interest to all in both Scottish and Irish communities, many of whom will realise that their knowledge and understanding of events in Ireland in 1922 has been woefully incomplete. Torn Edges will also appeal more widely to all who appreciate a good story well told."

TORN EDGES can be purchased on *www.ringwoodpublishing.com* for £9.99 excluding p&p or ordered by post or e-mail for the same price.

The e-book version is available for £7.20 from the Kindle Book Store or Amazon.co.uk from October 2012.

Paradise Road by **Stephen O'Donnell** is the story of Kevin McGarry a young man from the West of Scotland, who as a youngster was one of the most talented footballers of his generation in Scotland. Through a combination of injury and disillusionment, Kevin is forced to abandon any thoughts of playing the game he loves, professionally. Instead he settles for following his favourite team, Glasgow Celtic, as a spectator, while at the same time resignedly and with a characteristically wry Scottish sense of humour, trying to eke out a living as a joiner.

It is a story of hopes and dreams, idealism and disillusionment, of growth in the face of adversity and disappointment. Paradise Road examines some of the major themes affecting football today, such as the power and role of the media, standards in the Scottish game and the sectarianism which pervades not only football in Glasgow but also the wider community. More than simply a novel about football or football fandom, the book offers a portrait of the character and experiences of a section of the Irish Catholic community of the West of Scotland, and considers the role of young working-class men in our modern, post-industrial society.

The road Kevin travels towards self discovery, fulfilment and maturity leads him to Prague, enabling a more detached view of the Scotland that formed him and the Europe that beckons him.

"Written in a thoughtful, provocative yet engaging style, Paradise Road is a book that will enthral, challenge and reward in equal measure. It will be a powerful addition to the growing debate on some of the key issues facing contemporary Scotland"

Paradise Road can be purchased on *www.ringwoodpublishing.com* for £9.99 excluding p&p or ordered by post or e-mail for the same price.

The e-book version is be available for £7.20 from the Kindle Book Store or Amazon.co.uk